Hig

The
Orphanage

OTHER BOOKS BY LIZZIE PAGE

When I Was Yours
Daughters of War
The Forgotten Girls

Lizzie Page
The Orphanage

FOREVER

New York Boston

Copyright © 2021 by Lizzie Page
Reading group guide copyright © 2024 by Lizzie Page and
Hachette Book Group, Inc.

Cover image © Tanya Gramatikova/Trevillion Images. Cover design by
Debbie Clement. Cover copyright © 2024 by Hachette Book Group, Inc.

Forever
Hachette Book Group
1290 Avenue of the Americas, New York, NY 10104
read-forever.com

Originally published in 2021 by Bookouture, an imprint of StoryFire Ltd.

First Forever Edition: June 2024

Forever is an imprint of Grand Central Publishing. The Forever name and logo are registered trademarks of Hachette Book Group, Inc.

The publisher is not responsible for websites (or their content)
that are not owned by the publisher.

The Hachette Speakers Bureau provides a wide range of authors for speaking events. To find out more, go to hachettespeakersbureau.com or email HachetteSpeakers@hbgusa.com.

Forever books may be purchased in bulk for business, educational, or promotional use. For information, please contact your local bookseller or the Hachette Book Group Special Markets Department at special.markets@hbgusa.com.

LCCN: 2023946759

ISBN: 9781538766088 (trade paperback)

Printed in the United States of America

LSC-C

Printing 1, 2024

To Ernie
Who never fails to make me smile

"To view children as individual human beings with both shared and individualized needs, rather than an indistinct mass."

The Children's Act, 1948

The
Orphanage

Suffolk County Council
September 1, 1948

Dear Miss Newton,

Referring to your interview today, we shall be pleased to engage your services as a housemother at Shilling Grange Children's Home in Lavenham at a starting salary of twenty-eight shillings per week.

You will work every day of the week, with the exception of the eight hours between Sunday 10 a.m. and 6 p.m. provided there is sufficient cover. The children have a two-week holiday in August—this is when you will take your annual holiday (paid).

Please provide yourself with a one-way ticket from London, the cost of which will be refunded to you. We shall be glad if you would commence your services after breakfast on Thursday, September 9, 1948.

We hope you will have a long and happy service with us.

Yours faithfully,
P. P. Sommersby

CHAPTER ONE

September 1948

Suffolk

Clara Newton rang the bell. After about twenty seconds, the door opened slightly and a nun appeared from behind it. Nuns had been running Shilling Grange Children's Home until recently, Clara knew that, but she hadn't expected to find a live one on the premises. She'd been hoping the kind-eyed, stiff-haired lady from the interview would be here to welcome her.

The nun wouldn't let her in but held the door on its latch and squinted out. Her face was white and powdery. She had tiny black eyes like stones in the snow.

"In trouble, are we?"

"Beg pardon?"

"Pull open your coat. Let's see. Twelve weeks, I'd say, no more."

Regretting the cress sandwich she'd had on the train, Clara muttered, "I'm here for the job. I'm the new housemother."

The lock made a rasping sound as the nun drew it back.

Clara followed the nun to a large kitchen at the back of her house.

"I'm Miss Newton—Clara. At your service."

Nothing.

"What should I call you?"

"Sister Eunice will do."

"Didn't the council let you know I was coming?"

Sister Eunice sniffed. "I was expecting an older lady."

Clara decided to take this as a compliment.

"And...and...the children?"

"School."

Of course they were at school.

"What time will they be returning?"

"Just after midday," said Sister Eunice. "For their luncheon."

"And then back to school?"

"Where else?"

It was only nine thirty a.m. Clara had tiptoed away from Judy's home at six thirty, careful not to wake anyone, caught the 8:15 train and waited half an hour at a platform in Chelmsford for the change.

Midday felt like many moons away.

"I see. And...and...are there some files I could look at while I'm waiting? Bit of background always helps."

This was Clara's way to get a grip on a situation. Hadn't she turned Harris & Sons round with her systems? Invoices. Expenses. Miscellaneous. Everything had its place. For ten years she had been the company "godsend" and then, out the blue, she wasn't needed anymore. Dismissed. Small payout, yes, but to all intents and purposes, dismissed. She hoped her replacement, the luminous Miss Barber, was suffering in Clara's swivel chair, at Clara's beloved typewriter, but she doubted she would be. Unfortunately, Clara had made her systems foolproof even for that fool.

Sister Eunice stared into the middle distance.

"I said, the files? About the accommodation or the children?"

"There was never any need." Sister Eunice spoke to the air. "We *know* the children."

"Well, there must be *some* paperwork...just to get started."

"Start with the laundry."

*

There were four bed sheets in the basket, various smaller items like towels and one cuddly toy. It was a warm insect-y kind of day, summer seemed reluctant to let go of its hold and Clara grew hot at the mangle. When the washing was satisfyingly done, Clara lugged it outside. The garden was a lovely green space, defended by trees lining every fence and a garden shed like a fairy-tale house tucked at the back. It was a big change from the rubble-and-broken-glass playgrounds of London. Clara pegged up the sheets and admired them fluttering prettily in the breeze like reports unwritten.

She had applied to the advertisement "Do What Women Do Best—Caring" because it was the only one in the *Evening Standard* she *could* apply for.

She was not an ex-serviceman with exemplary driving skills or a chef for a high-class Mayfair restaurant. She was not looking for a new and exciting sales opportunity.

But she was female, between 20–40 (26), responsible and sensible (quite) and she *was* looking for a stimulating job, accommodation in an attractive location included, no experience required.

She hadn't expected to be offered an interview—and, when she was, decided it would serve as a warm-up or practice run for a *real* job. She borrowed Judy's good shoes and the suit Judy wore for meeting parents at school and, perhaps because she didn't think she stood a chance, she hadn't come across as nervous. She had gaily chatted away to the panel of two men and the kind-eyed, stiff-haired lady as though she had nothing to lose.

Indeed, she had surprised herself with the things that came out of her mouth. It wasn't that she made anything up, but she *might* have exaggerated her skills and interests a teeny bit. No, not exaggerated, it was like putting something under a magnifying glass. It became big or intricate when actually in real life it was…insignificant. So under the magnifying glass, having attended boarding school was "a great training ground for working in a children's home," her role at her old employers, Harris & Sons, was "vital to their smooth running" and "protecting children from nefarious influences would always be her number one priority," et cetera, et cetera.

Although it was Suffolk County Council that had interviewed her, Clara also hadn't thought much about where the attractive job location might be. After all, the interview was held in a dimly lit office over a greengrocers in Islington...but then to be allocated a home in Lavenham of all places—that was the push that made her say yes.

Tremulously, she had read the offer over and over again and then made Judy read it too. Clara wasn't usually superstitious—she took a cheeky pride in bringing open umbrellas into a house or walking close to—if not quite under—a ladder, but on this occasion, it was just too much of a coincidence.

Lavenham? The job was meant to be.

Sister Eunice was nowhere to be found. Some potatoes were heating in a pot and a chunk of ham was out: presumably lunch was taken care of. The washing was drying, the house was tidy, the children were at school.

In her room, Clara unpacked her case. She hesitated about putting her framed photos out on display before deciding: why not?—this was where she lived now. If she acted like she was comfortable, then the rest of her would hopefully catch up soon.

Photo one was a faded picture of Michael as a baby, a woolen cap tied under his chin, in a pram with great wheels, proudly showing a rattle to someone out of shot—the photographer, perhaps. This was one his mother had sent, after Michael wrote to her in those sweet carefree months that they were getting married.

There was a photo of her and Michael together at a dance hall in Clapham. The Roxy, was it? (They went to so many.) It was the night Michael had proposed and, still breathless from the lindy hop, she'd said yes in a flash—she'd been scared he might change his mind. There'd been no hesitation about it—not only would they marry, she would go back with him to America. Their future together stretched out like some great adventure. How happy she looked in black and white, her shirt brilliant, her lipstick luminous. It was like she was a different person.

The third photograph was her favorite: Michael in uniform propped against a plane. The plane was so big, it made him look small when he wasn't small at all—he was a broad fella—in a brown leather jacket, at RAF Cockfield, or RAF Lavenham, as it was sometimes known. Sometimes Clara found looking at that photo unbearable, but you had to bear it, you had to. Today, she gazed at it fondly. Michael would be proud of her, she knew he would.

Clara got out her papers, her pen and ink, from her handbag, and set up her desk just as she liked it. Enough dreaming. She was here at Shilling Grange Children's Home to work. Clara was not a shirker, that was one thing that was the same about her, magnifying glass or not. She began her first report:

THE ACCOMMODATION AT SHILLING GRANGE,
3 LAVENHAM HIGH ROAD AS OF SEPTEMBER 9, 1948
by Miss Clara Newton, new housemother.
Initial Observations

Shilling Grange is a picturesque medieval house with beams and chimneys. It is old and feels old too—you wonder if these walls could speak, what would they say?

There's an enormous sign outside like an advertising billboard, impossible to miss. The Grange has been a children's home since the 1900s, run by nuns, most of whom left this year. Sister Eunice seems a woman who knows what she is doing and runs a tight ship. I endeavor to learn as much as I can from her.

The kitchen is ample-sized, complete with stove and chill cupboard. I think almost everything we need is here (check?).

Larder looks adequately equipped. There is a lot of flour and not many tins. I presume Sister Eunice bakes.

I have a nice-sized room on the first floor. Simple, but all I require. There is a bathroom next door, which I think is mine to share with Sister Eunice. It is clean.

I presume the downstairs parlor is not used much, since the chairs are covered by plastic. It is not dusty though. Whoever does the cleaning is doing a fantastic job. Pleased to note there is also a wireless!

There is a dormitory room on the first floor and another on the ground floor. Both have four beds each, but I doubt there are eight children here now (check?). The children's bathroom is in the basement and it is dark, damp and smells as you'd imagine. There are large puddles around the boys' toilet (possible leak?) but the girls' seems fine.

There are four washbasins and four cubicles. Not a bad ratio. The children's belongings are all numbered. I don't know why they don't have their names on them. By belongings, I mean their mugs, their toothbrushes, their flannels, towels and combs. All of them have seen better days... There is one mirror, cracked. Talk to Sister Eunice about a replacement?

There is also an outside lav with newspaper squares all over the floor. Only the spiders seem to use this one.

I wonder if it's possible to change some of the rooms around so that older children can have some privacy and so that there is a play area? The shed in the garden might be suitable for play.

Actually, I've just realized, I haven't seen any pictures, toys or games anywhere. I don't like to say it, but the impression is rather bleak. Talk to Sister Eunice and/or designated contact at council asap.

*

Three and a bit hours after Clara first arrived, all manner of small people piled into the Shilling Grange kitchen. They were wearing dresses or shorts. Knee socks or ankle socks. The state of their shoes—the polish couldn't disguise the holes. They wore matching black capes that gave them the air of bats. Some stared at her. Some ignored her.

Clara realized suddenly it had been a long time since she had been around children. In fact, the only time she had spent a substantial amount of time with them was when she was a child herself. Judy was good with little ones. Clara had always been more at ease with graphs and charts.

The littlest child strode over, put her hand in Clara's. Clara froze.

"Do you know where Mama is?"

"I don't, sorry."

The girl snatched away her hand.

Sister Eunice had disappeared again. She had a knack for not being in the same room as Clara at any time. Clara had hoped to watch her interact with the children. They'd have to get together and do an information handover over the next few days.

"Who are you?" one of the boys asked.

"I'm your new housemother." Clara tried to speak small child. She had not tried this obscure language before. "Do you know what that is?" she asked slowly, as if he were a foreign person. They had those at Harris & Sons sometimes.

The children shook their heads.

"Why do you speak like that?" said the boy, imitating her.

Clara sped up. "A housemother is a lady installed by the council to see that every child—like you—gets the *best* possible care."

"Are you going to find Mama?" the smallest child persisted.

Clara knew she shouldn't make promises she mightn't be able to keep, but it slipped out: "I can try."

The girl jumped up and down.

"Find Mama! Find Mama!"

A bad start. Clara looked at the others: big ones, skinny ones, ones whose hair fell into their faces. Ones whose hair was tangled, ones whose hair was shiny, two boys who looked exactly the same.

"Are you a nun?" asked one boy with a shaved head and pink ears that stuck out so far, Clara feared for the plates balancing on the dresser he stood next to.

"Not quite."

Not quite?

"What do we call you then?"

"You can call me…" Clara had anticipated saying "Aunty Clara," but now thought that would be too informal. "Miss Newton."

"I'm Alex." The boy presented a grimy paw. Clara dreaded to think where it had been, but she couldn't not shake back. "That is Rita," he said, pointing to the girl, who was still jumping.

"Mama, Mama!"

"And this is Peter." He gestured to the lad next to him.

"Nice to meet you," Peter said with a shy smile. Peter was much taller than Clara, that age in between the adult world and the child one. He had so many freckles, she could hardly see his skin beneath them.

Peter, she told herself. She must try to remember them as quickly as she could. *Alex with the ears, Peter with the freckles, Rita with the mama.*

Another child pushed forward.

"And I'm Terry!"

"Hello, young man."

One of the identical boys laughed.

"That's not a young man, that's a girl."

"I see. Teresa, is it?"

"It's Terry." Terry's bottom lip stuck out and she put her fist to her chin.

"I was just wondering at the derivation of the nickname."

"Deviation?"

"Um, derivation, it means...where it's from."

"I'm from London."

"Right. Excellent."

The identical boys jumped forward as though for inspection. Toes lined up, white hair, red cheeks, they saluted.

"We're twins."

"I suspected it."

"I'm Billy."

"I'm Barry."

"What are your real names?" Clara asked more confidently. She stopped at their expressions. "Riiight-O. Billy and Barry it is."

The children went to wash. Clara let out a sigh of relief, but just when she was on her own again, the back door opened and a man with a small child on his shoulders entered the kitchen. He was singing about fishes and dishes while the child's feet tapped rhythmically on his chest. He had very dark hair, jet-black even— and a strong jawline. Not quite Desperate Dan territory but a few centimeters more and it might have been. He sang neither well nor badly, but with great enthusiasm.

"When the boat comes innnnnn!" he chorused, while the child did rowing motions with her arms.

He startled when he saw Clara. "I didn't know there were visitors. Forgive my...entrance."

"I'm the new housemother." Clara was thrown. "I...I...rather enjoyed the song."

She wiped her hands on her skirt. She shouldn't be hot and bothered at the proximity of a handsome man—at her mature years especially—but she was. Judy's eyebrows would have shot straight to her hairline at this one.

"And what's your name, sweetie?"

"Ivor Delaney," said the man, straight-faced.

Clara blushed. "I meant the little girl. Little girl, what do they call you?"

The girl's eyes widened before she buried her face in the man's shoulder. He swung her feet down to the floor with an "Oop-la! This is Peg."

"Well, hello, Peg!" said Clara in the brightest voice she could muster. Peg's ruler-straight hair swung into her own snot. What was it with small children that they never had handkerchiefs? Clara would make this a priority.

Ivor held out his hand. "I live just over the road—which is where I found Peg. Please call me Ivor."

"Clara. Clara Newton."

As they shook hands, Clara's eyes were drawn to his other arm, which ended in a curved nub just before where the elbow should have been. It made her shiver. It wasn't that it was ugly—just unexpected. When he noticed her looking, he swung it slightly behind him, biting his lip. She wanted to explain she did not find it repulsive, just curious, but how do you put that into words?

"I was wondering where she was," Clara lied. "How do you do, Miss Peg?"

"Peg doesn't speak," Ivor said quietly.

"I'm sure she does."

"She doesn't."

"Well, why not?"

Shaking his head incredulously, Ivor muttered something—possibly an expletive—under his breath.

"What a lovely..." Clara cast around for something to compliment poor Peg on. "...blouse. Is blue your favorite color?"

The girl grabbed Ivor's leg and hid behind it. She was even tinier than the Rita child.

"Red is mine," Clara gabbled on. "For clothes, that is; for other things, like eyes, I think brown is most pleasant and I suppose I like blue sky and grass is best when it's green..." She laughed nervously. "What about you, Peg?"

The girl shook her head from side to side vigorously.

"What part of *doesn't speak* did you not understand?" Ivor sounded cross. The little girl ran out of the kitchen. At the same time, an older girl, she must have been about thirteen, came in the back door. Clara was relieved at the interruption.

"Hellooo and welcome!"

Welcome? Who was she to welcome anyone?

"So, you're the new nun?"

Clara gave the girl her broadest smile, for here was an ally. The girl was almost an adult!

"I'm not a nun, my name is Miss Newton." This girl had masses of light brown hair and beneath that sullen expression, you could tell she was bright as a button. "As you're older, you can call me Clara."

"You've got something in your teeth, *Miss Newton*."

"Maureen," said Ivor in a low voice. "Try to make Miss Newton feel welcome, could you?"

"Welcome," Maureen parroted.

Ivor made for the door. "Good luck."

"Thank you for bringing back Peg." Clara wanted to add "and correcting Maureen" but she didn't want to say that in front of her.

"It's my pleasure." Ivor paused, his hand on the handle. "Just so you know, I don't agree with the changes."

"The changes?"

"The changes going on around here. Since the Children's Act. Things were working all right before. Now," he surveyed the kitchen, "all the nuns have gone away."

"Sister Eunice hasn't."

"And it's just…kids being divided, moved around for no reason and…" He paused, looked at the floor. "Council bringing in a lot of inexperienced pen-pushers."

Inexperienced pen-pushers? Clara blushed. *He meant her.*

"With no idea what they're getting themselves into. And who have loads of unsuitable ideas," he added, to hammer the point home.

If there was one type of person Clara disliked, it was someone who hammered a point home.

"Well, thank you for your opinion."

"When I see something wrong, I say it."

"An interesting quality."

Clara noticed with alarm that his eyes were brown. He might have thought she was referring to his eyes earlier. Should she mention that she liked blue eyes equally?

"Especially when children are involved."

"Right."

"Sorry if that's not what you wanted to hear. Goodbye."

Clara thought she could already write a whole file on Ivor, title: bad-tempered neighbor. Maureen was smirking as the other children clattered back in, each taking a place on the bench. There was no argument about who sat where, but it soon become clear there was no place for Clara. There was barely enough space for the children. Sister Eunice steamed in like a great ship, positioned herself at the head of the table and gazed disapprovingly about her. Maureen brought the potatoes to the table. Billy or Barry presented the ham. The children eyed their cutlery. Epochs passed before Clara could bring herself to say, "Oh, I don't seem to have anywhere to sit."

No one moved until the freckly boy—was it Peter?—scraped back his chair. "I'll find something," he whispered like he had done something wrong.

Sister Eunice hadn't even looked up.

Peter staggered back with a footstool and dropped it at the free end of the table. Unfortunately, it was very low, and once she had sat upon it, Clara could barely see over the table edge. She was a full head smaller than everyone else. She hoped that someone might offer to swap, but no one did. Indeed, some of the children—the twins, for example—sniggered and even Peg-who-didn't-speak was grinning. They may as well have plonked Clara in the corner wearing a dunce's cap for all the dignity it offered.

Sister Eunice recited the Lord's Prayer. Clara mouthed the words, keeping one eye open the way she used to as a child. Eight children! Eight *individual* children. Eight people, each with their own wants and needs. When she had pictured eight, it did not seem as many as there were in front of her right now.

Still, she supposed, she would pick it up. Sister Eunice would guide her and Clara prided herself on being a quick learner. When Harris & Sons had been instructed to switch their entire operations from manufacturing domestic appliances to munitions, Clara had been at the vanguard of the change. She had adjusted then and she could adjust now.

"Well, I'm delighted to be here!" Clara said once the Amens were done. "How wonderful to meet you—"

"We eat in silence!" Sister Eunice held her fork closer to heaven, then slid it into her mouth.

"What? The whole mealtime?"

Sister Eunice inclined her head.

"I didn't expect..."

Sister Eunice chewed and swallowed slowly.

"I see."

To return to school, the children put on the identical bat-capes over their clothes again.

"Why do you wear those things?"

They ignored her.

"I asked a question," Clara snapped and finally they jumped to attention, the smaller ones looking at each other warily. Terry trembled and Alex's ears went red. "Why do we wear these?" The oldest girl—Maureen—plucked hers with disdain. "So everyone knows we're from Shilling Grange. Otherwise, we'll look like *normal* children and we can't have that, can we?"

What to do now? Sister Eunice had once again vanished. This was Clara's free time until the children came back at four. She decided she may as well go out and get her bearings.

She had been too glued to her map to notice much about the village earlier, but now she saw Lavenham High Road was a beautiful parade of shops and private residences. Whitewashed fronts and hanging flower baskets, cobbled pavements, even some thatched roofs. It was like going back in time and it was every bit as beautiful as Michael had told her. She had thought he was exaggerating—he loved everything English and he wasn't discerning. But now she felt emotional as she looked at all the shops that Michael must have seen and the White Horse public house, where he may have gone for a drink in the evenings (she wasn't sure if he'd mentioned it. She hated that she couldn't remember).

She remembered other things though. He had said, "Lavenham is like a film set." Yes, it was, it was a change from London that was for sure and it was exactly what she needed. Now that she was in the countryside, Clara wanted woods, foxes, squirrels, ferns and kissing gates. No, not kissing gates, she wasn't ready for that yet. And no cows either. Every so often she'd read in the papers about a fatal cow-trampling incident; honestly, you'd think they were just as dangerous as the Nazis.

As she wandered through the village, drinking it all in, a fashionably dressed woman bowled toward her, surprisingly quickly given the uneven state of the cobblestones and the height of her heels.

"Hello. You look lost."

No one would approach someone like that in London, a city of strangers cradling their own business to them, but Clara was delighted.

"I am—but in a good way. I'm feeling my way around."

"Staying long?"

"Hope so."

"Wonderful." She gripped Clara's hands. "This town could do with some new blood. You will instantly halve the average age of us residents."

She laughed at her own comment, then stepped in companionably beside Clara as though they knew each other well. She looked about Clara's age. Fitted jacket, pencil skirt, all in a pretty sky blue. Wedding ring on her finger, naturally—most women their age were married—but of course she might be a war widow. Her hair was bleached white-blonde, Hollywood style. Clara loved celebrity fashion—if she had the guts, she would have done the same. She hadn't experimented with her own style for years. On the other hand, dyeing it must take an awful lot of upkeep and, Clara regretted, she probably didn't have the stamina. To be honest, nowadays she found even powdering her nose a bore.

It was great luck to meet someone straight away who could be a friend.

"I was just thinking to myself, what a beautiful village."

"And we are *such* a community here, I can tell you all about it. I'm Dotty, Mrs. Garrard—oof, I love saying that. I've only been married six months. My husband—love saying that too—Larry is over there." She pointed to a man in a hat staring at the signs in the post office window. "LARRY. Come and meet…"

"Miss Newton. Clara."

"Miss?"

Clara didn't have to wait long for "the look." Mrs. Garrard sucked in her lips sympathetically, causing lipstick to stick to her teeth. "Never mind. I love a project and I know we will be absolute friends. Where are you based? The Lavender Arms is a dream. I hear their breakfast is to die for. Larry has promised me a night there for our anniversary. Wood," she added. "Or lead, I can never remember."

"I'm at Shilling Grange."

Mrs. Garrard stopped dead.

"The Grange? But that's not a hotel."

"No, it isn't."

In a hushed voice, she continued, "The orphanage, the Grange?"

"That's it."

Mrs. Garrard's demeanor had changed completely. Hands on hips, she demanded, "What on earth are you staying there for?"

"I'm the new housemother there."

Clara liked the word "housemother." It suggested her chief task was to take care of a building. She could do that with her eyes shut. At Harris & Sons, they used to say that efficiency was her middle name.

"Oh? Is that what it is?"

"Yes?"

"That place doesn't belong here. It should move out of the high road. This is a respectable town. We're the home of Jane Taylor."

"Who?"

Mrs. Garrard shook her head in despair. "The poet. And Constable. And you must know Sir Munnings, the painter? And his horses?"

"Sir Munnings and his horse paintings?" Amused, Clara pictured a man and his horse painting at easels side by side.

The husband had joined his wife. He was holding a small brown dog under his arm that matched his wispy mustache. He was a cheerful-looking soul. Judy would have said he looked "pleased with himself."

Mrs. Garrard poked him in the elbow.

"This... she has come to work here. At the orphanage of all places."

"Oh, yes, we want them out!" he chirruped. He had such an unexpectedly high voice that despite her confusion, Clara wanted to giggle. "Nothing personal. Just standards. And property values."

"And the rest," sniffed his wife.

"We think they would be better off in Ipswich," he squeaked. The dog put its paw on its master's arm protectively. *It's not him that needs protecting*, thought Clara.

"Or Clacton? An orphanage would do well in Clacton."

The two sauntered off.

"It's paper!" Clara shouted. "It's definitely paper. For your one-year anniversary. Not wood."

Clara had just arrived back home, Mrs. Garrard's words still ringing in her ears, when Sister Eunice appeared, wrapped in an overcoat, carpetbag in hand.

"It's goodbye from me, dear," she said in a more affable tone than Clara would have thought her capable of.

"What?"

"I'm off. For good."

"Already? It can't be…What? Who is…who is to tell me what to do?"

Sister Eunice couldn't contain her happiness. "You'll pick it up, dear."

"Won't you…" Clara grasped at straws. "Won't you want to say goodbye to the children?"

"Wouldn't want to make a fuss."

"And…and…" There were so many things Clara wanted to say, she didn't know where to begin. "Do you have any last words of advice?"

"Whip them." Sister Eunice's face was close to Clara's. "Hard. When they wet. Bye."

There was a telephone number for the council among the papers in the dresser, but it said it was only for emergencies. Was this an emergency? Hard to say. Clara also hadn't found an actual telephone in the house yet. She had no telephone, no plan, no strategy, no schedule, no information, nothing.

It certainly felt fairly emergency-like.

A nice cup of tea, Clara decided. That's what she and Judy had done throughout the Blitz and it had never failed. And at least there were no bombs. At least there were no children in crocodile formation wearing gas masks, at least there were no body parts engulfed in rubble.

Deep breaths. She could do this.

As soon as the children came back from school, freckly Peter—who had fetched Clara the stool—scrubbed the oven, his whole head in it, while Alex laid the table for breakfast. The twins peeled vegetables for the pie they would have the next day. The girls swept and polished the floors. The smell of wax was everywhere.

All the children washed their ankle socks and left them to dry on the bathroom pipes. Then they polished the pile of shoes. Clara had wondered if they might sit down together and listen to *Children's Hour* on the wireless, but they were clearly too busy.

At six o'clock, Alex informed her that the older ones had crackers with cheese and Spam for tea. The younger ones had their crackers plain, but everyone could do themselves, Clara need not worry.

They ate silently and efficiently, cleared the plates away and then each sat reading (or pretending to read) the Bible.

Clara had initially thought seven thirty was too early for bedtime—*surely the children need free time?*—but by the time the big hand touched the half past, she was desperate to be away from all of them. They mightn't say much, but their constant presence was imposing.

"Goodnight, all," she said as they trooped to their rooms like clockwork soldiers.

The kitchen was clean and ready for the next day. Tomorrow's pie had to go in the oven; that was all she had to do.

For a first day, despite Sister Eunice's shock exit, it hadn't been too terrible. The home obviously ran like a well-oiled machine. Its inmates were out most of the day, they cleaned, tidied and now they were asleep. They were a bit like animals in a zoo: nothing too sad about it, they were just so used to their captivity, they got on with it without complaint. Her first day at Harris & Sons had been no picnic either, Clara reminded herself. Someone had scratched the "-on" off her name badge so that for a short while she was *hilariously* known as "Clara Newt." It wasn't until Judy had arrived about three years later that Clara really started to enjoy working there. Judy was the new forewoman, in charge of all the new girls on the factory floor once war had broken out. She was five years older than Clara, and seemed light-years more grown-up, but somehow the pair of them clicked. They used to lie next to each other in the air raid shelters whispering about what they would do when the war was over. Judy wanted to work in a school—that came true—and Clara wanted to stick with her paperwork, but in America, with her Michael.

A cry from upstairs. Clara hesitated, just for a second, then raced up, heart in her mouth. Her first problem.

Rita was standing in the middle of the room, hands over her face. Maureen, Peg and Terry surrounded her. If it hadn't been for their incredulous expressions, Clara might have thought it was a game.

"What's happened?"

"This!" Rita held aloft a tiny gray woolen mouse like a trophy. "You washed Molly Mouse!"

Maureen was looking at Clara like she'd witnessed a bloody murder.

"I didn't know I wasn't supposed to," Clara began. "It was in the washing basket, how was I to—"

"Mama!" called out the weeping girl. "Smelled of Mama. MAMA!"

"I'm sorry."

At this, Rita stepped up her tears and they became wails, desperate, shirt-rending wails.

Clara felt like crying too. Had Sister Eunice let her do it on purpose or had she just been stupid?

"I didn't mean for it to happen, Rita, I promise."

But Rita wouldn't look at her. She faced the wall and cried so loudly that all four boys thundered up the stairs. Billy—or was it Barry?—grabbed Rita and stroked her hair.

"What has she done to you?"

"Nothing!" protested Clara. "I didn't know..."

All of the children were gazing at Clara as though she was coming for their precious things next. Terry hugged herself and Peg covered her ears with a pillow. Rita wept on.

"Smelled like Mama."

"Please, Rita," begged Clara, "hush."

"I'll look after her." Maureen gave Clara a scathing look. "She likes *me*."

As Clara left the room she trod on Terry's toes, sending her howling too. Then she slipped on the overly mopped floor in the bathroom and, although she was only giving Peg a warning to please be careful not to do the same, the girl burst into tears too. So now three of them were wailing, while Maureen's scathing looks multiplied.

Barry—or was it Billy?—asked her for a shilling and when she refused, he asked for two. Then he said it was a joke.

"How is that a joke?" demanded Clara. She had heard the phrase "at the end of my tether" many times before and had never really gotten it—she did now. "For something to be a joke, it has to be funny."

"To be fair, a joke might be funny to one person and not another," Alex with the ears pointed out. Clara told herself not to change her expression one bit.

"Are you in pain, Miss Newton?" Alex continued. "You look like you are."

The other twin came out of the boys' dormitory. "Bad news," he said. "I've got visitors again."

Clara waited for another disappointing punchline. He held out a gray handkerchief. Clara backed away but he said, "Look, look!"

Tiny black dots. Tiny moving black dots. It was disgusting.

Clara sprang away from him.

"What on earth are they?"

"Nits."

"No!"

"Have you not seen them before?" Alex was amused.

His shaved head made more sense now.

"No, yes, no. Oh God."

By the time Clara finally made it back to the kitchen, it was filled with smoke. She had only gone and burned the pie. Maybe in ordinary times it would be inedible, but these were extraordinary times. Charcoal crust for dinner tomorrow or nothing.

It must have been about eight fifteen by the time Clara went back to her own room—after having discovered that the wireless didn't work. Within minutes there was a knocking on the door. She guessed it would be Alex, the one who explained everything and made her feel like a two-year-old. She had probably done something wrong again.

But it was the weepy Rita, still holding Molly Mouse.

"I can't sleep."

"Just lie down and try."

Rita looked downcast.

"What is it?"

"Maureen is being silly."

"Ask her to stop."

"I have."

"Tell her I said to stop."

"She won't listen."

Clara tried not to be resentful, but she couldn't help it. A woman needed time to herself. No matter how hard she had worked at

Harris & Sons, at least the evenings had been her own. How *did* you manage without it? This evening she felt like she couldn't even take a breath without someone interrupting.

Back in the girls' room, Maureen was leaning out the window overlooking the street, wearing a gray flannel nightie that was far too short. She might have been smoking before Clara came in; Clara was too slow to see. Certainly, the room smelled of cigarettes, but then the whole house was now burnt-pie-scented.

"Shut that window, now." Clara tried to be calm about it. Hadn't Maureen done her a favor earlier by calming Rita? "You'll catch a chill."

Maureen shouted to someone outside. "See you tomorrow. Keep your trousers on!"

She shook her head at Clara, muttering, "Why don't you leave us alone?"

Clara tried to give Maureen a censorious look, but it was difficult now that Terry was tugging her arm.

"What is it *now*?"

Clara looked down, then let out a shriek. Blood. Drops of bright red blood—on the floor *and* on Terry's face.

"Oh, for goodness' sake!" hissed Maureen. "It's a nosebleed, not a blooming massacre!"

By nine o'clock, Clara was exhausted. As she lay in her room, which smelled of smoke and cleaning fluid, she thought of her father's sudden and unwelcome recent return from Africa and the crunchy film of sand he had left all over the house that she had once loved.

She remembered the patterns in the carpet in Judy and Arthur's living room, where she had been staying, on the sofa in front of their new electric fire. And Arthur's stricken face when Clara had said, "Just a few more days, Arthur? Judy thought it would be fine."

It was strange to be here, alone with eight children. Between them, they could be plotting anything; they could come at her with machetes and chop her head off while she slept for all she knew.

Don't think like that, they're good children. Think of Michael instead. The way he smiled when they met after a long time apart, or his habit of rubbing his eyes first thing in the morning, murmuring, "Hello, sweetheart."

Just then, something astonishing happened.

As Clara lay in the darkness, the desk under the window moved. *But it couldn't have. Inanimate objects don't move.*

But it did.

An inch at first, no more, its legs wobbling. It was moving by itself. Just a tiny amount, but yes, it was movement.

"Michael?"

She had expected a sign for a long time. In fact, that's what helped get her through at first, looking for that sign. Everyone got signs. Fiancées got red robins at their kitchen window, wives got feathers on their front paths and mothers got rainbows in the sky on their birthdays.

But she had never had one. Not a single one. And she had decided: there couldn't possibly be ghosts or signs from the dead or anything like that, because if anyone could have found a way to communicate with her, Michael would have.

It was probably about this time of night that he'd died. It couldn't be a coincidence.

"Michael?"

The desk continued to wobble as if in answer, just a little at first, and then more. Yes, it was definitely wobbling more—in fact, it was shaking now.

At last, he was trying to communicate with her. He was sending her a message. What was he trying to say?

Her papers edged to the side of the desk before clattering to the floor. If that wasn't a sign enough. It was ridiculous. It wasn't ridiculous. He had promised to be with her always and...here he was.

"Are you there? Oh, my darling! Michael?"

The bedroom door was opening, by itself. Clara gazed at it, transfixed. She couldn't move. Suddenly there was a ghostly figure illuminated in the doorway. And as it moaned, Clara screamed as loud as she possibly could, then fled over to the shaking desk. She slipped under it and clasped her knees to her chest, burying her head in her knees in terror.

When she dared look up next, she saw a sheet fluttering in the air. Two boys appeared from underneath. They looked as scared as she did. It was Billy and Barry, the twins.

"HOW DARE YOU!" Clara bellowed at them.

"Don't hit us!"

"Get out of my room!" Clara had never heard herself sound so furious.

"Is she going to use the slipper on us?"

"Not the slipper!"

"Get out. GET OUT. GO!"

As they slammed the door, Clara rose up. *Those toerags.* It had not been Michael. There was no such thing as ghosts, however much you hoped there was.

And she saw now, in the light from the open doorway, that it was a slim line of black cotton threads that had been causing her desk to wobble, not her darling. Clara felt as if someone were yanking her strings too.

Right, that's enough.

She pulled on her day-clothes, but waited until she heard the hollow click of the light switch go off in the girls' room before she silently repacked her trunk, her files and her photographs.

How she yearned for the predictability of Harris & Sons—neat columns and darling rows of figures, a currant-bun tea break, the flirtatious fellas in the factories. This new job was just a ridiculous state of affairs.

This wasn't her. *Children* weren't her. She'd blown it with every single one of them—the mouse, the cigarettes, the...everything. How had she imagined she could swan in here and enjoy clean accommodation in an attractive location? She should have known. You pay a price for everything.

As she waited until she was certain the children were asleep, Clara couldn't help thinking about the last ten years—no, about the whole of her life. She had gone through such a lot, not only the war and Michael's death, yet the one thing she had always known was: all she had to do was get through it. By herself.

An albatross round your own neck was bad enough, but eight of them? The responsibility was all-consuming. Why, there would be no room for anything else! Sometimes she could barely make it through the day herself, carrying just her own grief and loneliness. The thought of carrying along all these orphans was just too much. It was too great an ask of anyone.

They would cripple her, they would ruin her, she didn't doubt it. It wasn't even much of a dilemma.

There would be other jobs.

Dear children,

I am afraid it's all been a most dreadful mistake. I am not the right person for you. I don't know what I imagined, but it wasn't this. It's not you personally, you're all fantastic human beings—it's me. It's just since the war and...things...I'm an empty shell of a woman. I don't know how to look after people, emotionally, I mean. I can do it on paper, but not in real life.

Maureen or Peter, as soon as you get up, please find a telephone booth and please phone the council on this number (I have provided a shilling). Ask for a Miss Bridges or the other one involved in children's services (sorry, I can't remember the name).

For anything else, the man from across the road with the dark hair and the brown eyes might be able to help.

Sorry to let you down, you deserve better.

I wish you all the best of luck in the future.

Sincerely,

Miss Newton, Clara

CHAPTER TWO

Clara's trunk made such a noise as she dragged it down the street she feared she'd wake the entire town, but she didn't see a soul all the way to the station and the dark windows overlooking her journey did not light up to shame her.

She felt liberated suddenly. The heavy burden she had been carrying since she arrived at Shilling Grange evaporated. Working with children was not for everybody. No shame in that. She had told herself that it would be mostly about paperwork. Or that it was enough that it would be in Lavenham. Or that she didn't have any other options.

Well, she had been wrong.

She tried not to think of Billy's (or was it Barry's?) tearstained cheeks and the plaintive way he cried, "Don't hit us!" Or the bitterness in Maureen's voice: "otherwise, we'll look like *normal* children." Or how Rita gripped her ridiculous mouse. "Mama!"

She wouldn't let herself dwell on Sister Eunice's closing words: *Whip them.* Was she serious? Just what had these children gone through?

Well, it wasn't Clara's concern anymore.

But when she got to the station, there were no trains to London. The last had gone fifty-five minutes earlier. *Damn the trains and damn me for dithering! Was there ever a more clueless runaway?* Clara sniffed back her tears. What to do now? Go to the fancy-pants hotel, the Lavender Arms, as recommended by Mrs. Garrard, for one night of irresponsible money-burning? Or give up the plan for tonight and try again tomorrow?

Turning round, she set off back to Shilling Grange.

Clara became nervously aware that someone was walking along the same side of the road as her before realizing, first with relief but then disappointment, that it was the sulky neighbor. The last thing she needed was more disapproval from the man with a chip on his shoulder.

She was marching straight past him when he called out a "Good evening," and a sob caught in her throat as she tried to reply. Yet he didn't take the hint, but ambled toward her. He was in an overcoat and hat, and looked even more striking than before. What was it about a nice-fitting hat that sent her doolally? Now he looked at her in much the same way he had looked at Peg when Clara had made those excruciating attempts to get the girl to speak.

"Where the hell can I get a timetable from? I can't even catch a train right!" Clara cried.

"I don't think there's a right or wrong way to catch a train, is there?"

Clara let out another sob and his face contorted in concern.

"Oh, Miss Newton. You poor thing!"

It was the worst thing he could have said. She couldn't handle kindness. Not now. She didn't have a handkerchief either. For shame! She'd given her last one to Terry. He peeled one from his pocket and she watched his empty sleeve flutter.

Why must her eyes always be drawn to his lost arm?

"The next train out is tomorrow afternoon, I think. Can it wait till then?"

"It'll have to."

"Let me take that trunk for you, Miss Newton."

She was still weeping. She was as bad as Rita. An errant tear rolled down her nose and she was ashamed that she should let a man, a man with only one hand for goodness' sake, carry her trunk when she had two perfectly good hands. He kept giving her worried looks, which was annoying because she couldn't help but note that his eyes *were* the color she liked best.

"What've you got in here? Weighs a ton."

"Letters, files, photos, that sort of thing. Oh, and some clothes."

"Not a dead body?"

"Ha, ha."

Clara had to keep focused. She couldn't let Mr. Ivor Delaney's attractiveness in a hat or his sudden turnaround to Prince Charming—grateful as she was for that—distract her from her mission to get away. When she spotted the public telephone box, she seized the opportunity.

"I'll just…make a call. Would you watch my trunk?"

He stood next to it, his face soft and sad. "I'll guard it with my life."

Judy answered on the fifth ring. Clara had known she would pick up. No one was more reliable than Judy. Nevertheless, she sounded sleepy.

"It's me, Clara. I'm getting a taxi back. Right now."

Judy would rescue her. Like she did in the Blitz. Like she did after Michael.

"What? That will be so expensive, Clara!"

It would be.

"All right, I'm going to come back in the morning."

"But Clara, why?"

"Because there are no trains tonight."

"I mean, why…why are you leaving so soon?"

Clara whispered, "It's rubbish here. *I'm* rubbish. I can't do this."

Judy lowered her voice. "Course you can. They wouldn't have employed you if they didn't think so."

Wrong.

"But where will you go? What will you do?"

This was *not* promising.

"I thought…I could come back to yours, just until I get back on my feet."

Judy sighed.

"You're always welcome, but Clara"—*there she was with the "but Clara's"*—"we don't have room."

Clara waited. If she waited long enough, Judy would feel bad and give in. There was a reason all the children at Honeywell School wanted her as their teacher: Judy was infamously soft.

"And actually, I don't think it's fair on Arthur."

Just because Arthur had had a tough time in the Far East, he oughtn't take it out on them.

"So, Arthur doesn't want me there?"

"It's not like that. Don't say it like that."

"Once I have a regular wage, I'll find a place to lodge." Clara had an awful feeling this battle was lost.

"How long will that take this time?"

Judy was never usually so unreasonable. Clara supposed Arthur was behind her, whispering furiously in her ear, *Don't let her stay here again.*

Judy had only once admitted to Clara that it wasn't happy families at their place all the time. Arthur had nightmares, sweats, the lot, but then many ex-soldiers did. It didn't make Clara like him any more.

"If you must come back to London, have you thought about going back to your father's?"

Clara slammed the receiver down and wept.

"Do you want to come to my workshop?" And now Ivor Delaney was talking to her like *she* was a child. "It's a bit of a mess, but…"

Clara sniffed. "What kind of workshop is it?" *As though that would make the difference.*

"Upholstery mostly, but I sew, fix, do anything really."

Clara pondered this. She couldn't understand how he could do all that with just one working arm.

"Things sometimes seem better over a nice cup of tea." His cheeks were flushed. "I hope I'm a good listener."

She didn't want to tell him about the ghost of Michael. *That* was embarrassing. She, who mocked seances, horoscopes and all the hoo-ha other widows and daughters had indulged in during the years since the war, had turned out to be just as silly.

Failure upon failure stacked up like a tower of stones within her. She couldn't tell him about the humiliating low seat at lunch. She couldn't tell him about washing Molly Mouse. She couldn't even tell him about Maureen's smoking at the window or the fella she had presumably been shouting to in the street. He would either think she was incompetent or that the children were bad. Neither was fair.

She blew her nose again—*his poor handkerchief.*

"I'm fine." She remembered the cold way he'd said "inexperienced pen-pushers" just a few hours earlier. He was no friend. "Thank you for your help."

"Any time." He paused. "I'm very fond of the children. I've known some of them for a long time and—"

Clara cut in decisively. "I won't need any more help."

"Suit yourself." His tone changed. "Good luck with your decision."

"Decision?"

He shifted uncomfortably.

"Wh-whether you're going or...staying."

Clara blinked at him.

"I *have* decided, thank you. I will be gone by tomorrow afternoon at the latest."

He shrugged. *Like he cared!* "That's probably for the best."

CHAPTER THREE

Bread and dripping for breakfast. There should have been porridge too, but Clara hadn't worked out where it was kept and by the time Alex showed her the cupboard, it was too late. Once again, it was the oppressive silence as much as the food that made the whole affair so dismal. The older boys cleared the plates as soon as they had put their spoons down and raced to the sink. Clara didn't know what to do with herself. The girls were being supervised by Maureen. Rita and Peg set the table for lunchtime. It was weird just sitting there, letting it happen around her. Billy and Barry were both scratching their heads. She thought she may as well try to have a conversation with them. A *last* conversation (they didn't need to know that, of course).

"So, you all go to the same school?"

Peter looked puzzled. "No, we go to the high school. The younger ones go to junior school."

"Of course." *Goodness, she was being ridiculous. Capital R ridiculous.*

At the back door, Rita held out her palm, her fingers outstretched. Clara stared at it. *Was she supposed to give the children something before school?*

"What's this?"

"I wet," Rita prompted. Her sad eyes met Clara's.

"Oh."

Rita leaned in, looking over her shoulder secretively. "Terry and Peg did too."

"Well, thank you for letting me know."

"Aren't you going to beat us?"

"I don't think so."

Rita stuffed her hand back in her pocket. "Fine, see you later."

Clara waved goodbye unsentimentally. Okay, she would never see them again and that would be for the best. She pondered whether she should wash the sheets of those—*three?*—who had wet. She didn't want to, but leaving them didn't seem fair either.

It was as she was scrubbing them that a woman from the county council came by, full of apologies that she hadn't made it along to welcome her yesterday. Miss Bridges had curled gray hair, thick-rimmed glasses and reassuringly solid heels that clicked rhythmically on the kitchen floor.

She was part-time children's services, part-time cemeteries.

"We're overwhelmed." She beamed. "Can't bury them quick enough. But we'll work this out together, right? I bet you've had an adjustment to make too."

She seemed so enthusiastic, and so overworked, that Clara couldn't immediately tell her what she needed to tell her.

Miss Bridges made a pot of tea, which was nice; Clara couldn't remember when someone had last made her a drink. Then she unpacked her bag—rubber linings for the mattresses and combs for the nits—and as she did so she talked nonstop. She didn't seem to need to draw breath.

"You'll be needing more of these. And I have to tell you about the new policies, the guidelines do change all the time. So, we believe it's better to get the children into permanent homes as soon as possible. Think of this place like a cog in a wheel, or a part of a long assembly line."

She took a long, luxurious gulp of tea, then peered into Clara's face.

"Oh no, not assembly line, not like making weapons or anything. I mean, like—like—oh, I know, like jars of jam. Get them ready for family life. We just want to disperse them to good homes as soon as possible, so they do not become institutionalized. You are here in the meantime. It's all in the Children's Act. Did you manage to read the Curtis Report? Dame Myra is a genius. We needed a shake-up and that's exactly what we got."

Clara had read some of the Curtis Report before her interview and had found it an extraordinary document. It detailed everything that was wrong with the fragmented charity system and how smaller, more family-like children's homes and more careful adoption and fostering were the future.

"You agreed with the findings?"

Clara nodded. She was hardly listening now. She was wondering how to tell Miss Bridges she was leaving. The fact that she was so sweet, understanding *and* talkative was making it difficult.

"We've tracked down some living relatives for some of the children." Miss Bridges looked around her before patting the chair. "Touch wood, I don't want to speak too soon, but there are two possible placements in the pipeline, we've even got a few adoption inquiries on the go. By my calculations, if we push, push, push, you could be down to four by spring. Which is such good news, isn't it?"

Miss Bridges chuckled. She really was a cheerful soul. She was launching into another soliloquy when Clara took her chance.

"I have something to tell you, Miss Bridges. I don't feel I'm the right person for the job, I'm afraid."

The effect on Miss Bridges was devastating. Her mouth fell open. She blinked rapidly. She put her hand over Clara's, trapping it. "I know it can be overwhelming at first, we all know that, but you learn to relax in the day while the children are at school and then it's action stations later. You'll be right as rain."

Clara tried to pull away her hand, but she couldn't.

"Sister Grace comes over every second Sunday, so you will have time off then."

"But I have no idea what to do with them."

"There's nothing mysterious about it." Miss Bridges allowed Clara's hand to escape, then placed her hand on Clara's knee, where she tapped reassuringly. "It's like looking after any family, only larger."

Clara decided not to say the truth, which was that she had no idea about looking after any sized family. She had not even managed to keep her houseplants alive. She swallowed her tea and even when there was none left, kept on raising the cup to her mouth for something to do with her hands. *This was awkward.*

"There is not even any paperwork."

"There is this!" Miss Bridges produced a slender—3mm thick at most—folder. "Keep it away from prying eyes, obviously. You'll have to update the records and start new ones."

"I already did." Clara felt proud. She was not a *total* waste of space after all. "But Miss Bridges, I don't think I made myself clear. There's a train back to London this afternoon and I intend to be on it."

It came out harsher than Clara had anticipated. But there was no better way to spell it out and at least she'd done it.

Miss Bridges lost her smile altogether.

"There's no way you can leave. Who would look after the children?"

"As you say, all the jars will be going to their new larders soon enough."

"We can't go through another round of advertisements and interviews. You can't imagine how time-consuming it is."

Clara murmured that she *could* imagine. *Sorry, sorry.*

"This is really difficult. The usual notice period is three months. Minimum."

Three months?

Miss Bridges looked flummoxed, but then she gathered herself.

"I suppose under the circumstances, if we say it's a family crisis, we might be able to bring it forward to say, two months?"

Two months is just as unmanageable. Clara's stomach clenched. "Six weeks, and I'll work the hardest I can for each of the children until then."

"Done."

*

After Miss Bridges had left, Clara sat out in the garden. This *was* her time off, although she had no idea what to do with it. Her day was upside down. The children were at school for six hours—apart from lunchtime—and the rest of the time she belonged to them and they to her. It was daunting but now, with a finish line in sight, she felt she could do it. Miss Bridges was right, she *should* see out her notice—even if only not to damage her chances of getting another job.

The garden occupied a corner plot, giving Clara a view of the comings and goings on the pretty high road. Resigning had been horrible, yet she was not displeased with the outcome. Although it would doubtless be dull, a stay of six weeks was probably more practical than running away with a bee in her bonnet. She would have time to find a new place to live and get another job. Harris & Sons wasn't the only place where she could be happy. Although right then, she'd have given anything to be back at her old desk with her old sense of purpose.

A dog sidled up next to her, placing his furry paw on her thigh. She stroked him in wonderment—this clever dog with bulging cutie-pie eyes. It felt like he was trying to tell her something. A voice came from beyond the garden.

"What *are* you doing, Bandit?"

It was a man in a tweed cap, blazer, jodhpurs and boots. He was the epitome of the country gentleman and something about him made Clara both want to giggle and sit up, back straight, stomach in.

"Get down, Bandit."

"Don't worry, he's lovely," Clara called.

"Bandit does have good taste in people." The man came to the gate and Clara rose to meet him.

"I'm White," he said. "Julian." *Posh name*, Clara thought as they shook hands. "Good to meet you."

"Miss Newton. Clara. Pleased to meet you too. And you, Bandit. Hello."

Julian had a nice smile. Floppy blond hair, even features, pale eyebrows and pink cheeks as if he'd been running. "We're neighbors," he said. "That's my office just there."

For the first time Clara noticed, properly noticed, the building diagonal to the Grange: a large, well-maintained property with Grecian pillars, windows glistening in the sun, freshly painted white walls and a golden plaque that read: "Robinson, Browne and White, Solicitors."

So, he was that White. She'd never met a solicitor before. She told him that.

"Well then, firsts all round. I've never met a...what are you exactly? You're not a nun, are you? Unless nuns have changed their...habits." He was in his mid- to late forties and the way he was eyeing her up and down suggested he was unmarried, although you never knew—*Clara* never knew.

"I am the new—what they call a 'housemother.' I'm employed by the council."

"To look after the children here?"

"That's the plan."

Should she tell him she'd be gone in just six weeks? No, it was none of his beeswax and it was hardly compulsory to tell her life story to strangers. Even charming solicitors who smiled at her like this.

"And how are you enjoying our fine town of Lavenham?"

"I haven't seen much of it yet."

"Well! Allow me to be your guide."

He had twinkly eyes, though she wasn't close enough to make out the color. You wouldn't imagine a solicitor with his own plaque would be so twinkly. And anyone with an adorable dog like Bandit had to be fun.

"Thank you. Absolutely!"

The next six weeks mightn't be so long and dull after all.

*

At lunchtime, Clara took Sister Eunice's seat at the head of the table—the children hadn't even asked where the nun was—and once they were tucking into the charcoal pie, she spoke up.

"Tell me about your mornings, children."

Nothing.

"Come on, I'm sure *something* interesting happened?"

Nothing.

"Anyone? All right, shall I go first?"

Nothing.

"Well, I met Miss Bridges from the council and we made lots of plans." Clara decided not to pass on the tenuous analogy about assembly lines and jams. "For your futures, I mean. It's all very exciting. Now, who's going next?"

"We have silence at mealtimes," freckly Peter muttered.

"It's the rule," added Alex with the ears.

"I appreciate that's the way it has been, but I'm in charge now, and we don't need to do it that way anymore."

Maureen bristled. "That's how it's always been."

Clara wouldn't have expected Maureen, of all people, to fight this. But perhaps Maureen would fight *anything*.

"Things change."

Clara had nothing to lose. What would the council do? Fire her?

"Maybe we *like* not speaking. Maybe we don't have anything to say to you."

No one else spoke. There was only the sound of forks scraping against china plates. A car hooting its horn outside. And was that the postman or the milkman calling out, "Nice day for it"?

"Billy, Barry? Peter? How was school? Terry? Rita?"

They all stared at her.

"Cat got your tongue, has it? Peg? No, not Peg. Um, Alex?"

"Thank you for asking." Alex looked at the others helplessly. "In maths we are learning the Pythagoras theorem. Do you want me to explain it?"

"Please," said Clara.

God help us.

CHILDREN'S REPORT 1
Rita Jane Withers

Date of birth:
August 21, 1939
She is nine but acts younger.

Family background:
In 1944, the family home in East London was hit by a stray incendiary bomb and subsequently there was a house fire. There were five of them and only Rita was discovered alive—the rest are missing, presumed dead. It seems Rita was found late the next morning with her little woolen mouse, about two miles away from the site. A relative took her in in Southend-on-Sea but she couldn't cope with the demands of yet another traumatized child and Rita was bullied there, apparently (according to a neighbor). Rita came here in 1947.

She mentions her mama, Gloria Withers, at least six times every day. Sometimes more.

I will try to find out what happened to the mother.

Health/Appearance:
Rita is a healthy girl with large eyes and long eyelashes. People in the street often say, "She'll break a few hearts." She is fond of her long hair, which Maureen brushes for her, 100 times, most nights.

Food:
Buns, rice pudding, macaroni pudding. Anything sweet. She eats well—so well, it is a mystery she is so weeny. Maybe she has hollow legs.

Hobbies:

She is good at needlework and art. She likes the Janet and John series of storybooks.

Other:

She gets frightened by loud noises and fire. The older children are kind to her—she seems to bring out the protectiveness in them. She is very attached to her woolen mouse (do not wash!). She closes her eyes when she says her prayers before lunch.

CHAPTER FOUR

Michael used to say opposites attract. Michael was serious about things Clara wasn't serious about, and funny about things that were deadly serious. He was smooth, she was edgy. He was strong, she wasn't. But Clara struggled with some of the children who she supposed could be considered her opposites.

She was most similar to Peter—his mannerisms, his demeanor reminded her of herself at that age. He was quiet yet helpful around the house—a loyal presence. Billy's and Barry's playfulness and Alex's brilliance she could also understand, or at least tolerate. If only they were all like that...

But they weren't. There was Maureen and her moodiness, Peg and her silence. And they deserved better than Clara, they needed someone who knew what was what, someone with authority, someone with gravitas. *Someone more like Judy.*

But Rita. *Oh, Rita...*

They hadn't gotten off to the best start. First, the incident with Molly Mouse. Then, the next night, Clara had picked up a hairbrush and that had made Rita scream.

"Don't hit me!"

"I wouldn't!" Clara set it down carefully, raising her hands in surrender. "Look, see?"

"She used to," Rita wept. "Sister Eunice beat me. I want my mama."

"I'm not going to hit you," Clara said. "Ever, I promise."

Maureen, who was standing looking out the window for something, or someone, crossed her arms. "They all say that at the beginning."

Rita never wanted to go to school unless everything was just right. Not a hair out of place, socks pulled to the exact same length, shoes shinier than anyone else's.

She stared in the cracked bathroom mirror. "Am I pretty?"

"Perhaps you should ask, 'Am I kind?'" Clara suggested once.

Rita gazed at her uncomprehendingly.

"I mean, pretty isn't everything, is it?"

Rita walked off and Clara was left once more with that "I didn't get that right" feeling.

None of the children slept well, but Rita struggled the most. She wet the bed during the early hours of the morning, then came into Clara's room. Clara began to dread that whispered wake-up call of "Need new sheet" or "Can I sleep here?" She liked to talk then too: "My knee feels different," or "I thought I heard a cat. Can we get a cat?"

"They all wet during the war," Miss Bridges said and promised to dig out an article about it.

Clara tried to be as patient as she could with Rita, but it required superhuman effort. Rita had days when she was not a problem, days when she would skip merrily in the garden for hours, wash her socks without quibbling and sing the national anthem, loudly. Other days, she couldn't or wouldn't stop crying. She told Clara that she had to keep her hair tidy in case one day, Mama came to collect her.

Clara wondered if she would ever sleep again, ever read in privacy again, ever use the lavatory in peace again without someone knocking: "Rita's crying," or "Terry's got another nosebleed," or "Barry hit me," or "My shoes don't fit."

Two weeks after her arrival, Clara had stomach cramps—her monthlies—and all she wanted was a deep sleep. Her bones ached. The evening's mince dinner had been another tasteless failure, memories of Michael were pressing down on her and as she fell asleep, she was wondering if she could last the four weeks left until October 14 after all.

In the middle of the night, she was woken by the instinct that she wasn't alone. Opening her eyes, she saw a face next to hers, cast in shadows. Clara shrieked.

"Don't creep in here!"

The face burst into tears. "Miss Mama."

It was two thirty in the morning. "I miss my mama too," barked Clara, she couldn't stop herself. "We all do, that's why we're stuck in this dreadful place."

Rita's mouth fell open.

"I didn't mean it," said Clara quickly. *This little girl has lost her mother! Awful, awful.* "Rita, I'm sorry. I am just so tired tonight."

"What happened to your mama?" Rita asked.

"She's dead." There was nothing Clara hated talking about more. Rita, however, nodded with understanding.

"Where?"

"In Africa." Clara knew that Rita deserved so much better than this.

"I know Africa. It's near Birmingham." Rita wound her arms round Clara and sank her head into her neck. "Makes me sad."

"Me too." Clara patted the little girl awkwardly and soon they had both fallen asleep.

The doctor's surgery was on one of the grander roads off the high road, only a five-minute walk from the Grange. There was a sign on the frosted glass, but otherwise it looked like a normal residential home. Clara took Rita there the next day after school. Dr. Cardew was tall, rangy and blond—the men in Lavenham didn't suffer from rationing looks-wise.

He greeted them at the door, military-straight.

"Ah, I wondered if we'd have the pleasure."

The doctor led Clara and Rita through a plain waiting area to a bright room at the back. Wooden cabinets covered three of the walls and each was filled with jars, jugs and boxes. His surgery smelled—not unpleasant, but super-clean. He listened to Rita's heart, her pulse, looked at her ears, got her—laughing—to stick out her tongue. "There is nothing *physically* wrong with this little one," he pronounced as Rita gazed up at him, the purple crescents under her eyes prominent in this brightly lit room.

There was a sudden noise, a melancholy sound that made Clara freeze. It was a violin, she realized almost immediately, but played like she had never heard before. It was so haunting. Clara didn't know much, but she could hear that whoever was playing was very talented indeed. Rita squeezed her hand and said, "Pretty!"

"Excuse me," Dr. Cardew called to the other room. His voice was measured, but he seemed annoyed at the interruption, as if it happened a lot. "I've still got patients."

The sound stopped abruptly—so abruptly, it too sounded annoyed.

"My wife." He turned back to Rita. "See that jar of sugared almonds there? Take one and go and have a look at the frogs at the pond."

Delighted, Rita did as she was told and slipped outside. The garden was lush with tall trees in a U-shape around the water. Clara heard footsteps and then, moments later, a tall dark-haired woman joined Rita in the garden.

"She's been through so much." Clara told the doctor the information she had on Rita: the bombing in London, the bullying family in Southend-on-Sea, the fear of being hit.

He paid such close attention to her story that Clara couldn't help being taken aback. She wasn't used to being listened to by men. "She's obsessed with finding her mama. I don't know how I can get her to think about anything else. Or if I should try."

"She will just have to get over it," he said.

"I don't know if it's that easy."

"I didn't say it was easy." He picked up his pen and wrote a few words. It was a grand kind of fountain pen, the type Emily Brontë might have used. *A notekeeper*, Clara thought approvingly.

"There must be something we can do?"

"We used to talk about shellshock after the Great War. It's a recognized condition. Rita is suffering from a form of that."

"What's the treatment?"

Now that he'd finished writing, he stared out the window, not at Rita but beyond.

"There isn't any one solution, I'm afraid. Time, maybe, understanding. Miss Newton—I just want to say, I'm glad you decided to stay."

Clara chewed her lip.

"I saw you leaving." He didn't look at her, but at his pen. "You went to the station with your trunk."

Clara couldn't think of anything to say to that. The clock ticked. There was the drone of a distant appliance. A car went past.

"I wanted to tell you, it's normal to have doubts."

"I...thank you."

"After all, it's a huge responsibility. Many of the children of Shilling Grange have suffered a great deal already. So, to see someone come along and offer them consistency, reliability, commitment is great news: not just for the children, but for the whole town."

In the garden, Rita was now standing next to the tall, impossibly slender black-haired woman.

Dr. Cardew opened the French doors and motioned to Clara to join them outside; Clara did, feeling terrible. She should have told him she was leaving in a month instead of accepting his accolades like a bouquet of flowers meant for someone else. She just hadn't felt able to.

Outside, there was a gray stone patio and a hutch in front of which Rita and the doctor's wife were crouching.

The woman raised her arm in greeting, then dropped it as though she regretted it. She had the most extraordinary cheekbones and violet eyes; she looked like a film star, or at least someone who belonged in a world of five-star hotels and posh restaurants. And then Clara saw that her sleeve was rolled up and below it was the blue imprint of a row of numbers on her upper arm, like a bruise or a scald. They held the eye. The woman was looking at Clara now, intently. Their eyes met above a gray rabbit with floppy ears being squeezed in Rita's arms.

"Sorry to bother you," whispered Clara.

The woman looked away.

"I want a rabbit," said Rita. Joyfully, she sank her face into the creature's fur. "Can I, please?"

CHILDREN'S REPORT 2
Teresa Seraphina Carter

Date of birth:
July 13, 1938

Family background:
Terry's mother, Patricia Carter, died in the Blitz with Terry's baby sister, Bernadette, in May 1941. Terry was not living with them at the time. The mother was apparently planning to evacuate the family to the countryside where they would be together again but had delayed the move because of caring responsibilities in London. Terry was eventually moved from her evacuation home in Wales to a children's home in Norfolk. Terry didn't know her father—it seems he was a career soldier killed in operations in Egypt in 1943.

Health/Appearance:
Bedwetter two out of seven nights. Terry likes shorts instead of skirts, pajamas instead of nighties and insists on having her hair cut short. This is sensible since she is particularly prone to nits.

Food:
Ham. Cheese on toast. Popcorn. Black coffee. She has surprisingly adult tastes.

Hobbies:
Not sure.

Other:
Although friendly and lively in a one-on-one situation, Terry tends to shrink in crowds.

CHAPTER FIVE

Shilling Grange, Mr. Delaney's workshop and Robinson, Browne and White Solicitors were at the bottom end of Lavenham High Road. The railway station and the Lavender Arms Hotel were at the other end. In the middle were various shops, including the butchers, the bakers and the post office. Beyond them were fields, which Clara was both attracted to and nervous about for she knew there were cows, and not just cows but mud and mess. That was the thing about the countryside—it got everywhere. But on the other hand, Clara loved a wildflower as much as the next person, she loved the trees, she loved the open spaces—she was just not used to them.

By late September, the chill in the air had begun to feel more permanent and it was never as warm as it looked from inside. The children kept bringing home heaps of autumn leaves and piling them on the table, like cats bringing in maimed mice, and Clara didn't know what she was supposed to do with them. Even after twenty-four days at Shilling Grange, she still didn't know what she was doing at all. And the longer she stayed there, the less certain about *anything* she was.

The children were getting more used to her, but were still jumpy, especially if they made mistakes. After Billy knocked over the milk jug he had fetched a slipper, and when Peg fell over, she still held out her palm for a smack. As time went on, hopefully they would begin to realize that Clara didn't punish children—not like that anyway—and Clara hoped her replacement wouldn't either.

But what if they did?

*

Toward the end of the month, Clara was out with Terry in the high road when she realized Terry was no longer with her but was three or four shops behind, gazing into the florist's window. Terry was terrible for dawdling. Alex had said she was often punished at school for being late.

Clara went back and found her, fingers pressed against the glass. The shop door opened with a clang.

"Do you *mind*?" It was the woman with the bleached hair, Mrs. Garrard.

"Sorry?"

"That little boy is steaming up the glass."

"Oh, but *she* is just looking at the sunflowers."

Mrs. Garrard shook her head. "He gives me the creeps."

"She likes them, that's all."

"She can go and like them somewhere else. Move along, please."

"Let's go." Clara grabbed Terry's hand and walked her away. Terry seemed unperturbed, but you never knew.

"That woman!" Clara said, exasperated, when there were a few shops between them.

"Those flowers!" said Terry. "It's like they're trying to say hello."

Miss Bridges was especially busy these days—there had recently been a flood at a local cemetery—so they sent Mrs. Harrington to do Clara's check instead. Mrs. Harrington was also part-time children's services but her other part was "social care."

Clara was putting out the milk bottles when Mrs. Harrington turned up: a blustery young woman with red hair in a net and too much rouge.

"Thank you for coming—" began Clara but Mrs. Harrington flapped her arms around her like an injured bird.

"Is that Mr. Delaney I see over there?"

She had an unexpectedly posh voice. Judy would say plummy.

Ivor was just leaving his workshop. In his hat and overcoat, Clara couldn't help thinking, he might have come straight off a film noir set. He definitely had a bit of a bad-tempered Humphrey Bogart about him.

"Mr. Delaney the dashing upholsterer?"

Clara blinked at her. She hadn't spoken to Ivor since the evening at the train station nearly one month earlier and she didn't want to get involved now. Unfortunately, she was ever alert to his presence, because he left his workshop door open most of the day and his lights on most of the night. (Clara was convinced this was to annoy her.)

"I've got some bits that need stuffing," Mrs. Harrington called out to Mr. Delaney, winking at Clara. "When can I bring them in?"

"You can drop them off at my workshop any time."

"*What* an invitation!" cooed Mrs. Harrington.

"And you too, Clara." Ivor addressed Clara directly despite her efforts at pretending he did not exist. "I used to darn and mend for the children. If you have anything…?"

Clara decided to ignore him. Oh, he was being all friendly now in front of the council staff. He probably thought she was staying. Well, she didn't need him. Even so, the display of familiarity between him and Mrs. Harrington had taken Clara by surprise and it irked her somewhat, although she didn't know why.

She shuffled Mrs. Harrington inside.

"Isn't he a dreamboat? I haven't seen a one like him since the Americans left. And *what* a hero. They say he saved twenty men. Dunkirk."

Clara wanted to laugh. *Twenty men*? As if. War stories, like war wounds, got exaggerated, everyone knew that.

She laid out cups and saucers as Mrs. Harrington rambled on. "Shame about the arm but I'd put up with it, wouldn't you? Only joking, I'm a married woman, but good grief! Puts a spring in your step!"

Clara endeavored to keep Mrs. Harrington on track, but it wasn't easy. Mrs. Harrington was more interested in discussing Ivor's war record, her own mother's arthritis, her husband's favorite meal ("he says there's nothing like a chop") and her hopes to have a baby—"it will be bye, bye, Suffolk Council!"—than anything to do with the children.

The moment she paused to drink her tea, Clara questioned her about the council's quest to find living relatives or adoptive families for the children. Miss Bridges had suggested it was urgent, she said, or at least a priority?

Disgruntled at the subject-change, Mrs. Harrington drew out a folded piece of paper from her bag.

"Oh my! It looks like Peter has an uncle who is to take him out for a contact visit."

This was big news indeed. Peter had someone? Of all the children, gentle, freckly Peter was Clara's favorite. (She knew she shouldn't have favorites—the fact that she did was further confirmation that she was ill-suited to the post.) The thought that dear Peter might soon be on his way to a permanent home was delightful. At the same time, it was annoying no one had mentioned it sooner.

"Anyone for Alex?" It seemed inconceivable that clever Alex also hadn't been snapped up.

"Not a snifter."

"The twins?"

"Would you be prepared to separate them?"

"Oh!" Clara was surprised by the question. Billy and Barry were joined at the hip. "Erm, no, I don't think…"

"Then no." Mrs. Harrington picked at her nails. "Not a hope."

"What about Rita's mother?" Clara pressed on. "Does anyone know what happened to her?"

"Gawd, it's been years. Surprised Rita remembers anything about it."

"She remembers an awful lot."

"Oh, me too. Mother says it's a curse. My husband says I'm like an elephant."

Clara let that sink in.

"I know it's awkward, but do you think you could investigate? Rita seems so convinced she's still alive."

Mrs. Harrington didn't write it down, but maybe she didn't need to because of her amazing memory.

"It would be helpful to uncover something definite," Clara added. "Either way." *And*, she thought, *it would be a nice note to depart on*. She had only two weeks left in which to make a difference and she was feeling determined to try.

CHAPTER SIX

The trip to Dr. Cardew's had gotten Clara thinking. There could be no rabbits or guinea pigs at the Grange, pets were strictly against council rules, but what about a musical instrument? Rita's pleasure at the sound of the violin was undeniable. A violin probably wouldn't work (too expensive, too complicated!), but how about something smaller? Recorders, whistles, maracas? There was something tangible about learning music. It had measurable outcomes. It would do them *all* good.

"Have you ever played a musical instrument?" she asked Alex at breakfast.

"Professionally?"

"Er no, for fun?"

"Oh no, actually I haven't."

"Would you like to?"

Alex rubbed his chin. "Nothing ventured, nothing gained."

Clara called Mrs. Harrington. "The effects of musical education can be transformative," Clara said, a line she had rehearsed several times. "Is it possible I might get money to buy some instruments?"

Mrs. Harrington had laughed her plummy laugh and Clara had quickly added, "Only small ones. Penny whistles perhaps?"

"Miss Newton, I don't think you realize your position. You, we, are financially strapped. I can't imagine what the council would say if I requested something as frivolous as that! Anything additional to the budget will have to come out of your pay." Clara had a sinking feeling. Her pay wasn't terrible for a young woman, but it wasn't much either. How would anyone be able to afford anything extra for the children? It wasn't possible. They would be stuck in a miserable cycle of scrimp and save—which was yet another sign that this wasn't the job for her.

"How's that lovely neighbor of yours, by the way? Tell him I need some more things darned."

Clara promised she would, knowing that she would not. Absolutely she would not. She was not the house matchmaker!

Despite Mrs. Harrington, Clara remained keen to acquire musical instruments before she went. It was a mistake being here, and she had managed to make all of the children either cry or sulk, but at least she would have left one good thing.

The telephone conversation Clara had had with Judy the night she almost left had bruised her, so she didn't call her friend again for a while. When she finally did, Judy was once again her warm and interested self, so Clara resolved to put it behind her.

"Whatever you do, don't get recorders," Judy said darkly about Clara's plans. "They're the devil's work." And, "Arthur says to look out at the auction rooms."

Arthur says, Arthur says. Judy was barely able to begin a sentence without mentioning him these days.

Judy offered to go to the Newton family house in London to see if Clara's father was still there. If he wasn't, she would let Clara know immediately. Clara thought longingly of returning to her old bedroom and her responsibility-free life post October 14. It was unlikely that her father had cleared off though. When he had appeared out the blue, the first thing he had said to his daughter was he had had it up to here (indicating his forehead) with "uncivilized natives" and he was sticking with Blighty. "At least you can get a decent cup of tea here."

Judy also said that if Clara *genuinely* didn't have anywhere else, she supposed she could stay, but Arthur wasn't happy about the idea and please don't let it be for more than three nights this time.

Three nights?

After Michael died, Judy had been a rock—*her* rock. Judy had made sure Clara ate of an evening, she had made sure she got out of bed and washed her face. She had been a prop, an ally, she went way beyond the call of duty. Even once the war ended, when Judy left Harris & Sons and got her dream job at Honeywell School, she had been a devoted friend. Then, a demobbed Arthur had turned up, all handsome and yet *another* hero with his St. George's Cross—if Ivor Delaney had saved twenty men, then Arthur would have saved thirty—and had set up a popular homework club at St. Mary's Primary. After that, things had never been the same.

"He'll be headteacher within eight terms," Judy had said yet, rather than being annoyed as she usually would that an upstart male had leapfrogged the female teachers with all their years of stalwart service, she was impressed.

Clara had never gotten on with Arthur. Arthur had told Judy that the reason Clara didn't like him was jealousy: Judy had her man and Clara did not. Clara didn't think that was the reason, but it was hard to argue with someone so certain about everything.

A few evenings later, when Clara and Alex were walking back from the post office, they ran into Mr. White, out with Bandit.

"I've had bad experiences with the canine species," Alex said, shying away, but Clara encouraged him to pat Bandit and eventually he dared. Bandit responded. Before long, they had become great pals and Alex couldn't stop grinning.

Julian winked. "Miss Newton, I don't know who you are more pleased to see: me or Bandit."

Clara said she was delighted to see them both, *equally*, she refused to have favorites. Julian laughed. "I love a woman with a sense of humor," he said, and she blushed because she hadn't been joking.

Julian was debonair in a cream-colored suit, matching hat and shirt and Clara regretted that she wasn't wearing one of her more fitted going-out dresses, like she had been when they first met in the garden. Still, he gave her his appreciative once-over. *It's only because there aren't many young women in the countryside*, she reminded herself. Possibly she and Mrs. Garrard were the only women under thirty in town—no doubt Lavenham was a small pond in which to fish *romantically*.

When Clara asked Mr. White if he knew where she might be able to secure some low-priced musical instruments, he thought for a moment.

"We might have an old piano in the office somewhere."

Clara was amused that his office was so big he wasn't certain if he had a piano or not. Then she realized he was being serious.

"Oh no, a piano is much too much. For a start, I can't afford to pay and...Mr. White, I was thinking of maybe recorders?"

"Not recorders," he said firmly, his wrist over his forehead. "Clara, the piano is all yours—on one condition: you will go out for lunch with me this weekend."

For the past four years Clara had had a line ready for the men who asked her out at dances and pubs (and once while waiting at the Elephant and Castle bus stop): "I'm not ready, thank you."

And she was just about to deliver her go-to line with just the right sprinkling of regret when she thought, *why though? Why not go out with Mr. White the solicitor?* Why *shouldn't* she try something a bit different?

Michael was gone and it wasn't like anyone else was asking.

Anyway, Mr. White was only offering a nice meal. And a piano, certainly, but yes. When was the last time she had eaten well? It would be hard to say no to that without coming across as a bit uppity. Plus, there was Bandit. Who could fail to adore this bug-eyed, tail-chasing dog? And she *was* free on Sunday. Sister Grace had turned out to be a lifesaver. She scrubbed the oven, she swept, she brought little treats, she listened to Rita's ramblings and admired Peg's dancing.

"I'll consider it."

He grinned at her and whispered, "That's my girl." And that gave her a little thrill too.

"Bad news," Miss Bridges said on her next visit. "Norfolk council have placed fifty-eight children in the last six months. That's a fifth of their children."

"That's good, isn't it?"

Miss Bridges quickly corrected herself. "It is good. But we really have to get a move on at Suffolk. Otherwise, we're going to look incompetent."

"So it's a competition?"

"No!" Miss Bridges denied before laughing. "Well, since you put it like that, Clara."

Later, Miss Bridges explained that a possible adoption for Terry had fallen through. The family—"lovely people, salt of the earth"—went with a boy in the end ("from where do you think? Norfolk!"). And a cousin for Alex had turned out to be not related. "Dead ends all round," she admitted.

A few days later, Clara watched two workmen maneuver the piano out of the solicitors' building—"Watch out for the hanging baskets!"—through the gate and to the Grange. Passersby stopped walking and gaped. Unfortunately, the front door was too narrow for the piano, so the men set it down and walked off for their supper. They'd only been paid for removals.

Ivor was watching the kerfuffle from his workshop window. It was annoying to Clara that he was the Grange's nearest neighbor, especially since there were so many other, much nicer people in the town. Dr. Cardew, the petrol attendant and the butcher all called out greetings to Clara now when she passed by, so did the women from the bakery and the couple from the grocery store. The woman from the post office had even chased after her when she had left behind her book of stamps and had said, "What you're doing is nothing short of miraculous. God bless you!" Clara had gulped in reply. There really had been no point in announcing that she was leaving when she could just slip quietly away.

By the time Clara and the children had managed to jam the piano halfway inside the doorway, Ivor had disappeared. Ten minutes later, however, he sidled over, probably to gloat.

"We're fine, Mr. Delaney!" The man was *such* an interfering so-and-so.

"Of course." He backed off a little but then countered, "It looks stuck to me. What were you planning to do?"

"Smash the bleedy piano!" shouted Barry and Clara sent him to his room for swearing. He went, kicking the ground as he did. Barry had a vile temper sometimes.

"You can't leave it there."

"I'm aware," sighed Clara. The exchange with Barry had upset her—and in front of Ivor too. She wanted to look competent not just in front of him, but especially in front of him.

Ivor felt around the piano and then got under it. He obviously had some kind of hero complex, Clara decided. Twenty men at Dunkirk *and* a piano.

Suddenly, he pulled the piano free one-handed with a shout, dragging it from its trap so it was no longer stuck. When he emerged, his hat had fallen off and his hair was stuck to his forehead. Clara noticed he had dark bags under his eyes and suddenly felt less animosity toward him.

She picked up his hat.

"Is there another place you could put it?" he asked.

"What about the garden shed?" Alex suggested.

Clara thought Ivor would laugh, but he said, "He's so sharp, he'll cut himself," and ruffled Alex's hair.

"Mr. Delaney, I don't think that'll work."

"We'll be able to take it round the side. Alex is right—if we clear it up, there'll be plenty of room. I'll make sure it's watertight." He met her eyes. "It's up to you though. Just seems a pity to let it go to waste."

Ivor walked backward taking the strain, Clara mostly guided from the front. She moved a box full of child-sized gas masks and found a place for the piano next to a rusty wheelbarrow and an even rustier saw. It was not what she had hoped for, but it was better than nothing. She fetched the stool from the parlor and found, serendipitously, it was just the right height. And the piano itself was a thing of beauty. Julian had been very kind.

Clara brought Ivor out a cup of tea—he had been kind too, of course so she used an unchipped cup.

Rita ran her hands along the keys. Peg jigged from foot to foot and Peter popped his head round the door, blushing. "Cor, I never thought we'd have something like that here! Thank you, Miss Newton."

A few minutes later, even Maureen came for a nose. "Wow. We're posh now."

Ivor said, "Miss Newton's not so silly after all, eh?" and Maureen flushed.

Clara bristled. It sounded like those two had been discussing her behind her back.

Ivor sipped his tea as Clara tried not to notice his arm. "So, you're going to teach the children to play, Clara?" he asked.

"I can't play a note," she admitted. "My parents didn't believe in music."

"Christ."

"They didn't like swearing either."

Ivor laughed. "Poor Billy, is he still in his room?"

"Barry. No, he has apologized and I have set him free."

Rita asked if she could learn to play the piano. "Mama would be amazed!"

Ivor raised his eyebrows at Clara.

"Of course," she said. "I'll just have to get you some music."

"And a teacher?" persisted Rita.

"I ... yes, maybe a teacher."

Once the children had wandered off, Clara dropped her head into her hands. "I didn't think this through."

Ivor grinned sympathetically. "Oh, a teacher will turn up. Probably when you least expect it."

"There's no way I can afford to *pay* a teacher," Clara said. "I can hardly afford to get a piano book. I have to beg the council for every single boot, every single vest and half the time, they say no. If I had more, I'd pay for it all myself, but..." She trailed off, already regretting being so candid with her least favorite neighbor. "I don't have a lot."

"Well, I think it's nice. You're doing the best you can."

"Thank you. And at least the Grange garden is wonderful, isn't it?"

"Yeah, Terry loves it. You know, that's her thing."

Clara remembered the sunflowers in the shop window reflected in the girl's eyes.

"Oh yes," she agreed. She'd add that to Terry's file. She smiled at him, gratefully.

"Alex said you have some time off on Sundays?"

"Every other week, yes, Sister Grace comes."

Ivor tucked his thumb under his braces. "Once a month, I go to Felixstowe market to sell. It's this weekend. Alex asked if he could come."

"Oh, that sounds wonderful."

"It's not wonderful." Laughing, he pinged his braces accidentally. "But it is fun."

"Well, if he wants to, why not?"

"Alex wondered…" Ivor stuttered slightly. "Well, we both did, if you'd join us?"

"Ah!" Clara blushed. "Oh!" This really *was* the hand of friendship. "Well, yes, thank you," and then she remembered. "Gosh, I'm sorry, I…I…already promised to go out with Mr. White this Sunday."

"Oh, I see."

"It's just for the piano…" Clara's voice trailed away.

"Never mind. Another time." Ivor pushed his hair out of his eyes, smiled at her. Dark eyes that noticed everything.

"I suppose I should tell you—I've given in my notice here. I'm leaving on the fourteenth."

"The fourteenth of what?"

"October." Clara smiled, confused. When did he think she was talking about?

"That's just a few days from now…"

"Ten days, isn't it?"

He squinted at her, deliberating. She supposed he, like the doctor, had assumed she was staying. Well, people shouldn't assume. Hadn't they learned enough about that during the war?

"Great." He stood up abruptly, grabbing his hat. "I'll be off, Miss Newton."

"I thought you'd be pleased."

"P-pleased?" He stuttered, struggling to find the words. "I think it stinks."

"What?"

"People like you, coming and going, going and coming without a care for the children. You council crowd just don't know what you're doing, do you? At least in the old days, working here was considered an act of love, or of compassion or care. Not just a job or a paycheck. I thought better of you."

"It's *because* I care that I'm leaving here!" Clara was so shocked the words simply flew out of her. "I'm *totally* the wrong person for the task. The children deserve much better than me. I'm just a... what did you say? A stupid pen-pusher!"

He stomped away, slamming the side gate behind him.

The next morning, Clara called Terry into the garden. She slouched out, hands in the pockets of her shorts, staring at her muddy shoes.

"Am I in trouble?"

"No, why?"

"They used to say I was bad when I did something wrong. Even when I didn't know it was wrong. They used to lock me in the larder in the dark."

Terry spoke like a weary old woman. Clara couldn't think what to say. She went to pat the top of the girl's head, then decided not to.

"You're *not* bad, Terry, and I know you like being out here, so I was wondering, would you like to grow some things in the garden—your own patch, all to yourself?"

Clara had watched the transformation of parks into farms, and private gardens into chicken coops, during the war. It could be done.

Terry burst into tears. Clara watched her for a moment before nervously asking, "Is that all right?"

The girl put her arms round Clara's waist.

"Thank you."

They avoided Mrs. Garrard's flower shop, but there was a plant shop nearby that was part of a walled estate. A kind couple there gave them seeds—some of them free—and lots of advice.

"Be quick though, you're running out of time."

They didn't mean her, but still Clara blushed. She tried not to think of poor Terry, crying in confinement, but the image was stuck there now and there was nothing she could do to make it go away.

*

Clara had to explain to the children she was leaving. They were growing used to her being there (*too* used to her) and she regretted not saying anything earlier. Maybe subconsciously she had arranged the piano and the vegetable patch in recompense.

Now that it was October, the fourteenth no longer seemed like a distant star, or a finish line, but a large, hulking shadow moving toward her. Ivor's unpleasant reaction to the news had made her anxious too. She was doing the right thing by leaving, wasn't she? *One more week to go.* She would have felt better about it if she knew the children would be in safe hands once she'd gone. And if she didn't have pictures of some of them being ignored or locked up in her head. And if she knew where she was going or staying. And if every time they spoke, Miss Bridges hadn't kept making little comments, like, "It's not too late to change your mind" and "You are getting on remarkably well."

That evening, she told them she was going back to London. Rita kept saying "why?" and "Mama," then covering her face with her hands.

"Because I think someone else will do the job better than I will. Record-keeping is more my thing. I'm good at that," Clara explained. "I'm not so good at childcare," she added guiltily. "You deserve more."

Peg stopped hanging off Clara's arm and raced upstairs. Clara's arm ached where she had been.

"What are you planning to do in London?" Alex asked politely.

"Not sure yet," admitted Clara. "I'd love my old job back, but that's not going to happen."

"Is it wise to be focused on that?" he asked before correcting himself, "I hope you find it fulfilling, Clara."

He was such a little professor.

Billy asked Barry if he'd seen his best conker and said if he had taken it, he'd kill him. Barry leapt on his back. Clara hadn't impacted much on their lives, she realized. Well then, at least they wouldn't miss her.

"What do you think, Peter?" Clara ventured nervously. Peter's opinion mattered.

Startled, the boy looked up from buttering his bread roll.

"Nice ones never stay."

Maureen nudged him and he dropped the knife.

"Told you," she crowed, flicking his ear. "You owe me a shilling."

Judy suggested that the children were too used to people coming and going to react strongly, but Clara didn't know what she had expected or why she felt so down. She knew that relationships worked on trust and her lying, or at least withholding information for so long, had chipped away at their trust. *I will never do that again*, she told herself. *Never.*

And Judy wasn't right—they *did* seem to feel it strongly. Not surprise, not sadness, but a kind of resignation. As though they hadn't expected any better and she had proved them right.

The child who had the most painful reaction was Terry. She had been out in the garden when Clara had told the others, so Clara had to tell her at bedtime instead. Terry would only go to sleep with her hands and feet firmly under the covers—otherwise she feared the devil would get to them.

"I thought, I thought..."

"What?"

"I thought we were growing things together."

After that, she just lay there, silent and still as anything.

CHAPTER SEVEN

Mr. White, or *please call me Julian*, was handsome in a delicate, golden way. He was also older than Clara had guessed. He was fifty, he told her in the car. Fifty! Maybe it only sounded older than it was? Clara's father was in his fifties, although he was right at the other end.

Because of his age, Julian had missed the draft. He explained it in a way that suggested he had been explaining it often over the last ten years.

He had, however, been in the Home Guard, where he made what he called "Friends for Life." Clara liked this. It was a sign of a loyal person. Michael had been a great one for his friends too.

Clara enjoyed the drive to Bury St. Edmunds. Julian drove them through a shallow ford and the water splashed right up to the windows and somehow it was gorgeous that someone else was taking fun risks *and* responsibility for her.

I need this, she thought. It felt as though part of her had disappeared since she had been at Shilling Grange, swallowed up by the needs of the children. Time without them felt restorative—it made her whole again. She had thought she was getting used to the tiredness—by now she hardly woke when a child slipped next to her under her blanket, and she almost sleepwalked through the sheet changes or reassuring them that they weren't being chased or falling off a cliff: "it's just a bad dream"—but now that she was away from the Grange, she realized it was more that she was getting used to operating with lower energy levels.

Julian had a nice profile; neat features. There was something about his manicured nails on the gearstick that made her think— or hope?—that lunch was not *just* about the piano. It had been a long time since she'd had even a mild flirtation with someone.

Bury St. Edmunds was a bit disappointing, though. It was a charming town, but it made Clara restless. She had wanted a change of scene from Lavenham, not more of the same. There was something stifling about Lavenham's tweeness, sometimes one found oneself looking for something a bit more rugged or imperfect. It felt as though she was wearing a coat with the buttons too tight and this place was the same. She began to explain that to Julian, but it was a half-formed idea and she couldn't put her point across.

He said, "Well, there's better shopping here and better pubs."

Julian had planned not a restaurant, but a picnic.

"I expect you find stuffy restaurants a terrible bore!"

Clara, who had been looking forward to her first big meal out for years, smiled enigmatically.

"We'll go to a restaurant another day, Miss Newton." Even though she had told him she was leaving in just a few days it felt nice that he was still lining up plans, like buses. It gave her a frisson. "Presuming you will permit me another day?"

Although he was blustery and confident, Clara was surprised to find that he was shy when it came to her. He was perhaps a "man's man"? Clara thought that a positive. Who wanted a ladies' man? You couldn't trust them as far as you could throw them.

"I'll take you to a fancy London one. I'd like to see you all dressed up."

Clara *did* like getting dressed up. She had met Michael at a party—he was with friends from the Eighth Air Force and she'd been with Judy's friends. They had taken one look at each other and were smitten. The first thing he said was, "I need sunglasses, you're so dazzling." Michael had a corny line for every occasion, but she *had* looked swell that day.

Unfortunately, it was too cloudy and cool for Julian's picnic, so they found a tea room instead, and if Julian was fretting about the food he had prepared sweating in the basket in the back of his car, he didn't show it. The tea room was a lovely choice—an airy place with immaculate white tablecloths and glasses that brilliantly shone. Clara was rather relieved. She enjoyed outdoors, but not that much.

Clara liked the way the waitresses in their white aprons and hats beamed when Julian spoke to them. He was *commanding*, that was it, not in a horrible way, but he asked if they could move tables so Clara could see out the window onto the street and he sent back one of the glasses because amid the brilliant shine there was a thumbprint—"We can't have that."

He was never rude, though. And they *did* get better service because of it.

He certainly had charm. She wondered why he wasn't married or a father already. She didn't know anyone aged fifty who wasn't—although to be fair, he looked a lot younger than Miss Bridges, who was probably about the same age.

Later, in the car home, they ate chocolates he had brought especially for her. He said, "This may be premature, but I like to know where I stand."

"How do you mean?"

"Are you looking for a relationship, do you think, Clara?"

"I'll be back in London next week, you know that, Julian."

"London is only an hour away."

"Longer by train," she said. *Why was she being so petulant suddenly?* She shook herself. "Maybe."

"You could always stay though, couldn't you?" he added gruffly, "I bet they don't have a replacement lined up yet."

Clara couldn't think what to say. *Should I not go? After I've made all that fuss?*

What would the children say?

Staying had never before been a realistic option in Clara's mind.

She looked at him again. Julian was smart and generous and he was a solicitor with his name on the door! He clearly wasn't struggling financially.

Scrimping and saving for the next forty years was such a depressing thought that Clara rarely allowed herself to entertain it.

Julian also had a slight air of detachment about him, which was appealing after the intensity of her relationship with Michael. Plus, it was unlikely that he was going to go and die on her. One, because they weren't at war anymore and two, because he was the picture of health. She'd learned: these things were important.

She wouldn't let her heart break again. So, she smiled at him and muttered something like, "Nobody knows what the future will bring," and he took his hand off the wheel, grabbed her palm and kissed it. No one had ever done that to her in her entire life, not even Michael.

"I'm patient," he said.

CHAPTER EIGHT

You could feel the changing seasons in the countryside. Of course, you could in London too, but in Lavenham, the seasons were exaggerated. Early October and colorful leaves piled up in the road, the wind whistled through the air and the air smelled that heady mix of burning, cinnamon and the possibility of snow. The older children taught the younger ones how to pierce holes in the conkers they found below the chestnut trees and how best to tie them on to strings. Rumor had it that the children from Shilling Grange had the strongest conkers in town. Billy and Barry came home with handfuls of their prizes. A man she didn't know stopped Clara in the street to say they'd won all his Bernard's conkers. Clara was about to apologize but he tipped his hat, saying, "Impressive," and "Good luck to them!" Less impressive was finding conkers everywhere: when she was making the beds, sweeping the floor or doing the laundry.

"Who taught you?" she asked them.

"The Master of Conkers, Ivor!"

That figures, Clara thought. She hadn't realized until recently how enmeshed Ivor was in Shilling Grange. Still, only a few days to go and she would have thoroughly detangled herself. She wished she and Ivor were not parting on such sour terms but he really was an insufferable man.

Clara had still not yet packed. She seemed to have a block about it. She did not have a job in London to go to and she was dreading staying on Judy's sofa, peering at the classifieds under Arthur's watchful eye again.

The day after their tea-room date, Julian dropped around some flowers, which was unexpected. He didn't pressure her for another date, but did say to get in touch "when she was ready."

There was a flurry of poorly typed letters from the school and the council: it seemed as though the council did not believe she was leaving either.

Did Miss Newton know about cod liver oil?
   Was Miss Newton alert to the risk of polio?
   Was Miss Newton making and mending? (Yes, though she would have liked to outsource this to Ivor, but she had burned her bridges there.)
   Had Miss Newton applied for all the right coupons?
   The children will be weighed next Wednesday.

Clara busied herself with making her files as informative as possible to make the handover smooth. That was something she could do but nearly everything else was out of her hands now.

As the fourteenth approached, Clara was finding her work at Shilling Grange more enjoyable than she had originally anticipated. When the children told her about their school day, when Billy and Barry brought home a jar of pickles because she'd told them she loved them (they'd helped themselves at the harvest festival), when together they tore down the Shilling Grange sign—"We'll tell the council that it blew away in a storm!" When Maureen came home with a 7/10 at school or when Peg showed her a new dance, it felt brilliant. *It's only because I'm leaving soon*, Clara told herself, *everything has become intensified under the magnifying glass, that's why.* But other times, she wondered if maybe she should have given this job and this quaint film set of a town a proper chance.

Two days before she was due to go, Clara was finally about to start her packing when the doorbell rang. It was Mrs. Harrington. She had stopped by with big news for Rita. Clara asked what it was, but smiling, Mrs. Harrington insisted she should be the first to tell the little girl. Clara felt a sudden spring in her step. This was the high note she wanted to go out on.

Clara went to fetch Rita from the shed. Rita, Alex and Peg went there every day after school. They liked dancing, pretending they could play the piano, and doing goodness knows what else.

Peg wanted to come and see Mrs. Harrington too. "Not this time, Peg." Clara winked at the silent one and Peg winked back. Peg warmed Clara's heart. Yes, she was unusual, but it seemed incredible that she would be, as Miss Bridges phrased it, "very hard—nigh impossible—to place."

Mrs. Harrington had already made herself at home in the kitchen and was drinking tea out of Clara's favorite cup.

"Ah, here you are, Rita. I have something to tell you about your mama."

Rita's dark eyes lit up. She looked up at Clara for reassurance and Clara nodded at her excitedly. Rita smoothed down her hair and bit her lip: she was ready.

She had been ready for this for a long time.

"Well, you know that there was a bomb and she went missing and you think you remember seeing her alive…is that right?"

"Yes!" Rita could no longer contain herself. "She was in the dust, holding her head! I saw her!" She gripped Clara's arm, her other hand had found her mouth. She bit down on the palm in excitement. Clara was beside herself too. *This. This made it all worthwhile, surely?*

"Well, we've done some investigations and we've found out that she has indeed passed away."

Cold shock and goose pimples. Like being back in the war and finding the house next door had disappeared. You don't know what to do with yourself. No—this was worse.

Oh, Rita.

For a long moment Rita didn't move, then she crawled into the crook of Clara's arm, tears rolling down her hot cheeks.

"Mama," she breathed and her breath was damp and stale. "Mama. My mama."

"Do you think she'll want to have a look at the death certificate?" Mrs. Harrington asked Clara.

"No, I don't." Clara couldn't believe the woman's insensitivity.

"Don't be overdramatic, Rita, it has been years! Now, don't squeeze Miss Newton like that," Mrs. Harrington said. "You know she's going soon."

Mrs. Harrington shook her head at Clara. She didn't even lower her voice. "You don't know how resilient they are, Miss Newton. She'll get used to it if she knows what's good for her. It's better you're going, so they don't get too attached. Now," she winked, "I'm off to see my favorite upholsterer."

Rita threw up three times that afternoon, tears rolling down her face, her whole body trembling. Clara held back her hair as she knelt on the bathroom floor. Peg and Terry came in to have a look. Then Rita lay down right there.

"You have to get up, darling." Clara didn't know if she could carry her all the way upstairs to the dormitory. Rita did eventually pull herself upright and let Clara lead her to bed. Clara tucked her in and the little girl said, "Don't leave me as well, Miss Newton. Please."

"Sssh," said Clara guiltily. "Try and get some sleep. You've had a terrible shock."

When Maureen got back, Clara left the younger children with her and ran to the telephone box: "Hello?" The money fell straight through the slot. The telephone had no sense of urgency.

Clara paid and dialed again. She knew the ten-digit council number off by heart now.

"Miss Bridges? It's Clara. There really should be a telephone in the house."

Miss Bridges' voice was fuzzy. "Is that why you called? We're awfully busy with cemeteries, Clara, can it wait?"

No, thought Clara, *it can't*.

"Have you found a replacement for me yet?"

Miss Bridges cleared her throat. "We've been so over—"

"Because—"

Dammit. The phone had stopped again. But then it started up and this time Miss Bridges was whooping—Clara hadn't even had to say her bit. "Attagirl, I knew it! You're staying with us?"

"Yes, Miss Bridges. If I'm not too late?"

You could tell Miss Bridges was smiling down the wires.

"Never too late, Clara. Welcome back."

They played a celebratory game of mini-rounders in the garden. Even Rita got out of bed to join in. Peter said to Maureen, "I'll have my money back then," and Maureen said, "Sod off," before insisting loudly, "Miss Newton will change her mind again soon.

It's only because of her *love life* she's staying—it's nothing to do with us."

Mrs. Garrard walked past the garden with her nose in the air and Clara had the chance to catch Alex out but missed it on purpose, leading to howls of disapproval from her teammates. Then they went in and had milk and crackers, and Clara taught them to do cheers with their glasses—"GENTLY, Barry, for goodness' sake"—before they went up to bed.

That night, Clara slept like a baby. Perhaps it was because of her three home runs, or perhaps because Rita, exhausted, slept through—bless her—or perhaps it was because committing to a decision after the weeks of uncertainty at long last was good. It felt right.

Clara found she was also looking forward to telling Julian. She certainly hadn't changed her mind just because of her love life— but it helped. There would be more dates, there would be more tea rooms and restaurants and perhaps even more than that. She should let herself have a little romance, it wasn't a crime. And who knew where it could lead?

In the morning, Clara opened the window wide and breathed in the fresh country air. She was growing to love this historic town, to love the sense of all the generations who had lived there before, the way they felt evident in the Tudor and medieval buildings, the gardens and even in the cobblestones. Somehow, this linking of the present with the past warmed her through and even made her feel like she too might belong, one day.

It was possibly the first time she'd had a good night's sleep since her father had turned up out of the blue in London. And it was the first time since Michael died that she had gotten up with a smile on her face and a sense of raw possibility. The children were getting used to her. And she was getting used to them.

Perhaps the most surprising thing of all was: she felt she could do this.

There was good news the next day too that seemed to further confirm the rightness of Clara's decision. She was outside the house with Alex when an impressive car screeched from the top of the high road all the way down to the Grange. Clara could see it was driven by a dashing fella in a fedora. She went over to say hello. Up close, she could see he wasn't as young as either his driving or his hat suggested; he was mid-thirties perhaps, but he was good-looking. It turned out he was Peter's uncle, his only living relative, here to take Peter out for the afternoon. This was possibly a first step toward adoption. Miss Bridges and Mrs. Harrington chanted, "Older ones are harder to place," so often, Clara had been led to believe it was like asking for the moon.

"Nice car," Clara said, suddenly aware that Ivor had come out of his workshop and was surveying them all.

"It's an Aston Martin," Alex clarified from behind her.

Peter's uncle said, "Clever kid. Is this the one?"

Clara laughed. "No. Yours is Peter...Hang on, he'll be down in a minute."

"Shame it's not a girl, could do with some help with the house-work." He winked at her. Clara reddened, wishing he hadn't. She smoothed down her dress.

Peter came out shyly, holding the ball they used for rounders. He was all awkward, long legs in too-small shorts, his hair stuck to his sweaty forehead.

"Leave that." Clara took the ball and waved him off. She felt proud; like her baby was taking his first steps. The uncle sounded the horn as he left; he didn't care about the neighbors. Peter was looking out of the back window, his freckly face full of nerves. Clara nodded enthusiastically, showing him it was going to be okay. *One down—seven to go.*

Ivor had gone back inside.

Alex looped his hand into hers. "I wish I had a nice family."

"Mm, Peter is lucky." Clara squeezed Alex's fingers. She doubted he would be with her for long either. "Your time will come too, one day."

And the extraordinary thing was, she would be here to see it.

When Clara told Julian she was staying, he was "ecstatic"—his word, a nice word, if a little keen. He had all sorts of plans for her and the way he raised his eyebrow at her said he wasn't just planning on taking her *out*. Clara demurely brushed off this suggestion, saying she didn't want to get a reputation. He laughed. "At my age, a reputation would be a fine thing." Clara worried about his age, but then again, her father had been twelve years older than her mother, so on another level it felt normal. What felt less normal was how much money Julian had—but, deep down, Clara suspected she could, if she had to, get used to that too. They arranged to go to a restaurant the next Sunday she was free. He said he was "delirious with anticipation."

The Jane Taylor Society met every few months in Lavenham Library. They had been meeting since 1912 and had managed to keep the group going through both world wars, a feat they were proud of. Miss Bridges suggested Clara go along to their autumn meeting, although Clara couldn't tell if she was being sarcastic or not. *Why on earth would I want to do that?*

But on the Wednesday of the meeting, Clara didn't have anything else to do; all the children were in school, lunch was ready, washing done, the house was clean enough. *Why not?*

She was surprised to see about twelve people sitting in the Biography and Travel section of the library, including the butcher, Mr.

and Mrs. Garrard, the post office lady and Dr. Cardew's wife—the glamorous lady she had seen that day in the surgery garden with Rita. Trying to avoid the Garrards, and noting that Mrs. Cardew was so slender that when looked at from the side she was almost not there, Clara grabbed an empty seat. Unfortunately, it was right behind Ivor Delaney.

What is he doing here?

The speaker, who was also the librarian, was the old, dusty type, with an ill-fitting suit and a cough. Clara thought it was a mistake coming and then when the speaker said today he was going to concentrate not on Jane Taylor but on older sister Ann, she was even more disappointed. If she could have crept away without drawing attention to herself—without Ivor noticing—she would have.

Born in 1782, Ann Taylor was the practical, capable sister—the one who had a go at everything and didn't let convention hold her back. She married and had a large family with her religious husband, Joseph Gilbert, while continuing to write children's poetry, memoirs, pamphlets and articles for journals. Her writing helped financially support the family at a time when it was unusual for women like her to work. Clara's mouth twitched in sympathy. She was glad she had come and heartened that even here in conservative Lavenham, which seemed in some ways far more conservative than London, women's contributions were being noted.

In the tea break, Clara dashed to the lavatory and stayed in there, determined to avoid both Ivor and the Garrards.

In the second half of the talk, they learned that Ann Taylor was anti-slavery and campaigned passionately on the issue.

"I am pleased to hear that," said the doctor's wife and everyone murmured their assent. Clara thought approvingly, *Oh, she does speak then!*

The strange thing was that Ann Taylor was also anti-suffrage and had not believed women should have a vote. There was a pause.

"I don't find it strange." Mrs. Cardew spoke up again. "You

can be right on one thing and wrong on another. It is part of the human condition."

It was the most Clara had ever heard Mrs. Cardew say and she decided that she liked her. Just then, Ivor turned round and smirked at Clara.

He was infuriating.

While people were still clapping, Mrs. Cardew gathered her things and left, greeting both Ivor and Clara unenthusiastically on her way out.

Ivor was walking the same way as Clara and unfortunately, they fell into step together.

"I didn't expect to see you here," he said.

That put her back up right away—to be honest, her back was already up.

"Why wouldn't I?" If Ivor was going to be confrontational again, then she would be too.

"I thought you couldn't wait to leave this cultural backwater."

She didn't know where he'd gotten that from. "That has never been the issue."

"When are you off then?"

"Oh! I decided to stay in the end."

He looked at her, then shook his head and kept shaking it incredulously.

"There's a song about you, isn't there? *One foot in, one foot out, in, out, in, out, shake it all about.*"

Clara stalked off. *Idiot.* She wouldn't give him another chance. There was no rule that said you had to get on with your neighbors.

Clara cut fresh flowers from the garden and put them in jugs in each of the rooms. She opened the windows wide—Sister Eunice had been averse to an airing, apparently—and she took on some of the chores so the children didn't spend all their time at home mopping and scrubbing.

She thought up questions to ask the children at mealtimes, just basic things like: "What did you do at school today?" and "What are you going to do at the weekend?" When she did, she could see it took them by surprise—their mouths would drop open—but eventually they started to come up with answers.

She tried to fix the wireless, but couldn't. Then she let Billy and Barry try and somehow it worked again. As she had hoped, *Children's Hour* became a hit with the younger ones.

Turning the kitchen into a gallery of art was Judy's idea. Peg was particularly prolific; she drew stars and sunshine, clouds and umbrellas. Clara laughed and said Peg must look up a lot.

Rita drew potato-looking people, which she said were Mama. Terry said she'd do a picture later, thanks. She was a dab hand at putting things off. Alex said he'd rather not, if Clara didn't mind—"We do enough of that sort of thing at school, thank you."

Clara didn't ask the older children for pictures. Billy and Barry were strangers to the idea of sitting down and using pens—they struggled to sit still for dinner, and jiggled and waggled and rolled on the floor at any opportunity. Maureen would have sneered at her, she sneered a lot—and Peter; well, lovely though Peter was, he would probably have swapped the pens for the cigarettes he now smoked *constantly*.

Clara peeled the numbers off the bathroom things and put the children's names on everything instead. That was better. She made everyone try on shoes and put names on them too so there'd be no more sharing. All the shoes were too small for poor Peter and too big for little Peg—why had no one noticed? At the Saturday-morning market on the other side of the station, they were allowed to pick a pair each. That dug into the allowance that Clara had put aside for some games and toys, but shoes were a priority, unfortunately. She submitted another request to the council for boots and vests and surprisingly, this time Miss Bridges came back with a yes. Clara also told the children they did not have to wear the "stupid" Shilling Grange capes to school anymore and they were overjoyed (apart from Terry, who said she liked looking like a bat and kept wearing hers).

She took the children to join the library and the old dusty librarian—Mr. Dowsett—was as brilliant with them as he had been about Ann and Jane Taylor. Peg loved Rupert the Bear, although reading it sent Clara to sleep. Rita and Terry became great Enid Blyton fans. Maureen kept sloping over to the adult section where the Mills & Boon romances were—*"Not yet, Maureen, you're only thirteen."* Billy and Barry just loved having membership cards: they pretended they were secret agents with them. Clara and Mr. Dowsett joked that Alex would move his bed into the factual section if he could have. When he found out it was six not three books that he could take home, he was over the moon. When Maureen said he could borrow her card to get more, well...

Throughout October, whenever Clara was out, she would see Ivor, in his workshop with his doors wide open, and he would nod curtly at her while making a big fuss of the children. Clara decided not to let it get to her. After all, the town was full of nice people, people like Julian, who were making her feel rather more than welcome.

CHAPTER NINE

It rained a lot in early November. Clara felt sorry for the children traipsing to school wet through, but they didn't seem to mind. Rita and Peg liked balancing on the low walls while Maureen and Peter had to hold their hands to steady them. Billy and Barry preferred hiding behind trees, yelping out "boo" to strangers.

The headmaster at the Lavenham high school greeted Clara warmly and asked her how she was getting on. When she said it was "an eye-opener," he laughed. "You've only got eight. Try one hundred and twenty! We've never had a worry about the Shilling Grange lot. At least we know they're being fed and clothed."

This seemed a low bar.

It had been Judy's idea to go into the schools—"to find out how they are doing." Clara wanted to kick herself that she hadn't thought of that—but come to that, no one at the council had suggested it either. She knew she had to start thinking for herself. She couldn't always rely on Judy, however much she was tempted to.

It transpired that the high school headmaster was, like Clara, a fan of data and advanced record-keeping, so they sat in his study and he read reports on the children. Clara learned that not only were Maureen's academic performance and punctuality below average but her attendance was poor too. She scored 14 out of 16. At first, Clara didn't understand—"That's not bad…"—but the headmaster set her straight: "This means overall she comes fourteenth in a class of sixteen."

"Oh well, at least she's not sixteenth," said Clara, looking for a silver lining.

Billy and Barry were tricksters and the headmaster laughed as he related their escapades, before adding sternly that their reading, writing and arithmetic were all below average. They presented at 12/16 (Billy) and 16/16. (Barry). Clara was about to question this ranking system when the headmaster continued that Peter was good all round and was at 2/19 in several subjects and even 1/19 in some.

At last, thought Clara jubilantly, *one sensible child out of eight isn't bad!*

The headmaster said, "By rights, Peter should probably have gone to the grammar school." To Clara's astonishment, he explained that there was a more academic school at Ipswich that led to university, whereas his school generally prepared the children to go into manual or domestic work at sixteen. She had had no idea.

"It's too late for him to change," the headmaster said after fending off Clara's questions. "And Peter is the kind of boy who will succeed wherever he is."

Clara felt a warm glow of propriety. *Her* boy would do well anywhere.

She thought suddenly of Alex and Terry. They were nearly eleven and they were both unquestionably smart.

"How do you get into the grammar school then?"

"Now that," the headmaster said, "is a good question."

It was an informative meeting and Clara was feeling upbeat when she went to Lavenham Primary, the younger children's school. And although her umbrella dripped over the wooden floor of the reception area, the woman behind the front desk put down her pen and tilted her head in greeting.

"I'd like to speak to the headteacher. It's about the children from Shilling Grange?"

The receptionist vigorously screwed the lid onto her ink. "Oh, I know, I *know*. Feral monsters. What've they done now?"

"I am the new housemother." Clara stood on her tiptoes. Every inch counted. "If you ever have a problem with the feral monsters, do let me know."

The receptionist sucked in her teeth. "I'll ring the bell."

After this inauspicious start, the headmistress said she could give Miss Newton five minutes, no more. In those minutes, the headmistress walked her along some maze-like corridors, her pale lips set grimly.

Clara found out Rita drank other children's free school milk, Peg did not drink hers. Alex was forever correcting teachers and Terry had to be caned frequently because of her poor attitude and approach to timekeeping. Clara scowled at this. She was surprised they turned up at all if this was the way they were treated.

Back in the reception area, Clara got to the point. "I was wondering about the eleven-plus exam and applying for the grammar school."

It was the first time the headmistress let herself smile. Then when she realized Clara was being serious, she stopped herself.

"That's not possible."

"Why is that?"

"Well, we don't recommend it for *certain* children."

"Certain children? Could you elaborate?"

The headmistress shook her head. "It's only for exceptionally bright children."

"And?" Clara remembered Alex and Pythagoras and Ivor's verdict—*He's so sharp.* "I'd like them to take it and I'd like you to prepare them for it."

"No one has ever passed from the Grange before." The headmistress took out her pocket watch. "Time, Miss Newton, thank you."

Clara didn't know what got into her, but: "That's not good enough!" she said firmly. She was the housemother of Shilling Grange and she was here to get the best for her children. "They will take the exam, whether they pass or not. They deserve the same opportunity as the others."

"How ever would they afford the uniform if they got in?"

Clara talked about bridges crossed, turning points and forks in roads. The headmistress resisted.

"Not suitable." "Not done before." "Not appropriate."

Her resistance made Clara more determined.

"I will contact the council. I will say you are discriminating against them. They are concerned about things like that," she added, unsure if they were or not. "Ever since the Children's Act."

The headmistress steadied herself against the wall. The woman at the front desk looked anxiously between them both.

"There's no need to do that, Miss Newton. I will send in the applications."

"I want to see confirmation in writing." Clara didn't trust her at all.

The headmistress acquiesced.

Each time Clara stood up for the children, she felt better about herself. It was a strange thing. It was a *good* thing.

As Clara left, the school bell rang and, within seconds, children were pouring into the puddled playground for their breaktime. Looking for "her" children, she spied Alex with his best friend Bernard, a boy the mirror image of Alex but double his size. She saw Peg swaggering over some hopscotch. Saw Terry playing at skipping in a happy bundle of children.

"Turn around, touch the ground!"

At first, she couldn't spot Rita. She scanned the playground, growing ever more worried, until she spied her, standing next to a drainpipe, eyes down, pretty hair, hands in her pocket, all on her own.

Later that afternoon, Clara saw Mrs. Cardew walking up the street holding her large holdall and tentatively avoiding puddles.

Remembering her tenderness with the rabbit, her directness at the talk in the library, Clara raced over to her. Seize the day, she told herself; Ann Taylor, the practical sister, would have done.

Mrs. Cardew surveyed her, not coldly exactly, but without interest.

"Mrs. Cardew, I just was wondering…" Clara wasn't sure exactly what she was wondering, but nevertheless she persisted, "if you would ever like to spend some time at the Grange with us?" She smiled in a way she hoped was inviting.

"Why would I want that?"

Mrs. Cardew didn't have a strong accent, but it was stronger when she was confused.

"For a cup of tea or…I don't know."

Mrs. Cardew's gaze was boring holes in her head. It was best to be honest.

"Truth is, I am out of my depth sometimes and some adult company would be lovely! I'm an outsider here in Lavenham, just like you."

"I'm *nothing* like you."

Okay, so that was the wrong choice of words.

"No, I didn't mean it like that. I hear you're German?"

Mrs. Cardew's face was a picture.

"No."

Oh God.

"Sorry. Yes. Poland, wasn't it? And what was it you did back there?"

Mrs. Cardew looked like she was considering walking away but instead, with a sigh, she said in a taut voice, "I was a high school teacher."

To Clara, this was as though all the auspicious things had joined up together. Serendipity again.

"Oh! What subject?"

"Music and maths."

"Why, that's perfect!"

Mrs. Cardew stared at her. "Why?"

"We've got a piano in our garden shed."

"In your garden shed?" Mrs. Cardew repeated slowly.

"And some of the children would love to learn. And of course I know *you* know music…I heard you playing your violin that time and it was so beautiful."

Every single muscle in Mrs. Cardew's face was clenched tight. "What did my husband say to you?"

Dr. Cardew?

"Nothing. Why?"

"He did. I know he did."

"He didn't. But even if he had…wouldn't you consider it, please?"

Mrs. Cardew drew in her breath. Something had made her furious.

"I can't be fixed. I won't be mended. The answer is no."

CHILDREN'S REPORT 3
Maureen Amy Keaton

Date of birth:
November 23, 1934 (Maureen was premature)

Family background:
Maureen doesn't know much about her origins. I think if she does remember, she's probably blocked much of it out.

There are some notes of her arrival in Suffolk. She came from her family home in 1940 when she was five. Her father bludgeoned her mother to death in the kitchen with a hammer while Maureen was upstairs and then he left—she sat with her mother for some time, perhaps twenty-four hours, maybe more. Police couldn't understand why her mother was covered in tissues and initially thought it might have been something the father had done: it wasn't that. Maureen had wrapped her mother in "bandages" and had to be dragged away from her body.

Father is now in jail in North London. No contact.

Health/Appearance:
I worry about her teeth, which don't look too strong to me. NB. Some mornings, her toothbrush is bone-dry. She feels the cold—blue lips—needs hat, scarf and warm gloves. (Inquire)

Food:
Maureen likes to cook and bake, especially biscuits and cakes. Future job?

Hobbies/Interests:
If she could just focus on her education and keep her head down, I think she might do well. The school staff say she looks out the window too much. She makes no effort in most subjects.

Other:

Maureen is an opinionated young woman who doesn't respect anyone much. Given her horrendous background, that's perhaps not surprising.

Clara wanted Maureen to have some time to enjoy herself. She shouldn't have to do chores all the time she wasn't at school, she was only thirteen. Perhaps also if she had more time off at home, her performance and attendance would be better at school?

When Clara told Maureen that she could be let off some chores, Maureen didn't react at first, but then a smile spread across her pretty features and her expression said *really? Honestly?*

With fewer tasks, Maureen did relax, she relaxed too much. She started staying out late, long after dark; she stayed out past bedtime. Only at weekends, but still. While Clara wanted Maureen to have more freedom, this wasn't the freedom she'd had in mind. She had been Maureen's age only twelve years ago, but the world had changed beyond recognition. And so had she. She knew now what terrible things could happen if you dared look away, just for a moment.

Clara felt uncomfortable sharing her worries about Maureen with Miss Bridges, who had insinuated that giving children more free time was just asking for problems: "You know what they say about the devil and idle hands, Clara!"

"Where've you been, Maureen?" Clara asked whenever she came home late, whispering because the last thing she wanted was for the other girls to wake up.

"Out."

"I know that." Clara resolved to stop asking questions she already knew the answer to.

"Where?"

"Nowhere."

"You can't stay out so late," Clara tried in a breezy voice that she could barely recognize as her own. "It's not on."

"Fine!"

Clara thought she had won the battle until Friday rolled around again and Maureen wasn't back until two hours after her curfew.

It was hard to be strict on Maureen though. Not only because of her terrible past, but because she could sometimes be so kind too.

One day in November, Maureen came home part pushing, part guiding Rita. Rita had mud on her cheeks and could hardly speak for gulping tears.

"All I said was that I'd be the best May Queen because of my hair!"

Clara didn't know what she was talking about, but apparently the girls at school hadn't been able to stomach it.

"There, there," said Maureen, dabbing Rita's face with a flannel with such tenderness, Clara felt moved. After Rita went to lie down, Maureen cheerfully explained.

"They call her Big Head, Shirley Temple and Mama's Girl."

Clara sucked in her breath. Of all the names, that last one must most compound poor Rita's heartache.

"I hit one of them." Maureen was putting jam on bread. Even her swipes seemed boastful. Clara grabbed the knife from her.

"You hit a child? You can't *hit* a child!"

"Well, I did."

"Wha-at? How hard?"

Maureen's mouth was full of sandwich. "Hard enough. It's the only thing that stops them."

Thing was, over the next few days, Rita did seem happier so maybe Maureen was right.

*

Saturday morning. Clara had been at the Grange for eleven whole weeks and they were tearing back from the library. Billy and Barry had run ahead and now Billy or Barry was shrieking in the street (just as Clara had told them not to).

"Visitor!"

The last thing Clara needed was more nits. But it wasn't that. Terry was also whirling around in great excitement.

"There's a man at the gate, Miss Newton, a *man*!"

The man at the gate was in a black suit and he probably belonged to the badly parked car on the road. Was it someone from the council? Or prospective parents who she hadn't been informed about? Or was Peter supposed to go to his uncle today?

She couldn't work it out until she drew closer, when she saw it was Harris—Harris Jr. from her old workplace, Harris & Sons.

"Mr. Harris!" She hurried over with her shopping bags. A hug would be too much, but a handshake seemed too little for her ex-boss and old friend.

"Miss Newton!" He reached for her delightedly.

"Do you know Mama?" demanded Rita.

"Are you two going to get married?" asked Billy, his eyes narrowed.

"You'll have to come through us first," said Barry, arms crossed.

"She's going to marry Ivor, isn't she?"

"Terry, that's a ridiculous thing to say!" Clara rarely got annoyed by Terry but she was then. "What *are* you suggesting?"

"Do you know what pi is? In maths? I can explain it to you if you like."

"Mr. Harris knows what a pie is, Alex."

Clara realized "introductions" were another thing the children needed work on. And Terry was being daft.

She explained to them all that Mr. Harris had been her boss for ten years, he was the third of the three generations of Harrises, and then told them to go get cleaned up.

"Mr. Harris, you will stay for lunch, won't you?"

Clara was embarrassed to serve up the watery chicken soup and hard bread that was their usual Saturday fare, but Mr. Harris said he didn't eat so much himself these days. He always had lovely manners. He was thinner than before and he had always been thin.

Clara noted his pale oval face. He had never been an outdoorsy man, and though he was much the same as he had been, he looked more exhausted somehow. This was including the nights Clara had spent with him in Aldgate tube station during the worst days of the Blitz. She wondered what he had come for; why had he not just called or written? She had already established that his father, Mr. Harris Sr., was in good health, enjoying his retirement, and eighty-four-year-old Harris Sr.-Sr. was still fishing; in fact, he caught prize-winning carp.

You can win prizes with carp?

The children did not come back to the kitchen after their wash. After several minutes had passed, Clara said, "Help yourself, Mr. Harris," in an overly jolly voice and went to look for everyone.

In the boys' room, Billy was throwing a pillow around. Barry was attempting press-ups, Alex was reading on his bed. Peter was gazing out of the window, smoking.

Clara had already called out several times but now she kept her voice neutral.

"Lunch is ready, didn't you hear?"

"We're not coming."

"What?"

"Why should we be friends with him?"

"What's going on?" she asked Peter, who just shrugged.

Barry explained. "He wants you in London."

Clara's brain worked quickly. "No, it's just a visit, boys."

As she said it, her heart was beating louder. *Was that what Mr. Harris was here for? What would she say if he was?*

"Don't be so clueless, Miss Newton." Barry gave up his exercises and lay spread-eagled on the bed.

In the girls' bedroom, there was a similar air of discontent.

"Need help packing?" spat Maureen.

"What?"

"We knew you wouldn't last three months."

Rita was clutching Molly Mouse. "But you pwomised."

"This is unacceptable. That's not why he's here and I'm not going anywhere."

Terry piped up. "But you always talked about how happy you were at Harris & Sons."

"Well, I was. But I'm also happy now."

Eventually, they all sloped into the kitchen. Mr. Harris stoically tried to make conversation with the children as they ate.

As soon as their bowls were empty, they asked to be excused.

"I suppose," sighed Clara and watched them race to the sink. They were not exactly adding anything to the occasion.

It was Maureen's turn to wash up. She slouched into position, shooting daggers at poor Mr. Harris.

"So how is it working out with Miss Barber?" Clara's voice was level but even mentioning the name of the young woman who had her place was painful. Mr. Harris ceremonially laid his spoon on his empty plate.

"She is the worst secretary you could possibly imagine," he said, dabbing his mouth with his napkin. "And that's putting it politely."

Clara laughed. How sweet it was to be vindicated. That girl, who had put her through so much turmoil, had turned out to be a mistake. *Quel surprise.*

"To be honest, Mr. Harris, I never liked her." Clara was in the mood to be candid. "I didn't believe a word that came out of her mouth at the interview. It was obvious from the start she did not have the skills or the personality to be a secretary."

"Oh," said Mr. Harris. "You didn't hear we got married?"

Clara was as scarlet as he was. "Um, no, I didn't. Congratulations."

Her back to them at the sink, Maureen was shaking with silent laughter.

As Clara walked Mr. Harris to his car, the wind was picking up and leaves were jitterbugging in the air. She saw Ivor over the road, sweeping. Their eyes met briefly.

Mr. Harris said they were seeking to diversify the business. He had always been the one with the plans.

He started up the engine, then, hat in hand, returned to her.

"We *are* struggling on the paperwork side of things," he said, with a lopsided smile. "Wondered if you'd consider coming back? We should never have let you go. We'd like to offer you a much better package, improved remuneration."

Clara wished he hadn't said that. It was all tempting, but *improved remuneration* was, in particular. Scrimping and saving might look good in stories but in real life, it was pretty ugly. And never mind the money, the job was what she had loved six months ago. You don't throw that away for nothing.

"Thank you so much for coming. It is an amazing offer," she said.

"I trust we will hear from you soon?"

"Definitely." Clara took a deep breath. She was giving up something precious here. "But not for the job. I can't leave the children now, I hope you understand."

Mr. Harris opened the driver's-side door. "I do."

"You're not angry with me?"

"Angry? No. This is your place, Clara. Anyone can see that."

Her heart swelled. *Her place?* That was how it felt to her sometimes, but for someone else to say so...

"I don't know if it is...I'm not actually sure if I'm achieving anything here."

Terry ran out. Her face was radiant.

"You're not going to believe this! The tomatoes are growing. Real ones. To eat!"

"Oh, that's wonderful, Terry. I can't wait."

Terry ran over to Ivor's workshop to tell him the news.

Mr. Harris raised his eyebrows. "You can't say you're not making a difference here."

When Clara went back into the kitchen Rita was hovering at the table, her eyes huge in her paper-pale face.

"Well?" she asked petulantly, crossing her arms. "When are you off?"

"It's all right, darling, I'm really not going anywhere."

Rita, Alex, Peg, then, unbelievably, Maureen enfolded her in a hug.

She was here to stay.

CHAPTER TEN

Throughout November, Maureen stayed out later and later. She would sneak out when Clara thought she was home. She used the old trick, a pillow stuffed under the blanket to make it look like she was sleeping. Clara was insulted that Maureen thought she'd fall for it—but then realized she probably had before, several times.

When she was out, Clara had an overwhelming sense of powerlessness—it reminded her of waiting for the bombs during the Blitz. Nothing you could do but make yourself tiny.

And then Maureen would come back, bright-eyed, either out of breath or humming "Shine on Harvest Moon." Clara began to hate the tune. The cheek of her. At her lowest, Clara couldn't help thinking: *After all I've given up for her too!* She could have been at Harris & Sons, where her biggest problem was the faulty E on the typewriter and getting dates wrong in the minutes.

Don't say anything in anger. You'll regret it tomorrow. You'll lose the upper hand.

One night, it was after eleven and Maureen still hadn't returned. Clara paced. No one had warned her that looking after a teen-ager could be the loneliest place on earth. And then, just when she thought she might explode with anxiety, Maureen was back, cocky as a small dog.

Clara couldn't stand it. She stormed out the front door. There was less chance of saying something regrettable if she and Maureen weren't in the same building.

Across the road, Ivor was putting out his milk bottles.

Don't speak to him, don't.

He straightened up. "It's late for you, Miss Newton."

How did he know her schedule?

Despite herself, the urge to talk about what was going on was overwhelming. Clara couldn't contain it anymore.

"It's Maureen, she sneaked out. She never listens to me."

"Want me to go and look for her?"

"No, no... it's all right, thank you. She's back. For now."

She crossed the road toward him, her legs cold under her flapping housecoat. It wasn't because she wanted to speak to him—in fact, he was the last person she would choose, bloody war hero turned upholsterer—but she needed to speak to someone and it was far too late to telephone either Miss Bridges or Judy. "It's not the first time and I feel so weak. I don't know what to say and I don't know where she goes and—"

"Sometimes the local kids hang around the graveyard," he said.

"That sounds fun."

"Come in," he said. "Let me make you that cup of tea."

His workshop was like a sultan's hideaway or an Aladdin's cave. It was like nowhere she'd ever been. There were masses of long rolls of material stacked up against every wall. There were three—three!—sewing machines on the central table. There was a cabinet with tiny little drawers with brass handles. And there were overflowing boxes of ribbons, lace, buttons and velvet. Thick, thick books of fabrics. A sofa or four. Some upright, some on their side. Cushions. Stuffing. Tape measures and rulers. Clara wasn't sure what she had imagined, but it wasn't this.

Ivor glided in between everything; here, in his world, he had a grace about him she hadn't noticed before.

"This is amazing. I had no idea."

He scratched his head. "I don't know about amazing, but I like it."

She watched him boil water on the small hob at the back of the workshop. She noticed that the skin on one side of his face was scarred. The war. Virtually no one came out unscathed. His experiences and hers were possibly as far apart as could be—wars weren't the great equalizers some people liked to believe—but she would never pretend otherwise.

"I need to apologize," he said eventually. "I shouldn't have said what I said to you."

He turned and faced her as steam rose behind him. He seemed to mean it, thought Clara, although you never knew.

"The hokey-pokey thing was pretty awful," she muttered.

"It was."

"I always hated that dance."

"I had no right to say it, Clara. It was stupid *and* it was untrue. Please forgive me."

"You still think I should go, don't you? That I've got no business being at the Grange. You made it clear."

"I didn't give you much of a chance, did I?"

"What did you call me? An inexperienced buffoon, with all sorts of silly ideas and—"

"I didn't say buffoon. You are the opposite of a buffoon."

"Pen-pusher then."

"I might have said that," he admitted. His hair was falling over his dark eyes. "Is that such a bad thing?"

Clara snorted.

"Well, I liked the nuns—"

"Sister Eunice hardly inspired devotion..."

"Not her, no. Some of the others. I was brought up by them—here at Shilling Grange."

Clara hadn't known that. She swallowed. It made sense, she supposed.

"Poor you."

"It wasn't a bad place back then." He said it like she wasn't going to believe him. "I was in the boys' room. Ground floor, the bed under the window."

That was Peter's.

"And I was well looked after. We didn't call them housemothers back then. But some of them were kind and Sister Kate, who looked after me, was lovely."

"What made her different?"

Ivor paused, contemplating. "She listened. She took time to get to know us all. She wasn't perfect by any means, but she had our backs, you never doubted it. But the thing is I've just...I can't help notice; the kids seem happier now." Finally, he handed her the cup. "That's because of you. I was wrong about you."

Clara let that sink in. They didn't *have* to be enemies. He really did seem to have changed his mind about her. Could she try to do the same about him?

They talked a bit more about Maureen and her background—again, Ivor reassured her on her handling of her—then they talked about Alex and Peter, who he was particularly fond of. She told him how thrilled she was about Peter's uncle and the talk of adoption and that another family was looking at Peg, but the fact the little girl didn't even say her pleases and thank-yous was getting in the way.

Clara drained her tea, wondering if he might offer her some more. She told him how cold it sometimes got at the Grange, particularly in the upstairs rooms, and he shivered.

"Mm, I remember it all very well."

She felt so comfortable here, in his workshop, and that surprised her. And his honesty and his vulnerability had moved her. She should repay him with her own. "I still don't know if I'm doing the right thing, to be honest. I seem to have upset every single one of them."

"Not all of them, surely?"

"Maybe not Alex."

He laughed. "Alex is a very placid kid."

"I could probably do with some help, but the council are so constrained by budgets."

He nodded. "They say children's services are always the brides-maid, never the bride."

She smiled at him. Talking to someone who understood made her feel lighter.

"I wonder... have you asked Mrs. Cardew to help?"

"The doctor's wife? Mm," Clara said ruefully, for this was another conversation she was keen to forget. "She's another one I may have upset."

"I see." Rubbing the scarred side of his face, he said, "Look, Clara, try not to be too hard on yourself. Even Maureen came back in the end. She knows where she needs to be."

Clara felt a rare surge of pride. That was true. And maybe she wasn't a total failure after all. It was easy to count her mistakes; maybe she should count her successes too. Harris & Sons wouldn't have wanted her back if they didn't believe she was good at something.

"I already have gotten them sorted—you know, I've organized everything a bit better. Done a lot of report-writing."

"Riight..."

"And two of the children are signed up for the eleven-plus exam and they all go to the library now—and we do have a piano."

"Ah the bleedy piano." Ivor grinned.

"And Julian and I are getting on well too. That doesn't happen every day, does it? The solicitor. Mr. White? And he has a dog. I do love a nice dog."

Ivor had gotten up and now he went over to the window. She couldn't make out his face in the darkness. Nights were so much darker in the country; it reminded her of the blackout, when you had to rely so much harder on your other senses.

He didn't say anything for a moment, then he said, "I'm glad for you. Do you mind? I'd better get back to work."

By the time she got home, Maureen was snoring away innocently in bed, Peg tucked in beside her.

They didn't usually celebrate birthdays at the Grange. There were too many of them, Alex explained. *Too many to bother.* It made Clara sad. Even though her parents hadn't made a fuss of her either, her boarding school, her colleagues at Harris & Sons and Judy's family all had.

She had had only one birthday with Michael. He couldn't get the day off, but he appeared the Sunday after: *I'm taking you out dancing*, kissing outside the clubs, kissing inside the clubs. Hand in hand on the top of the double-decker buses, promises of holidays.

A nice memory.

Clara couldn't think what to do for Maureen's fourteenth birthday. When she told Maureen she was allowed a friend to come over from school, Maureen had stared at her blankly.

"No one wants to come here. Are you kidding?"

Don't overreact, that's what she wants.

"Why wouldn't they?"

"Because it's a dump, that's why."

This hurt, as it was intended to. Ever since she had committed to stay, Clara had been shining, polishing, brightening and rearranging. Now that they had reached a neighborly truce, Ivor had been over with cushions, a rug and new curtains—"Just remnants and samples," he said. Clara had even saved up for a sweep to clear the chimney, so they could get a fire going in the parlor. It warmed up the whole house *and* it looked lovely.

"It's not about the *place*, it's a chance to spend time together."

"Everyone hates me anyway," said Maureen.

"That's ridiculous." Clara laughed, but Maureen was being serious.

Clara offered to make a birthday cake, but Maureen turned up her nose. Maureen's disdain about Clara's culinary skills was mortifying, but she was probably right. In London, Clara had happily lived on cans, egg and toast and a Friday-night treat of fish and chips. Here, everything had to be made from scratch and some of the vegetables that turned up were as mysterious as they were uninviting.

Clara eventually persuaded Maureen to help her make a bread-pudding birthday cake from left-over crusts. Maureen had an instinct for cooking and somehow the result smelled appetizing and didn't look too unprofessional either.

After lunch, they stuck a candle in it and the children sang "Happy Birthday" while Maureen scowled and went scarlet.

Peg had drawn Maureen a picture of the whole household: in the middle, Maureen and Clara were holding hands. Maureen put it down. "Thanks, Peg, but we don't look *anything* like that." Which was harsh, for Peg had tried her best.

The winter coat Clara got her wasn't the Dorothy Perkins one Maureen had wanted, but it did look almost exactly like it. Maureen bit her lip. "I don't think it will fit."

Why couldn't she be more grateful? Clara was about to lose her temper when Mrs. Cardew appeared in the doorway in a fur stole and high heels, looking as though she were about to go to a ball.

"I think you like sugared almonds, Maureen," she said. "You took a whole handful when Dr. Cardew had turned his back in the surgery last visit."

Maureen looked like she wanted the floor to swallow her up.

"So here, a box just for you."

As Maureen took it, her hands were shaking. "Thank you."

"Not every day a girl turns fourteen," said Mrs. Cardew. "Make sure you share."

Maureen scuttled away. Mrs. Cardew dragged her finger along the kitchen table and scowled at the plates. Even the bread pudding seemed to slump under her disapproving gaze.

"All right then."

"What?" said Clara.

"I can help them with music and I hear you've put two of them in for the eleven-plus?"

"Yes."

"Good. So, I will tutor maths as well as the piano. When do you want me?"

"I can't pay you, Mrs. Cardew," Clara stuttered.

"Call me Anita. And I know."

This *was* a turn-up. Clara wasn't sure how to react.

"Would you join us for some birthday cake?" she asked tentatively.

It took Anita an age to unbutton her coat. Then she pulled out a chair and peered around at them all, her large bag tucked under her.

Clara cut her a slice and she eyed that suspiciously too.

"This is cake?"

"It was the best we could do."

"Looks like I'm going to have to help you with the cooking as well."

Clara had to laugh. She had never met anyone so forthright. Eventually Anita managed a weak smile.

Clara supposed that Ivor had sent her and now she had appeared, like a fairy godmother.

She wasn't going to say no.

CHAPTER ELEVEN

By mid-December, Clara and Julian had been out on four more dates. Could you call them that? He used the word "rendezvous," which made it all sound a bit more Parisian than it was. *Can we rendezvous again? Are you free to rendezvous?* The good thing about the word was that it avoided the problem of: *Is he or is he not my boyfriend?*

They had been to one restaurant (which was as smart as Clara had hoped), a pub lunch (fantastic), a drive with sandwiches (surprisingly fun), a theater trip where the play was so incomprehensible that they'd left at the interval—something Clara would never have dreamed of doing by herself and had found exhilarating.

"Life's too short!" Julian had said, a philosophy he seemed to live by.

"Why do you like spending time with me?" she inquired once over lobster in the pub. He could have any Hermione or Octavia at the fancy parties he frequented.

"Apart from the fact you're gorgeous?"

"No, really, Julian?"

"How about 'you're a breath of fresh air'?"

"Unconvincing."

"It never seems to work out for me with some girls. I prefer someone who's a bit of a challenge."

"I'm a challenge?"

He considered. "No…you *are* different though. I just like being with you."

But there was more. There had to be. For a start, statistics—there were more women than men nowadays. The newspapers said, "We face a surplus of ladies!" and "Men can do the picking!" The magazines advised women to up their game if they wanted a coveted diamond on their finger. This included getting false eyelashes, being thin and not speaking much to appeal to that rarely spotted creature—the eligible bachelor. "He won't want to hear about the time you had in the war while he was sweltering in Egypt," they said. Julian hadn't been in Egypt, but still.

What was her particular appeal? Clara wondered. She asked him again. She didn't know what she wanted to hear, but she wanted to get to the heart of it.

"A kind woman is hard to find," Julian explained. "Some of my circle can be slightly cold. I want someone who has a soft heart. That's not too strange, is it?" He cleared his throat. "I was in a relationship with a woman for some time. I left her."

"Oh. Why?"

"She didn't want children."

This was surprising. A bombshell, in fact. Never had she heard a man so openly declare it. Not even Michael had gone that far.

"And you do want children?" Clara prompted nervously. Her stomach was skittling.

"I do," Julian said. "Now, what is it you see in me, I wonder?"

Clara dearly enjoyed being with Julian. He provided her with such a complete change of scenery. It was as though her day-to-day life were a kind of show, a pantomime perhaps, then Julian came along and it became an altogether different kind of production, something much more mature.

Having both worlds in her life—both sides of her, perhaps—was great, even if she sometimes felt like those paper dolls that Peg and Rita got from the library. You cut out their clothes and put them in different outfits so they got to live different lives: actress, party hostess, princess, bride.

Clara didn't let herself think about it too much and she would never tell anyone, not even Judy, but the other thing she saw in Julian was that he was financially stable. If one day she decided to marry, he would make a good catch. She would never have to go through the bottom of her handbag to pay the chimney sweep again.

One afternoon, once the children were back at school, Clara and Julian went out for a post-lunch walk and Julian tried to take her hand. It probably shouldn't have, but it took Clara by surprise.

"I don't go in for hand-holding much," she explained although she wasn't sure if that was true. She had held Peg's hand all the way to school. She had held back Rita's hair when she was being sick, again, and she had washed down Alex when he wet the bed and was all confused in the dark. She had held Terry when she got stung, again, by stinging nettles.

That was enough physical contact, thank you.

Julian laughed. "I thought *all* women liked holding hands."

Julian was given to generalizations like that and once she'd noticed it the first time, they came thick as snowfall. "I thought all Londoners smelled of smog." "I thought all French people liked cheese." It was surprising. He could be so intelligent in some ways, so unworldly in others.

"I'll try," she said.

"Don't force yourself," he said spikily, so Clara quickly said, "No, no, it's fine," and it was. Their fingers fitted nicely together and she felt silly that she'd been so reticent.

Clara no longer told Julian about the more negative incidents at the Grange, because she didn't like how he reacted. One time, she told him that Maureen frequently stayed out late and he said, "She must have bad blood." Another time, she said that Barry was in trouble for fighting at school and he responded, "Can't they do National Service yet?"

"He's twelve years old, Julian."

"Oh, bring back the birch."

Now, in the park, they kicked through the leaves, then sat on a bench watching the squirrels hop from tree to tree; and all the while, they kept holding hands. It felt cozy, thought Clara, surprised.

"There is a way out, you know from the Grange," Julian said suddenly. Clara wasn't sure what he meant, but she felt cautious about asking.

"Oh, I don't mind it. Sister Grace is great," she said. "And Miss Bridges has lots of advice."

She now took the sewing over to Ivor. He let down Maureen's hems, *that girl grew fast*, darned socks, Peter's shirts, Billy and Barry's ripped trouser knees. Well, he *had* offered. But she decided not to tell Julian about that, on some instinct.

"And Anita is a fabulous help, too."

Anita Cardew worked on maths with Terry and Alex at the kitchen table. She was a strict tutor—given to drills and scoldings—but both children were leaping ahead in their work. She was also a fine cook. Dr. Cardew did not like anything exotic, which meant that the residents of Shilling Grange were sometimes beneficiaries of Anita's vegetable bourguignons or her potato cassoulet.

"Who is Anita?" Julian asked.

"Dr. Cardew's wife."

Anita thought Julian was fantastic. "You are going to meet Mr. White again? The solicitor!" she said every time Clara mentioned one of their dates. You could almost hear the exclamation marks in Anita's voice—she might as well have said, "You are going to meet Mr. White? The Movie Star?"

The feeling, however, was not mutual.

"Ah, the crazy Polack. He found her in Bergen-Belsen, you know."

Clara remembered Anita's tattooed arm. The way she could be

lost sometimes, just for a minute; her thoughts would go far away, her expression dark. "I don't know the details."

"Half-starving, half-dead, desperate, among skeletons."

"I can't imagine."

Julian pulled Clara to her feet suddenly. Time was up. "Do you really trust her with the children?"

Clara hesitated. The question hadn't even occurred to her. Perhaps it should have? Rather than thinking about her own line at the interview all those months ago about "protecting children from nefarious influences," she had thrown herself at Anita's feet.

"I suppose I do."

"That's another thing I like about you, Clara. You're wonderfully optimistic."

Clara didn't feel she was. But it was awful to correct him on that, especially if that was what he particularly liked about her.

They walked back to his office, still holding hands, even though Clara had an itch and could have done with rearranging her hat too. For their next "rendezvous," Julian proposed tennis, or riding, or... He paused, but it was a different pause, heavy with expectation.

"How about you come over to mine?"

Clara was not sporty. Nor was she ready to take things further physically, which she feared might be the meaning of option number three. You could never keep still with a man though, they always wanted to wade in deeper, or retreat to the shoreline.

Hmm.

They agreed on the Lyons tea rooms in Bury. *A halfway house*, thought Clara, and Julian seemed content because he was partial to a bit of their shortcake.

"I'm in a pickle," Clara began on her weekly call to Judy that evening. "There's this fella..."

It was one of those odd calls where her best friend sounded distant again. These were becoming more common. If ever Clara mentioned it, Judy would say, "I don't like talking over the telephone," which was a new one on her, or "It's a funny line."

That might have been true, only it rarely if ever happened when Clara was speaking with the council.

"Surprise me."

"I'm not sure but I think he likes me, you know, in *that* way."

"*All* men like you in that way."

Judy was what the teachers used to call "a late developer." When she was sixteen, she still looked nine and she hadn't even had her monthlies until she was eighteen. Boys looked through her. That was probably another reason she had been so thrilled to attract an eligible bachelor like Arthur; she still felt like an ugly duckling.

"I don't know how I feel about him though."

Clara couldn't help thinking, *I'm in a relationship with eight children at the moment and my head feels so full of them, I think I might burst.* And yet, Julian was a professional. *Don't forget that.* With him by her side, her life would be a thousand times smoother.

"Michael would want you to be happy," Judy said, as she always did.

"I miss him so much," Clara breathed. The windows of the telephone box had misted up, but she could still see the golden lights of Ivor's workshop, where he was still putting in the hours over his work, and the restful, soporific darkness of Julian's office.

"I know you do," said Judy.

Soft Judy.

But Arthur was calling for her and soon she hung up.

Maureen sneaked out less in December—whether it was because of Christmas (and wanting to be good) or because it was too cold to hang around in the local graveyards was anyone's guess. Whatever the reason, Clara was pleased. Maybe she was getting through to her. Sometimes, they peeled onions or carrots side by side. Maureen was good company when she wanted to be.

The children at the junior school made paper Christmas decorations. Rita made an elaborate card with the wise men and a solitary sheep made from cotton wool. "For Mama," she said. Alex's card depicted an unhappy robin on a log. He apologized as he handed it to Clara: "Art is not my forte."

Forte, huh! Clara had to go and look the word up.

Terry had a card of brown and green painted shapes that she said were trees. "Very Terry," Clara laughed when she showed it to Ivor. Peg's card was of a jolly Father Christmas with a sack full of toys. Peg also wrote in it, "To Mama Newton," which was a moment. It was a shame Peg didn't speak, especially since it diminished the hope of getting her adopted. Clara had at first tried to get her to say something, but it had distressed the girl so much that Clara now just talked away to her as though she were replying. Peg might not have the words, but she soon put you right if she wasn't happy.

The twins complained about why they didn't get to make Christmas cards at school although Peter and Maureen didn't seem bothered. Clara suspected Maureen might not be going back to school after lunchtimes. She was still on at Miss Bridges to get Shilling Grange a telephone, but the powers-that-be wouldn't budge.

Clara did get a letter from the high school toward the end of term but surprisingly, it was not about Maureen; it was about Peter.

He had slipped from second place to seventeenth in his termly tests. This was a shock. Perhaps now he was seeing his uncle regularly, he was preoccupied with his next turn in that fancy car or perhaps he thought there was less of a need to make an effort at school? He probably expected to be adopted at any moment now. It was something to keep an eye on.

Julian had also planted a small seed of mistrust about Anita

Cardew in Clara's heart. The woman was severe, but also some-what distracted. Clara asked Alex, who said, "She's the cleverest person I know!" and Terry, who said, "She knows all the flowers."

She decided to pursue the issue with Miss Bridges at their last catch-up before Christmas.

"Oh goodness, she's family and friends, isn't she? So that's fine," Miss Bridges reassured her.

Rita was the only one still learning the piano. The others had given up within the month. And Rita, who usually could chat the hind legs off a donkey, was secretive about her piano lessons.

Late one afternoon, Clara tiptoed outside the shed to listen to the lesson. It sounded as though things were in order, although you might have thought poor Anita was being taught the piano by Rita rather than the other way round.

CHAPTER TWELVE

Clara didn't know what she should do for the children for Christmas: *How do you celebrate?* but then she remembered everything Judy's mother had done the Christmases she had gone there and tried to reproduce an approximation of that.

Ivor brought in a Christmas tree, which the children decorated. Clara was pleased that Maureen took control, deciding which ornament went where as precisely as though placing armies across Europe. Peg had a cold, Billy and Barry were wrestling more than decorating and Rita was whining, but other than that it was bliss.

Clara took the children carol-singing. The list of places to avoid was as long as that of places she could go to. To avoid was the great big house off the high road where she had heard the artist Sir Munnings and his horse paintings lived, and of course Mrs. Garrard's home next to the florist.

Julian and his law partners stood at the door and made comments among themselves, then gave all the children a shilling each. Clara liked shy, compact Mr. Robinson immediately, but Mr. Browne was tall and bulky like one of those new refrigerators advertised in the newspapers. His suit didn't fit and his mustache was droopy. Something about him made her skin crawl.

The last stop was Ivor's workshop. The children sat cross-legged in a circle around his heater and Rita sang a solo, "Silent Night." She had a surprisingly sweet voice and everyone listened attentively. Anita had revealed that Rita could play "O Little Town of Bethlehem" on the piano, but when Clara had asked her to play it, Rita refused: "Mama first." Evidently, none of what Mrs. Harrington had told her had gone in.

The smaller children climbed over Ivor's knees or sat on him.

"Peg doesn't talk to you, does she?" Clara asked him suddenly. The pair of them were like peas in a pod.

His laugh was loud. "No, but I'm hoping one day she will, eh, Peg?"

Peg buried her head in his shoulder.

Clara wondered if she would ever be as at ease physically with the children as he apparently was.

Ivor had a beautifully wrapped parcel on his workbench. It had a great gold bow and ribbons.

"Is it a pet for me?" squealed Rita.

"It's actually mine!" Ivor said quickly as he shoved it under the bench out of view. Everyone laughed, even Clara, because that was ludicrous. *Who would Ivor be getting presents from?*

Alex was the first to realize it wasn't a joke, but it was only Maureen who dared ask.

"Who's it from then, Ivor? Spill the beans!"

"A friend." Ivor was blushing. Clara didn't recall seeing him go red before.

Not Mrs. Harrington? Clara wondered, while telling herself it was none of her business either way.

The children were like Bandit with a chicken leg sometimes.

"What friend? Who, Ivor, who?" they chorused.

"Her name is Ruby," Ivor finally said. "Enough now, who is going to sing next?"

Clara and Michael had had small anniversaries all over the place: the first time they met, their first kiss, the first time they made love, the night of the engagement, the date planned for the wedding. But there was no getting away from it, Christmas Eve—the night he'd died—was the most poignant anniversary of them all.

Clara managed to get the children to bed early—incentivized by promises for the next day—and she too went up early surrounded by her photographs. She had a good old cry. Perhaps it was the contrast with the hope of Christmas, perhaps it was remembering going to bed on this night only four years earlier not knowing the horrors yet to unravel. Or perhaps it was nothing to do with the date, it was just reliving the event: imagining him, tinsel in the cockpit—for Michael loved Christmas—sensing his fear. When the plane caught alight, did he know what was happening? She would never not be dogged by painful questions.

She hadn't had a card this year from Marilyn, Michael's mother, but then she hadn't told Marilyn her new address. She ought to write, but couldn't bring herself to. Had Marilyn sent a card to her father's house? Possibly, but maybe it was time to let go.

Some time, past eleven maybe, her bedroom door opened. Someone—she thought it might be Maureen, although she couldn't be sure—came into her room, then backed out again quickly.

For Christmas Day, Ivor had borrowed a great big red coat trimmed with fur and with a hood and a false beard held on with elastic. He had a potato sack on his back and had a present for each of the children and they roared and squealed when they were given them.

"Can we open them now?"

Father Christmas said, "If that's okay with Miss Newton?" which made Terry shriek, "How do you know her name?"

Terry got the spade she had wanted for her gardening. Peg got a new soft toy bear to cuddle, which she immediately held to her cheek, then christened Rupert after her favorite literary bear. Rita got a music box with a tiny mirror and a turning ballerina that Clara had found in the market and which had cleaned up a treat. Alex got a long-awaited geometry set. Billy and Barry were at that difficult age, but they leapt around at marbles. Clara hadn't known

what to get Peter, so she gave him some money and a pack of cigarettes. He went back upstairs, but she was relieved to see he was
grinning. For Maureen, a silver bracelet of her own, her first piece
of jewelry. It wasn't until Clara saw her delighted face that she
understood how much it meant to her.

"Won't you stay for dinner, Father Christmas?"

Father Christmas explained he had to get on. More deliveries.
Busy day. The children hugged him as he departed.

"How did he know where the back door is?" wondered Terry,
eyes narrowed.

Ten minutes later, Ivor came back, grinning nonchalantly and in
his normal clothes. Clara couldn't stop smiling. He was a nice chap,
she realized suddenly. It was like she had never noticed it before.

"See? It couldn't have been Ivor," said Billy.

"Of course it wasn't Ivor!" protested Rita.

Ivor laughed. "Hello everyone, are you having a good Christmas?"

They rushed to show him their presents.

Judy had knitted Clara a wonderful red scarf, sent with a
note, "sets off your eyes," (typical Judy), which made Clara laugh.
Clara had sent her some Suffolk fudge, which wasn't imaginative
but hopefully Judy wouldn't mind, plus she could share it with
Arthur—it might help put her in his good books for once.

While the children argued over who had the best gift, Ivor
nudged Clara.

"A word, Miss Newton?"

"You can have more than one," Clara said coyly. "It is Christmas after all."

He held her eyes as he handed over a large, squashy-looking parcel. For a moment she imagined it was the gift from the workbench,
from whoever that Ruby was. *Ridiculous, he wouldn't do that.*

"Who is this for?"

"You," he said in a voice that sounded like he'd changed his mind.

It was a massive quilt, pillar-box red and soft as a blossom.

"I remember you said you liked red," he said. "The first time we met. And..." he paused, "that you got cold at night."

It was lovely. Clara pressed it to her cheek, feeling suddenly overwhelmed. She couldn't meet his eye. And sweet as it was, Clara couldn't help feeling mortified that she hadn't thought to get him anything.

Anita and Dr. Cardew had given them Christmas crackers. Clara wanted Maureen to win the cracker prize. Ivor whispered to her to hold it higher than Maureen and they pulled and Maureen *did* win, thank goodness. She pretended to cut Rita's fringe with the tiny prize scissors. Rita howled.

Peg laughed so much at the jokes she fell off her chair.

And they all put on their paper crowns, even Peter. Billy's and Barry's ripped, naturally, but Maureen's stayed aloft, floating almost like a halo over the cloud of her hair.

Billy and Barry produced some mistletoe they had gotten from the market and very pleased with themselves they were too. They hung it from the light fitting, even though Clara said that they mustn't. *If Miss Bridges saw...*

After lunch, Clara was surprised to find she was under it—right next to Ivor.

"Kiss, kiss!" shouted the children, gathering in a circle and clapping. Clara glanced over at Ivor, who was looking suddenly agonized.

"Nooo!" But he was mumbling it like he was in two minds and the children's determination was greater than his.

As they moved closer, Clara caught a flicker in his dark brown eyes. *Is that embarrassment, compassion or desire?*

They did a childlike smacker of a kiss on the lips, then laughed loudly. Clara made a show of wiping her lips like Peg did. She felt ridiculous suddenly, she wanted to hide. Alex saved the day with a convoluted story about how the Christmas tree in Trafalgar Square was given as thanks from the Norwegian people.

"We *know*!" shouted Billy. "Professor, can we have one day off?!"

"This is the best Christmas ever," Rita squealed.

Even Maureen and Peter agreed.

It was pretty high up on Clara's list too.

On Boxing Day, Sister Grace came to relieve Clara—and she also brought presents for the children to unwrap. Clara left them all tearing at brown paper as she went to Julian's. The plan had been to set off out at midday, but Julian kept her waiting in his entrance hall while he thumped around upstairs. He was surprisingly poor at timekeeping, even while admitting he was never late to his own office. Clara had bought him the same fudge that she had sent Judy.

I only have until six o'clock, Clara thought, but Julian had to do this and that.

"You don't mind, do you, darling? You know how it is."

I managed to get ready while looking after eight children, Clara thought, but didn't say anything. You didn't say that sort of thing to Julian unless you wanted a debate.

His hall was a large room—as large as the parlor at the Grange, with black and white impeccably shined floor tiles and antique furniture. Julian's family were wealthy, although Julian, who only mixed with or compared himself to extremely wealthy people, didn't think so.

Julian's laundry was taken out and food appeared for him five or six times a week. "Mrs. Wesley from the next village," he had explained to Clara. "She could do your washing too."

"Don't be daft, Julian."

But the thought of not washing, not cleaning, not shopping, not cooking, did of course have a certain appeal.

After about fifteen minutes, Julian came downstairs with a parcel. It was beautifully gift-wrapped in shiny silver paper; she'd never seen anything like it before.

"It's too good to unwrap!" she told him and he gazed at her admiringly.

"Oh, you are such a *darling*!"

It was hard to be annoyed when he was like this.

"I wasn't expecting anything."

Truth was, she *had* expected something and knowing Julian, she had presumed jewelry.

Instead, it was a first edition of a book of poems by Jane Taylor.

"Well, you said you enjoyed that meeting you went to and I know you like local history and well, here we are."

Clara flicked through the pages. It was exquisite. It was one of the nicest things she'd ever been given. Its loveliness—and the fact she hadn't anticipated it—made her burst into tears. Julian hugged her.

"There, there, did I blow it?"

"Not at all, it's just so thoughtful of you."

"I can be thoughtful." He laughed. She decided not to give him the fudge present. It was too cheap, it was probably worse than nothing.

Julian had reserved a table in a country pub. He had given Mrs. Wesley the week off. (More thoughtfulness.)

"Was it sheer hell? Alone with those feral beasts for Christmas?"

Clara laughed. "Not at all." When she added, tentatively, that she had not been alone all day, that her neighbor Mr. Delaney had come by, did she imagine it or was there an edge to Julian's voice?

"He hasn't got family of his own?"

"He grew up here, in the Grange."

"Oh yes, of course, I knew that."

"Then you'd know he's sympathetic to the children's situation."

Julian ordered some champagne. "Only the best for my girl," he said to the waiter. Then he turned back to Clara.

"Sympathetic to the children, I see. The lone war hero."

What's that got to do with it?, thought Clara. She didn't tell him about the gift of the quilt. What would be the point?

As usual, being with Julian was a wonderful escape in beautiful surroundings and Clara adored the sophisticated conversation about "adult" things. She felt like the paper doll again, in her finest clothes, and she couldn't stand the thought of not wearing them again until possibly next Christmas.

Julian had friends in high places—and it was delightful to hear about the latest comings and goings. Many of his friends were downcast about the Labour government and were hoping for Churchill to take control and roll back lots of the new laws.

"They wouldn't get rid of the National Health Service though, would they?"

"Well, we can't have people abusing it," Julian said. "They'll be wanting everything free soon."

Clara thought of her regular visits to Dr. Cardew, who had said, "Of course, you *must* bring the children to me, Clara, never hesitate." Of the visits that had proved to be nothing—and the visits that had proved to be life-changing or even life-saving. Was Julian annoyed about them?

But then the next minute, Julian was stroking her hair and reading a poem from her lovely new book:

> *Then the traveler in the dark,*
> *Thanks you for your tiny spark,*
> *He could not see which way to go,*
> *If you did not twinkle so.*

She blushed. The way he read it implied that she was the spark. She was helping *him*! Or was she being ridiculous? One thing was for certain, he had a wonderful reading voice. When she told him that, he purred.

"Thank my mother for the elocution lessons."

"They've paid off."

In the car, she took the initiative and kissed him. *He seemed so happy*, she thought, *I should do that more often.*

When they had parked up back home, Julian said, "Won't you come back to mine? For a drinky? It is Christmas, after all." His voice had a slightly—what was it?—whiny quality to it. *No, it doesn't. Be nice. He's just nervous.*

But it was already nearly five. Sister Grace would be wanting to depart and the children would be waiting for her. Clara had promised a round of gin rummy and there were carols on the wireless and leftover mince pies from Miss Bridges. She apologized.

"Ask me another time."

He kissed her slowly, lingeringly, and nibbled her earlobe, which made her go all hot, and he said, "Oh, I will, sweetheart. Don't worry about that."

As she climbed into bed that evening, Clara thought of Michael. So much longer dead than she had known him and now she was older than he was when he died. She could—and this shamed her—hardly remember him. Only phrases: "Michael liked Spam," or "Michael adored Glenn Miller," "Michael did not like *Moby Dick.*" But these were just his preferences, his tastes; they didn't begin to tell the essence of him. She could not remember the essence of him; whereas once she could recall his smell, his skin, now it was slipping away.

The one thing she could remember was how he had made her feel. Deliriously content. Stupidly safe. He had made her feel like she could conquer worlds.

Julian sometimes made her feel like she was a world he wanted to conquer.

But she couldn't go through that again, she couldn't. She would never give herself a hundred percent to anyone again, never. She was older and wiser. A working, sensible relationship was what she was after—if she was after anything at all.

She told herself to push all thoughts about men to one side: *focus on the children.* Concentrate on getting them ready for their new homes and making sure they were happy at Shilling Grange in the meantime. That would be her New Year's Resolution.

The grammar school was an austere Victorian building, up on a hill in the town of Ipswich, and Clara had to pretend not to find it overwhelming. A few days after Christmas, the school held their annual open day. Clara's two—Alex and Terry—were dressed once more in their bat cloaks, to cover up their scruffy uniforms. The other children visiting were all dressed up to the nines, polished and smooth, in blazers so expensive even Julian would have found them over the top. Some children arrived in swanky cars with ornaments on their bonnets, while Clara, Terry and Alex dashed up hot and flustered from the train station, smelling of steam.

"Don't be intimidated," Clara advised the children—and herself. "It's a wonderful place. You'll have to work hard to get here *and* when you get here."

The idea, *Anita's* idea, was that knowing what they were working toward would give the children some extra momentum for the last few months before the exam. Anita said both children were definitely bright. They soaked up knowledge "like flannels." Clara assumed she meant sponges. Alex leaned toward maths and Terry the sciences. They each had real potential.

Now they both nodded. They were both earnest-faced, abnormally so.

"Yes, ma'am!" saluted Alex.

"Fine," said Terry.

"I believe in you both, remember that," Clara said, before they joined the others and walked nervously through the arched entrance.

Anita agreed to look after the children on New Year's Eve so Clara could go to a party with Julian. It was embarrassing because Julian wrong-footed Anita in the street and only told Clara about it afterward. Anita could never turn Julian down. "He's eligible," she kept reminding Clara, "but he won't be for long."

Clara worried that she had been absent from the children a little too much over the holidays, but when she suggested it to Miss Bridges, she said, "Oh no! A little of what you fancy does you good."

Before she left, Clara read poems to the younger girls from her Jane Taylor book. There were lovely verses about flowers and children. Peg adored them and that made Clara warm to Julian even more. She couldn't wait to tell him. Anita's enthusiasm about him helped too.

When she arrived, all dressed up, he swept his hand over his forehead as if in shock and when he kissed her hello, he whispered, "Maybe we should stay home instead."

Clara was startled. "Are you embarrassed about me?"

"Good grief, no!" Julian hugged her. "It's not that. You will be the best-looking woman there!"

Julian's hand traveled tentatively to the top of her skirt. "I'll be the envy of the Solicitors' Union. And I will, if I may, introduce you as my girlfriend?"

Clara blushed. "I would like that."

He kissed her on the tip of her nose.

The party was in a white brick mansion, the trees outside lit up with tiny fairy lights. Inside, mistletoe and ivy, holly, bells and candles. It was a look Clara would have loved to pull off at the Grange.

Men in bow ties held trays of champagne. Julian's world was so different from the home she had just left—sometimes it was hard to make the transition. Back home, the Christmas pudding hadn't agreed with Alex and she had been arguing with Maureen about staying out late again, as well as stopping Billy and Barry from throwing water bombs at people in the street. "A person wears many hats," she remembered Judy's mother once saying. It felt like since September, her hats had multiplied.

She was introduced to some of Julian's old friends from the Home Guard. They had all gone to the same school of firm handshakes.

"You're not one of these new-fangled career women, are you, Miss Newton?"

They never said that about the men, did they?

Clara drew herself up. "You might say so. I am a housemother at a children's home."

"See, I don't see why the government only cares about orphans—they don't care about the children stuck with horrible families!"

The man speaking, Lester, was a fragilely built young fellow with a prominent Adam's apple and wire-rimmed glasses.

"I think that's another area to look at—" Clara said.

"So, you'll agree the Children's Act didn't go far enough for children in difficult family situations?" He peered at her closely as though the answer would be in her face.

"Absolutely," Clara said, although she'd never thought about it before. "It was limited, but it's on the right track."

"I had a terrible time when I was a boy."

Clara's heart went out to him. "I hope they look at that soon."

"Tell me, how does your Shilling Grange work then?"

"I try to make sure it's not too much of an institution," Clara answered, honestly, and he clinked his glass against hers.

Julian joined them with his colleague Mr. Browne, who was holding a bottle of red wine and a full glass. Mr. Browne must have overhead Clara's conversation with Lester, for he launched right in.

"Flogging with cat-o'-nine didn't do me any harm. I've always wondered what goes on in there. Fantastic property—seems wasted on the little ingrates. Can we come and have a nose around inside?"

Just as Clara opened her mouth to speak, Julian gave her a warning tug on the sleeve. She ignored him.

"A nose around? The Grange is not a museum."

Next to her, Julian was tensing up. *Well, he shouldn't have brought me here if he didn't want me to be myself.*

"Or a zoo."

"More's the pity. What if I wanted to adopt? You'd be all over me then, wouldn't you?" Once again, Mr. Browne was standing too close. How could a man his age be so unaware of social boundaries? Clara moved away from him. He *was* aware, he just didn't care.

"You'd have to go through due procedure, like everyone else."

He ignored her and addressed his friends. "Could do with a filly to clean up after me. Got a pretty nine-year-old by any chance?"

"No."

"I wouldn't mind working in a children's home. Spankings all round!" He held out his glass as a "cheers." The other men joined in and laughed. Even the mild one, Lester, with wire-rimmed glasses, chuckled. They were all a club, a tribe here, and for a billion reasons she wasn't part of it and her voice was not welcome.

Julian managed to pull her away.

"Keep Browne sweet," Julian said into his drink. "He's got friends in all the right places."

"I don't like him." The champagne was making Clara bold. She glared back over to where Mr. Browne was still going on. "I'd pay for one. Not a lot, but..."

Awful man.

"Anyway, what's Lester been saying to you?"

"Oh, *Lester* was lovely, it's Mr. Browne who—"

"Don't be getting any ideas. Lester bats for the other team."

"What?"

Julian chugged his drink. "Funny case, he is."

Surprisingly, Julian wanted to leave early. He made eyes at her as he said *early* and it was; it was just after nine. *Fine*, thought Clara. She was dispirited by the conversations and the bubbles now whipping around her head. But while Julian went off to fetch their coats, a large, bald-headed man who was propped up against some nearby bookshelves started talking to her.

He had the self-confidence of someone who knows he's been rather successful at life and could no longer be bothered with anything he didn't have to. Clara suddenly knew who he was and she blushed.

"You're the one who works with the orphans, is it?"

Everyone knows everyone in a small town.

"Sad little life, isn't it?"

"I'm trying to make a difference," Clara said primly.

You had to count your blessings and it had been a good Christmas holiday and Clara could see improvements everywhere. Not only in her reports or the look of the house but in Rita's piano playing, Alex and Terry's schoolwork, even Maureen's improved attitude.

"Come and see me. I'll see if I can make a difference too."

"Sir Munnings wants me to go to see him," Clara told Julian in the car.

"Are you sure?" Julian swallowed. For a while he seemed not to be able to speak, but then he said, "I've never been invited. Not once in the twenty years I've known him."

"He said he wants to do something for the children."

"Well, well..." Julian looked at her like he was seeing her for the first time. "You *are* exceptional, Miss Newton."

That night was the first time she went back to his. It had been on the cards for some time. After all, as Julian was fond of saying, they'd been courting for three entire months. Or, as Clara laughingly told Judy, he'd paid for a lot of lobster.

She didn't want to think about Ivor, but she did wonder if he would be looking out of the open doors of his workshop that evening, or if he would see them kissing in front of Julian's impressive double doors.

Imagine if he did.

Anyway, Ivor had this Ruby—whoever she was—sending him golden gifts with bows.

She thought of the children at home. She had promised to be back by twelve, like Cinderella, but she knew Anita wouldn't hold her to it. Anita would be thinking, *My goodness, Clara, get on with it! A solicitor!*

Clara wondered idly if Anita and Dr. Cardew actually loved each other or if perhaps it was his being a doctor that Anita loved.

Perhaps it was a bit of both.

Clara hadn't waited this long with Michael. But things were different then; they were in the middle of a world war and you did lose your inhibitions somewhat, even if at the time you didn't realize it.

She was older now, obviously. She didn't want to be making mistakes. Not that it would be a mistake. She was nervous, but she was keen. Julian was attractive. In fact, he grew on her each time she saw him.

This was a different kind of relationship. *Mature. Adult. Befitting a woman approaching thirty and a man in his fifties.* She no longer worried about the age gap, she understood it.

They'd both gone through a lot. That changes you, whether you like it or not. The days of intensity—the days of *we might die tomorrow so...*—were over and a more sensible approach was called for. Julian was a serious person, which was exactly what she needed. She didn't need fiery passion or to lose her mind. She wanted someone reliable, someone she could lean on. Someone with a dog. There was no doubt about it—Bandit was a definite bonus.

"Whisky?" Julian interrupted her thoughts.

"Please."

He handed her a glass, then kissed her on the neck, then throat.

"Happy New Year, darling. Nineteen forty-nine...Let's have some fun."

CHAPTER THIRTEEN

Sir Munnings lived in a big house and his hallway, as Clara expected, was full of horse paintings, as was the living room. Black horses jumping hedges, white horses racing across a beach, chestnut horses in the snow; they were so vivid, you could almost hear the sound of hooves.

"And smell the muck?" Sir Munnings laughed.

"That too."

At the New Year's Eve party she had thought he was younger, but now she realized he must have been over eighty. He spent ages stuffing his pipe: he had liver spots all over his hands and his fingers were trembly. She wondered if he could still paint. She tried not to cough at the smoke, she didn't want him to think her rude or feeble—and she suspected he found a lot of things rude or feeble.

His housekeeper had one of those soft Scottish accents that make you feel looked after and she fetched them tea in a beautiful service even more elaborate than Julian's favorite one. Clara had horrible visions of smashing a china cup or spilling it all down herself. Sir Munnings said his wife was out riding and Clara thought, *I didn't even know you had a wife.* And then, *I don't know anything about you. What am I doing here?*

"I had an idea for your children."

Clara feared it would be something to do with horses. She disliked horses only slightly less than she disliked cows.

"Cinema club."

Cinema club?

"The Ritz in Ipswich does an ABC minors on a Saturday morning."

All she knew about Ipswich was the grammar school and that Mr. and Mrs. Garrard thought the children should live there rather than Lavenham. Was this a ploy?

"It's a lovely idea and the children would love to, but... Ipswich?"

"It's the nearest cinema. I want you to borrow my car, complete with driver."

Clara coughed. "All nine of us?"

"Plenty of room. Make sure they're ready on Saturday."

"This is too kind."

He patted her hand. "It's the right amount of kind."

The children went *wild* for Sir Munnings' idea. Even Peter, who had been quieter than usual that Christmas, managed a smile.

"He'll do that? For us?"

When the morning came, Sir Munnings' car rolled up and hooted and they all tumbled in. For once, there had been no chivvying the children to get out of the house promptly. They were all ready to go.

For three of the children, it was their first ever journey in a car. For five of them, it was their first time in a picture house. Peg squirmed until she got used to it, but the others settled in as if they'd been born to it. It was dark and crowded, but their seats were ticketed and the children were quiet in anticipation. When Mickey Mouse came on the big screen, everyone squealed or clapped. Billy and Barry grabbed each other's collars, whooping.

Mickey did his thing, then there was the full feature, which was Daffy Duck.

Clara drifted off in the darkness, sleepy suddenly even though she'd slept well the night before and only been disturbed two or three times. She remembered the note from the school about Peter's results. He was laughing today, but whenever he saw her looking, his freckled mouth curved downward. She'd have to speak to Miss

Bridges and perhaps the headmaster, but there was nothing she could do about it just now. She remembered being cuddled up to Michael in the cinema those days when she could give one person her absolute full attention.

When Rita found out about an animal rescue center in King's Lynn, she wanted to go there to release the animals. She cried when Clara told her she couldn't.

"They are just like us," she insisted, her face blotchy with tears. "They just need people to love them. Some of them have been there YEARS. They're all going to DIE."

She had transferred her passion for Mama to piano and animals. Clara wasn't sure it was healthy. Well, she knew it wasn't healthy, but what could she do?

Miss Bridges said that because of Rita's "obsessional nature" she was difficult to place. Prospective adopters weren't keen on that. *Just like the pets at the sanctuary who'd been there for a long time*, thought Clara.

"It is never-ending," Clara said on the phone to Judy when she called to thank her for her scarf. "If it's not one thing, it's another."

Judy sighed. In agreement? Clara wasn't sure.

"So, how are you?"

"Busy," Judy said.

"What with?"

"Oh, you know."

Clara wished she knew. "How is Arthur?"

More sighs. "He has his issues."

"How do you mean?"

"Oh, pretend I didn't say anything."

"What?"

"I knew you'd overreact if I told you."

"I haven't...what won't you tell me?"

"Because I knew you'd react like this."

They were going round in circles again. Judy was trying to tell her something, but what?

Clara didn't have time to dwell on Arthur and Judy that evening though, for that was the evening that Clara found a man in the girls' bedroom. He was on Maureen's bed, feet dangling over the side, no jacket, a tie, no cap. Maureen was on her side, legs tucked under her, laughing. They were smoking, using a saucer as an ashtray, and there were glass bottles around them which they had made no attempt to hide. *Were they drunk?*

The other girls were asleep, or pretending to be.

"What's going on here?" Such a flagrant, blatant transgression as this; Clara could hardly believe it.

"Just hanging out."

"Out. OUT!"

Now she saw he was more boy than man. He put his hands out either side of him, palm up in a play of innocence. "I meant no harm, missus!"

"Out!"

He grabbed his cap but then stopped at the door to blow kisses at them all in turn, little simpering air kisses, *arrogant little git*, then he was whistling a jaunty tune as he went down the stairs. "*Shine on bloody Harvest Moon.*"

Maureen was getting up to go with him.

"Not you. What are you thinking?"

"You never said," said Maureen. "You're always asking me to bring friends home. So I did." She flopped back on the bed. "Make your mind up."

Clara had to report it to the council. No question. Unfortunately, it was Mrs. Harrington rather than Miss Bridges who answered, but Mrs. Harrington passed it on straight away and that afternoon, Miss Bridges came over not only with the Inspector who was in charge of the area, but also the Head of Children's Services. It was *that* serious. Mr. Sommersby, the Head, was a smooth, earnest-faced man with a shiny briefcase that he seemed to take pleasure in clicking open and shut. Mr. Horton the Inspector wore spectacles and had a mustache and seemed to think he was still in the military. Although Clara had now been at the Grange for over four months, she had met neither of them before.

"If she does it again, you must call us immediately and she will be taken to a special institute for offenders or..."

"Or what?"

"She's nearly old enough to live by herself."

"She isn't though, not at all. She's so..." Clara searched for the word, "vulnerable."

"She can't bring men here at night. Tell her that. She will be thrown out. No exceptions."

"Thrown out?"

"Yes."

Miss Bridges jumped in gently. "You did the right thing reporting it, Clara."

"Thank you."

Mr. Sommersby clicked the lock of his case.

"Miss Bridges, excuse us for five minutes, we're just going to see Mr. White."

They were going to see Julian?

The two men left.

"They're all Home Guard buddies." Miss Bridges shrugged but she didn't look impressed.

"Is that why they both came, do you think?"

"The council works in mysterious ways," Miss Bridges said before brightening again. "We've had more adoption inquiries, Clara. Not long now and we'll get a result, I know it."

But there had been so many false leads lately, Clara could hardly bear to get her hopes up again. "Who is it this time?"

At first, Miss Bridges tapped her nose—"Wait and see," but Miss Bridges also hated a secret. "I could have sworn we wouldn't get any interest for an older girl, but the Nelson family are keen on the idea of Maureen. Nearly everything's in place, so she might not be your problem much longer."

Clara related some of the conversation back to Maureen in her sternest voice. Miss Bridges' support made her feel as if she had been reinforced with sandbags.

"If you ever do anything like that again, you won't be able to live here. Do you understand?"

"Why?"

"It's inappropriate, Maureen. There's a time and a place, and this is not it."

As Maureen stared at her feet, Clara told herself that she nodded in agreement.

Clara couldn't tell her yet about the possibility of adoption, but she soon found out more about the Nelsons. They had fostered five girls in the war: they'd grown up and left home and now they had a place for another. *Good people*, everyone agreed, *salt of the earth*. The type who'd save an old dog from being put to sleep.

Clara hated the "stick" approach of punishments, preferred the carrot of incentives, so she talked to Maureen about getting some material Ivor could turn into a dress and about next month's film at the Ritzy, anything to keep her engaged.

"Let's make rock cakes!" she proposed, yet was surprised Maureen agreed.

"*Is* he your boyfriend then, that young man?" Clara asked as she stirred the stodgy mixture.

Maureen shrugged. She put her finger in the bowl and circled it round the edge.

"Let me meet him properly. In the day. Downstairs. Introduce us."

Maureen licked her fingers, said nothing.

Do people who've been through a lot deserve more love? wondered Clara. When she heard what some of the children had gone through... It made you understand, but did it make you sympathize? One problem was that some of those who'd been through a lot were sometimes less likable than those who hadn't. She liked Alex, who had had an easier life, and Terry, but often struggled with the more traumatized Rita, Maureen and Peg.

I must try. I must.

Then her thoughts turned to the men in the war: Michael, Ivor, even Julian, each with their different experiences. And Arthur, to whom she had given no leeway at all despite what he had suffered.

I should, she thought suddenly. *Poor Arthur.* It would also help Judy if Clara was slightly less antagonistic to him—not that Clara was *horribly* confrontational, but they both knew she didn't like him.

She resolved to be loveliness personified next time they met.

One evening, Maureen followed Clara upstairs. She wanted to borrow some curlers.

Maureen had rowed with Peter at tea—"You're all right, you've got relatives interested in you!" And to Billy, "You're a twin—you've got each other!" Even Terry, minding her own business, was the victim of her spite. "You can't just pretend you're going to stay in the garden all your life. They won't let you."

Clara almost wished she'd kept the silent-at-mealtimes rule.

Maureen walked around Clara's room, touching everything. She did it gently, but it felt as though each item was being walloped. It was invasive. Maureen looked at the photos of Michael, but to Clara's relief didn't say anything. She was most intrigued by the boxes under the desk.

"You keep absolutely everything, don't you?"

"It's just what I do."

One of Clara's earliest memories was butterfly hunting. The first time she caught one—a red admiral perhaps—in her net she immediately felt everything was safe and accounted for. That was how it felt when she had her boxes of paperwork around her. Once written down it was caught, it was hers. It was evidence, and evidence kept you in the clear.

"Are there any notes on me?" Maureen ran her hands along the desk.

"There are reports on everyone here."

"Can I see?"

Maureen's face was eager for once, which made her look younger. Clara was startled at the request. But her precious files were the one thing she was consistently strict about.

"No, they're just for me."

"But some of them are *about* me."

"They aren't."

"You said they were."

"I hear what you're saying," said Clara. "But no."

The next morning, Clara tentatively asked Miss Bridges for a safe to put her paperwork in. Surprisingly, Miss Bridges said the council *would* pay, and she would have one by the end of the week. In the meantime, Clara was to lock her bedroom door every time she left the room.

CHILDREN'S REPORT 4
Billy Coulson

Date of birth:
January 19, 1936

Family background:
Billy Coulson is a twin. He and his twin, Barry, are very close. His mother died three days after childbirth in a London hospital. His father was in the military, so a neighbor took them in. Father was killed some time later—in the war in Burma. There was talk of an uncle but it seems he emigrated to Australia. No other known relatives.

Health/Appearance:
Billy is a good strong boy although he suffers with his feet. His hair is white as a ghost's!

Food:
Billy eats anything and everything. He can't be trusted with a fly biscuit or a coconut ice and has little self-control.

Hobbies/Interests:
Fly biscuits. Saturday-morning cinema. Magic tricks. Not-magic tricks. Mending things. Kicking and throwing balls, leaves, walls, stopping Barry fighting, stopping Barry swearing, shouting at Barry.

Other:
Billy needs entertainment and activity. He struggles with academic work, but is practical and generally great fun to be around.

CHAPTER FOURTEEN

Mrs. Harrington had handed in her notice at the council because her husband didn't like her working. Clara had never forgiven Mrs. Harrington for the poisonous way she had delivered the news to Rita about her mother and she didn't like the way she simpered over Ivor or the way you could smell her perfume until long after she'd left. But still, to be told to leave work by your husband? Hadn't women made any progress at all? It made Clara wonder what Julian would be like if they ever took things further.

"You don't mind?" Clara asked. "What would he do if you said no?"

Mrs. Harrington's expression was unreadable. "It was bound to happen sooner or later," she said. "He didn't mind me working for the war effort, but we're not at war now so..."

A Miss Cooper took over from Mrs. Harrington. Miss Cooper was young and idealistic. Miss Bridges warned Clara that Miss Cooper was a member of the Labour Party and "frighteningly political." "She would have been a suffragette," Miss Bridges added, not altogether approvingly.

For the introductory visit, Miss Cooper was wearing trousers, and a clip in her gloriously unfussy straight blonde hair.

Clara started to tell her about her worries with Maureen, the files, the safe, but Miss Cooper interrupted.

"I have the most wonderful news, Clara. An adoption plan!"

"The Nelsons?"

Clara had—without intending to—put her hopes into this. If Maureen could be taken away from the bad influences—in the graveyard, that boy with the cap—maybe her prospects would improve.

But Miss Cooper didn't know anything about any Nelsons. She was talking about a match for Billy and Barry.

This was unexpected.

The Petersons were coming to meet them the next day.

"Tomorrow? But I've arranged to go out with one of the children."

Clara was going to take Terry to the garden center.

"This is a priority."

Miss Cooper shuffled her papers and then twirled her pencil. She seemed disappointed with Clara's reaction. "We can't let them get away. People who don't mind older children are as rare as hen's teeth. You know the policy."

"I do, but it seems rushed."

"It's not rushed." Miss Cooper had a way of making Clara feel stodgy.

Would Clara make sure the boys were clean and humble?

Clara agreed, thinking, *that will be a first.*

She asked if there was any news about Peter's uncle. Was he ready to move toward adoption yet?

"Slowly is best with him," Miss Cooper said. "Miss Newton, we do know what we're doing. We run a highly professional service."

She'd been in place for one week.

When Clara told Terry that their trip was canceled, tears came to Terry's dark eyes, but she nodded bravely.

"Another time, that's fine. Thank you, Miss Newton."

Sometimes, it was worse when children were stoical.

Shilling Grange looked lovely for the prospective adopters' visit.

They would come at three thirty, have tea, then meet the boys when they returned from school at four.

Mrs. Peterson was taller than the husband, even though his hat and shoes were intentionally large. He was tubby and stout, like a teapot, she was tall and lean. They reminded Clara of Jack Sprat and his wife.

"You keep a lovely home here," Mr. Peterson said admiringly. Ivor's cushions and rugs had worked their magic. He stroked a blanket and Clara noticed he only had three fingers on one hand. More war wounds?

"We've been to other orphanages and they weren't like this," Mrs. Peterson said, wringing her hands. "Oh my! It's fit for a king."

They lived in Colchester. "Our house is only small," she added, suddenly embarrassed, "but suits us fine. There is room for a little one."

Billy came into the parlor with his hair slicked down.

"Oh, he looks just like you, Sidney!"

It was true. Sidney, Mr. Peterson, had a similar flop of white hair. "People will think he's yours," Mrs. Peterson added.

Funny how important this was to them. Maybe it was easier to love someone who looked the same. *Mirror image.*

Then Barry came in and everyone stared at each other like they'd landed from Mars.

"What's going on?" asked Mrs. Peterson, open-mouthed.

"Um, they're twins."

So much for rigorous process, Clara thought. The Petersons clearly had no idea.

"Twins?"

"Did nobody explain?"

I will have words with Miss Cooper.

Before her eyes, Mrs. Peterson's look of horror turned to awe. "I've always dreamed of having twins. This was meant to be. How old are you twins, nine?"

"Nearly thirteen," said Barry incredulously.

"It doesn't matter!" Mrs. Peterson was breathless. Mr. Peterson was staying in the background. "We don't mind."

On her fingers, she listed: *boating on the river, trips to the beaches, fruit cakes.* All dangled over them like conkers on a string.

"You'll like that, boys, won't you? Twins! My stars! I can't believe our luck!"

A few days later, Billy and Barry both hugged Clara goodbye and left for their trial weekend at the Petersons'. Clara tried to keep the other children cheerful, but they were blue about it. Rita was bawling about anything and everything again. Peg was doing her Lambeth walk up and down in the garden. She'd stay there for hours, never mind the drop in temperature. Terry was doing whatever she did in her vegetable patch. Alex was poring over his encyclopedias in the parlor. Peter was in the bath and Maureen was out.

It was rushed, she thought.

Clara went to the telephone box, hoping Judy would have some wise words, but Judy sounded distant again.

"Is something wrong with the line?" Clara asked.

The reply took a long time coming. "No."

They chatted about this and that, then, just as Clara was about to announce her intention to go, Judy asked, out of the blue, "Are you happy, Clara?"

Clara paused. The question seemed heavy with something.

"I *am* happy. It's strange though—when the children are happy, I am, when they're not, I'm not."

"You sound like a…"

"A what?"

Clara guessed she was going to say *a proper mother.* But she didn't. Instead, she said, "I don't know—like you've settled in."

"And are *you* happy, Judy?" Clara meant, *with Arthur.*

Her best friend laughed. "Ninety percent of the time everything is brilliant."

It was only *after* she had put the phone down that Clara wondered about the other ten percent.

Now that Clara and Julian were exclusively rendezvousing or courting, it felt disrespectful to spend so much time with Ivor; but if Ivor or Julian minded, neither of them said. Well, Julian perhaps was unaware and possibly Ivor was too?

Clara had been wondering for some time why Ivor stayed in Lavenham—or more precisely, why was he alone? Had he too lost someone in the war? The questions had multiplied after Mrs. Harrington's visits and indeed after the shiny Christmas gift. She had wanted to bring it up, but all the conversation openers she rehearsed in her mind seemed clumsy or childlike. However, one evening in February, as she was delivering a pile of clothes to Ivor's workshop, she decided to seize the moment.

"So, is there no Mrs. Delaney on the scene?"

On the scene? What was that?

Ivor stopped smiling. "There is and there isn't."

Uh-oh.

"I *was* married."

"Oh... I'm so sorry to pry."

Clara wasn't sorry. She was more intrigued than ever.

"She left. A couple of years ago."

Left? Not dead then?

"I didn't know."

"Why would you?" He didn't look up. "Her name is Ruby."

So! This did have something to do with the Christmas present after all!

"Is, was. I never know whether to talk about her in the past tense. She was good with the children at the Grange. She used to take them out sometimes with the nuns. Up to Ipswich or even London sometimes. They once went on a boat trip down the Thames."

"Oh." Clara found she couldn't care less about what Ruby did with the children. She wanted to know more about her and Ivor. "Do you know where she...I mean, where did she go?"

"New Mexico," Ivor said flatly. "She met an American." He drained his cup. "Bastard. There were a lot of them in Suffolk during the war, you probably heard. Swept the women away while we were getting annihilated in France or Egypt. All that candy and chewing gum did it for them."

"I'm sorry."

"She's got all the nylons she wants now." He hesitated. "What about you?"

He didn't say exactly *what about you*, but she knew what he meant.

"There was someone," Clara admitted. "He was a bastard American, he swept me away."

Ivor looked distraught. "I am *so* sorry. I didn't mean..."

"No," said Clara and grinned. It had been a long time since she had been able to smile while talking about Michael. "I completely understand."

"I am ashamed, Clara. I've got into a habit of saying stupid vindictive things. Please forgive me. I'd hate you to think I was some kind of—"

"It's fine, honestly."

"So...what happened to your American?"

"He was based here—at RAF Cockfield as part of the Eighth Air Force. Christmas Eve, 1944..." *Hard to say it.* "Our dreams were blown away."

Ivor was silent for a while and so was she. No matter how many times she said it, it still took it out of her: it still seemed unbelievable.

"I'm so sorry to hear that," Ivor said eventually. He picked up the empty cups, then gave her a searching look. "So is *that* why you came here, to Lavenham?"

"Not really. It just happened. I like to think it was serendipity. How about you?" It felt like a big question, but she wanted to know. "Are you waiting for Ruby to come back?"

"Not anymore."

Clara had stood up to go back across the road when Ivor asked gently, "Is your American buried near here?"

"Yes, he's at the cemetery in Cambridge."

"Have you visited?"

Clara shook her head.

"I can go with you, if you want…I don't mean to overstep."

"It's kind of you. It's not something I plan to do, but you never know. Thank you, Ivor. I mean it."

"You're welcome, Clara. I mean it too."

The Sunday was an-every-other Sunday, which meant Clara could spend the afternoon with Julian, reading the papers in bed. His home was less than one hundred meters away from the Grange, but it was a different world. Such an elegant and peaceful setting for her paper doll. Clara didn't tell the children she was there for fear they would throw pellets at the window or knock down the door, but she suspected the older ones knew.

All the rooms were creamy and large, the lightshades were glass and the floor was smooth. The money was in the details.

Clara was telling Julian about Billy and Barry's practice run with the Petersons when he said, "Well done on getting rid of them."

"Getting rid? Finding homes for them, you mean?"

"Absolutely—and then when you've found homes for them all, you're done?"

Clara laughed. "It'll never *be done*. There are thousands of children in care across the country. There will never be enough families for them."

She remembered her conversation with his friend, the sad Lester. "And that's not even counting the struggling children who *should* be in care."

"Can't help *all* of them, Clara."

"*Can* help some of them."

"I see," he said.

Clara thought Julian didn't see at all, but he kissed her on the cheek—he was good at distraction, like it was his life's work—and said he'd make tea—"not that muck you have at the Grange. And some of those macaroons you like."

How Julian got around the ration was anyone's guess.

Recently, Clara felt like there was more unsaid between them; but there was more unresolved in her head too, so maybe that was why. *Where is this going? Does it have to go somewhere?*—yes, it did. She wanted it to. *But where?*

The twins returned worn out from the Petersons', having left one sock each there as a memento. They had though brought back ten slices of plump fruit cake *and* brand-new gray woolen caps.

"Did it go well?" Clara asked tremulously. This was so important, not just for them, but in setting an example to the younger kids too. It would send the message that finding a permanent home was within the realms of possibility even for Shilling Grange children, even for older children.

"They want us!" Billy jumped on the bed with his shoes on. "They absolutely do."

"Barry, shoes!"

"I'm Billy."

"Whoever you are, shoes."

"Both of us." Barry tugged at the knots in his tie and threw it on the floor where Billy could jump on it. "They want both of us to live with them. We can be together forever."

"Or until we get married and have children of our own."

"So, what do you think?"

Billy stuck up two fingers in a reverse Churchill. "No, thanks. They can go whistle."

Miss Bridges and Clara took it in turns to have "serious" talks with the boys—in the parlor, the venue for such a thing.

"It's such an opportunity. And they might take you to the picture house every Saturday." Clara had no grounds for saying that, but maybe she could persuade the Petersons. As conditions go, it wasn't too bad.

Usually, Billy was the talker, Barry was the do-er. This time, Barry spoke up. His voice was deep—it had gotten manly recently.

"Thing is, Clara, I dunno if Mum would have wanted us to have another mum."

So, there it was. Clara took a deep breath.

The boy looked at her under fringed eyelashes. He trusted her. And this felt scary because Clara had no idea what she was talking about. But she knew what was good for him, didn't she?

"Your mum would have wanted you to be loved." Clara suddenly had a lump in her throat. *Would she though? Was it a given?* Is that what her mum had wanted for her? If she had, then why had she left?

"But we're loved plenty here," piped up Billy cheerfully. "All the other kids love us."

"You don't need to worry about them..."

"And Ivor. He calls me his left hand."

Clara laughed. "Ivor will be fine."

"And you," added Barry. "You do too!"

Clara smiled. When they said things like this it was hard to remain unmoved.

"I do, but things are changing. This is a chance for a permanent home."

As she said it, she thought, *isn't that what everyone wants?*

"A permanent home," repeated Billy. He slid the window open and shouted out into the garden, "A permanent home!" Then he closed the window with a fat clunk. "What's *permanent home* mean?"

"A family, a forever family."

Billy screwed up his nose. "Sounds a bit serious."

In an earnest voice, like a bad radio presenter, Barry repeated, "A forever family."

They fell onto their beds laughing, grown-ups no more. Barry was cycling his legs in the air.

"You'll give it a go, though, boys?"

They looked at each other. "We'll give it a go."

CHAPTER FIFTEEN

Not long after the "incident" with the boy in the bedroom, yet before the arrival of the safe, Maureen disappeared. She didn't come back from school. Even more shamefaced than usual, Peter admitted, come to think of it, he hadn't seen her after lunch. It was Clara's shopping afternoon so it would have been easy for Maureen to slip home and then away—and Maureen knew that Clara wouldn't be home because she'd actually checked with Clara if she was still going to town. She never normally took an interest—Clara should have known.

Clara pelted around the house looking for clues. Maureen didn't have many clothes, but Clara worked out that the pink cardigan that was too tight and her Sunday best dress were missing. She must have squashed them into her schoolbag.

Then she saw the door to her own room and it was obvious—someone had broken in.

Papers were scattered on the floor. Her reports, her private, stupid reports. They were everywhere, but Maureen's had gone.

Her photos had also been moved. No, her photos had been smashed. Darling Michael by his plane. The glass was shattered. Why would Maureen do that? And the others? No, not broken, just face down on the floor.

Oh God. What was in that damn report?

She knew it wasn't great. It was a dreadful story, but worse than that, it had been written as though Maureen was just...just a specimen of interest to science, a disembodied brain in a glass jar, not a living, loving girl with every right to find out where she came from.

Her Jane Taylor poetry book remained undisturbed by her bedside—that was a relief. Not only would it have been difficult to explain to Julian, but Clara adored the book. Some nights, those poems were the only thing that made sense.

Frantically, Clara went over to Ivor's workshop. He put down his sewing straight away and listened, worry creating long shadows on his face.

"Maureen disappears sometimes though, Clara. You know it."

"It's different this time." Clara painfully told him about the report, the damn reports, which she had put her faith in, that were now skittering out of control, and the photo smashed on the floor.

The thought that it was deliberate made her heart ache.

"I'll take the bicycle out to look for her."

"Please."

They walked out to the street together, stood next to each other bathing under the streetlight, which somehow reminded her of being in London. He was warm and reassuring in his overcoat.

"I feel such a fool." She'd tried to tell the council Maureen was struggling. She should have gone to someone more senior.

"Clara, it's not you. There's nothing more you could have done. Maureen is...well, she's difficult."

"But..."

Julian was walking over to them, a peculiar expression on his face. Clara hadn't done anything wrong—at least not with Ivor—but she imagined it might look that way from the outside.

"Well...what have we here?" Julian stared at them both, his mouth twitching with undelivered words. He looked so smart, so professional in his suit and his tidy hair. He must think she and Ivor looked an absolute state.

"Maureen is missing. Ivor is going to help look for her."

"Oh, bad show." He puffed on his cigar. "Jolly...bad...show. Which one is she again?"

*

As Ivor rode away on his bicycle, ringing his bell and calling out Maureen's name, Clara went to the telephone box. She had to queue behind a middle-aged man having a colorful argument. Ten minutes of wasted time. How far would Maureen go? Would she go to London? Wasn't that where every runaway went looking for their fortune? Or was she somewhere with the young man from the bedroom?

Miss Bridges was away and Miss Cooper was attending to cemeteries, so Clara was passed around until she got to speak to someone in educational services, who said snippily, "I don't know what you expect us to do. It's nearly the weekend. Did you try calling the police?"

So, Clara did that, only once the police realized Clara was calling about a child from Shilling Grange, they were even less interested than the council. One officer said he'd come out the next day and make a report.

"Not today?"

"It's nearly six."

Ivor didn't return until after seven, by which time he was hot and regretful. "Sorry, Clara, I'll look again tomorrow."

No one came by the next day. This time, at the telephone box, a giggling teenager got in ahead of her, poured her savings into the machine and Clara was forced to wait ages. She was glad she had changed out of her slippers at least.

"Are you one of them nuns?" said the police officer when she finally got through. She pictured him gesturing over his mug. *I've got a right-nun here.*

"I'm with the council."

"Then you'd better speak to them."

"They told me to call you."

"We'll make some inquiries." The officer sounded more interested in the horse racing she could hear on his wireless than Maureen.

"A child is missing," said Clara, exasperated.

"She's likely to have run away, no? She'll be back when she's cold and hungry."

"You need to help."

"And we will."

"What exactly are you going to do?"

"As I said, we'll make some inquiries." He snorted with laughter. "Are you *sure* you're not a sister, Sister?"

Maureen didn't come back this time. And no one seemed to care. Clara wept at Miss Bridges over the kitchen table.

"She's only a child!"

"But, dear," Miss Bridges unfolded another handkerchief, "she's not like you or me." This was infuriating, especially from Miss Bridges, who Clara had thought understood. "You said yourself, she often comes and goes."

"Well, she shouldn't. It's not safe."

Miss Bridges was distractedly reading a new order about limits on coal. "Some girls are like that."

"If they are, it's because something has gone wrong." Clara wanted to swear but she knew what Miss Bridges thought of cursing.

"Probably, but it's too late to do anything about it now," said Miss Bridges. "I called the Nelsons, the prospective adopters, remember?"

"And?"

"No longer interested."

It wasn't a surprise, Clara told herself, but it still felt as though Maureen's future was being trampled on.

"They've already gone to Norfolk Council."

Clara knew that the Nelsons going to their rivals must hurt Miss Bridges, but she couldn't help being angry at her too. And it was easier being angry with Miss Bridges than being desperately afraid for Maureen.

She is only fourteen. Clara wanted to burn it in letters in the sky. She had been the same age as Maureen when her parents had left the country. She remembered feeling terribly young—but her parents had a desire to do God's work and God had not included teenage girls in the plan, apparently. In the holidays she would stay at school. The hurt she had felt then poured into her hurt for Maureen.

"Is Maureen missing?" asked Rita that evening. Maureen's empty bed was like a finger of accusation.

"No…yes…kind of," Clara stuttered. "She's not missing *as such*, we just don't know where she is."

Goodness, I talk nonsense sometimes.

"Like Mama?" probed Rita from behind her blanket.

"I don't know."

"Can I sleep in Maureen's bed?" asked Terry. "It's softer than mine."

"Have you done your eleven-plus exam work?"

"Ye-es! Can I?"

"I suppose so."

Terry leapt onto Maureen's mattress. Peg carried on silently reading her book, her finger pressed on Rupert the Bear's checked scarf and trousers, a place where nothing much changed.

Ivor was also worried about Maureen. You could see it in the way he sliced through cloths or hemmed a curtain like he was subduing a beast. Every time Clara spoke to him, he had a face full of bad news.

One day he came to the Grange to drop off some darning and it was as if he was continuing a conversation with himself.

"It's clear to me the changes haven't worked."

"What?"

"The Children's Act. It's been a disaster."

"No, it hasn't." Clara didn't know what to say. *What about our lovely Christmas?* she thought. *What about the children doing the eleven-plus exam? What about Terry's tomatoes?* "It's been mixed. There have been lots of improvements but—"

"It's much worse than mixed."

Clara was as hurt as if he'd slapped her. "Are you trying to say it's because of me that Maureen left?"

"Not you *personally*, but she's been messed around all her life and this is just yet another way she's been let down. All the interference and the change."

"It wasn't working *before* I got here," insisted Clara. "All those children, the nuns, the violence, no accountability, all the smacking, the slippers, the silence and the massive institutions, no one to report to... No *systems*."

Ivor wasn't having this. "It wasn't, Clara. I know. I was here. As a child. Some of us had good times, good homes. Maureen would never have run away before, never."

"Look, I know the new system is not perfect—"

He laughed hollowly.

"I know it's not nearly perfect, Ivor. It's not nearly good enough. But you're not telling me you'd rather go back to the days of the poorhouse, of workhouses? Ivor, you had a good home with the nuns, but I'm telling you, many, many people didn't. Children were whipped, hit, starved and worse. And you know what, no one cared. At least *I* care."

She galloped upstairs to her room, to her desk, and fumbled around for the Curtis Report. Maureen hadn't taken that, thank goodness. Racing back down, she shoved it under his nose.

"You need to read this."

Ivor shook his head. "We're dealing with people here, not numbers, or policies, not systems, Clara, when will you get that?"

"And this *is* about people. Read it, Ivor, please."

He took it, but he was just doing it to keep her quiet, not because he believed her. Everything about the conversation stung. Partly because there were some truths there and partly because she hadn't been able to put across her own truths.

Clara had an intuition (which she didn't tell anyone, not even Ivor) that Maureen had run away with that young man she had brought to the house. It might even have been he who broke Clara's bedroom lock. She hoped, she dreamed, that maybe he had a nice family somewhere who would look after them both. Other times, she doubted this and thought of Maureen somewhere on the streets of London.

It was the not knowing that hurt most. That and the crushing sense of guilt. All her old doubts came back, now doubled—no, tripled. She wasn't right for the job. She wasn't a people person. She'd thought children could be filed as easily as paperwork. She had been so proud of all the little changes she had instituted at Shilling Grange; now, to realize that nothing had been helpful, not really, was horrifying. If you took away the magnifying glass, you couldn't even see what she had done. She had thought she was "busy changing lives" or "making a difference" but in fact she was simply overseeing a series of minor disasters. Her stupidity clung to her like a mist.

She had had one job: keep them safe; and she'd failed.

CHAPTER SIXTEEN

It wasn't just Norfolk Council; Lincolnshire had adopted or fostered seventy-nine children in the past year. Suffolk was hovering at a paltry five. It didn't look great. And Shilling Grange's zero didn't help.

A young couple were interested in Peg but decided her "speech problems" were too big for them. Inquiries had been made about Alex but subsequently dropped. Those prospective adopters had gone overseas instead. The twins were going to live with the Petersons but not for several months.

However, there was some good news. They had found a living relative for Terry, in London. A grandmother. Correspondence was under way. Miss Cooper was having palpitations about it and Clara thought she might too. Terry might be able to go and live with the woman. Well, why not?

This was the goal, this was everything, but Clara couldn't help feeling sad too. She had grown attached to the little girl. And the little girl had grown attached to the garden. She was out there for hours, digging, planting, watering and waiting. Would she not see her tomatoes come through?

And the eleven-plus preparation was going so well, too.

Clara told Lavenham Primary that Terry was going to London for "medical reasons." She didn't dare give them an opportunity to scold her. Terry was wearing long gray shorts, a school white shirt that was more yellow than white and braces that were hand-me-downs from Peter. Clara didn't argue about the clothes, but in one concession to expectations, she made Terry put a clip in her hair.

On the train, Terry asked, "Did they have trains when you were little, Miss Newton?"

Clara laughed. "Yes, we did! You pest!"

"Were there no airy planes, back then?"

Terry wanted her lunch and although it was only ten o'clock, Clara let her. She was fed up enforcing rules that she didn't want to obey herself. Outside, the view was becoming less natural, more man-made. The sky shrank and the telegraph poles became more frequent and more intrusive. At Chelmsford station, a mother got on with a small baby and said, "I apologize in advance for any squawking," but the baby just fell asleep and the mother got on with reading her Penguin edition of *1984*.

Clara asked what Terry remembered about her grandmother, but Terry sank her teeth into her apple instead.

"Pippin," she said.

The man sitting opposite laughed. "She knows her apples."

Terry's grandmother lived in a nice part of London where the roads were well swept and the lampposts stood erect and shiny. It was a good sign. They must have avoided much of the bomb damage here. Clara could picture Terry playing out, all tidied up, with nice friends with nice names like Marigold and Faye. Perhaps she might take up ballet instead of rolling in the mud?

Terry was nervous though. She'd already lost her hair clip. Her lips were set. She held Clara's hands in her mittens as they marched. The newspaper seller called out, "Ask yer mother if she wants the *Standard*."

Terry yelled back, "She's not my mother!" and the seller chuckled: "Alwight, mate, keep yer hair on!"

As they grew closer to the address, a sense of anticipation settled upon them both.

"Do you think you'd like to live here, Terry?"

Terry glanced around her. "Maybe."

The gate of the lift was clanked across and a lift-boy took them up to floor four. *Nice.* Terry was ever more wide-eyed and her grip on Clara's hand tightened. At the end of a corridor with a flickering light, Terry's grandmother met them in front of her front door. She had whiskers and she wasn't wearing her teeth. She had white messy eyebrows and white hair and she walked using a stick. Letting them in must have exhausted her; she went straight to an armchair and plonked herself in it, breathing loudly. The files said she was seventy, but she wasn't a young seventy.

"Oh, is this it then? Looks like a boy."

"She's a girl."

"Then she should wear a dress."

Quickly, Clara evaluated that this was a non-starter. What *were* the council thinking? The flat smelled stale, not helped by the jammed-shut windows. The grandmother reluctantly showed them round.

"This would be Teresa's room. Cozy. You like it?" It smelled musty, of mothballs. The mirrors were so dusty, you could hardly see in them. There were ornaments of dogs and frogs. Some insects buzzed against the window as though even they couldn't stand it anymore.

"You like it?" asked the grandmother.

Terry sneezed in response.

The grandmother put her veiny hand on Clara's shoulder.

"If we come to an arrangement I'd see her right, you know."

"I know you would," lied Clara. *How long could the woman keep her hand there?*

"I used to get money for babies."

"What?"

"In the war."

"Oh."

"Oh yeah, we'd sell them on. Got you a good price those days."

"What? Whose babies?"

The grandmother pointed to Terry and laughed.

"Her mother's for one. You'll be giving me the cash, right, lump sum?"

"No, that's not how it works."

Clara had a sudden and powerful yearning to be on her own, to be away from all this. All of it. Away even from lovely Terry. From all the children and all the responsibility. To be tapping the keys at Harris & Sons with nothing to worry about but what to get in for supper.

Terry didn't want to let go of Clara's hand, not even when the tea was served and the grandmother said, "Get that down your gob." Only after Clara gave Terry a severe look did Terry release her grip. Clara winked at her to tell her it was all right.

The biscuit she took out of politeness was a mistake—Clara wanted to spit it out immediately. It must have been around for years. When Terry reached for one, Clara tapped her hand lightly and shook her head. She got them up to leave as soon as it was decent.

"Thank you so much for your wonderful hospitality. We'll be in touch."

"No money—no girl," the grandmother said as she led them to the door.

"Did someone actually tell you there would be a financial compensation?" Clara asked, mystified. What had been going on at the council? Maybe she was the one who had got it wrong.

"It's normal, isn't it? Why else do they think I'd 'ave her?" She cackled. "Out of the goodness of my own heart? No, thank you, madam, no."

Even once they were outside, even once yards and yards were between them and the smell had worn off, Clara still thought she could hear the grandmother's peals of laughter and her, *I used to get money for babies.*

*

"I'm not sure that placement would be suitable for you," said Clara when they were back in the relative sanity of the train. Terry pressed her forehead against the window, saying nothing. Then Terry got out the eleven-plus workbook Anita had made her, put it on her knees and wrote in it. Only she wasn't writing words, she was drawing lines through questions. When Clara asked what she was doing, she said it just meant "Done."

"Do you like learning with Mrs. Cardew?" Clara asked suddenly.

"She's strict."

"Oh dear."

"If I went to live with my grandmother, I wouldn't have to take my eleven-plus, would I?"

"I don't think you'd be able to." Clara watched Terry weighing things up. She was going to put in a strong objection to the council, that was for sure. In her mind, she composed a list of all the ways it would be an inappropriate home for Terry. "So that would be a disappointment, wouldn't it? When you're doing so well." Clara crossed her arms and gazed out the window, thinking of starting with the expectation of compensation.

Terry closed her book and stared at the floor.

It was not that Anita Cardew wasn't a nice person, it was just she was so rigid. Clara had hoped for someone warm and cozy, like Judy or Judy's mother maybe, or Miss Bridges or even Sister Grace. Anita was more like an occasionally visiting glamorous aunt; you respected her, but woe betide you if you crossed her.

The evening after the Terry grandmother trip, Anita was in the kitchen shouting at Alex over the presentation of his long division.

"How can I help you if your ones look like sevens and your zeros look like eights?"

Alex scribbled on regardless, but still. Julian's words echoed in Clara's head: *Do you really trust her with the children?*

All Clara said was a mild, "He's trying his best," but Anita slammed her book shut and gazed open-mouthed at her.

"You think I don't know how to teach?"

Clara sighed. She knew Anita was defensive, but this was ridiculous. And Clara was fed up with letting Anita's defensiveness silence her.

"Maybe in a school setting, but we're a children's home here." Alex was pretending not to listen. "The children have been through an awful lot."

"You think I don't know what these children have been through? Or you think it's acceptable to confuse a zero with an eight?"

Clara gave up. She was impossible. "I didn't mean anything."

"No, no." Anita grabbed her books and threw them into her bag, then she hoicked it up and over her shoulder. "No more. Finished."

The altercation with Anita weighed heavily on Clara. She had spoiled a beneficial arrangement by letting her mouth run away with her. Alex and Terry were largely happy with the tutoring— why had she picked a fight with one of the few people capable of helping them? When she told Rita Anita wasn't coming for piano anymore, she cried, "Mama, want Mama."

The next evening, Clara looked across to Ivor's workshop, where the lights were golden against the blackness elsewhere. She had never known anyone to work so hard as he did. She found herself yearning to be in there too, escaping everything at the Grange, for just a minute or so.

She pushed open the door. Ivor was not at his workbench, but at the back, in the shadows. She called out "Hello" and he immediately responded.

"Clara? Is there anything wrong? The children?"

What could she say? That she needed a respite and this was the only place she could think of? Would that make her seem silly or useless? His opinion of her was already low.

"No, I just...I...Sorry to disturb you."

But when he came out, he was smiling. "Actually, I was done for the day...I was just stargazing."

"Stargazing?"

"Come."

At the back of his workshop was a telescope. Ivor swiveled it so it came down to Clara's level and she held onto it. Then he moved the adjustor round and told her to say "When."

The stars were beautiful, the sky was beautiful, it was so distinct from everything she was used to looking at that Clara felt transported by it and forgot where she was. She suddenly thought of Michael, killed in this sky; then Maureen, somewhere lost out there, doing goodness knows what with goodness knows who.

She'd heard people say you feel small when you look at your place in the universe, but Clara felt big suddenly. This was her moment in focus—yes, she was tiny in the overall scheme of things, but for the time being, in the universe she had she was the biggest thing.

And then she did remember where she was and she could feel Ivor so close to her, guiding her. She could feel his breath over her head and the rise and fall of his chest. She wished he would come even closer—she was being ridiculous, but she did. Ivor was correct and gentlemanly though, and kept a safe distance. As far away as the stars.

She could hardly breathe. *This is wrong... This is wrong?* She wasn't even making sense to herself.

"Why do you like looking at stars so much?" Her voice was husky. "Aside from the fact it's pretty, I mean?"

He didn't answer right away, then eventually said, "I think it's because the stars don't require anything of me. With work, with life, it's all about fixing, mending and repairing. But with the stars, they just are—and—sometimes, that's what I need."

His tone was different too. Clara felt like she couldn't possibly move away. She would have to stay here, with him right behind her, forever.

She stirred herself. Good grief. She had only come over because she was lonely.

And it *was* ridiculous because she had been out with Julian again just a few days earlier and he was making it abundantly clear how attractive he found her *and* that he saw her as a "prospect." And Julian was a handsome professional—with both hands intact and an excellent salary.

Snap out of it.

"I'd better go," she told Ivor hurriedly, "the children…thank you."

"Good night, Clara."

School home time on Monday, Clara was upstairs making beds (again) when she heard a hammering on the front door and the children calling for her. Was it Maureen? Had she come back? Please. No. She heard something about Terry. Was it the grandmother? Clara chased down the stairs two at a time and saw Billy and Barry heroically propping the girl up between them, like soldiers back from the Front. Terry was so white, she appeared tinged with green, she was holding her wrist and it didn't look right.

Clara directed them into the parlor, put Terry on the sofa—there, there. Arranged a cushion—there. Good. Terry was so small, she only took up half of the sofa.

"What *on earth* happened?"

"She fell down the stairs."

"At school?"

She fell? Or was she pushed? Clara didn't trust anything about Lavenham Primary.

"Teacher put her in sick bay, then said I should bring her home," Alex said. "I saw Billy and Barry on the way."

"Jockey, Jockey!" called Terry in a pathetic voice, then threw herself back on the cushions, her good arm crossed over her face obscuring her expression.

"What's Jockey?" Clara called out helplessly. *A bear? A mouse? The person who did this?*

"Her favorite potted plant," explained Alex.

Wide-eyed Peg was dispatched to the garden to fetch it. Clara sent the twins to Dr. Cardew. They were back less than five minutes later and reported excitedly that he would be bringing his car.

That wasn't good.

Dr. Cardew examined Terry's arm, then said he would take her and Clara straight to the hospital. As Clara began to protest, he said Anita would come by to check all was well at the Grange. It was more important that Clara came with him. No buts. Clara didn't mention the row she had previously had with Anita. She had the impression Dr. Cardew hadn't heard about it either.

In the car, Clara couldn't speak for worry, Terry's little body was trembling next to her on the back seat. Clara found herself sliding all over the leather.

"Would you mind slowing down?" she asked Dr. Cardew after one particularly violent corner.

He ignored her.

Clara wished she had had time to go and tell Ivor what was going on. At St. George's Hospital, Dr. Cardew strode off, the master of this universe, and a starchy matron took Terry away. "Your little boy is in the best place," she said. Clara waited on her own in the corridor, her elbows creating red marks on her knees and her chin in her hands.

Some time later, Dr. Cardew was in front of her. He took off his hat and held it against his chest. It felt like a pose. His shadow on the hospital wall was double the size of him. Clara, who was feeling hungry and worried, waited for his verdict.

"Miss Newton, it *is* a break, but it's not too bad."

"Thank goodness."

But Dr. Cardew and his shadow still looked somber. "That's not all."

Clara flinched. He had a way of making her feel trivial somehow.

"I can't help wondering if it's self-inflicted."

Clara faltered. "How do you mean?"

"Is there any reason, she would... She seemed keen for it to have been broken. And it is her writing hand, isn't it?"

Clara experienced the strange sensation like she was not there. She was far away and it was someone else chatting with a doctor about a small girl in hospital. Just think, just eight months ago, she had known none of these people. Now she was expected to make decisions about them and their futures. This seemed topsy-turvy. Was there no one better qualified for the task? If only Ivor or Judy were here. She herself was so insubstantial. One gust of wind and she would blow away.

No, this was on her. She had to stand up for herself and the children. What was wrong with Terry? Was it connected to the bizarre grandmother? *I used to get money for babies.* To friends at school? To the garden? No, Clara had an idea what it was. She couldn't deny it any longer.

Dr. Cardew was waiting for her response. "Miss Newton?"

"I'll speak to her."

She remembered what Ivor had said about Sister Kate and the way she had listened to them. She remembered from her own life asking for things and being ignored. Not just the time when she was begging her parents not to go to Africa; there were other times too, small inconsequential things that added up had big consequences.

That feeling. It never does go away.

*

The hospital was quiet and smelled of cleaning fluid. A long ward. One little child, quite bald, was sitting up reading *The Magic Faraway Tree*, others were asleep, clutching soft bears or dogs. Another was sitting playing with elastic; Clara recognized it as cat's cradle. She should get some elastic for the children, she thought. *Ivor would have some.*

Where was hers—*hers*? There she was, second from last: Terry, gazing at Jockey the plant in her outstretched hand. The other arm was in a plaster cast.

Her mouth was twisted down, but when she saw Clara, she beamed. Clara asked her about her arm and if they had fed her. When Terry was relaxed, Clara gently smoothed the wiry blanket and began.

"I want you to be honest with me."

Terry's eyes were huge. Had they always been that huge or was it being here in the hospital that did it?

"Whatever you say, I won't be angry with you, I promise."

Terry whispered something to Jockey's leaves. Clara reached out and firmly moved Jockey to the drawers next to the bed.

"Terry, did you do this on purpose?"

Terry wouldn't look up. Clara waited. "You can tell me."

The matron walked in and filled up Terry's glass with water and then, kindly, splashed a little into the plant pot. "Bit dry in here." She smiled.

Only once she was back out of the double doors did Terry nod.

Even though she wanted to screech, Clara was determined to keep her voice even. "Why?"

"I don't want to do the eleven-plus exam because I don't want to go to the grammar school in Ipswich. I want to go to the local school, where Peter and Billy and Barry and everyone goes."

Clara gulped.

"The grammar school is a good school, Terry. And Alex will probably be going there too."

"I don't want to."

"You can't let the other girls influence where you go, you know that."

"It's not about the other girls. I just know it's not for me. Thank you, Clara, but I just want to grow my plants."

"You can grow your plants *and* go to the grammar school."

Terry stuck out her bottom lip.

"I'm listening," Clara prompted.

"I do not want to go to the grammar school, Miss Newton."

Clara's heart plummeted. *After all I've done. The row with the headteacher. The work with Anita. The visit to Ipswich.*

"In that case, you don't have to."

"Are you sure?"

"Absolutely."

They shook hands on it, like serious people making a deal.

Then Clara told Terry that throwing herself down the stairs was an incredibly daft thing to do and she could have terribly damaged herself, and that she must never do anything like that again.

On the way out, someone said, "What happened to your son?" and Clara didn't correct her but called back, "She has broken her wrist…it's not too bad though."

Bless him, Dr. Cardew was waiting for her in the car outside. Clara didn't want him to know that she had pushed through like a steamroller without being aware that it wasn't what the child wanted. It had implications for Anita Cardew too. She had thought she knew best. At the same time, she was disappointed at Terry's choice and in herself for being disappointed.

CHILDREN'S REPORT 5
Alexander "Alex" David Nichols

Date of birth:
September 9, 1937

Family background:
Alex has something of a mystery about him. No one seems to know where he is from or even how long he's been in care. His parents probably died in the war. I imagine he came from a well-to-do family and a loving home. I wouldn't be surprised if one day an aristocrat came to us and said Alex was a Lord or a Baron or something, like in *Oliver Twist*—he is such an exceptional boy.

Health/Appearance:
Sticky-out ears, long teeth, curly hair that needs frequent cutting. Propensity to nits. Aversion to baths.

Food:
Allergies. Does not eat enough vegetables. Likes grapes but can hardly ever get them.

Hobbies/Interests:
Alex is the young intellectual. We call him the professor. He knows countries and flags and capital cities. He collects stamps—he already has two albums—and coins (I suspect this is a money-raising scam!). He does so well with his schoolwork—if he doesn't pass the eleven-plus then I have told him, I will eat my hat!

Other:

Alex has beautiful social skills and table manners—I have never seen anyone hold their cutlery so decisively. Most of the other children struggle with a spoon.

I can't understand why he hasn't got queues of people wanting to take him on.

CHAPTER SEVENTEEN

Alex took the eleven-plus exam at Lavenham Primary in the school hall with sixteen other candidates. Terry did not. Clara was on tenterhooks all afternoon—as she peeled potatoes, as she did the sheets. Alex was well prepared and clever, but what if he were seated somewhere where he couldn't see the clock, or what if he got his timings muddled? What if the pages were stuck together, or he had a nosebleed or locked himself in the loo? What if he forgot his fractions or his decimals—or suffered a strange bout of amnesia? Clara's thoughts turned ever more fantastical. What if he choked on his breaktime biscuit? What if he hit his head on the water fountain?

He came home grinning. He recited all the questions *and* his answers.

"You remember it all?"

"Oh yes." He looked behind him, checking to see if anyone was nearby. They weren't. "It was easy, Miss Newton. Too easy," he whispered.

He said he thought the verbal reasoning was not just easy, it was a piece of cake. Clara had wondered if he had a photographic memory. Judy had said it sounded like he might.

Still, you had to be cautious. Anything could happen.

"It sounds like you've done well, if what you've remembered is correct. Alex, I'm sure your parents would have been so proud of you."

His lips trembled. She thought he might cry but he didn't.

*

Naturally, he wanted to go and tell all to Mrs. Cardew. Clara inwardly groaned. She hadn't seen Anita since their argument but she couldn't justify saying no to Alex.

Anita was leaving the surgery with her big bag when Alex went bumbling up to her and she gave him her small, hard smile. *How difficult would it be to hug him?* thought Clara but she couldn't say anything. Alex didn't seem to mind anyway.

"Thank you for teaching him," Clara said, embarrassed, as they stood some distance from each other. "Sounds like he did well."

"You never know." Anita wouldn't let down her guard for a moment. "Now the long wait for the results."

"Yes," agreed Clara.

"And Terry?"

Clara flushed. "Terry decided not to take it in the end."

Anita nodded thoughtfully. She didn't seem surprised. Perhaps she had already put two and two together.

"Do you want me to come over tomorrow for Rita's piano lesson?"

"Oh, Anita, yes, please. And I'm so sorry I upset you, I won't interfere with your methods again."

Anita nodded curtly. "Tomorrow then."

Clara was grateful. She supposed that was as good as she and Anita were likely to get.

By contrast to Alex, Terry was a little forlorn that evening. She wandered into Clara's bedroom, a sorry sight with her plaster cast and her grubby arm bandage, and Clara's heart went out to her. She had big burdens for a not-quite-eleven-year-old. Clara waited for her to say something, but she did not, so eventually, Clara asked, "Are you glad you didn't do the exam, Terry?"

"I am," she responded, her eyes lowered. "Are you still angry about it, Miss Newton?"

"Not at all, my girl." Clara stroked Terry's hair. "I'm proud of you for knowing your own mind."

And it was almost true.

CHAPTER EIGHTEEN

Clara left the Grange as soon as the children went out. If she wasn't back from London by the time they were home, Peter was instructed to take charge.

Judy and Arthur's house was a modest terrace in Clapham, not far from Clara's father's home in Battersea. On the rare occasion she went into London, Clara felt nervous about running into her father, but he would generally be out and about performing good works and they were unlikely to cross paths. There'd been no word from him, even at Christmas, which was both a relief and a disappointment. They'd both agreed there would be "no point."

Judy had an unexpected day off work. Clara was determined to tell her about her new resolve to be nicer to Arthur. Arthur had gone through a lot and, like the children, who'd also gone through a lot, she had realized that he deserved a bit more leeway and understanding.

Clara was learning, she told herself, not just about orphans but about all sorts. She couldn't wait to tell Judy about life at the Grange. She even knew how she was going to phrase it: "there's never a dull moment." She had suggested meeting at a favorite tea room in Clapham High Street, where they did cheese muffins, but Judy had asked Clara to come to the house first.

Clara hadn't understood why, until she got there. Judy had two black eyes and her lips were swollen up like cushions.

She let Clara in, shaking her head furiously. "Don't say anything. I fell, Clara."

"Did you, really?"

"I said so, didn't I?!" Judy was nearly shouting.

Clara didn't know what to think.

Judy asked all about the children as if she knew them—even though she had never met them—but batted away any personal questions. Clara found it hard to look at her—when she did, she saw Judy's eyes weren't actually black: one eye was dark purple, the other was completely swollen shut, and was yellow, pink and green. If it had been a sunset, it would have been exquisite.

As she made tea, Clara tried again.

"How did it happen, Judy?"

"I walked into something. A door."

"Oh, Judy." Clara felt like crying. "Which was it? You fell or you walked into something?"

Judy's less-sticky eye filled with tears. She waved her hands around feverishly.

"It's nothing, Clara, please."

Clara remembered something else that had happened while she was staying there last summer. Judy had sprained her ankle in the night. Arthur had made a big deal of massaging it in the morning, yet he wouldn't let Clara so much as look at it.

"Your leg that time, was that nothing too?"

Judy picked up the cups silently and stacked them next to the sink. Then, with her back to her friend, she sobbed. When Clara tried to put her arm round her, she said, "Don't make it worse."

The thought that Arthur had done this—*and* that he had hurt Judy before, was hurting her while Clara herself had been snoring obliviously downstairs, made Clara's blood run cold. That *bastard*. What had he put her friend through? Had Judy desperately begged him to keep the noise down? The memory that she had lapped up Judy's excuses the next morning: "I fell out of bed, you silly sausage," made Clara feel small and ridiculous. Judy should have trusted her.

Judy stopped crying, blew her nose and repeated, "It's nothing," and "Don't look at me like that."

"How many times?"

"It's not as bad as you think. It's only if I get in his way. Clara, CLARA! Stop staring at me. It's *nothing*. He loves me more than anything else in the world."

"That wasn't the question."

"Never mention it again. Promise me. I won't… I won't see you, if you keep going on about it. I've told you, it's over. It'll never happen again."

"How do you know?"

"Because I'll leave him if it does. And he doesn't want that. Now let's talk about something else."

Judy talked about the old members of staff at school who were stuck in their ways and the new members of staff who had absolutely no idea, and the difficult students—many of whom came in hungry or cold.

"Arthur works wonders with them."

When he's not scaring the wits out of them.

And Judy asked about adoption and living relatives and Clara explained that Suffolk Council's figures were down and they still needed a success story soon otherwise *questions would be asked*.

"If I know anyone, I'll send them your way."

"Please do." All Clara was thinking about was poor, poor Judy. She could hardly look at her; Judy had become Medusa—only when Clara gazed upon her, she turned not to stone but to jelly.

Judy admitted she hadn't left the house for three days, so Clara persuaded her out for some fresh air. During Clara's darkest days after Michael, Judy used to make her go for a lunchtime walk. Judy could wear a hat, no one need see her face. Even though she promised Arthur wouldn't be back, Clara couldn't help being anxious about it. What would she do? Fight him off with her umbrella?

Clapham Common was coming back to life after the dark war years and there, Clara allowed herself to relax. Maybe, she told herself a few times, it wasn't that serious. But then she just had to take one look at Judy's beaten face, now in the shadow of a ridiculously large straw hat, and she could see exactly what it was. Arthur was disgusting.

Later, as they said goodbye, Judy grew all jolly again. She was acting, thought Clara, she had to be.

"Please stop worrying about me, Clara. Things are fine."

"I'll always worry. This is what friends do."

"You can worry, but it won't make any difference. Arthur is fine, we're fine."

She walked off, holding on to her crazy straw hat. She was like an anachronism, Clara thought, a figure in the wrong place and in the wrong time.

On their every other Sundays, Clara and Julian usually had whatever food the versatile Mrs. Wesley had left. Sometimes it was fish, mostly it was unspecified meat that was probably mutton, but Mrs. Wesley disguised it well. Although Clara loved the food at Julian's, it felt like a rebuke to the dishes she served the children. While Clara was confident that their lifestyles had improved since the nuns, their diets had probably got worse.

After lunch, Clara and Julian would go upstairs and make love. In bed, in satin sheets, naturally. Julian was attentive and accomplished. It was just what she needed. She dismissed the word "mechanical" but it was slightly that, and no bad thing either; mechanics are important.

And for fifty, Julian was energetic.

Afterward, Clara was always pleasantly surprised that Julian would let Bandit into the room—he would have been waiting behind the door and they would laugh as Bandit came bounding over to them as though he hadn't seen them in years. She loved this time with the dog. Julian often joked that she preferred Bandit to him and there might have been a grain of truth in it. Goodness, though, it was good to get away for a few responsibility-free hours. Everything was easy with Julian; he made everything smooth. She'd be crazy to rock the boat.

Julian liked the finer things in life. He didn't spend money easily, but carefully. That was another way in which he was different to Michael. Michael could be impulsive, although maybe in peacetime he would not have been—who knew? War affected everything, from spending habits to sexual proclivities. You knew someone at peace, you knew someone at war and they could be entirely different people. Everything was out of character. You became confused about what one's real character was.

Anyway, Julian said he was serious about her and it was peacetime so...

Still Clara wondered what that meant. Serious as opposed to frivolous, perhaps?

Ever since Ivor had suggested it, Clara had been wondering about visiting the American military cemetery where Michael was buried.

It was too much to ask of Julian. Asking a boyfriend—she could call him that now—to go and see the grave of an ex-boyfriend was not the usual order of things, even if everyone had been through a war together. Even if Michael had been on their side. Even if Michael had died for the good of Europe. Even if he'd, you know, had a proper role in the war. She thought it best to ask Julian anyway; it might be better than him finding out after the event.

"I wonder if you would come with me to visit an old friend's grave?" She felt hot and stupid. Funnily enough, she hadn't told Julian much about Michael before—he hadn't exactly asked, and telling Ivor had been hard enough, she didn't need to rehash it over again. "Would that be something we could do together?"

Daft. Daft. Daft.

But Julian came good immediately.

"Do you know what?" He patted her thigh. "It would be an honor."

Clara felt like he had passed a test. Perhaps he did too, for he leaned over and kissed her cheek joyfully. He smelled of apple and cinnamon, which was probably something to do with Mrs. Wesley's unique washing methods. Clara was becoming addicted to the smell. Her defenses melted away.

"Today?" he suggested, sitting up.

"Not today."

"Why not?" He leapt out of bed. "No time like the present."

So he drove and as he drove they talked a little more about their war experiences—a subject they had both largely avoided before. Clara told him about her work at Harris & Sons and then about the bombings. She told him of this night and that; it felt like she was testing the water before she could tell him how horrendous it really was. The Blitz was so awful that most people didn't like reliving it, but sometimes you had to, it kind of burst out of you. But then it was awkward because you could start talking about it and then realize that the person you were talking to had had it even worse. And then you felt bad for complaining, but everyone needed to complain sometimes.

Clara had feared Julian might have had it worse—in some places, young men, or young-*looking* men like Julian, came in for a lot of abuse if they weren't away fighting, but Julian said, "Not at all, everyone around here loved the Home Guard. We really excelled ourselves."

"And did you have lots of girlfriends during the war?"

Oh, to be a single man on the home front. Didn't they say it was like being a child in a candy store?

"I had all the girlfriends." Julian laughed, then corrected himself. "I wish." He took his hand off the steering column and patted hers. "I've always been more interested in hunting and law—in no particular order—until I met you."

She wasn't sure if he was being serious or not. But all in all, she was glad she was going to the cemetery with Julian, not Ivor. How would she and Ivor have even gotten there anyway? The cemetery wasn't near a train station and Ivor couldn't drive. With Julian and his never-empty wallet, practicalities melted away.

A man with no legs was selling flowers at the gate, flowers to put on the graves. It was like he was there as a warning sign—*brace yourself, this is going to be emotional.* As they approached the entrance and saw crowds of people, Clara felt woefully unprepared. For some of these people it was the pilgrimage of their lives, their whole goal, whereas she had only recently thought it would be a good idea.

Clara rummaged through her handbag for her purse. Had she even brought any change? She wasn't wearing black. Should she be wearing black? She felt ashamed of herself. She had approached this all wrong.

Julian, however, had no qualms—he strode over to the flower-seller in three easy steps and handed him a crisp note.

"What do you think your friend would like?" he called.

"Oh, anything."

She hadn't even anticipated this. Flowers! Obviously. This was basic stuff.

Julian said there wasn't much choice. He paid for poppies and Clara was reminded of the Jane Taylor poem "The Poppy" and how the flower was described as "pert and vain, a gaudy weed." Clara usually loved this poem but at that moment, she had the horrible idea that she was those things too. Suddenly she wanted to just take the flowers back to the car and not go anywhere but have a good old cry for Michael on her own; that would suffice, wouldn't it? But Julian was with her now and you didn't do that kind of thing with Julian. In fact, she'd never once cried in front of him, although she still did often enough on her own.

It had rained in the night, so the ground was squelchy under-foot, reflecting Clara's unsteadiness. Families were moving in front of her, in and out of her way. A bored teenage girl with a bobble hat dawdled. Two small boys were pinching each other. Mothers, oh, lots of mothers, carrying lots of flowers for their lost boys. Clara didn't think she could stand the heartache around her. It was bad enough dealing with her own.

She thought of her mother's grave somewhere in Africa, another grave that she had never laid flowers on.

You had to read the graves. And then, there it was; his was sud-denly in front of her:

CAPTAIN MICHAEL ADAMS
OF THE EIGHTH AIR FORCE, 838 BOMBARDMENT SQUADRON
Beloved son to Michael Sr. (deceased) and Marilyn

She hadn't gotten a mention. It wasn't deliberate; someone told her no one's English girlfriend got a mention. It was just the way it was. Three months later and Clara might well have had her name on it. But then three months later and they'd have been married and Michael might not be dead, and right now she might have been living in Massachusetts with two corn-fed children growing American accents.

It *wasn't* deliberate.

She put down the poppies and moved on. It was too much to stand there staring. Not while Julian was jiggling next to her.

Working out their ages, you just wanted to weep at the blistering cut-short youth of them. One had been nineteen years old—and she had thought Michael was young at twenty-six. There were crosses and a couple of Stars of David.

She had received the telegram on the morning of Boxing Day 1944. *The whole plane together. Six of them.* The war would be over less than ten months later. At one grave further along, a mother had brought a folding chair and was sitting there eating sandwiches. She was talking to the grave. "Did I tell you about Cousin Sue?" she said. "She's marrying that Italian fella. They don't mind him, actually. You know, things have moved on."

A whole generation had been affected, hardly anyone left unscathed, and even the ones who appeared unscathed, well, some of them were pretty damaged too.

Clara found Julian's hand. It was like a reassuring crevice on a cliffside. He squeezed her fingers. He was there for her.

"He must have been special to you, Clara."

"He was."

She suddenly felt connected to Julian *and* Michael, all of them at that moment, for what they had been through. Julian understood the war and what had been lost. He understood her and he wasn't jealous or anything. He was so respectful. He would never hit her. He would never push or shove her or make her tell her best friend in all the world that she'd fallen or banged into a door. This was exactly what Clara needed. Reliability was underrated.

Clara was dabbing at her eyes as they drove to Cambridge town center and Julian was still trying to make her laugh. He was teaching her a rude song that he and the Home Guard used to sing.

"…And she was left without her drawers!"

There wasn't a song about a woman whose clothes fell off that Julian didn't know.

She wanted him to stop, she wanted quiet to think about Michael, but he had been so good to bring her and so sympathetic. He had taken her there on his day off, he had organized flowers. Now he would treat her to supper. It was the kindest thing, beyond the call of duty. Her heartache was safe with him and that was a relief.

"Feel better?"

"Much. I probably should have gone years ago."

Hard to put a finger on why she hadn't. She hadn't even thought of it until Ivor suggested it and then she just couldn't face it. Seeing it had made it true and maybe she hadn't been ready for it to be true. Perhaps for the last few years, she'd been pretending that Michael was simply on another mission and any day now, he'd call her: "Get your glad rags on, sweetheart, we've got dancing to do."

It occurred to her suddenly that she loved living in Suffolk—it wasn't just that Michael lived here, that he had died here, just that she did and that was that. It was a peaceful place. The countryside suited her after all.

She would write to Michael's mother tonight. She might be pleased to know about the visit. Clara resolved to tell her about the poppies. Fingers crossed, they were a flower that Michael had liked.

Cars and horses in the streets of Cambridge; here too, it was coming back to life. The shops were more indulgent than in Lavenham, the luxury type: clothes shops, bookshops. The university colleges with headlights at the windows, the great gates open wide. They passed an American bar, Frankie's, with a Stars and Stripes stretched over the door. In the dark, there was an outline of a small woman and three men. They were smoking. It looked like they'd just left the basement. But the thing that caught Clara's eye was the red scarf.

"Wait."

Julian drove on.

"Please, Julian."

"I couldn't stop there."

"I think it was Maureen. Can we turn back somewhere?"

"Maureen?"

"One of my girls, the missing one... Can we stop?"

"You want to careen around town searching for someone who doesn't want to be found on a rare day off?"

No, she didn't *want* to. But she had to.

"Please."

He swung his head round, reversed the car and they drove back round the corner in silence. They were back in front of Frankie's Bar in minutes. But it was too late. Whoever they were, they had long gone. There was just a fat man there now, in a black suit, cricking his neck.

"I told you it was pointless," Julian said.

It should have been a lovely evening. It *was* a lovely restaurant. Candles and warming stew and a surprisingly successful starter of parsnip soup, but Maureen's whereabouts were gnawing at Clara. *It couldn't have been her, could it? But if not, where was she? And it had to be her, didn't it?* The red scarf was a giveaway, a beacon in the darkness. Poor Maureen, with her blue lips and sore hands; she always felt the cold.

Julian said to order whatever she liked. "Push the boat out, sweetheart."

"It's been a long day. I'm probably a bit..." she didn't know, "overwrought from the cemetery."

Julian kissed her hand, meaning, *it's fine.* She suspected he was going to ask her to come back to his place again, "Round two!" but was glad when he didn't. They needed some time off.

"Everything all right, Miss Newton?" Sister Grace had done the oven, mopped and baked. She was an angel.

"I'm just exhausted," Clara lied. Sister Grace said she would pray for her, on top of her usual prayers, and Clara said she would appreciate it. Clara imagined her father used to pray for her too— for all the good that had done.

CHILDREN'S REPORT 6
JAMES "PETER" DOWNEY

Date of birth:
October 29, 1934

Family background:
His mother died in or shortly after childbirth and his dad abandoned him either immediately or not long after. He has been in and out of children's homes for most of his life. He moved to Suffolk with Sister Eunice. Before that, he was in Leicestershire. There has been little or no continuity of care. He has a charming uncle, Mr. James Courtney, who has been taking him out on Wednesdays for the past few months ever since I first arrived here (September). Whether the uncle could take him on full-time doesn't seem to have been arranged yet, but we are working toward that.

Health/Appearance:
Peter is a heavy smoker. I don't know where he gets his cigarettes from but doesn't seem to have stunted his growth for he is six foot tall and shoe size 6. I had to go to the shop and get him new ones. He grows so fast.

Peter is a nice-looking boy with lovely green eyes and freckles.

Food:
Eats anything. Loves fruit cake.

Hobbies/Interests:
He takes frequent baths, especially recently. He doesn't like wearing his school tie.

Other:

Peter is responsible, kind, quiet, but has grown moody of late. His school rated him 2/30 in his form but at Christmas he dropped to 17th. Probably a mistake. Inquire?

CHAPTER NINETEEN

Peter was out in the street, with a long stick, making circles in the dust. It annoyed Clara; dust had become her enemy since coming to the Grange, especially now that the children did fewer chores, but she told herself it was Peter, sweet Peter. *Don't be too picky with him.* She must try to bring him out of his shell, not push him back into it. *Always keep in mind everything he went through before I knew him.*

"Would you like a pen and paper instead of that?"

He shrugged.

"I mean, it looks fun but..."

He didn't look up, just carried on moving the stick. Dust rose, making her eyes sting. It was annoying, especially when she was just trying to be nice.

"Look at me when I'm speaking to you, Peter."

Dear God, I sound like my father sometimes.

His freckles were like someone had dotted all over him. *She had our backs, you never doubted it,* Ivor had said. She'd have Peter's back too. If only he would let her.

"I'm happy to get you some art materials. Is that something you'd like?"

"I suppose."

It was as though the words had to be prized out of him. *Why couldn't he be more grateful?*

Her request for stationery was not well received by the council. Somehow, it did not come under essential or educational items.

"We're not spending on entertainment," Miss Cooper explained. "And paints are entertainment."

"Oh, for goodness' sake, I'll get him some," Ivor said when Clara told him about her latest tussle with the department. She kept hoping he would suggest stargazing again, but the one time she asked, he said it was too cloudy.

"No, it's fine. Julian has plenty in his office, I'll ask him."

Ivor frowned.

"It'll save you a trip."

"Sure."

"Julian loves doing things for the children."

"Right-ho."

"He does!"

Ivor laughed. "I'm not arguing, Clara. I'm sure he does."

The next day, Julian produced a single pen and pencil for Peter. "Don't the schools provide all this? Or the council?"

When she complained to Judy about Peter's recent bad attitude, Judy laughed. "Ah, the terrible teens." That made Clara feel much better. They were like toddlers, but worse apparently. Being rude was a thing, it was a *phenomenon*. Judy said new research was coming out of America that showed that "teenage brains are different."

"Peter's certainly is."

Judy was also in a much better mood. Eyes all healed up and lips recovered. She said things were going her way now, and although Clara didn't know what things and what way, she did enjoy chatting with her friend now that she was more upbeat. Judy had been out dancing with Arthur and to a show: they were having fun.

"You'd tell me if he—"

"There's nothing to worry about. All that is ancient history."

Through the telephone-box glass, Clara saw Mrs. Garrard putting out flowers in buckets in the street. She wanted to carry on speaking with Judy so she wouldn't have to engage with her, but Judy said she and Arthur were going to the cinema to watch *Gaslight* and she would have to hang up.

Peter struggled to get up of a morning these days, but also struggled to get to sleep at night. She heard the ball thumping against the walls or sounds of him moving around. Luckily, the other boys slept through it. Peter wouldn't read, he wouldn't do his schoolwork, he wouldn't join in games or listen to the wireless. He still did his chores, but he never talked or whistled while doing them; he seemed lost in his own world.

Clara thought maybe it was just her being paranoid, but Ivor had noticed it too.

"Nothing's wrong with Peter, is it?" He was redoing a chair for the Mayor's residence. Clara watched him tilting it on its side, then hammering the tacks into place. She always marveled at how he managed with one hand.

"How do you mean?"

"He just seems lethargic recently, not into anything."

"Do you think he's ill?"

"You could see Dr. Cardew..."

There was no way Peter would consent to go to the doctor's.

CHAPTER TWENTY

For every story Clara told Julian about the children at Shilling Grange, there were probably ten or more she couldn't tell him. She curated their life at the home to make him feel better—and in truth, to make her feel better. Julian wouldn't want to hear anything alarming—like how Billy and Barry would throw knives at the shed. ("It's so we can run away to join the circus.") He didn't get to hear anything rude—like Rita misexplaining the birds and the bees to a stunned Peg: "The man does a wee-wee in the lady"— and he didn't get to hear anything personal, like Terry saying she didn't want boobies, ever.

The version of Shilling Grange that Julian heard was like something out of Rupert the Bear—not that Julian saw it like that. He seemed to think they lived like something out of the Vichy regime, with Clara as the oppressed French and the children as Nazis.

There were loads of things Clara *could* talk about with Julian though, she didn't have to talk about children. They both loved talking about Bandit: they found him endlessly fascinating, from his eating habits—he ate anything—to his antipathy toward water and baths. And did you know he was good at fetching a ball? Clara also liked hearing about Julian's work, even if some of it sounded a little dry. And surprisingly, and rather delightfully, Julian was a gossip. He had enough information on everyone in Lavenham *and* its surrounding villages to fill any silences (whether the stories were true or not was another thing). The Garrards—*what does Dotty see in Larry?*; the petrol attendant, who was a widow, *sad case*; the couple who ran the post office and lost a son in the war, the grocer—that plain fat man—had a daughter who looked like Audrey Hepburn and a son who looked like Rock Hudson. The butcher who couldn't say no to his spoiled little girl.

Oddly though, one of Julian's favorite subjects was Ivor. Julian didn't like him, although when Clara asked him why, he acted offended: "I think he's a perfectly fine fella, why would you say that?"

Julian was as intrigued by the absent Ruby as Clara was.

"There must be something wrong with him, otherwise why would she have left?"

"How do you mean?"

"Saved all those men at Dunkirk, all those medals...Must be something wrong with him. Apart from the old handy-pandy, of course. Down there, don't you think?" Julian gestured below his waist.

"Julian!" Clara was both fascinated and appalled by this suggestion. "He's never mentioned it to me!"

"Hardly think he would, darling. It wouldn't show him in the best of lights, eh? I reckon that's why she left."

Another time, Julian said, "They were together at your orphanage, you know."

"Who?"

"Ivor and his Ruby." He said it in a weird way, elongating the "oo" sound in her name, as though he found saying it distasteful.

"I didn't know."

"Yes, they were what everyone fondly refers to as childhood sweethearts. Must have come as an enormous shock when she upped and left." He grinned. "Childhood *cheat*-hearts."

Poor Ivor.

It was none of her business, but Clara couldn't help thinking about Ivor's Ruby. She wished there was a photograph of her just so she could have some idea at least. It was hard relying on just her imagination. Clara had thought to open a file on her, just for keeping those little tidbits of information in one place, but she knew if anyone found out they would think it strange—and if Ivor found out, it didn't bear thinking about!

Clara pictured a young woman with home-dyed hair and a lot of makeup, which she might not take off before bed but simply layered on more of the next morning. She was probably attractive—she couldn't imagine Ivor with someone plain. And Ruby had found herself an American, hadn't she? Michael used to talk about the girls who hung around the airbase, not disparagingly—he was too fair-minded for that—but not altogether warmly either.

What *had* happened between Ivor and Ruby? That was the one downside of Mrs. Harrington's departure—she was another one who knew everyone's stories and had always been happy to divulge.

When Ivor took his stock to the market at Felixstowe he usually employed a local boy to help him unload and load the van, but occasionally he took a child from Shilling Grange instead. Alex loved going and he often begged Clara to come along too.

By contrast, Anita couldn't understand why Clara was even considering it. "What about Mr. White?"

"I saw him last weekend," said Clara. She couldn't help reacting against Anita's enthusiasm for Julian.

"I mean, what would he say?" Anita pursed her lips.

"Nothing," Clara said, which was wrong, Julian had plenty to say about *everything*.

Anita made the face that Clara had learned meant: *You need to make more of an effort with Mr. White, Clara, men like him don't come along often.*

But Sister Grace said, "What a lovely idea, Clara," and offered to arrive a little earlier to allow Clara to get away.

When Clara arrived, the area was filled with trucks and vans and trailers of all different sizes and filled with different things: flowers, shoes, groceries and fruit. Ivor and Alex were still unloading, with the help of another trader, Lenny. Ivor gave her a half-smile, but it was hard to tell if he was pleased she'd turned up or not. They were talking about Alex's upcoming eleven-plus results. Lenny said, "You go to that grammar school and you'll be prime minister one day! You'll be better than that Clement Attlee, you will."

Alex scowled. He was fond of Prime Minister Attlee.

"Whatever the outcome," Clara said smoothly, "you can be sure your parents would have been glad that you tried your best."

Alex blushed and didn't say anything. Clara felt duty-bound to continue.

"A few weeks ago, I went to the cemetery to see an old friend's grave. It was helpful, you know, to see his final resting place. Perhaps when your results are in, we could ask the council where your parents are buried, to go and visit, let them know. How does that sound?"

Alex said it sounded all right.

Ivor sent Alex to get hot drinks from the tea stand. Once he had traipsed off, Ivor grabbed Clara's arm. "Clara, what are you saying?"

She felt suddenly guilty. It had been Ivor's idea that she visit Michael's grave. And she had taken his idea and had gone with Julian instead of him.

But it wasn't that.

"Alex's parents aren't dead!"

"Eh? Yes, they are."

"No, they're not."

"But Ivor, they must be." Even though Alex was several stalls away, she lowered her voice. "Anyway, no one knows for sure. It says in the files."

"Well then, the files are wrong. Alex's father is definitely alive.

He used to turn up at the Grange occasionally. He's a drunk, he used to beat Alex black and blue."

Some people with big shopping bags stared at them. Ivor smiled blandly until they'd walked on.

"I've been around here a long time, Clara. I know this for a fact. What *have* you been saying to him?"

That clever boy, the little professor, who she was sure was like some Little Lord Fauntleroy. He came from a troubled family? She had always imagined someday, a long-lost and ridiculously well-to-do relative would turn up, claim and restore him to his rightful place in society.

Clara took a deep breath. "I mucked up—I had no idea."

Ivor softened. "It's one thing being an orphan, it's another being abandoned…Well, both carry a different kind of stigma, I suppose."

"That's something I do know about."

Clara leaned on a display of blankets, her face in her hands. Would she never cease to make mistakes with the children of Shilling Grange?

"You'll make it up to him, I'm sure." Ivor pulled a blanket out from under her. "You helping us today or not?"

It was a glorious morning. The market was packed with cheerful people looking to spend.

"Maybe people are finally feeling more optimistic," Ivor suggested, "and it's the day after payday."

There were no price tags on Ivor's products; he kept them all in his head, so Clara put labels on everything—good to get him organized a bit. Ivor also didn't have a receipt book of which items sold or didn't. How else could he keep track of what was popular? Ivor shook his head vaguely but in a quiet corner, Clara devised a record-keeping system for him to use.

Alex threw himself into selling.

"These will endure anything!" he shouted, holding up Ivor's tea towels and gazing wide-eyed at his audience. "Monsters, alien attack, drought, disaster, these will be there for you."

The customers loved Ivor's products and they seemed to like Ivor too. He also had a great sales patter, if slightly less ambitious than Alex's, and there were never fewer than five people pressing around the stall at any one time, hands outstretched, looking for a bargain. When it got even busier, Clara nervously came out to help. She didn't feel confident with the customers. An old man was stretching over the boxes with some coins for Ivor.

"How's the lovely Ruby?" he asked.

Clara's ears pricked. *Another clue?*

Ivor stroked his chin. "I haven't heard from her for a while now."

"She was a one, that one." The old man's eyebrows met in the middle and the wiry hair on his head stood up as if he'd had a shock. "I could never understand why you let her go."

Peter was asleep (or pretending to be) when they got back. Billy and Barry were playing pontoon in the parlor. Terry was in her allotment, Peg was skipping backward in the garden and Rita was "composing" in the shed with Molly Mouse. Later, Alex allowed Clara to tuck him into bed. He was such a small figure in his pajamas, yet he still had something of a wise man about him.

"Do you forgive them?" Clara asked. She had to say something to acknowledge her mistake. "Your parents, I mean, for giving you up?"

"I don't bother with them," Alex said, smiling up at her from the whiteness of the pillow.

"Do you remember anything about them?"

He hesitated. "I don't really want to."

"That's understandable, Alex, but don't let it hold you back in the future, love-wise."

"Nor you, Miss Newton." He smiled up at her. His sticky-out ears and his big front teeth were the only things about him that had grown. "Don't look back—keep looking forward and all will be well."

He looked so sweet, dishing out the advice, that she leaned in and hugged him. "Never change, Professor."

"Can I change a little bit as I grow up?"

"No." She laughed, flicking his hair out of his eyes. "Oh, all right, just a little."

The next Sunday was the last Sunday in the month and Clara and Julian drove out to another pub. Clara instantly fell in love with the King's Head, enjoying its warm ambience and attractive mahogany furnishings. There was even a beautiful placid dog lying in the corner next to the fireplace. Clara fussed over it while Julian got the drinks.

Clara drank her whisky. She did enjoy her Sunday afternoons out. Julian knew the best places. Sometimes she wondered what she would do without them. They were on their third round of drinks when Julian placed his hand on her knee.

"So, Clara…"

"Look at his little face! Is it a Labrador, do you think?"

"I have something to tell you."

"It looks like he's smiling. I bet he's wonderful with children too—"

"I went to see your father."

"What?" Clara's heart began racing. Mention of her father always did that to her.

"Well, I was already in London. And I had the address. It was

near to where I was working…I just thought…Don't look so surprised, Clara. We've been together nearly six months now."

"What were you *thinking*?"

"I was thinking I was doing the right thing, Clara!"

"How would that possibly be the right thing?"

"Well, I didn't realize it wasn't."

"But you should have realized. Is the fact that I don't speak to
him not enough for you?"

"He wasn't there anyway, Clara, I didn't meet him."

"What?"

"There, is that better? I didn't get to see him. No one was home."

"I just don't understand why you went."

Clara knew Julian had meant well. No, actually she didn't know
he had meant well. *What on earth had he meant?*

"You need to calm down," Julian whispered, looking surreptitiously at the other customers. "I've never seen you like this."

No, he's never seen me express any emotion except gratitude before.
Clara felt as though something was squeezing her throat. She had a
sudden memory of Ivor explaining the stars. Then she had a vision
of Michael getting shot in the sky.

He would have died instantly, they said. *But what if he didn't?
Did he know what was coming? Did he call out for me?*

It was difficult to breathe. It was bad enough that her father was
in London. Worse that Julian had tried to contact him. The dog
came over and rested his head on her thigh. She put her hand on
his head. *What a lovely boy. Slow down.*

"What is it, Clara? Tell me."

"Give me a moment. I need some fresh air."

Clara stumbled outside and found herself in a changed world:
a world of fresh snow. When had it started snowing? Why was
she so far behind on everything? The branches were covered in
thick whiteness. It was a completely different view to when they'd
arrived, a clean view. It was a picture of new starts and wasn't that

what she was after? Unsullied, unspoiled. A new job, a new life, no more anger at her father, no more sadness about Michael.

And breathe. Breathe.

It wasn't long before Julian came out, but her hands were already growing numb with cold.

Julian looked serious and even a little sheepish. His cheeks were burning. She stared at his shoes, they were polished and refined—a bit like him, she supposed. Michael's had been great clodhoppers.

"It seems I made a mistake." Julian never usually spoke so quietly and he rarely admitted a mistake. "I've gone about it all the wrong way, but the sentiment is still there. Can you guess why I went to your home?"

He had a black box in the palm of his hand. Now, he peeled back the lid and held it out to her. His cheeks were never pinker. Inside was a ring, a sparkling diamond ring. It was like one from a magazine.

"I was going to ask him for your hand in marriage. I went to see him because I love you. Clara, will you marry me?"

When Clara got back to the Grange that afternoon, the garden was full of snow angels and half-dressed snowmen. She opened the gate and snowballs whizzed over her head, missing her by inches. She wasn't in the mood.

"Go indoors," she called, but just as she said it, a second smacked her on the cheek. It was a blow and it was wet, and then it was the last blooming straw.

"Very funny," she snapped. "Billy. Barry. In. The. House. Now."

Alex, Terry, Rita and Peg were sat around the kitchen table in candlelight and Anita was reading. It was like a scene from Dickens.

"I like reading to her," she said, pointing at Peg, who was resting her head on the table. "She's the best audience. All the others interrupt me or say, 'Hurry up' or 'boring' or," she eyed Rita bleakly, 'I want your rabbit.'"

Clara shooed away the children to get ready for tea. Anita packed her book into a bag that contained a spare cardigan, walking shoes, a scarf and a wallet, glasses case, books. It must have weighed a ton.

She narrowed her eyes at Clara. "Something happened with the solicitor?"

"No, yes, no...I don't know."

Anita clutched her bag to her. Clara watched her. It was the bag of someone ready to escape at any moment.

"Marry Mr. White, Clara," Anita instructed as she pulled on her fur coat. It was as simple to her as multiplication. "Your life will be so much easier."

It snowed most of the week, snow on top of snow on top of snow. The children were in heaven. Clara was not. She feared chilblains or ice-related injuries. She submitted an emergency application to the council for gloves, only to be told the children had had some last year, please look again. Clara did, but no luck. Ivor started knitting some. He held one of the needles in his teeth. His dexterity, his resilience was admirable, but she didn't tell him. He didn't like it when people gushed, she knew that.

She needed to talk to someone about Julian's proposal. Anita was too adamant, too black and white, but Ivor wouldn't be any better. He would ask her what her answer was—and she still didn't know.

Thank goodness dear Judy didn't let Arthur or the snow put her off accepting Clara's invitation to visit. And the trains were still running. *God bless the Liverpool Street line.* Judy arrived the next Saturday morning, six days after the proposal. Clara had somehow managed to avoid Julian all week.

"Nothing could keep me away!" Judy laughed, throwing her arms round Clara. "I would have walked here if I had to! It's about time I met the brood."

What a relief it was to see that familiar Judy face. Clara had thought Arthur wouldn't let her come. Well, maybe he wasn't that bad after all. And there was no sign of bruises, black eyes or sprains. Clara thought she was checking discreetly but Judy knew: "I'm fine, *we're* fine, honestly, Clara, let it go!"

If Judy was short sometimes on the telephone, there was no sign of any disagreeableness about her now. She had a spring in her step. She came clutching a paper bag of licorice and a suitcase full not of clothes but of things for the children. It was mostly old books for "the brainy one? Alex, right?"

There was also a game of Monopoly—"Arthur bought us the latest version, so we don't need this now"—that the twins would like, and some costume jewelry; "Arthur isn't keen—" she began, then added casually, "And nor am I. I thought it would be nice for the older girl, Maureen?"

"Maureen's disappeared." For a moment, Clara's heart dropped. *Had Judy forgotten?*

"I know that, silly, but she'll be back soon, no?"

Judy put her arm round Clara as she used to when they were in Aldgate station and the bombs were rattling their teeth. "Have faith, darling."

They went to meet the children in Ipswich after cinema club. They poured out, blinking, surprised at the exquisite brightness of the snow after the darkness indoors.

Everyone looked at Judy nervously.

"You're not from the council, are you?" Billy folded his arms. He would have looked menacing if his tongue and lips weren't blue from goodness knows how many gobstoppers.

"Do you know my mama?" Rita asked.

"I'm here to see my friend."

"She is my oldest friend," Clara said proudly, for Judy was, and she looked what they used to call a right bobby dazzler, "and my best friend." They linked arms.

Judy had come to meet the children. At last.

The children said the film, *Little Women*, had been brilliant, amazing, the best *ever*. Back in Lavenham, they went to the park, where they could show off their excellent tree-climbing skills and do some sledging on tea trays. Judy indulged Billy and Barry, was tender with Peg, curious about Rita.

She was especially taken by Alex.

"You are just as Clara said," she told him. Moments later, when Clara tried to catch up with them, they were deep in discussion about the Medici family.

"He's our little professor," Clara said later.

"He's perfect," said Judy.

Judy was so good with the children, *such a natural*, Clara couldn't help feeling envious. She couldn't tell if it was the questions or the way she asked the questions, but whatever it was, it got them interested. Back at the Grange, over hot Bovril, she asked them what they wanted to do when they were older.

Billy and Barry said they wanted to be magicians so they could saw ladies in half. If not, Barry would be a rag and bone man and Billy said he'd like to be a waxwork at Madame Tussauds. Judy laughed. Alex aspired higher: he said scientist or historian, he was undecided. Judy patted his hand. "You'll make a brilliant scientist or historian," she said. "I don't doubt it." Peter said he didn't know, and his snarl said he didn't care. Clara felt ashamed, but Judy's smile said it was all right, she knew what teenaged boys were like.

Terry said if she couldn't be a gardener, she'd want to be a lift-boy like the one she'd seen in her grandmother's house. She liked the way the metal cage doors clanged open and shut.

Rita said a hairdresser—that came as no surprise to Clara—or a roofer, which did.

"A roofer?" repeated Judy. "I didn't expect that."

Rita collapsed in heaps of laughter at her own mistake. "Not a roofer! I mean an *author* and I will have lots of pets."

Peg mimed writing, typing and then doing something with files.

"A secretary?" suggested Judy.

Peg shook her head fiercely.

"A librarian?"

That wasn't it.

Clara got it first. "A housemother?"

At this, Peg nodded so hard that she rocked off her chair.

Clara and Judy looked at each other and laughed.

"Following in your footsteps," Judy said and Clara felt herself go red.

Of course, Judy hadn't flinched at Peg's not speaking. She took it in her stride. Passed over the issue, but not the child. Clara watched and learned. It was so easy to neglect Peg—she reminded herself often enough not to, but the fact she did still have to remind herself said it all. But Judy and Peg wrapped up and went outside again, this time to build snow houses. Peg was all smiles.

Later, Judy and Clara prepared a ham and pea soup. That side-by-side female togetherness in the kitchen was something Clara had been missing. Maureen had never been keen on cooking with her, but Clara and Judy had always got on and they moved seamlessly around each other. *Like an old married couple*, Clara used to think. *Or like a dance—with dear Judy leading, of course.*

Ivor popped over with the last of the gloves. He shook the snow off his boots like a horse. Judy stood a little straighter and laughed a little louder when he was there. After he'd left, she made eyes at Clara.

"Well, no wonder you look like the cat who got the cream! Julian is—"

"Oh, that's not Julian. That's Ivor," said Clara. "And he's married." She sliced the bread, avoiding Judy's searching eyes.

"Oh?"

"*And*...I'm not interested."

"How do you mean 'not interested'?" asked Terry, who'd just come in from the garden.

"I mean children should be seen and not heard," laughed Clara, before grinning at Judy, "We'll talk later."

Once the children were in bed, Clara lit the fire in the parlor and poured them both some gin. She'd been looking forward to getting Judy alone all day. That was another thing about the children. You could never get to the juicy bits in front of them. They didn't listen most of the time, but try talking about something private and then they heard everything.

"So, Arthur didn't mind you coming to visit?"

"I told him I'm staying at my brother's." Judy stared into the glass.

"Really?" So, Arthur didn't want Judy spending time with her? She *was* right about that.

"It's fine."

"You shouldn't have to lie to him."

"If I need your help, I will ask."

"Promise?" Clara didn't know why it was so important to her, but it was.

"Yes." Judy poured them both another glass. Her reflection looked beautiful in the mirror, her blonde hair smooth and bouncy at the ends. She smoothed the back of her skirt down. Arthur was so lucky—a shame he didn't realize it.

"So, how about you? You're going to tell me what's going on with the men?"

"Men?"

"You and Ivor and you and Julian."

"First off, there's no *me and Ivor.*"

"Ri-ight. What about Julian then?"

"Well, yes." Clara grinned stupidly. "He has asked me to marry him—"

"Oh my gosh! Congratulations!"

"Is it though? I don't know."

"Don't you want to?"

"I do," said Clara lamely, before adding, "but then again, part of me thinks—why can't we just carry on as we are?"

"Clara, you have to get over Michael."

"I know."

Clara couldn't bring herself to tell Judy about Julian's visit to her father. And that was odd. She knew Judy would understand her feelings. But the thing was, Judy might take against Julian. And Clara didn't want that either. Which probably told her something too.

She had no idea what to say, what she wanted to say even. *Ivor wouldn't have done it*, she suddenly thought, and the thought was unwelcome. *He wouldn't have inveigled his way where he didn't belong. Michael hadn't. What was Julian thinking?*

He had gone to seek permission from her *father*? Of all the people in the world! She would better understand it if he had gone to Harris Sr.-Sr. (if he could be distracted from his carp), to Judy's father; come to that, even Judy herself—but no, he had chosen to go to her father! But then, he was only trying to do "the proper thing"—the proper thing was important to Julian—and she usually liked him for it. How could he know what she felt about her one remaining parent? She had never spelled it out to him. Perhaps she was the one to blame?

"So, what are you going to do?"

She thought of Anita. Full of certainty that girls like Clara Newton did not turn down men like Julian White. Not if they knew what was good for them.

"That's the question."

"Will this help you find the answer?" Judy unfolded a piece of paper from her handbag and started reading aloud.

Parish Newsletter
Battersea

It is with great sadness we beg to report that Mr. Augustus Newton will be leaving our parish at Easter time to return to Africa to continue his important work there. Mr. Newton lived in Rhodesia between 1936 and 1948. In 1937, he lost his loving wife of twenty-eight years, Agatha Newton, after a brief pain-free illness. He has one adult daughter, Clara Newton, with whom he is close. It is understood Mr. Newton has trained and helped thousands of young minds to take the true path of Jesus Christ.

There will be a collection for items of children's clothing for the needy children there.

CHAPTER TWENTY-ONE

The toothache started almost immediately after Judy left. Clara didn't tell Ivor—she usually would have, but she had decided to stop relying on him so much. Miss Bridges told Clara peppermint tea would ease the pain. Sister Grace told her to rub clove oil into it. Anita suggested salt water. Billy offered to punch it out. Barry, who always had to escalate a situation, said he'd kick it. Dr. Cardew said he'd find a dentist for her and in the meantime "eat on the other side." Nothing worked and over the next few days it got worse. It was impossible to concentrate on anything. It obliterated all Clara's concerns: the children, the melting snow, the soon-to-be vacant house in London and Julian's proposal swirled around in a soup of choices, but she could do nothing about them. Everything except her tooth would have to wait. Her cheek swelled. Food tasted terrible and she felt backed into a corner of pain.

Turned out, it was an abscess. Clara was lying back in the sloped-back chair, vulnerable and tearful. Fortunately, the dentist was a gentle sort—he came recommended by Dr. Cardew—and was not too expensive either.

"Do you want them all out?" he asked.

A sudden memory of her mother's impeccable teeth came to her—and the story that she'd had them all removed for her eighteenth birthday and replaced with shiny dentures, so they'd always look lovely. They hadn't looked so lovely in that smeary glass beside the bed. Clara felt tearful, but she kept her mouth open and allowed the treatment to begin. She squeezed her eyes shut and told herself that the children would die if she didn't comply: a ridiculous thing to think, but it worked.

Clara was woozy all afternoon. Thank goodness for Peter, who silently made cheese on toast for everyone at lunchtime and sliced carrots for an evening snack with crackers.

"You're a wonderful boy," she said but it came out slurred. He slid away from praise. She remembered the note from the school before Christmas, almost six weeks ago now, which she had neglected to follow up. She presumed all was now well. She would have heard otherwise.

Her being poorly seemed to alarm some of the children; they kept away from her. Perhaps it made them feel untethered, as though no one were in charge. Alex uncharacteristically asked her if she was drunk. "Just a thought," he said before wandering off, nose in a book. But Peg knelt by her side at the sofa, stroking her hair, Terry brought in some wildflowers, Billy left her a cup of tea and Barry an aspirin.

Her father was soon to be gone. She might have her old home back. She could probably still get her old job back. She could be back to where she was in London ten months ago. She could rewind to a time when she had been pretty content.

Or she could marry Julian and be a country solicitor's wife.

Or she could pretend nothing had happened and hope everything stayed just as it was—although deep down, she knew that was impossible.

By bedtime, Clara was feeling much improved and offered to brush Rita's hair as usual. Funny how she had become so completely familiar with the back of the girl's head, it was automatic to her.

That evening though, Rita insisted she do it herself.

"Can you watch instead?" Rita asked and Clara nodded, flattered. Rita divided her hair into six, then turned, pulled and twisted it into rolls. There was a big fashionable roll at the front and she curled the sides. Clara didn't know how she did it and told the girl she had quite the talent, although she was thinking, *that style is far too old for you, Rita. It's a woman's do.*

"Ruby does it like this."

"Is she a new friend from school?" Clara asked hopefully.

Rita giggled. "No, silly, Ruby is Ivor's wife. He showed me photographs. She has the most beautiful hair in the world."

Julian sent a lovely spray of flowers, like little stars on sticks. Clara didn't realize at first that they were from Garrards. When she did realize, she had to laugh even though she was all swollen. *Ouch.* She wondered what Mrs. Garrard had said when he ordered them.

Julian came to the door later that day to check she had received them. The sun had come out. He leaned toward her, tottering on the doormat like a tin soldier.

"Are you avoiding me, my English rose?"

"I am but only because of the toothache."

"It's not contagious."

"I didn't want you to see me looking like this."

She was wearing a shapeless shift with an apron on top. She could hardly bear her own reflection.

He said softly, "If we were married, I would see you every day. Is it too much to ask for an answer, Clara?"

What *was* her answer? Clara didn't know.

For the first time in a long while, she had options. She had responsibilities, yes, but she could make choices too. It wasn't easy to decide. She tried to speak to Judy again, but her friend's phone rang and rang.

When Miss Bridges visited, Clara asked again about installing a telephone, but Miss Bridges had something else on her mind: Billy and Barry were going to live with the Petersons. Finally, it was all arranged.

"They have been vetted," Miss Bridges reported. "All present and correct. Lovely and clean. Your own room, boys, one each! You'll love that, won't you?"

As soon as she had recovered, Clara went to London to see her family home. *Has my father actually left?* And if he had—*what does this mean for me?* Might she have an empty house in London, a home of her own?

She approached slowly, holding herself back, but she could see from several houses away that the lights were on in the living room at the front of the house.

Father?

No.

There *was* a family living there, that became clear. It wasn't just the lights; the garden was well looked after and the grass trimmed; there was an empty milk bottle on the step.

As she came closer, she saw there were three people in the living room, *her* old living room: a father reading a broadsheet, a mother sewing and a child, a boy with dark curly hair, playing with a wooden train on the carpet. A family of three. Just like the one she had once belonged to.

They must have sensed they were being looked at; the mother said something to the father and he looked up, scratched behind his ear, muttered a reply. Clara moved on, self-consciously. She was not here to make a scene. The mother got up and ostentatiously pulled the curtains. Clara's mother's curtains. Clara had put them back up after the blackout ones came down. Gray with white birds, white feathers.

Her father must have let it out. Or sold it. As Clara stood on the pavement in front of the house that she knew so well, it was a disappointment but also a kind of relief. She wrapped her fingers around the cold door key. So, this is what it was. At least the house hadn't been abandoned—that was good. And at least she knew now, which was better than not knowing.

Well, he had gone. And so had her home. He had already made sure it was no longer hers. Once a bully, always a bully. She had that in common with Alex and like Alex, she wasn't going to let it hold her back. Keep looking forward, wasn't that what he said, her little professor? Nothing stays the same.

She had her answer.

CHAPTER TWENTY-TWO

Julian and Clara went out for dinner to a restaurant in London where the waitresses were wearing costumes so skimpy you didn't know where to look. Times were changing, thought Clara, not just for her but for everyone.

Julian managed not to stare at them and this made Clara even more confident that he was a proper gentleman. He wouldn't stray like so many men did. He wouldn't show the children photographs of women with glamorous up-dos.

"Thank you for this, I needed cheering up," Clara told him.

Julian looked alarmed. "Why? What's happened?"

"The twins! They're going next week."

"Of course!" It was clear Julian didn't remember despite her telling him several times. "Going where?"

"New home. The Petersons. They live in Colchester," she added, although Julian seemed more interested in inspecting his wine glass for lipstick. "They seem nice."

"So, then you'll be down to four? That's good news, isn't it?" Julian's glass had passed its test. He threw back his drink.

"Five," said Clara testily. "Can you remember their names?"

"Alec, Terry, and...the freckly one."

"Alex, Terry, Peter, Rita and Peg."

He bowed his head. "Oh, darling, you know I'm useless at names. Test me on the names of military aircraft and tanks instead, I'm good at those."

Julian was still waiting for her answer to his proposal. Every time he looked at her was like an open question, a box that needed ticking. Unspoken words were swirling around them, like circling wagons in the Saturday matinee.

She had her answer. She just wanted to make sure she told it to him in the right way. He might be useless at names, but she didn't want to be useless at proposals.

They went to a secret bar at the back of the restaurant—Julian knew all the places—where it was quieter and even more expensive, and there were photographs of silent movie stars on the walls. The girls in the pictures posed with their hands on their knees, in flapper dresses and with curls plastered to their foreheads. The men were in suits, with cigars and superiority complexes. It seemed like an uncomplicated time, but Clara knew it wasn't, it couldn't have been—this was just after the Great War, after all, and it mirrored today in many ways. A nation recovering. So many dead.

Julian sat so close to her that their thighs were touching. She liked it. She had to stop thinking about Michael, it wasn't fair. She didn't want to be trapped in the past—like Ivor so evidently was with his Ruby. In a way, it was pitiful. When would he move on?

And a future with Julian—well, there was no getting away from it, a future with Julian looked bright. He offered security—long-term security, that was. Life with him offered permanence. After a time of uncertainty, that was welcome.

"Are you going to make me the happiest man in Suffolk?"

"You already are, aren't you?"

He laughed. "They *are* a miserable bunch."

"I do have an answer for you—but there are a few things we have to thrash out first…"

"Ah, the romance!" Julian put his hands behind his head, crossed his legs and grinned at her. "Let's hear it then."

"I'm staying at the Grange until I'm ready. There's still such a lot I want to achieve there. I want to see Alex and Terry settled into school, I want to find good forever homes for the little ones. I want to help Rita come to terms with what happened to her mama. I want Peter's adoption to go through. I want to get them all on the right path."

And part of her *did not* want to be like Mrs. Harrington. She couldn't bear it, to have a man tell her she couldn't work. Not her, not after going through the war; it would suggest all that had been for nothing.

"So, I will continue working there after we've married." She raised her eyes to his. "I know it's not the done thing, but it's important to me. For as long as . . . for as long as I like. I want it to always be part of my life."

"Understood."

"I don't care what you think about it."

When Julian laughed, his teeth flashed. "I *said* I understood, Clara, and I do."

"How do you feel about a long engagement?"

"How long is long?"

Clara spoke nervously. "How does a year and a half sound?" *Maybe two?*

Julian broke into a smile.

"I thought you were going to say something much longer. Yes, my darling, fine. In fact, it's eminently sensible. As long as we can tell everyone and throw a party soon?"

"Oh, definitely." Clara hadn't expected Julian to take it so well.

"And you'll forgive me for the miscalculation? Vis-à-vis your father?"

"We need never speak of it again."

"That's my girl."

The ring was the perfect fit. She would never know how Julian had done it. Clara loved the way it looked on her finger. It changed the look of her hand entirely.

They would be one of those couples, together, yet not together. They would still have their own lives, their own secrets. They wouldn't be like Mr. and Mrs. Garrard, with only a dog's tail between them, or like Judy and Arthur excluding the world, but more like...more like...Princess Elizabeth and Prince Philip perhaps. And Clara was glad of this. She was too old for a relationship where two merged into one. That was for people and their dogs. She had been in a relationship once that burned with intensity—and look what had happened there. A pretty flickering birthday-cake flame was so much less demanding, so much more sustainable.

CHILDREN'S REPORT 7
Barry Coulson

Date of birth:
January 19, 1936
Sadly for Barry, he was born two minutes after Billy, a fact Billy is proud of and which is both the defining moment and the bane of Barry's life.

Family background:
See Billy.

Food:
His favorite is most definitely chocolate cake with sticky chocolate icing.

Health/Appearance:
See Billy. I still occasionally struggle to tell them apart—something they love to take advantage of.

Hobbies/Interests:
He's not a great triumph academically; however, teachers have said he can be kind and an asset to the class. He is quick to lose his temper and is often sent to his room to "think things over." He struggles with reading and writing but knows more swear-words than anyone I've ever met. Apparently, Sister Eunice washed his mouth out with soap. I can't say I blame her.

Other:
Success story! Barry and his brother Billy are due to be adopted.

FILE CLOSED

CHAPTER TWENTY-THREE

The fair came to the field behind the garden shop. The caravans had been pouring down the high road for days. Clara had enjoyed watching Mrs. Garrard grimacing at them over her carnations.

Clara had never been to a fair at night before—they had been canceled during the war—when she found out there was a "half-price night" she was almost as excited as the children. There was no reason not to go.

"Watch your purse," Julian said, and "I had a bad experience on the teacups once—they're not as benign as you'd imagine." Clara was a little disappointed that Julian wasn't going to join them on the night, but he said, "Sweetheart, me and fairgrounds don't mix."

The man at the gate threw their entrance fee in a bucket, winking at Clara. "You've got your hands full." She had guessed he was going to say it before he opened his mouth. She got that a lot. That and "wireless broken?" (which it often was!).

The children's eyes were like saucers. It was Billy and Barry's last night. Tomorrow they were going to the Petersons'. What better way to go out than with a bang!

Oh, the noise! And the flashing lights. It was a whirr of primary colors and machinery smells. And people were milling everywhere. As Clara steered the children through the stalls, not entirely sure where she was heading, she thought for one moment that she saw the young man from Maureen's room. Was Maureen here? It was ridiculous, spotting her everywhere. She had done it with Michael once upon a time. But Maureen was not dead, which meant, *It might be her, mightn't it?*

The children were under instructions to "stay where I can see you." Peg and Rita were waving madly at some teachers from school. Alex found his best friend, Bernard, with his large father, who was looking amiably at everything while smoking his pipe. Bernard's father asked Clara if she'd been to the crooked house yet. "I could while away a few hours in there," he said. "It's the mirrors, you see." Alex asked if he could go off with Bernard and his father and Bernard's father, who seemed never to have qualms about anything, agreed. Clara said only if Alex came to find her in one hour's time.

Sir Munnings was eating candyfloss by the fortune teller's tent—he was the last person she'd have expected to see here. He greeted her enthusiastically, completely at ease, and they talked about the latest films they'd seen at the cinema.

"I love the fair," he said. "The sense that just about anything could happen."

Clara agreed; it certainly felt unpredictable.

Peg was drawn to the circular stalls where you could win gold-fish in bags. She kept pulling Clara over to see. All you had to do was get the ring on the hoopla—then you'd have a fish for life! The bearded man in the center called out, "Come on, girls, win a fish! Three goes for a shilling."

Rita pushed forward. "I can hoop it, I'm excellent."

"No, no goldfish," Clara said, trying not to offend the stall-holder but also trying to get this across *strongly*. "It's absolutely not allowed. Council rules. Let's try and get a bear instead." The girls looked thrilled. "*Not* real bears, Rita, Peg, for goodness' sakes."

There were the spinning teacups—Julian's nemesis—and the dodgems. Hook the duck, shooting stalls, which was where Billy and Barry were voiding their pockets. She wasn't sure where Peter was until she saw him aiming fire at a coconut shy. He had a pow-erful throw, but his aim was off. Clara drove the children through the fair: she imagined she was a sheepdog, these were her sheep and they were all prone to wandering near cliff edges.

By eight o'clock, Clara had had enough of the lights, the crowds and the noise. Alex returned with chocolate smears on his face, clutching a handful of prize marbles and prizes for her—a bottle of gin and some sweets. Apparently, Bernard's father played darts like a professional. Clara was hoping to round up the other children and leave. Watching them climb up the helter-skelter, for the third or fourth time, she was reminded that the last few occasions when there had been accidents—Terry falling out of a tree and Peg tripping over a pothole—it always seemed to happen in that final window when they were just about to depart.

"One more time, Miss Newton, please!" the children were screeching, when a man in a pinstriped suit came over to Clara. He had a paisley cravat, a ruddy complexion and an impressive-looking camera round his neck.

"Four children, am I right? With a figure like that! Eat your heart out, Mae West! What. A. Mama."

Terry shouted, "She's not our real mama!" as she dragged her rattan mat to the helter-skelter steps.

"Have I said something wrong?" His breath smelled oniony.

"No, she's right. I'm not their mother, I'm a *housemother*."

He looked mystified.

"At a children's home," Clara explained. "And there are seven actually."

He was surprised, then delighted. "Wow! I'm Maurice Selby. *Enchanté!*" He held out his hand, so she took it. To her surprise, he wouldn't let go, but kept shaking it up and down. "And is there a housefather, Miss...?"

Clara dislodged his fingers and took a step back. "Miss Newton. Not a housefather, but yes, there is someone special." She wished she were wearing her engagement ring now, but she had put it in her safe, thinking it better to tell the children first.

"Shame," he said. "Isn't there always?" Clara ignored him, watching Peg soar down from the top, fearless, her arms in the air even though Clara had expressly told her not to.

"So, tell me, how can you afford all this?"

He gestured at the bears, the sweets and the bottle of gin in her arms. Clara looked down at them as though she hadn't seen them before.

"This? Well, they won these."

"Can't have won *all* of it," he said. "You have to pay to play."

What business is it of yours? thought Clara, but at the same time, she hadn't talked to an adult that evening since Sir Munnings and she was eager to set the record straight.

"The council give me a budget and I also set aside a small amount every month for treats, birthdays, Christmas and so on. And it's half-price today."

"You must be good at managing things."

Clara liked this. "I try." She smoothed her hair. He liked her, she could tell. "Administration is one of my strengths."

He considered. "Do they ever get to go on holiday, poor souls?"

"They go away for two weeks in August." Clara beamed at the child waving from the top—Terry or Rita, she couldn't be sure. "And we go to London occasionally too, day trips and things."

"Right. And someone told me they go to the cinema regularly?"

Clara wondered who he'd been talking to.

"Kids' Club," she said more uncertainly. "Only Saturday morning, reduced price."

"Can I take a photo of you with the children?"

"I don't know who'd be interested."

"A beautiful woman doing all this! There won't be anyone who isn't."

Clara was flattered. Just as Peg, Rita, Terry and Alex gathered for the photo, Billy, Barry and Peter came back, breathless, holding their loot out in front of them.

"Look what we won!"

"Oh no!" Clara looked around, hoping nobody had heard. What could she do with goldfish? But Billy and Barry were insistent she take them.

"It's our last gift to you!" Billy said emotionally.

"Oh, but the council won't let us keep pets." *You know this.*

"They don't need to know."

"They won't live two days."

That's what she was afraid of too. Bereaved children didn't need more loss, surely?

But Peg was jumping up and down and Terry was cooing into the bags. And when Rita saw them, there was no going back. Screeching and laughing and hugging the boys. There was nothing Clara could do about it, especially not in front of Mr. Maurice Selby, who was gazing at them curiously.

"Give us a smile, everyone, and you, Miss Newton—anyone tell you, you look like Olivia de Havilland?"

Clara blushed. The children stared cross-eyed at the fish, tails swishing in their little bags of water.

"Say cheese!"

They all cheesed. And as there were so many flickering bright lights everywhere, Clara was unsure when the actual flash went off.

She kept hold of the children so she wouldn't have to take Mr. Selby's hand again.

"I'll send you a copy," he said.

They trudged home. The soup on the stove she thought she'd turned off was burnt onto the pan and the potatoes she was going to chip had eyes. She didn't know where to put the damn fish, but Alex fetched the old chamberpot from the boys' room. Then Billy and Barry had a fight on the stairs because they disagreed about which fish was which.

In the middle of the night Clara woke, sick at the thought that something was wrong. One of the fish might have eaten the other.

Did fish do that? Perhaps she shouldn't have put them in together? She raced down to the pot and found them both quite uneaten and alive. Back in bed, she lay worrying about something else she couldn't put her finger on. She kept having thoughts of the swirls on Maurice Selby's cravat and his clammy hand.

The Petersons were coming to pick up the boys in a taxi!

"Since it's a special occasion," Mrs. Peterson had explained on the telephone and Clara could imagine her twisting her fingers raw. "Please make sure the twins are ready, so we can set off straight away. It'll be on the meter, you see."

Better like that, thought Clara. Long goodbyes were pointless.

They all made a fuss about the fish. Alex joked that he had peed on them in the night and everyone squealed.

Billy didn't eat as much porridge as usual and Barry spilled precious milk over his clean trousers. Feeling the tension, Peg clung to the backs of Clara's legs.

"Come on out, Peg, you're not a rabbit."

"Can we have a rabbit, Miss Newton? Since we've got fish now."

"No, Rita, sssh, just give me a minute."

Clara felt herself growing tearful. *This will not do*, she told herself. *This is all part of the job. It's how it's meant to be. The children move on. Like jars of jam. Easy come, easy go.* Except that seemed a terrible approach to people, especially orphans.

"You'll stay in touch, boys?"

"Course!"

They hugged her.

"No sawing ladies in half, please."

"And you'll look after our fish?"

"I suppose I'll have to. And you'll write?"

Now everyone laughed. There was *no way* they'd write, not Billy and Barry.

"We'll visit," Billy offered as compensation.

"Lots," Barry added.

There was more hugging and kisses. Then a taxi pulled up and within less than a minute, as the color drained from their faces, they were gone.

As soon as the door shut, Rita began to wail, "Mama."

It was their first "success." Clara called the council to let them know the departure had gone smoothly and Miss Bridges said she had already logged it in the race against Norfolk and Lincolnshire. Two down, several hundred more to go.

So then there were five children at Shilling Grange. Only five. Five felt too easy, too amateurish; five felt almost like a normal family.

Miss Bridges said, "We'll send more soon," and Clara couldn't help feeling nervous about that too. She knew her magnificent five, inside out. Who wouldn't be wary of unknown ingredients coming into the mix? *Keep looking forward*, Clara reminded herself as she left the telephone box. *Don't look back. At least, don't look back at the unhelpful stuff.*

In the afternoon, Ivor came over to fix the wireless. Clara went up to her room to catch a moment to herself.

She was still feeling tearful, but now she was also feeling ashamed of herself. Children leaving was a major part of the job. Sending the jam jars out was an integral part of her mission—she knew this. She should not have become so attached. These children were hers not to keep but to grow and pass on. And anyway, *Worse things happen at sea*, wasn't that her generation's motto?

While she appreciated Ivor coming over, part of her wished it was Julian. It should be Julian comforting her, Julian telling her everything would be all right; but Julian was hunting poor foxes again and had no idea of her woes. Clara lay on her bed, read a poem from her poetry book and found it worked its magic on her.

Ivor smiled ruefully at her when she returned, her face washed of tears and her hair freshly combed.

"I guessed you'd be a bit low today. It's natural."

"I'm not," Clara said determinedly. "In fact, I have good news."

He smiled at her.

"Can you guess?" Her voice was not her usual voice.

"Is it Terry?" he said. "Or Peg?"

"No, it's me." *This had been a foolish way in.* "I'm…" She couldn't breathe for a moment; she suddenly thought of that evening stargazing with him. And what he said: *The stars don't require anything of me.* What a strange thing to suggest. Almost an arrogant thing as though everything else in his life—including Clara presumably—*demanded* things of him. As though they were his burdens. "Marrying Julian. Julian White, the solicitor."

"What?" Ivor didn't usually show his emotions much, but now he looked… what was the word? *Repelled.* "Why?"

Clara looked at her feet. *Why?* For a few seconds, she couldn't think of an answer. And then of course she could; there was only one correct answer.

"Because I love him," she burst out. "Isn't that obvious?"

"Why?" he asked again and Clara thought of Ivor helping Terry dig up a particularly hard patch in the garden and Rita asking to play roly-poly. She thought of his face when he'd told her about Alex's drunken father, or when he tried to get Peter to smile.

"Because he takes care of me and…" The *and* stood there, spotlighted on an empty stage. For some reason the only word she could think of was "lobster." She couldn't think of another word, which was probably Ivor's fault somehow. "And that's what I want now. I'm at that stage of life when that's the most important thing to me."

"In and out and shake it all about."

"It's nothing like that, it's completely different."

"What? You messed the children around then and you'll mess them around now."

"I won't. I swear to you."

His voice was like something stuck. And it was clear, suddenly, that he didn't care about her at all—she needn't give *that* a moment's thought—he was just obsessed with the Grange.

"I'm *not* leaving, not this time. I'll carry on until, until...for at least another year. I'm going to make sure they're all doing well and then I'll be nearby—we're not going anywhere—and I'll always be part of their lives."

As Ivor breathed out, his chest puffed out like a barrel. His arm with its abrupt ending felt like a rebuke. His face grew shady again. She remembered that he and Ruby were childhood sweethearts and that Ruby had beautiful hair.

She could hardly look at his face anymore, never mind tell him things. The contours of his cheekbones, the scar on one side, the kind dark eyes, now devoid of warmth. Those lips. Kissing him under the mistletoe, for less than a second, as though anything more would be too...too petrifying. And then it came back to that moment again. Leaning against him looking at the stars, feeling his breath on the back of her neck. Would she never not think about that?

"I'm sorry. I..."

He gave a bitter laugh. "I've patched up the clothes. Please collect them as soon as you can."

"Why don't you believe me? I won't let the children down."

"They're taking up too much space."

CHAPTER TWENTY-FOUR

When Clara called the house meeting, two of the children were playing jacks under the kitchen table, one was in the garden. One was in the parlor trying to tune the wireless and one was in the bath even though it wasn't his bath day. But Clara had banged on a saucepan with a wooden spoon and eventually they had all gathered around. They were good like that. She was relieved she didn't have to start threatening them, especially not in front of Julian.

"Mr. White and I have an announcement to make."

Julian hadn't wanted to tell them about the engagement yet. She wasn't sure why. It wasn't because he was reticent about the news getting out—he had already submitted the notice to the *Telegraph*—so she had insisted they get on with it. Children hate being the last to know, even more than adults, perhaps because it happens to them such a lot.

She knew how to handle Julian. And he *did* need handling somewhat, like a frisky puppy. He didn't want to tell them about the engagement—but she did. She won. She knew she'd have to stand up for herself, that he was inclined not exactly to take advantage, but to ride roughshod over her—but this was challenging and actually it was exciting. She was no doormat and didn't want to be treated as such. And since when was standing up for yourself a bad thing? She and Julian were both determined to be right—and that certainly added an extra dimension to the bedroom.

"Why do I have to be there?"

"It's the unknown that's scary for children," she told him as Judy had told her. "So the more they understand, the better—puts their fears at rest."

"I'm hardly unknown," he had argued. "I've worked on the other side of the street for most of their lives."

"You know what I mean. Time to get to know them better."

Julian winced. "I'm marrying you, not Shilling Grange."

"We come as a package."

At this, he had nuzzled her neck. "I am looking forward to unwrapping this parcel every night."

"Seriously, the children will grow on you."

"Like a fungus."

"Exactly like a fungus." She sighed.

Julian kept his hat and coat on, making it clear he wasn't staying long, and he didn't sit but instead perched on the edge of a chair.

"Is there going to be another war?" inquired Alex. "It's all kicking off in Korea now. The thirty-eighth parallel."

"War?" asked Rita tremulously. Peg covered her ears.

"Don't worry, girls, that's not what this is."

"Where's Car-ree-er?" shouted Terry.

"It's not that, children. Korea is the other side of the world anyway. It won't affect us. Peg, out from under the table, please. You're not a pussycat."

"She *is* a pussycat."

Laughing, Peg clambered onto Clara's lap.

"This is *good* news, everybody."

Clara took a deep breath, then, taking Julian's hand, she said, "So, Mr. White and I are going to get married."

"Is this an April Fool?"

"That's not until next week, Rita. Put your bottom lip away."

"So, he will be our housefather?" asked Alex doubtfully.

"But Ivor is already our housefather, isn't he?" Terry was already annoyed at having to come indoors. She had mud down one cheek. Clara didn't know how she did it. Rubbed it all over herself like talcum powder probably.

Peter stood shivering resentfully in the doorway in his pajamas. He must have swapped his bath day with Alex again. Alex was looking more like his hero Albert Einstein every day.

"Ivor is a friend, and no, Mr. White won't be a housefather. There isn't such a thing."

"You won't leave us though, will you, Miss Newton?" Rita flung her arms round her. "My second mama."

Clara bent down and kissed the girl's creased forehead.

"You'll all have new homes and new families too one day soon. That's what we're working toward."

"Well, we won't, will we?" Sometimes Terry could be as cutting as the garden shears she had just started using.

"Well, you *might*."

"Lady from the council said we're too old," she said. "Everyone prefers babies."

"Who said that?"

"Miss Cooper."

Damn Miss Cooper.

"Miss Cooper is not right about everything. Anyway, never say never. Look at Billy and Barry. They're older than you."

"You promised us you would never lie to us."

"Well, yes, okay. So…Anyway, it's all in the future."

"So why are you telling us now?" Rita persisted.

"Miss Newton, I've got a nosebleed."

"Do you have a handkerchief, Terry? No? Go and find one in the washing. Okay." Clara clapped her hands. "Thanks, everyone."

She turned to Julian, who was still perched but was now also smirking. "I think that went well."

The Daily Telegraph
April 1, 1949

White–Newton Wedding to be held.

Plans for a wedding are being made by Mr. Julian Archibald Samuel White, son of Mr. Frederick White and Mrs. Helena Felicity White, and Miss Clara Newton of Lavenham.

Mr. Julian Archibald Samuel White is a graduate of Merton College, Cambridge. He attended School of Law, Queen Mary and is part of the partnership of Robinson, Browne and White Solicitors in Lavenham, Suffolk.

CHAPTER TWENTY-FIVE

"I saw you in the paper," said Mrs. Garrard a few days later. Usually, Clara and Mrs. Garrard managed to avoid each other by unspoken agreement, but today their paths had inauspiciously crossed. The Garrards' dog Bertie was ineffectually trying to get out of her handbag. Clara stifled a laugh.

"Do-gooder—such an accurate word, don't you think?"

Clara stared at her in surprise. Bertie whimpered. "I don't know. Anyway, I must get back...I'm off to the cinema with the children. Sir Munnings' treat."

"Sorry...who?"

"Sir Munnings? Horse paintings? I suppose he's a do-gooder too."

Realization dawned on Mrs. Garrard's powdered cheeks.

"Some people actually like to see children do good," Clara added haughtily. "Remarkable, isn't it?"

If she hadn't nearly tripped over a protruding paving stone as she retreated, it would have been a triumphant moment.

Miss Bridges turned up at the house that afternoon, one week before she was due.

It was only when she was halfway up the path that Clara remembered the fish. She galloped to the kitchen and carried the chamberpot off into the parlor.

"Won't be a minute!"

What was I thinking? The parlor was no good—Miss Bridges

often went in there. Clara raced the pot upstairs to her own room. The water lapped over the sides and onto her dress but the fish appeared unbothered.

It was a good thing Clara had the instinct to do that, since that day Miss Bridges did not want to stay in the kitchen. In the parlor, she peeled off her white gloves and sat primly with her handbag in her lap. The more annoyed she was, the less room she seemed to take up. Today she was tiny.

This was not good.

Which of the many things she might have done wrong was this about? Clara wondered. On the phone, she had told Miss Bridges of her engagement—she hadn't wanted her to be out of the loop— and Miss Bridges had been effusive if knowing: "I suspected this was on the cards."

So, if that wasn't it, then what was it?

"Well, this is nice…" began Clara, ignoring that Miss Bridges was shaking with repressed rage.

"Did you see the paper?"

"Our engagement notice in the *Daily Telegraph*? Yes!"

No, Miss Bridges did not mean that. She fumbled with the click of her handbag. She was too angry for her fingers to work.

"Can I help?"

"No."

It felt like ages before she produced a newspaper and unflapped it. It was a local one, the *Suffolk Times*. On the front page was a photograph of Clara and the children. Clara's first instinct was to shriek.

"What is that doing there?"

It was a lovely picture. Clara's hair looked surprisingly in order and her expression was indulgent and happy. There were the twins—she missed them already; there were the fish—enough said about them. Peg had her eyes closed and Rita was standing on one leg. Terry looked like a sullen little boy but Peter was almost

smiling and Alex looked radiant despite the two fingers someone—
Peter—had put behind his head like rabbit's ears.

But the photograph wasn't the problem.

EXCLUSIVE SUFFOLK COUNCIL
MONEY-WASTING EXPOSÉ
by MAURICE SELBY

We've all heard about the Labour government's flagship
policy—new children's homes. Our intrepid journalist,
Maurice Selby, has been running an undercover investigation of Suffolk Council's children's homes policy. He went
to meet one of the new officers in charge of local children's
home Shilling Grange in Lavenham.

He was horrified to find:

Children running wild at a fairground AT NIGHT.

Expensive day trips planned to LONDON.

Flagrant disregard for rules over PET ownership.

Poorly nourished children eating CANDYFLOSS.

For over fifty years, Shilling Grange was a serious institute run by celibate nuns. Now, it's run by a glamour-puss
do-gooder barely out of her teens. The inmates used to lead
simple honest lives and reflect on the horrors that had put
them there—now, they spend half the year planning their
summer holidays.

And who's paying for that? Yes, ladies and gentlemen,
that's where our hard-earned taxes are going.

Our money on their stays at the seaside.

The article was a demolition of her, the Grange, the council,
the Labour government... There was even a swipe at Dame Curtis
further down the page.

Clara's heart was in her boots.

Miss Bridges sighed, heavily. She was in worse spirits than on the day Clara had handed in her notice.

"I don't know how you got caught out, Clara."

"Nor do I."

"What *were* you thinking?"

What had I been thinking?

"They'll use anything to get at us."

"Who will?"

"People. The general public. The Children's Act wasn't popular. People would rather parents stepped up and took care of their own...Surely you knew this?"

"Yes, but I just...I didn't realize this was...a...question. I thought taking better care of children was a given."

"Most of them would rather step over children starving in the gutter than commit time and resources to them."

"Oh."

"Remember during the war when there was always someone ready to snitch? Act like that."

"I see. Someone might have told me all this."

"Is it not obvious? *Everything* is political."

"I'm sorry. I didn't realize that...that taking care of orphans could be wrong."

"It's not wrong, just being seen to do it is wrong. No one wants to know about it."

"Fine, I'll make sure the children look miserable in public in future." Clara was annoyed, mostly at herself, but she had enough left over for everyone.

Miss Bridges scowled. "That's not what I mean, Clara, and you know it."

"And for some of these children this presents a security risk. You are aware of this, Clara."

"I am." Clara bowed her head. What if someone saw this article and decided to hunt down a child? It didn't seem likely—there were no names or ages—but still, they were identifiable from the photograph...

"Well, it's done now. And the fish? What happened to them?"

"What fish?"

Miss Bridges was having none of it. She tapped the photograph until the newspaper crumpled—which was much how Clara felt.

"Those fish in this photograph, Clara. You know the policy on pets. No exceptions."

"Dead," lied Clara. "As dodos."

It niggled at Clara all week. She lost her appetite. Even eating Anita's superb cooking made her feel guilty. She pushed plates away unfinished. *That Maurice Selby, what a bastard.* She went over and over the events of the night at the fair and how stupid she'd been. She was usually far more cautious. How had she allowed this to happen?

When she walked past his workshop, Ivor called out but it was not about the article or her engagement. He thought Alex might have nits again. He had seen him scratching behind his ears.

"Is that it?" Clara shifted from foot to foot impatiently. She felt suddenly aware of the diamond, now on her finger at all times: would Ivor notice it? "Is that all you wanted to say?"

"Ye-s?"

Clara enjoyed turning her back on him and stomping away.

At lunchtime on Friday, Julian had a cancellation and asked her to the pub. She had already eaten with the children, but she said she'd sit with him and have a drink. She'd thought it would do her good to get out, but she couldn't escape the whirring in her head.

"Do-gooder?" she repeated. It burned. "It's better than the alternative. What would that be, a do-badder?"

"And there are worse names than glamour-puss," Julian said, making eyes at her. "Meow!"

He refused to take any of it seriously—but then it wasn't his reputation on the line.

"That's not the point." Clara tilted her glass despondently.

"He's right about the summer holiday though, isn't he?"

Clara felt a bolt of fury. "You don't think children in care should go on holiday?"

"I didn't say that." Julian carried on smashing his lobster.

Clara realized with horror that she too felt that all-too-familiar itch behind her ears. Ivor had been right about Alex and she probably had visitors now too. Dammit.

Julian leaned across the table, his expression inscrutable. "Don't spoil lunch, Clara."

By Monday, the children had learned all about the newspaper article from the children at school.

"Apparently we're scroungers, super-scroungers and spongers," ever-helpful Alex said. "Oh, and my particular favorite, 'parasites.'"

"All of them? At once? Goodness."

Peg leaned her head against Clara's hip. Rita said she was writing it all down in her book.

"Your book?"

"A book of rude words."

"That sounds bloody awful, Rita."

They were in hysterics at that.

CHAPTER TWENTY-SIX

Peter's attitude was getting worse. Clara wondered if it might be the announcement of her engagement to Julian? That had seemed to throw them all. No matter how many times she had reassured them *nothing will change for some time*, they all seemed worried. Peg had even wet the bed that same night. Terry had an on-off headache and someone—it must have been Peter, with his cigarettes although he denied it—had burned a hole in the parlor carpet.

It was a mistake to announce it so soon. Like telling Bandit "walk" when you weren't planning to go for a while—she'd learned that one the hard way too.

"Maybe it's Peter's past coming back to haunt him?" Miss Bridges suggested.

That seemed reasonable. They all had haunting pasts, but Peter especially was the age to dwell. Clara decided to make even more effort with him. She didn't want him going the same way as poor Maureen, who she missed dearly. In the past, spending time with Peter wouldn't have required making effort. He used to be quiet and polite. Now he was quiet and seething. He didn't even want to come down to smoke in the garden with her.

"But Peter, I have Lucky Strikes."

He rolled over in his bed. "Go away."

"Hey, that's not nice."

"*Please* go away."

It was funny to think that when they first met, Clara had

thought Peter was the one she was most like. *Still waters run deep.* Now she couldn't see it anymore. He just seemed such a grump: still water that was cold and uninviting.

Anita had an idea for the two goldfish—Billy and Barry 2, as they'd been christened by the children. Apparently, Dr. Cardew had been thinking about getting a fish tank in the waiting room for a while. Who doesn't like watching fish when they're waiting for their overdue verruca treatment?

Clara took the fish to the surgery while the children were at school. They were decanted from the chamberpot into a rectangular tank dressed with weeds and stones. Polishing the glass sides so that Billy and Barry 2 had a lovely view, Anita said, "Dr. Cardew needs a hobby," which made them both laugh.

They were getting on better. Clara still didn't understand what had gotten into her that time to criticize Anita, but fortunately Anita had forgiven her. Maybe she was sincere about believing you can be wrong on one thing and right on others, as she had said that time in the library.

On the bonus side, Clara had noticed Anita *was* more sensitive with the children recently. Perhaps it had just taken time.

Rita didn't notice the fish had gone for three whole days, but when she did, she took herself crying off to bed. Clara promised her some old face powder *and* some of Judy's costume jewelry and Rita soon cheered up.

"Still want a cat," she sniveled. "Although a guinea pig would do. Or a rat."

The thought of rats sent shivers down Clara's spine. She remembered nights in Aldwych station, when small boys would tell each other stories about being eaten alive by them.

The other children didn't mention the fish. Clara was happy not to bring them up again.

*

Usually, vegetables came wrapped in newspapers, but occasionally they were wrapped in comics. The garden beans, "hairy beans" as Terry called them, were wrapped in the *Beano*. As Clara unraveled them, she had a thought that they might make Peter laugh. The "Li'l Folks" comic strip used to be one of her favorites.

"I like this character. And the dog." Peter hardly glanced up, but Clara caught a glimmer of a smile and a glimmer of a smile from him was worth a full headlights' beam from anyone else.

Saturday morning, Clara found Peter out in the garden, in the shadow of the elm tree, still studying the comic.

"Want to share a cigarette?"

"Don't mind."

She wanted to say, *why are you so unhappy all the time, Peter, talk to me?* but she knew from trying that he would only turn away.

"You liked the cartoons?"

He grunted.

"I thought so."

Later that week, Clara went to the book stand outside the station, where she spent far too much money on new comics. One day soon, she supposed, she mightn't have to worry about finances so much.

It was nice to get Peter something. He didn't ask for a lot.

"Here." She dropped them proudly on his bed. "And why don't you have a go at cartoons, Peter? You're good at drawing. I could draw you some squares." He watched impassively.

This room was once Ivor's room—that bed under the window was his—and look how well he had done when just one person, Sister Kate, had believed in him. And she could do it too—and she could do it without Ivor. Still crouched on the floor, Peter leafed through the pages.

Oh, but it was already five o'clock. Sound of a car hooting outside. His uncle. Peter rose, seeming unsure what to do.

"Off you pop." Clara smiled at him. "They'll still be here tomorrow, don't worry."

And off Peter popped, or rather trudged, with his great walking-in-treacle feet.

The next day, Peter asked for more sheets of drawing paper.

"Do you want me to draw the squares on?"

Peter did, and Clara understood. There was something about the shapes that was helpful. Freedom in the constraint. She loved rows and columns too. Using her ruler, she created neat squares and rectangles for him. Another way of bringing order to chaos.

"I'd love to see what you do with it."

He shook his head. "You don't have to show me, of course," she added quickly, nervous that she had gone and spoiled it. "That's not what art is for." This sounded insincere. "You know what I mean, Peter. Just have some fun with it."

Dear Marilyn,

I'm sorry it's been so long since I last wrote. I hope you are well and that the family are in good health. I have moved to Suffolk and am now the housemother of a children's home. This probably will seem out of character—it does to me— but sometimes it's good to do something out of character: you get to find out what your real character is. You know Michael will always be in my heart. Always. He made me the happiest girl in the world. It's been over four years now and I don't think I'm wrong to want to find that happiness again. I have met someone. It is early days—well, maybe not, but he has asked me for my hand in marriage and I have agreed.

He is another thing out of character, but he is a good man. His name is Julian White. He is a solicitor.

I don't know if you wish our correspondence to continue. I have always loved talking, sharing stories about Michael.

Did I tell you about the time Michael flew low over Harris & Sons—so low that we could see him waving or at least imagine we did? I couldn't believe it. I had nearly flattened myself on the ground with fear! Another time, he said that he saw the fields of Lavenham and for a split second, thought he was flying home to you.

I want you to know, I am happy for us to continue writing and your letters have always given me great pleasure. I leave the decision in your hands.

With great affection,
Clara

CHAPTER TWENTY-SEVEN

One morning, Clara came downstairs to find Billy at the kitchen table and Barry at the stove, cooking porridge. It was still dark outside.

"What the heck are you two doing here?"

"We're back!" Billy held up a slice of bread. "Have you run out of marge?"

Oh my goodness. Clara would have to phone Miss Bridges. This would go to the head of children's services; it might even go to the head of the council. *What on earth had they done?*

"Don't worry, we left a letter explaining," said Barry cheerfully. *Oh, that's okay then!* "Milk?"

The thought of Mrs. Peterson discovering some scrappy farewell note made tears prickle Clara's eyes. Had they hurt her dreadfully?

"How did you get here?"

"Hitched—we got a ride to Chelmsford, then on to RAF Cockfield, walked from there."

"Good Lord," she said, and at the same time, she thought, *no one must ever know. Miss Bridges would shrink in fury, especially so soon after the newspaper debacle.*

"But why?"

"We haven't eaten burnt food for a week."

"We missed it!"

"Ha ha. No, tell me. What really happened?"

"At school, the kids called us farmers."

"Farmers?" *Is that so bad?*

"So, we smacked them in the nose."

Billy tucked into his porridge like he hadn't eaten in days. "The teachers were awful."

"Worse than here?" asked Clara, trying not to sound incredulous.

"Much! And the Petersons wouldn't let us out."

That made more sense. Billy and Barry loved roaming free in the countryside. They wouldn't take kindly to being made to stay at home.

"But…"

"The Petersons are good people, but they don't want us. They need little kids."

Barry nodded vehemently. "We're too old for them."

"She sang us nursery rhymes."

"That's nice, isn't it?"

"I don't care about the Grand Old Duck of York!" Billy yelled. The toast was burning.

"He was interesting actually," pointed out Clara, watching the two of them act like they'd never been away.

"She treated us like we were four."

"Three."

Clara pondered. "She really wanted twins though."

"Tell 'em Rita and Peg are twins," said Billy, scraping the bowl.

"And we missed the fish," added Barry. "They're not dead, are they?"

"Ah. About that…"

Shortly after nine, Clara steeled herself for the telephone call. She was not going to be too apologetic. The council's job was to look after the boys; if they had any doubts about the suitability of the placement with the Petersons, then *they* should have erred on the side of caution. She had already leafed through her files to a section—*If for any reason, an adoption breaks down…*

Fortunately, Miss Bridges had already heard. She sounded surprisingly airy considering the blow to their figures.

"I understand the collapse was fairly mutual. The Petersons have already gone to Norfolk Council and are making some inquiries there. They're coming in to sign the mutual consent forms—Billy and Barry will need to do that too: make an appointment and bring them in as soon as you can."

"So, the boys aren't in trouble?"

"Well, that's up to you, Clara."

Clara grinned to herself.

It was lovely to have the twins back. The rest of the children squealed at the sight of them. It gave her a new feeling of completeness. (If only Maureen would come back too, that would have been all her lovely brood.) She felt like a mother hen. Or mother cat with all her kittens. She just wished she had something to celebrate but she made sure to roast the potatoes instead of boiling them—Billy's favorite—and to crack open a box of marzipan donated by Anita instead of waiting, as she had planned, for a birthday. This was a special occasion, after all.

She told the boys about her engagement to Julian and they hugged her, like the grown men they were becoming, and she assured them she wasn't leaving, not for ages anyway, and she would personally make sure that her replacement was kind, easy-going, a good cook and hated nursery rhymes. She said she would only be living up the road anyway, they would be welcome anytime.

Billy laughed and asked if she was "moving to her forever home," and she said, "something like that," but it made her feel a bit choked too, so again she added, "Not for a long while yet."

Then Barry asked, "What does engagement mean?" and Billy said, "It means she's getting married, stupid," and Barry had looked shocked.

What had he thought it meant, wondered Clara.

Clara was just about to serve up the special lunch when there was a banging on the front door. Loud and intemperate. Someone was having a bad day.

First thoughts—it was about Billy and Barry. Second thoughts—Ivor?

Julian was standing on the doorstep, holding someone by the throat. He didn't look at Clara but was shouting right into the someone's face. "You despicable piece of work!"

Peter. It was Peter. Julian was holding him round the collar, with both hands, shaking him.

"If I didn't know you, I'd go straight to the police. You thieving little bastard! Don't you ever come near my office again."

Clara was frozen in horror, yet as she stood there, she remembered an interview question: *Would you get involved in a fight?* Yes, she had said, yes, she would.

"Julian? Peter? WHAT IS GOING ON?"

Julian threw Peter to the ground. Peter's face was tomato. Julian's wasn't much different, only Julian was also shaking with fury. She'd never seen him like this before. She looked over to the workshop. Good thing Ivor was not there. If he had seen this, he would probably have punched Julian on the nose.

"I'm sorry it's come to this, Clara, but we all knew it would one day. You've got one running amok out there, sleeping with God knows whom, and you've got this one thieving. Bet it wasn't the first time either. Get some control over these monsters. Or I will."

As he was launching into what Clara would later describe to Anita as his diatribe, Mr. and Mrs. Garrard happened to pass, on their constitutional with Bertie. The delight radiated off them. Mrs. Garrard even forced a tinkly wave.

"Mr. White, you agree, don't you?" she called out. "They don't belong here. Clacton or Ipswich are far better."

"It's not personal," agreed her squeaky husband. "It's just fact: Lavenham and orphanages don't go together."

Even Bertie wouldn't stop yapping.

After Clara had wrangled Peter away from a still-fuming Julian, she sent the others out of the kitchen and made him sit at the table. "Stay there and listen," she snapped, although she didn't know what she was going to say. The urge to call Judy, Ivor, the council or just about anyone for advice was overwhelming. *Compassion*, she reminded herself. Peter had a difficult past.

"Peter," she began. "Why didn't you just ask me for more paper?"

"I don't know," Peter mumbled.

Well, who knows, then, Peter, tell me that? If not you.

He twisted and shook. His face, that sweet freckly face, was so humble and ashamed, he reminded her of a poem she loved about the violet:

> *Down in a green and shady bed*
> *A modest violet grew;*
> *Its stalk was bent, it hung its head,*
> *As if to hide from view.*

"I'm so embarrassed, Peter."

It's not about my embarrassment though, or at least it shouldn't be, she told herself. But she couldn't seem to move away from that. She'd trusted him. And this is how he repaid her. Everyone in the village thought the children were feral and she had defended and excused them.

And now this. He'd only gone and bloody proved all those snobs right. And as for Julian...

She should focus on Peter, not Julian, nor the Garrards, but it wasn't easy. She needed to get to the bottom of Peter's behavior, but she couldn't. It was a bottomless pit of despair.

"Can't you just tell me *why* you did it?"

He shook his head.

Rita ran into the room. "All I want is a cat," she said angrily. "Or a rabbit. Why not?" Billy and Barry ambled in after her: "When's lunch?"

"Later!" she barked. "For goodness' sake, all of you, out."

They hurried away and slammed the door. *Some welcome home.* Clara turned to Peter again.

"We're going to have to apologize to Mr. White."

Peter shrugged. That shrug prompted another wave of irresistible anger. Did he think she wanted to sit down and compose a beseeching letter to her fiancé on his behalf? Did he think she had nothing better to do?

"Stealing!" She couldn't help repeating it incredulously. "Stealing! Under my nose. From my... friend. I can't see why you'd do it."

The roasties were burnt. The celebration lunch was ruined. Rita cried as soon as her plate was set in front of her. Billy and Barry muttered something about the food being better at the Petersons' and Clara raised her spoon at them. She wasn't having this today. Peg and Alex dutifully sawed off the charcoal bits. Terry quickly escaped into the garden; Clara could see her, tending her vegetable patch, probably praying that her vegetables met a different fate from those under Clara.

Later in Peter's room, under his pillow, she found there were other things too. Julian was right, today *wasn't* the first time. Even Miss Bridges' Zippo lighter was there. Peter was a thief. A common thief. It was much worse than she'd expected.

What else has he got? And why?

She wished she could talk to Ivor about it. But Ivor had made it clear he was no longer a sounding board for her. The one thing she knew was that she needed to punish Peter. Not hitting or whipping. Those were the old despicable ways. She was better than that. No, she needed to take away something he liked.

"I won't let you go to your uncle's on Thursday."

He looked up at her and laughed, right in her face.

Dear Mr. White,

My sincerest apologies for my intrusion earlier today. I
enclose a shilling to cover the cost of the materials and the
terrible shock. If there is anything I can do to further aid
your recovery, please acquaint me with the knowledge. For I
am in your debt.

I really am humbly your servant,

Peter

CHAPTER TWENTY-EIGHT

All she had to do was turn up on Saturday night, looking marvelous. Julian had the engagement party under control.

He's good, Clara kept saying to herself. *Quite the Renaissance man* (if Leonardo da Vinci had been bothered about where the cheese sticks should go).

Julian had apologized about losing his temper and she had apologized that she didn't have Peter under her control. They left it at that, not only because there was nothing more to say, but because they still didn't agree although Clara couldn't say on what exactly. Anyway, she and Julian often had their "quibbles" (his phrase) but they usually ended in kisses, tickles and the rest. Julian tended to overrule her, but he was usually right about entertaining and socializing, they were his things—so she let him. Why not? What did she know about hosting large events? Besides, she stood her ground when necessary. She had suggested inviting Miss Bridges and Miss Cooper from the council (not Mrs. Harrington) but he had laughed and then said, "I thought you were joking. You want to invite the childcare officers who come to inspect you to our engagement party?"

Later, she would admonish herself for backing down—she should have said, *they're more than that, they're friends and confidantes*—but it was too late, they had reached their agreed number limit of eighty.

Eighty? She hadn't met eighty people in her life!

Julian wanted her to get a new dress to wear, but there weren't enough coupons to get something glamorous, and neither was there enough time, so she selected the dress she had worn on New Year's

Eve. It was an old favorite (Michael had loved it) and it had worn well. She would have liked to ask someone—well, she would have liked to ask Ivor—to swish it up a little, bring it a bit more up to date—but she couldn't ask him. His feelings toward the engagement were obvious.

She would definitely get her hair done though on the day. Julian would kill her if she didn't. And she had her beautiful ring. It made her feel like she was going up in the world.

Friday lunchtime and Alex was trembling as he handed Clara the envelope from school.

"I think it's my results."

Clara couldn't believe he had waited for her to open them. What a good boy! She already had something in mind to say if he didn't pass. She hadn't dared think about if he did.

To whom it may concern,

We would like to offer Alex a place at Ipswich County Grammar School.

Alex received 484 marks out of a possible 500 for his test. This is the highest possible mark in Mathematics and the fourth highest score in English. His Verbal Reasoning was also exemplary.

We are holding a prize-giving ceremony for current students this Saturday evening. A small number of future students who have been identified as "potential high-fliers" are invited to attend. Since Alex attained the top score in his cohort, we would be delighted if he could join us. We will send a uniform list in due course.

Many congratulations
Dr. B. Harvey (BA, MA, PhD)

Clara pressed the letter to her heart. *He'd done it.* Here was evidence that not all was disaster under her tenure. She passed the paper to Alex.

"How do you feel?" she asked.

His cheeks were flushed, yet he was gnawing his lip. "Pleased, but…"

Clara looked at him in surprise.

"But what?"

"I don't want to make Terry feel bad."

Clara hugged him, then plumped a kiss on his cheek. *Such a sensitive professor.* He wiped it away, embarrassed.

"Don't you worry about Terry. It's fine. She's fine. You worked hard to get in there."

"Then I'm over the moon," he yelped, punching the air. He did the funny dance that he did with his best friend Bernard, the one that made them look even more peculiar than normal. If he did it at the local high school he would be mincemeat, but maybe at Ipswich County Grammar it would be more accepting. Maybe Alex would even be popular there!

Ivor was outside washing his workshop windows. Ever since she'd told him about marrying Julian they had retreated to their old positions of antagonism, eyeing each other over the road like enemies across the Maginot Line.

Still, Clara went to tell him about Alex's result. If anyone would be thrilled for him, then Ivor would be. Maybe this would be the thing that could get them back on good terms again? It had only been a couple of weeks they hadn't been talking, although it felt like ages.

"YESSS!" Ivor squeezed his sponge free of dirty water and when he smiled at her, unreservedly, she knew she had done the right thing. It was lovely to have someone to share this with.

"It is amazing, isn't it?"

"You did it, Clara."

Her stomach somersaulted. "Well, Alex did." It was important that Ivor knew she was humble.

"So, will you take him to the prize-giving for 'potential high-fliers'?" Ivor laughed at the phrase. "I can look after the others if you want."

"Well, I can't, can I? It's this weekend..."

Ivor was shocked. "So? You can't let Alex down."

"Well, we knew he was going to pass, it's not like it's a surprise." Clara laughed, then stopped since Ivor was scowling. She hadn't expected this. "And it's not obligatory." She waved the letter. "See, it says here—"

"But..."

"It's my engagement party this Saturday night, Ivor," Clara said firmly. It seemed incredible that he had forgotten.

"Oh." He paused. "Of course...so Alex will be there, will he?"

"Well, no, actually, he won't."

"Why?"

"Because Julian and I decided the engagement party is for adults only."

"Why?"

"Why what?"

"Why aren't you including the children? You know how much they would want to be part of your party. They love a chance to dress up. To sing and to dance. Especially Rita and Peg."

"Because this one thing is about Julian and me. I can't do *every-thing* with them. And I will celebrate Alex's success, of course I will, just not *this* Saturday night. I'll celebrate it when I have the time. Alex is so easy."

Ivor muttered something.

"What did you say?"

Between gritted teeth, Ivor said, "That's *precisely* why you need to make the effort. Alex asks for so little—he gets little. He is so undemanding, he gets ignored."

"I *am* making the effort, Ivor. It's just one night. One thing for myself. And I know how to deal with Alex, thank you very much."

Who put Ivor in charge? He was like some angel on her shoulder, always chipping in when she took a path he didn't see as holy.

CHAPTER TWENTY-NINE

On the morning of the engagement party, Clara took the younger ones to the library to look for more Rupert the Bear and to return the gardening books that Terry hadn't read, then took Billy and Barry to spend some time with the fish Billy and Barry 2 at the surgery. They were still alive—Dr. Cardew wasn't just good at looking after people. The boys pressed their faces against the glass tank and whispered to them. Even Clara suddenly felt fond of the fish. Perhaps having no memory was a good thing, she pondered. They didn't seem too unhappy living in the moment.

She hurried the twins along though, because Judy was arriving at midday and then they were going to get their hair done side by side at Beryl's Brushes, the best (the only) hair salon in Lavenham.

When Judy still hadn't arrived by one, Clara began to worry. At half past, Clara went to the telephone box. She'd expected the phone to ring out, or for Arthur to answer, but Judy herself picked up: "I'm not going to get there, Clara."

Clara tried to conceal her disappointment—*be a grown-up about this*—but it was hard.

"What's happened?"

She had helped Judy with her wedding: the dress made from parachute silks, the bouquet, the cake with its cardboard inserts; even while her own heart was breaking.

"Migraine," whispered Judy, but Clara's antennae were alert.

"Really? It wasn't…Arthur?"

Judy's voice came from far away. "Sssh. I told you that's fine."

"Have you been getting migraines a lot then?" It sounded curt.
It *was* curt. Clara didn't believe Judy anymore. What were the odds
she would have a migraine today? What had he done to her this
time?

"Now and then. I'm so sorry, Clara."

Clara relented. Judy sounded so sad. And maybe it was true.
If Judy said Arthur had turned a corner, maybe he had. Judy had
never been a liar before.

"I really wanted you there, Jude."

A memory of a different engagement. Her, Judy, Michael and
his squadron. November 1944. They climbed up lampposts, they
did the bumps, they were giddy, free, foreign triumphers, they were
going to jump in the Thames, but Clara and Judy begged them not
to. Instead, they found some boats shaped like ducks and pedaled
around a lake. So much laughter...

"I love you, remember that, whatever happens."

Had Michael really said, *whatever happens*? It was like he knew.
*Concentrate, concentrate on Julian. On becoming Mrs. White and
how much easier life will be.*

"You'll have a lovely time." Judy sounded choked.

Impulsively, Clara asked Anita Cardew to accompany her to the
hairdressers instead, although as soon as Anita agreed, Clara wondered if it was a mistake. They *were* friends, it was just that they
were not *easy* friends, not yet, not in the way Clara and Judy were,
with their anticipating of each other's words, the pet phrases that
could bring each other to tears of laughter.

By two o'clock Anita and Clara were sat side by side in the
salon, flicking through the fashion magazines. Clara was determined to put her best self forward with Anita. Now that they were
out together, alone and out of the house, she realized that they
hardly knew each other at all.

Anita was making faces at the pencil drawings of hairstyles in the magazines.

"You could have yours like this?" She pointed to a particularly ghastly up-do.

"I'm thinking of it." Clara pictured Julian's expression if she turned up at the party with bleached Hollywood hair. He got antsy when she pinned her brooch on the wrong side of her coat.

"You would look like that awful Mrs. Garrard." Anita sniggered. Since they'd never shared their feelings about that awful Mrs. Garrard before, Clara was glad they had that in common at least.

Beryl the hairdresser had a cigarette dangling from her lips and an unlit one behind an ear. Her hair was also uninspiring—it seemed to have a life of its own—but then beggars couldn't be choosers, especially when it came to hairdressers in the countryside, that was for sure.

"You never told me about your war, Clara," Anita mused while Beryl gathered her brushes, dropping ash along the carpet.

"There's not much to tell." Clara had no idea what Anita had endured in that camp in Europe, but she had seen enough newsreels before the features at the cinema to know the word "hell" wasn't an exaggeration. "I was working at Harris & Sons in London mostly and...that's it." If she started on Michael, she would get tears in her eyes and this was supposed to be her engagement party.

"Through the Blitz?"

"Yes."

"Your mother was in London too?"

The children asked about her mother sometimes, but adults rarely did. Most people were like tightly screwed jar lids since the war and understood that others were too. Don't ask, don't tell.

"No. My parents were missionaries. In Africa," Clara said flatly.

"You didn't go with them?"

"I didn't."

"They left you here?"

"Yes."

Anita had none of that stiff-upper-lip thing about her. When she wanted to know something, she just unscrewed the lid of the jar and gave it a sniff.

"They abandoned you?"

"No. Well, kind of. Yes. I suppose."

Clara suddenly felt like all the air was coming out of her. She had to say it. She had to get it out. Beryl was making her way toward them with a tray of curlers. "It was *his* idea that they went. And then my poor mother got ill and she died out there. Slowly and painfully, from what I heard."

Anita put a hand on hers. "Then you know about suffering too."

Mrs. Wesley catered. You couldn't see the table for the food. There was cheese, ham on the bone, puffed-up sausage rolls, bread pudding and peach crumble. A little bit of cash went a long way. Clara had not seen such a mouthwatering spread for years, but she was too nervous to eat and she didn't want to spoil the display. Even her green dress now seemed too showy, too London. She was glad she hadn't bought anything new. Her hair was unnaturally stiff—she was never going back to Beryl's Brushes. The tips of her ears still felt red, although Terry had assured her they were always that color.

Robinson and Browne were there. Robinson's and Browne's wives were there too—Clara instantly felt sorry for Browne's—and there was a Robinson child, a twelve-year-old in a bow tie walking around with a plate of cress sandwiches. Everyone was smiling indulgently at him. That made Clara feel guilty. If *he* was here, surely it made sense that her children should be here too?

Only she knew Julian would say they weren't hers, wouldn't he?

There were the clients Julian liked to publicly announce: the

Lords and the MPs, the engineers and the businessmen. And the ones he gossiped to Clara about: the art collector, the gambler, the homosexuals, the actors. As she wandered around the room, she heard lots of chat about the hunt or who was selling up, or who still hadn't gotten over what happened—in the war, they meant. They didn't say it directly: the popular phrase was "never been the same."

So she didn't have the children, Judy, Miss Bridges or Ivor there, but she *did* have Anita, who despite Beryl's best efforts looked dazzling, and also Dr. Cardew and the nice postmistress, whose name she embarrassingly couldn't remember: it wasn't *all* Julian's people.

Julian put his arm round her, he was more demonstrative in public than he was in private, then he went off: "Must circulate."

"Do you remember me?" a slender man asked and his face lit up when Clara said she did. Lester Burns! She wished she could spend longer with him—his fragility charmed her, reminded her of Peter somehow—but Julian spirited her away to introduce her to more of his friends.

"Here she is, the future Mrs. White."

"Childbearing hips," one of the men said to the other approvingly. It was like they thought she couldn't hear. No, they didn't *care* if she heard, she was that inconsequential to them.

She grabbed another drink from the display. "Must circulate." She winked at Julian.

Standing by the buffet, Clara thought how few of the people there knew her and how few she knew. Some couples were dancing and one glamorous-looking woman was trying to convince Julian to rumba. He wouldn't. You could say that for him, he wasn't swayed by a pretty face or a low-cut neckline. Mrs. Garrard raised an eyebrow at Clara, then whispered something to her husband, whose side she never left. Her hair was so blonde it was almost white. Clara wondered if hers was also a product of Beryl's Brushes. Mr. Garrard was selecting one of the cigars being passed around. It felt like it was their party, not hers.

Clara missed the children. What had happened to her, she who once loved a big night out? Nowadays, she enjoyed their unhurried bedtime routines. Fat-lipped kisses, the tucking in, socks in a row on the radiators, ducks in a bath, hair spread out on pillows. She might not know about hunting or property, but she knew all the words to "You Are My Sunshine."

Sir Munnings kissed her on each cheek, proclaimed her a stunner. If only she were a horse, he'd immortalize her. Clara laughed.

"You don't like the modern art, do you, old girl?"

"I don't know about any kind of art."

"If only I were fifty years younger, I'd teach you everything you need to know about horses and art."

"I'm not sure those are the subjects I most need to know about."

In a voice loud enough for anyone to hear, Sir Munnings shouted over the music, "He doesn't deserve you!"

This wasn't the sort of conversation you had at an engagement party. Sir Munnings didn't even seem conflicted about it. *Was he drunk?*

Clara tensed. "Julian is a good man. We may be different, but I think together we make a formidable team."

"Julian doesn't give a toss about anyone but his own sweet self," Sir Munnings said. "Now I'm going to go home and sketch some foals."

When Julian next came to find her, Clara told him, "I have to get back." She had promised Sister Grace eleven, but her head was beginning to throb not just from the circulating but from what Sir Munnings had said. It was unkind and it was untrue.

"They'll be fine." Clara hadn't realized Julian had drunk so much. He grabbed her round the waist. He swung her round and she obliged, because people—the Garrards in particular—were watching.

"You're like the old woman who lived in the shoe, who had so many children she didn't know what to do…" He had said this

before. Clara nodded. Let him get on with it. "It's our party!" he
persisted.

"I know it is."

But it wasn't, it was Julian's party; she was just an accessory
there and not a shiny one at that.

"You're marrying me, sweetheart. You don't need to worry
about them anymore."

"We agreed, Julian, don't start now."

"That Peter—"

"I know you don't like him."

"What's to like? They're feral, grubby-nosed, horrible little
children."

Clara laughed, before realizing he was being serious. "They're
not, Julian. They're lovely little things and they've had a tough
time. All of them. Terrible times. You wouldn't believe it."

She thought of the patchwork of background stories in her children's reports, the deaths, the missing parents, the violence, the
instability; bad enough if they had someone to kiss it better. So
much harder without.

"Why are you so attached to them anyway?"

"Anyone would be if they spent time with them."

"I wouldn't. Filthy urchins. They should put 'em down. No one
would miss 'em." Julian mimed shooting a gun. Sizing up the tar-
get, pulling the trigger. "I'd do it for you if you want."

CHAPTER THIRTY

Julian apologized the next day with primroses. He didn't seem to be able to say sorry without flowers. He said he couldn't remember a thing about the evening from nine onward. Must have been something he ate. He hadn't moved far from the lavatory since midnight.

Good, thought Clara, *serves you right.*

"Was I that awful?"

"Yes, Julian, you were."

They sat outside the Railway Arms in the midday sun. Clara raised the hem of her skirt so the heat could get to her stockinged legs. Bandit leaned comfortingly against her thigh. Today she preferred Bandit to Julian and Julian knew it.

Julian gripped her hand as though he sensed she was trying to get away. He rolled the engagement ring round on her finger and kept cricking his neck from side to side. Clara couldn't tell if he was contrite or doing an impression of it. Either way, she liked this new, contrite Julian. She felt powerful for once.

"I drink too much."

He was drinking a whisky now, but it would be churlish to point it out.

"Do you think that's what it is?"

"I'm going to cut down. How does that sound?"

Clara wondered if Julian's crude opinions would change if he gave up drinking. She doubted it. He might not remember, but unfortunately, *she* remembered everything about the evening before, from the conversation with Sir Munnings: *"Julian doesn't give a toss about anyone,"* and the crazy look in Julian's eyes when he talked about Peter. Her father would have said he was "possessed by the devil."

"And the other thing is, the council demand too much of you. It's too much for one woman."

Julian was painting her as a martyr, thinking she didn't love being a housemother. He didn't realize she had changed since the first time she'd met him that day in the garden, brittle with nerves and fear. She was different. She had shored herself up. And her work *wasn't* too much. It was the least she could do.

"It's a good idea to cut back on the alcohol, Julian," she said presently. "But you said some mean things: would you have said them if you were sober?"

"Absolutely," he said.

"Wha-at?"

"Absolutely *not.*" He chortled. "Clara, you know me. I try to be a good person, yet I don't always get there." He stroked her fingers, but let the ring alone. "With you by my side, I will be a better person. I can change."

"I'm inviting Miss Bridges, Miss Cooper, Sister Grace and maybe Mrs. Harrington to the wedding," Clara tested. *Why not?* "And all the children, of course, even the ones who will have left by then. And I'm not giving up my work. Not until I'm ready: you have to accept this. I won't be changing my mind."

"Done!" Julian sounded relieved. "You're not breaking up with me then?"

"Good grief, no."

"Can we…" Julian was almost childlike in his tone. "Can we say December then? I just want you to be my wife, darling."

"December this year?"

He nodded, little-boy nervous.

"I don't see why not."

Tit for tat. Clara knew how to play him. As if she'd really break up with him over this. And sooner rather than later worked for her too. Otherwise, she had an inkling, they'd both get cold feet.

"How was Alex last night?" she asked Peter as he was mopping the floor.

"Fine."

"He didn't mind not going to the school presentation?"

"He made us listen to him read from his encyclopedia. About Tyrannosaurus rex."

"Oh crikey. Lucky you!"

They both laughed. Peter could be great company when he wanted to be. He was such a lovely kid, deep down. He swished the mop around in figures of eight, like a country dancer.

"And then?"

"They played hide-and-seek." He sniggered. "Billy and Barry were useless. They hid under the table, you could see their legs from miles away. But Peg hid behind the dresser..."

Clara loved anecdotes like these. Why didn't she and Peter chat more often? Perhaps Peter too was changing since the incident with Julian, growing up a bit? Perhaps he just needed to understand there were consequences to everything.

"She could still fit there?" Peg was amazing at disappearing. She disappeared when she played hide-and-seek or sardines. Clara found it petrifying.

"Just about...it took ages to find her, Rita was crying—she thought we'd never see her again."

"I can imagine. How about you? Did you join in, Peter?"

At this, Peter hung his head. He dragged his mop to the bucket. It seemed to Clara that the floor was no cleaner than when he'd started.

"You would get so much more out of things if you did."

Dr. Cardew said joining in had helped Anita. But Peter hung his head lower, then sloped off, the bucket smacking against his legs.

So much for a breakthrough moment.

But maybe, for once, Clara's words did go in, for after school the next day Peter was out in the garden with the others, joining in with the cricket. Although cricket was new to the children, they had picked it up quickly and certainly the lawn looked like they'd been playing it for years.

Peter was laughing. He hardly ever laughed when she was around. And it wasn't just her. If Ivor or Miss Bridges were there, he closed up like an oyster.

He was batting now. They used a tennis ball for a ball and the wickets were three long sticks and a short twig for the horizontal. Bandit had broken in and peed up them twice to everyone's delight. Alex's best friend, Bernard, was bowling. Terry was backstop. Billy, Barry and their school friends, a pair of brothers who lived over the bakery, and the postmistress's daughter, were waiting their turn or making varying degrees of efforts fielding. Rita and Peg were not playing. Apparently, they were in the shed.

Alex, who prided himself on being as useless at sports as he was at art and music, came over to Clara. He pointed to Peter, who had just walloped the ball sky-high.

"He's good, isn't he?"

"He is. You should play, Alex."

"I *am* playing," he explained. "I'm in an important position!"

They'd made him an outfielder where his daydreaming wouldn't affect anyone.

The game continued. Bernard was a good bowler too, but Peter's batting was excellent. And then, he hit the ball into a beautiful arc toward them. A better fielder than Alex might have caught it, but somehow it sailed past him and hit Clara smack in the collarbone. It was a shock more than anything.

"Ow!"

And then she caught the terrible look on Peter's face. *Pure loathing.* Clara clutched her throat, tears stinging, partly in shock and hurt, partly in embarrassment at being distressed in front of all these young people.

Billy and Barry were running toward her. "Peter, you prat!" yelled Billy.

Alex was peering at her like a botanist studying a fly. "Miss Newton, do you need medical assistance?"

"PETER!"

"It's not Peter's fault," Clara whimpered. "It's mine for being so fumbly."

"Should I run to Dr. Cardew's?" Alex said. "He was good with my constipation."

"It's fine." *Oh, would they stop making a fuss!*

Peter hadn't moved. He stared at her, then shook his head like he was having terrible thoughts. He ran off out of the gate, into the street. The grass under the pads of his feet bowed down, then sprang back.

"Please, Peter," Clara called after him. "Honestly, I'm not hurt. I'm not hurt at all."

But he wouldn't come back.

After a short while, the children played on. Clara joined in too, but she couldn't bear it. Where had Peter gone? She couldn't have two children go missing on her.

He did come back, but only at lunchtime, and he wouldn't speak to her for the rest of the day. Not at lunch, not at tea. *It's not as though* I *threw it at him. He* hit *it at me,* she thought to herself. *And anyway, I know it was an accident…*

When she asked him to pass the salt he pretended not to hear until Barry shouted in his ear, "She wants the salt, stupid."

He might as well have thrown that at her too.

*

"Peter has always been odd." Miss Bridges, who had been baking all weekend, flipped some ginger biscuits onto a plate. "Leftovers."

"Has he? It's funny, he's the only one who has contact with any of his family, so you'd think he'd be more cheerful."

"Sometimes a little contact can be more painful. It's a reminder, isn't it? Of all that you've lost. Of what you haven't got."

Miss Bridges was dipping her biscuit in her tea, so Clara did too, thinking mischievously that Julian would be horrified. *Biscuits are not for dunking, Clara!*

"Anyway, tell me about the party. I heard you and Julian were dancing and drinking late into the night. It was like the VE Day celebrations all over again."

"Who told you that?"

"Everyone."

Everyone was Mr. Horton the inspector and Mr. Sommersby the children's services head. Clara hardly remembered seeing them, but then there had been a lot of gray men in suits at the party.

"It was fun." Clara would be happy never to talk about the evening again.

Clara wouldn't give up on Peter. She wanted to get him fixed, in whatever way she could, before the wedding if possible and, if not, definitely before next year. When he was sixteen he would be out on his own, having to face the big wide world—she didn't have long to shape him.

He stayed in the boys' dormitory most of the time, doing goodness knows what. She took him rolls of drawing paper, hoping to inspire more artwork.

His expression was cold.

"Peter, you needn't ever worry about hurting me. I am…" What

was she going to call herself, indestructible? A smile threatened
the corners of his mouth. "Impervious. Anyway, it's all part of the
game. Cricket, eh!" Quickly, he turned his grin into a frown.

He took the sketching paper.

"*Thank you,*" she said.

He considered, then nodded, and she didn't have the heart to
say she wasn't thanking him but cack-handedly encouraging him
to say thank you to her.

CHAPTER THIRTY-ONE

Alex had wanted to go to the Natural History Museum in London for some time and, since she had missed the celebration about his school place, Clara owed him. The other children would probably have enjoyed the trip too, but Clara thought it was time—it was long overdue in fact—for Alex to have something for himself.

Alex never seemed to get interest from prospective adopters either, although Clara had at least finally worked out why. An orphan was one thing, but no one really wanted a child with a drunken father who could turn up out of the blue.

Judy said it was sports day at her school and, since she'd never been a one for sports day, she asked if she could come along with Alex and Clara—if they'd have her.

"Of course we'll have you!"

They arranged to meet outside South Kensington station, where a man was playing the accordion and Alex had his first ever roasted chestnuts.

His verdict: "They smell better than they taste."

"So do lots of things." Judy appeared behind them, beaming broadly.

Despite the bright lipstick, Judy looked more tired than usual and she had a cluster of spots on each cheek. Or perhaps it was the cotton scarf she had tied under her chin, which made her look like a harassed housewife. But she hugged them both and said, "Am I glad to see you two! I've been counting the minutes."

"How many did you get up to?" asked Alex.

"Eighteen thousand, four hundred and seventy-six," shot back Judy, taking his arm like he was twice his age and shaking her head in wonderment at Clara.

If Judy said everything was better, then maybe it was. She shouldn't search out problems, Clara told herself. She had enough problems without imaginary ones to contend with.

The great hall of the Natural History Museum was dominated by four elephants. Poor dear creatures, here to be gawped at and prodded for eternity. Clara suddenly wanted to cry.

"Are they real?" she asked, regretting it as soon as she did.

Judy and Alex rolled their eyes at her in unison, they were like some music hall comedy duo.

They looked at the dinosaur bones (real) and the volcanos (they weren't real, they were just models, got that, Clara?) and the insects in glass boxes (real). Judy explained things to Alex as they went round, then asked him questions to check he'd understood. *She's so good at this*, thought Clara. *Where did she get this encyclopedic knowledge from?*

Judy tapped a case and the little information labels underneath. "It's all written here," she explained but it was much more than that; she reframed everything perfectly for Alex, making it interesting for Clara too.

Judy said that just before the war the exhibits were taken out of London, for safety, and were dispersed all over the country.

"I knew we did that with children, I had no idea about the things too."

"Country houses, even a mine in South Wales, and some of them found better homes than others."

"I liked where I was evacuated to," said Alex.

"You remember?" Alex could only have been three or four. Clara didn't think he could have, but then why say it?

"This boy knows his stuff," Judy said to Clara when they came to the end of the butterflies section.

"He is quite the clever clogs," Clara admitted proudly.

*

Alex wanted to look at the temporary exhibition of spiders. He wanted to take in *everything*, but after three hours, Clara had had enough of the overheated building, the creatures with gaping eyes or claw-like hands and the intensity of it all. Her brain was over-crowded. She suggested that she and Judy go outside to eat their sandwiches; Alex could continue exploring and save his lunch for the train home. Judy looked torn.

"Come on, Jude," insisted Clara, "It's our day out too."

"Go-go!" Alex was thrilled at the prospect of exploring on his own.

"Join us when you're done," Judy called out, but Alex was already galloping up the stairs toward the big photograph of tarantula that heralded "ARACHNIDS."

It's enough to put you off your lunch. Clara wished the sandwiches weren't cress. She always ate better with Julian. Still, she had a tea-cake for dessert to look forward to.

"How are your migraines then?" She had warned herself not to ask, but she couldn't help herself: Judy had missed her engagement party!

"All fine."

"You should get them checked out."

Judy nodded in a way that Clara interpreted to mean that she absolutely wasn't going to get them checked out.

"Everything all right with Arthur?" It was something to do with him, she knew it.

Judy sounded exasperated, as though Clara was always asking. "He's well." Before Clara could ask any more, she said, "And how are things with your fiancé?"

"Perfect."

On the train home, Alex wouldn't stop talking about all the won-derful things: the lizards, spiders and dinosaurs. Clara found herself thinking that while she had done it for Alex, she'd also done it to send a message to Ivor. Was that wrong? She couldn't help feeling pleased when, predictably, Alex insisted on running over to Ivor's workshop, keen to tell him all about it.

"Miss Newton took me to London to show me dinosaurs!" he called as he barged in.

There Ivor was, sewing curtains or some such. His dark eyes concentrating. He had pins in his mouth which he hastily removed. It made her wince to see them. Suddenly she imagined kissing him and felt a prickle of pain. She touched her lips.

"Did she now? Clara takes great care of you children."

Ivor looked over at Clara, eyebrows raised. It wasn't the apology she had hoped for, it wasn't an apology at all, but it was a compliment, an acknowledgment, and she felt a huge—possibly quite disproportionate—relief that they were still friends.

CHAPTER THIRTY-TWO

The next day, Clara came in the kitchen from pegging out the washing to find the children gathered around Rita, looking serious. Even Peter was there. Peg put her hand in Clara's and rolled her eyes.

Alex explained: "Rita didn't get it."

Clara had to work out what it was that Rita hadn't gotten. *Good grief. What had she missed now?*

"May Queen," added Alex helpfully. "They decided it at school today."

Oh, May Queen! Rita had been making a fuss about it for a while now. She had been trying out different hairstyles and saying, *When I'm May Queen, I'll rule everybody and make everybody put their toothbrushes in the right place and everyone wear yellow and no one will ever have to eat cheese, ever again.*

Clara hadn't thought much about it.

She knelt by the crying girl.

"It's all right, darling. We can't win them all." *To be fair, the children of Shilling Grange didn't seem to win any of them.*

"She didn't get any other role either."

Clara straightened up. "What other roles?"

Alex was more on top of this than anyone else, as usual.

"There were all sorts of positions she might have got: deputy princess or lady-in-waiting."

"I'm 'girl in the crowd.'" Rita chewed her plait. Clara remembered that Rita had done her hair especially that morning because it made her look "more beautiful than the other girls." She held back the temptation to say, "Don't chew." She also held back the temptation to say, "Welcome to the real world."

"Oh, Miss Newton, I wanted to do this. Why does it always happen to me?"

"So, who is May Queen then?"

"Betsy Hanshawe!" Rita almost spat the name.

"Betsy Hanshawe whose parents own the grocery shop next to the station?"

"Yes."

"And who is her deputy, did they say?"

"Milly Little."

"The butcher's girl?"

Rita burst out: "I hate them all."

Rita wailed for most of the evening. She cried almost as much as she had on the infamous "day of Molly Mouse," but this time there was no Maureen to calm her down. At teatime, Clara told everyone they were a family and they would get through it together. Rita nearly drowned her out with her sobs.

"And do you know what united means?"

"Manchester United?" asked Billy. "RUBBISH!"

"It means we're together. We work together and look after each other."

Clara said that this was Rita's darkest hour. They liked the sound of that. Barry did a terrific impersonation of Churchill. Alex fetched his encyclopedia. Even Terry took sympathy on Rita; she went out to the garden and brought in some plums she'd grown. Clara was proud of their resilience and told them so.

"Resilience?" asked Barry.

"It means people keep kicking you down but you keep getting up," explained Alex.

"Wouldn't it be better if people stopped kicking you?" asked Terry.

"Well, yes," admitted Clara. "I suppose it would."

Rita wept on. If only the May Queen were a weeping contest, she'd have won it by a country mile. "I wanted to wear a special dress."

"I know you did."

At bedtime, Clara lay next to Rita, but she wasn't doing a great job of comforting her. The sheets kept coming unraveled and the blanket was scratchy. Clara missed her own bed with its cozy red quilt.

"What can I do?" she asked Rita.

"A rabbit would cheer me up. A real one," she added threateningly. "Or a dog. You gave away the fish."

This set her off on a new wave of tears.

Clara didn't say, *and you didn't notice the fish were missing for three whole days*. She was better than that.

Rita clutched her. "I thought if I could be May Queen, they'd put a photograph of me in the newspapers. Mama would hear about it and she would come and find me."

"Oh, sweetie!" *She still believes that's possible?* Clara rocked her. She was such a tiny little girl with these big burdens. One day, she'd have to accept it.

"There's always next year," Clara began, but this made Rita weep more. When you're ten, next year might as well be a hundred years away—Clara should have known that.

The playground the following afternoon was full of children running around, freedom in their hair. It was embarrassing, charging up to the school, but Clara couldn't think what else to do. The woman at the reception turned salmon when she arrived and wordlessly sent her through. Clara stalked the corridors, losing confidence with every step, until she found Rita's classroom. She hadn't yet met Rita's teacher, Miss Fisher, but so far as she knew, Rita didn't dislike her.

The classroom was plain, somber almost. I WILL LISTEN TO MY TEACHER. MY TEACHER KNOWS BEST was chalked on the blackboard. It felt old-fashioned and not an entirely *hopeful* place, but looks could be deceiving.

Miss Fisher wore small oval glasses and a white Victorian-style blouse, which might have been an original—she was that old. Clara's appearance at the classroom door seemed to give her an awful turn, for both heels left the ground ever so slightly. She folded her arms.

"Did you have an appointment?"

"The children at Shilling Grange have faced many obstacles in their lives," began Clara once the introductions were done and after she'd explained she only wanted five minutes of Miss Fisher's time. The *My teacher knows best* was off-putting—probably the intention.

Miss Fisher narrowed her eyes. She had a small silver cross at her throat.

"Are you asking for special favors for certain children? If you are, that's unacceptable."

Clara reddened, but the thought of Rita crying in her bed over this setback spurred her on.

"I don't want exceptions to be made, but I'm curious—not one child from the Grange could have a role in the celebrations?"

Miss Fisher took hold of the window pole and began working the long thin windows shut. She was stronger than she looked. It was even harder for Clara to state her case while Miss Fisher was doing that. She could smack the pole onto Clara's head, for example. Or jab her in the stomach. Clara could imagine the damage Billy and Barry could do if they got their hands on one of those.

"The May Queen and her entourage are highly coveted positions," explained Miss Fisher once the windows were closed and the children's cheerful screeches could no longer be heard. "You'll appreciate pupils have to earn their place. None of it is given. And none of the Grange children did."

"How do they earn a place?"

"Is it not obvious?" Miss Fisher proceeded to stack her notebooks into a tower. The urge to give them a shove was strong.

"It's not."

"The children who have a place each have families who have assisted us in some way."

The grocer's daughter. The butcher's daughter... Clara stared at her in bewilderment.

"Assisted?"

"That's right."

"The idea is... we help you?"

"I didn't say that." When Miss Fisher raised her eyebrows, her spectacle frames slid down her nose.

"Then... then how do you mean, assist?"

"Meat? Books? Sugar? These are..." Miss Fisher took the eraser and wiped the letters off the board in rehearsed circular strokes, "difficult times for us all."

Ho, so this is how things are. Poor Rita. Clara thought on her feet. Ivor. Ivor was the answer. She thought of her own Christmas present.

"I could bring in... cushions... or a... a... quilt?"

"Next year then," said Miss Fisher warmly, as though she liked Clara after all. "I like greens and blues. No patterns or tartan, thank you."

Clara was still flabbergasted when she relayed the conversation to Ivor over tea in his workshop. He had invited her in for a cup and, relieved that things were once again on an even keel, Clara had accepted. Rita and Peg were in the shed with Anita. Terry was buzzing around her patch: she was expecting rhubarb and asparagus any day now. Billy and Barry were playing in the wild somewhere, Peter was mooching in his room and Alex was researching his latest passion: Neanderthal Man.

"So, to be the May Queen, or part of the entourage, you are supposed to bribe the teacher. Have you ever heard anything like it?"

"Afraid that's small towns for you... Have a slice, Clara, and take the rest later for the children. There's too much here for me."

It was a large, fat chocolate cake, with mouthwatering, ration-busting chocolate icing.

"Where *did* you get this from?"

He raised his eyebrows. "Mrs. Harrington."

So Mrs. Harrington, who had retired from children's services because of her husband, was still in touch with Ivor?

"How unexpected."

Ivor's expression was blank.

"You don't mind, do you? My offering up your cushions as a sacrifice to the May Queen gods?"

"Not at all." He hesitated. "And Rita is all right about waiting another year?"

"Yes. No. Maybe." Clara absentmindedly picked at her slice of cake. She'd gone off it suddenly. "She'll have to be. Oh, but Ivor, do you think you could make something for her out of an old dress of mine? A new frock might just cheer her up."

"Good idea."

Clara was just about to go back over the road, with a plate piled high with cake, when Ivor said, "Clara," in a different tone to usual.

"Ye-es?"

"Sorry things have been awkward between us."

A half-apology from Ivor was a whole apology from anyone else.

"I've never really got on with Julian."

"I guessed." Clara smiled. It was going to be all right.

"I'd love to give you my blessing."

"There's no ne—"

"But I don't. I won't. I don't think he's the right person for you, Clara."

"Who would you rather I married, Ivor?"

He didn't say anything. He'd insulted her and it hadn't worked. As if she would change her mind on his say-so! He got up, awkwardly put the lid on Mrs. Harrington's now-empty cake tin and went out the back.

Okay, so the air had not been cleared.

CHILDREN'S REPORT 8
PEG CHURCH

Date of birth:
Peg's birthday is celebrated on April 1, the day she was left at
a church door in Boston, Lincolnshire, with just a seashell.
No one knows more than that.

They think she was six months when she was left, in
1942, so she is approximately seven or eight years old.

Family background:
Inside the shell, someone wrote, "Please look after my precious Peg."

Health/Appearance:
She has mouse hair and brown eyes. She likes plaits. She is
waiting for her front teeth to grow. One drop of sunshine,
Peg turns nut-brown and her hair goes much lighter.

Peg doesn't speak. Ever. We don't think it's medical—it
must be emotional.

Food:
She doesn't eat much. She's a nibbler like a mouse but she
does love jam. Jam on bread. Jam sponge. Jam anything.
Hates Bovril.

Hobbies/Interests:
Dancing, skipping, listening to Rita play the piano, hopscotch, elastic.

Other:
She likes holding hands, walking in the countryside, building igloos and her seashell.

CHAPTER THIRTY-THREE

It was a beautiful summer day; the sun was high in the sky and managed to shine through the trees, even where the leaves were at their densest. Clara and Peg took a new walk, along a mud track next to some fields. Peg collected pretty stones, clambered over gates and smiled agreeably at whatever Clara said. She was lovely company. Clara was still mulling over the previous day's conversation with Ivor. *Silly fool*, she thought, what did he want her to say about Julian, her husband-to-be? He must know where her loyalties lay. But another part of her could think only, *oh, Ivor*... and that foolish compulsion she sometimes felt when she was with him, not to say anything but to put her arms round him and just be...

They had been out for a while when Peg tugged Clara's arm and pointed. Mr. Garrard and his dog were ahead of them. Clara groaned. Peg giggled. Mr. Garrard was waiting for them to catch up. Clara slowed her pace down but he was, definitely, waiting.

"What does he want?" she muttered to Peg. They should have stuck to their old walk. Who wanted to run into him?

"Well, hello, ladies," he said as they approached, doffing his hat, as though he and his wife had not spent the last six months sneering at her. He was dressed fantastically inappropriately for a summer's walk, in a waistcoat, and his dangling pocket watch caught the sunlight, blinding Clara momentarily. "How nice to see you taking your constitutional."

"Good day, Mr. Garrard!" said Clara brightly. She knew what he'd say next, she bloody knew it.

"And you, little girl, don't I get a greeting from you?"

"This is Peg," said Clara as Peg's hand tightened in hers.

"Hello, Peg."

Staring at the copse of trees ahead, Peg looked as though she'd like to disappear into them.

"Did you see the calves?" chirped Mr. Garrard. "Quite beautiful, aren't they?"

Clara, who never thought cows were beautiful, said they must have missed them. Mr. Garrard gazed down at Peg in a way that seemed to emphasize how tiny she was.

"What about you? Cat got your tongue, eh?"

"Peg isn't speaking today." Clara didn't feel like explaining it to him. Why should she? Why should Peg have to explain herself to anyone?

Bertie was bolting around in quite a frenzy. They carried on walking, all three abreast, Clara plotting how she could shake him off.

"Perhaps people would look more kindly on the Grange children if they had some manners."

"Peg does have manners." Clara wondered if she should mention his dog's weird behavior. Out of the corner of her memory, she recalled something about calves and dogs being a poor combination. But Mr. Garrard was a local; no doubt they were in safe hands with him.

"It's just a suggestion."

"She just doesn't have anything to say right now." Clara preferred to say *right now*, as though at any moment Peg might launch into a Shakespearean soliloquy.

But the strange thing was, at that moment, for the first time ever, Peg let out a sound, the likes of which Clara had never heard before. It was a screech or a howl. It was awful.

"Peg?"

Peg's face was petrified. Her mouth opened and shut, one, two, three times and then she breathed, "Cows!"

Oh my.

Seconds later, cows were coming at them from behind. Bertie must have aggravated them. The noise of their legs was like thunderclaps, hundreds of rumbling thunderclaps. The indestructible look of those cows! They were en masse and they were angry. Clara weighed up the distance to the next gate and the distance between them and it. *They could do this.* She was sure she and Mr. Garrard could. But maybe not Peg, with her little legs.

"Ruuun!" Clara scooped up Peg. Usually, the girl was light as a feather but today, pretty stones were weighing her down; they rained from her pockets as Clara jogged her, jiggled her back to the gate. She and Peg would not be trampled to death by cows. Not today, thank you. The earth was vibrating under the soles of her shoes. At the gate, she threw Peg over the other side. Bertie was on the other side of it too by now, woofing madly. Cursed dog. Clara expected Mr. Garrard to be right behind her, but a demi-second later, she realized he had barely moved an inch from their starting place. He stood in the field, his arms outstretched, his hat blown off, his hair whipping up unattractively in the wind. He could have been a scarecrow, only he wasn't scaring anything.

"Mr. Garrard!" Clara called. "The dog is here, come, come!"

She went back for him. Split-second decision. What else could she do? This time, she moved calmly and cautiously. She took his sleeve and backed away with him, facing the cows, and then, again, judging the distance, made him run.

Those enormous faces. Those flies. The clatter of their feet on the mud. They flew to the gate, then climbed breathlessly to safety. There might have been a moment—never to be mentioned—when she pushed at his bottom to help him over quicker.

Clara was still overwhelmed about Peg.

"Peg, you spoke! You said *cows*."

Peg shook her head. She was half-giggling, half-crying.

"You did, didn't you? You clever girl! You warned us."

Peg put her head in the crook of Clara's neck, moaning softly.

"We're all right." Clara patted her on the back. It was awful, but also quite exhilarating.

Mr. Garrard sat on the ground, his legs out in a V-shape in front of him, like a toddler, shaking his head in disbelief. There were twigs all over his waistcoat.

"My watch." He patted his stomach ineffectively. His watch must have fallen off and was somewhere out there in the mud with his hat.

"Thank goodness you were here!" He huffed and puffed. His face was as scarlet as the spots on his handkerchief.

"Glad I wasn't in Ipswich or Clacton then?" Clara couldn't resist.

Mr. Garrard laughed, then coughed and had to breathe deeply again. "Very."

CHAPTER THIRTY-FOUR

Alex explained to Clara there would be a maypole, and maybe some country dancing but no teacups rides, or more importantly, no goldfish stands at the junior school May Day event.

"It's just for kids," he added. He sounded like a fifty-year-old man sometimes. Speaking of which, Clara *had* asked her fifty-year-old man to come and he had agreed, but at the last minute he was invited to a hunt in Norfolk. Julian could never resist the chance to chase a fox.

"You don't mind? I'll make it up to you, darling." The next weekend, they were going to a hotel, he reminded her. But Clara did mind—or rather, she half-minded. Julian would likely hate the event and probably spoil it with witty but cruel observations, but she wanted to spend more time with him—she *needed* to spend more time with him—otherwise they would just slip away from each other and their planned future. And yes, she was aware, acutely aware thank you, that Julian lived only five minutes away. They *were* able to see each other more—it was choice, not war, that was stopping them.

The May Fair was a big event in the Lavenham social calendar. Most of the children were in their Sunday best and some of the parents were too. As Alex had said, there was a maypole but there were also refreshment stalls selling Bakewell tarts and orange and lemon squash, which was pleasing, for Clara had not eaten breakfast, and there were stalls with contests involving hammers and balls or pins and donkeys, which were less enticing. Fortunately,

there were no live creatures to accidentally take home—and hopefully no Maurice "stitch-up" Selby lurking in the bushes with his
camera.

Ivor had, as usual, done an incredible job on Rita's dress—it
was yellow, patterned with flowers with a gorgeous bow to tie at
the back, and Rita was thrilled with it. As soon as they arrived, she
darted off, although occasionally Clara caught glimpses of yellow
here and there like the first daffodils of spring. Clara was walking with Alex—"Did you know M'aidez, in French, means help
me?"—when she saw an unwelcome sight: Mr. and Mrs. Garrard
at the "How many sweets in a jar?" stall. Mr. Garrard stared at his
boots rather than catch Clara's eye; however, Mrs. Garrard, who
usually took great pleasure in ignoring Clara, gestured for her to
come over. If Clara had hoped Mr. Garrard had told his wife about
their escapade in the fields, it soon became obvious that he hadn't.
Mrs. Garrard was as antagonistic as ever.

"We're doing the flowers for your wedding, Miss Newton."

"Apparently so." Clara tried not to think of Mr. Garrard's trousers straining over his ample bottom halfway up the gate.

"You've got your feet nicely under the table, haven't you?"

Which table?

Mrs. Garrard nudged her husband, who shrugged at Clara
before he muttered, "Yes, dear" to his wife.

"Tell her then."

At least Mr. Garrard was less enthusiastic than usual. (Which
he should be, seeing as she had just about Saved. His. Life.) "We,
urm, you know, just think Ipswich—"

"Or Clacton would be a better location for a children's home. I
KNOW," snapped Clara. *The cheek of the man.*

She spied Mrs. Harrington at a darts stall—probably practicing
throwing Cupid's arrow at Ivor—and ducked out of her way. She
couldn't tolerate her today. Then she saw Alex in dispute with the
raffle man.

"But if they must end with a five or a zero then that's not fair."

Peg was skipping in a crowd. Clara noticed Terry squinting at a sweet stall. She waved, but Terry didn't wave back.

A short while passed before Clara saw Ivor, but before she could catch up with him, Mrs. Harrington did. Ivor didn't seem as pleased to see Mrs. Harrington as she was to see him. Clara heard him say, "I need to return your tin," while Mrs. Harrington flapped her arms. "Did you eat it all up, Ivor? There's more where that came from."

It felt like there was a never-ending stream of people to avoid. Clara had lost all of the children—although surely it was okay to lose them here, in the confines of the school playground?

There was a kerfuffle over by the marquee. A crowd and some screeching. Clara saw Billy and Barry running away from it, red-faced and chortling. She hurried to join them, sensing that what-ever it was, they were involved. Grabbing Billy by the arm, she snapped, "What have you done?"

"Nothing!"

"Served her right," said Barry.

"What? Served who right?"

They could hardly talk for laughing. Then Billy managed to control himself. He explained, "The May Queen and two of her princesses sat on chocolate cake."

"What? No! How?"

"Icing squelched everywhere. They're crying 'coz their dresses are ruined."

"How did the cake get there? Where on earth was it from?"

The boys looked at each other with palms up in innocence. "No idea."

This wasn't funny, but Billy launched into his new Churchill impersonation: "We fight them in the playgrounds. We fight them on the streets. We are a family *united*, Miss Newton."

He expected Clara to be impressed!

"That has nothing to do with being a family united! You, you...
humiliated some little girls on their special day!"

Clara might as well have told them they'd invaded Poland. They
couldn't have looked more stunned.

"We didn't!" protested Barry, his mouth wide open.

"That Betsy girl has been horrid to our Rita for years!"

"Betsy Hanshawe is awful and I'm glad she's upset."

The headmistress was marching over with the toady woman
from reception.

"Boys. And you. Yes, YOU, lady from Shilling Grange!"

Uh-oh, here we go. Clara's stomach was in turmoil. She didn't
know how to react. What would Judy have said? Julian would say,
see, I told you so. Miss Bridges would be scolding. Ivor would probably listen first.

Clara followed them into the school building docilely, then into
the headmistress's office. The boys were ordered to wait outside.
The headmistress wasted no time.

"Did you know about this?"

"Of course not, I just heard."

"Was this a planned assault?"

"A planned assault?" Clara rapidly decided which side she was
on. "Good grief. No."

There was a window high up in the door, about a meter and
a half up. Billy must have been sat on Barry's shoulders, because
suddenly Clara glimpsed his cheeky face pressed against the glass.
His nose was squeezed out of shape and his lips were puckered into
a fat kiss. Clara wanted to smirk. Then suddenly the face started
sinking lower and lower until there was a clatter, which must have
been him hitting the deck.

Now, Clara did laugh.

"Miss Newton?"

Clara suddenly felt as though she too were looking in from outside the door; she was up high, higher even than where Billy had

been, she was up in the ceiling and looking down on it all, and it was Michael's voice she heard and he was smiling: "Go on, sweetheart, you tell them."

"Those girls have been picking on Rita all year. I feel sorry about the outfits, but I have no idea what happened—if ever I do, I'll be sure to let you know. Now, I have children to round up. Good day."

Outside, Peg and Terry were dancing around the maypole. Alex and Bernard were part of a country dancing display. Bernard's father was cheerfully clapping along; Clara briefly wondered why she never saw Bernard's mother. But where had Rita gotten to?

Another teacher, gloriously oblivious to all the chaos, called out to Clara, then pointed over at the marquee.

"Rita makes such a lovely May Queen, doesn't she, Miss Newton?"

And there she was; Rita had ascended to the throne, in her beautiful make-do-and-mend yellow dress courtesy of Ivor, crown perched on top of her beautiful plaits, happy as Larry.

CHAPTER THIRTY-FIVE

"No one wears glasses," Terry ranted a few days later, before correcting herself, "no one good anyway."

Clara had taken Terry's squint to Dr. Cardew, who said to take it to the opticians in Bury as soon as possible.

Clara considered who *good* wore glasses. There *was* one boy at school, Henry Meekins, but he was a nose-picker and didn't come under Terry's definition of good. Miss Bridges did for reading and so did Miss Fisher at school. Neither of them would inspire a struggling little girl. Miss Bridges had already made the fatal mistake of saying, "They will make you look clever." Terry didn't *want* to look clever. An excellent gardener maybe, or a skilled muck-raker, but not *clever*.

Still, she sat patiently as the optician placed the spectacles on her nose and shoved a mirror in her face and waited for her approval. Terry was an obedient girl. She did not approve but eventually she held onto a pair, tortoiseshell with little wings at each side. They wouldn't have been Clara's first choice, but they weren't too terrible.

Julian was locking up his office as they walked from the station. Clara was delighted to see him and relieved at how warmly he opened his arms to her and that he kissed both her cheeks. When she didn't see him for a while—and she hadn't seen him for over a week—she wondered if he forgot about her; perhaps that was since she sometimes *almost* forgot about him. It was only because their worlds were so different, she told herself. Terry scuffed her shoe into the ground as Julian whispered into Clara's ear that he couldn't wait until Sunday.

"Do you like Terry's new spectacles?" Clara prompted him.

"I do."

To Clara, he raised his eyebrows. "You didn't tell me you knew Harold Lloyd."

Terry begged to visit Ivor before they went home. Clara didn't want to—not with the way things stood between them—but if anyone could cheer up Terry, Ivor could.

"You go, I'll wait outside."

But Terry went blundering in, before running out self-importantly: "Ivor says to come in."

Oh God.

Okay, so they would try to be friends again in front of the children. She could do that, she wasn't a total fool.

Turning her face up to Ivor, Terry pointed to her glasses. "They're awful, aren't they?"

"Let me see...so now you have two ways of seeing the world, and I only have one, is that so?"

"What?" Terry wiped her runny nose on her sleeve. Clara sighed. *Handkerchief.*

"How do you mean?"

Very gently, Ivor pinched the glasses at the bridge of Terry's nose and pushed them up to her forehead. "What can you see now?"

"It's blurry," Terry admitted.

"Right." Then he dropped them back into the correct place over her eyes again. "And how's this?"

"That's sharp."

"See—two ways of seeing the world. That's a gift, that is."

Tears came to Clara's eyes suddenly, stupidly, and she didn't know why. "Thank you, Ivor. You always make everything better."

He met her eyes over Terry's head, and he seemed to be saying something else, but it was too blurry for her to understand.

"You're welcome, Clara."

Her heart was pounding like crazy. She knew suddenly what it was. Attraction: it was what she had felt toward Michael and it was not what she felt toward Julian. Silly pointless attraction. They called it "lust" in the magazines and Ingrid Bergman and Carole Lombard were brilliant at showing it in the movies. But in real life it was ridiculous. It did not last. It did not pay the mortgage either. It did not help. Something always, always went wrong. Or someone died.

She should visit Ivor less often, now that she was an officially engaged woman.

And yet. "You've almost convinced me to get a pair!" she said brightly.

"You'd look lovely, Clara."

She put her hand to her cheek. It was on fire.

"Time to go, Terry."

CHAPTER THIRTY-SIX

A few days later, Clara was tidying up the boys' room. Was this also an excuse for prying?

Perhaps, yes, just a little.

Peter had been so difficult recently. Every day with him she felt as though she were taking two steps forward and three steps back. It was hard to believe he had once been her favorite child.

He had refused to come to the May Fair and when they got home, he was still in bed where they'd left him. In her mind, something about him lying there, wasting away, infuriated her, connecting him to all the lost boys in the war. They didn't get the chance to idle their days away in comfort—why should he?

She had flipped. "Go, get out, just do something," and he had gotten up and gone. She didn't know where he went and at first, she didn't care. Then she worried. He sloped back just before bedtime. He had missed his crackers. She had been waiting up to apologize (and hoping he would apologize too) and she had (but he hadn't).

Since then, he had barely spoken to her.

Each of the beds had a little bedside table next to it with a single drawer. It was one of the only things they had that was exclusively theirs. Tentatively, she slid Peter's open.

Comics. It was full of them. But not shop-bought; these comics were homemade. *He is an artist*, she thought with pleasure. It almost made up for the smell of socks and sweat. The windows were closed. There was no air in the room. Billy's and Barry's beds were unmade. Alex's alone was pristine. So much about their personalities there; and Peter's was a tangled web.

He hadn't shown her these comics. But yes, he was talented, no doubt about it. She rummaged through the pile of paper, feeling for the pages underneath. She sensed it wouldn't be the top pages that would be the most interesting. She took one out.

That first line made her start. The picture—a boy who looked like Peter, only desperate with despair and fear. And next to him, the words in a bubble:

Stop it. You're hurting me. No. I don't want to. No.

And suddenly Clara knew. The knowledge flooded her all at once. She knew Peter's ailment. It was his Thursday-night visits. She read on.

A living relative. Peter had been delivered to his uncle's every week. They might as well have served him up on a plate. She wrung her hands. She didn't know what to do.

And where was Peter now? A creeping, soaking fear filled her. She had told him to get out the other day. What if he had run away today?

He wasn't in the kitchen, the bathroom or the garden.

She found him in the parlor, lying on the sofa with his eyes closed. Was he asleep or pretending?

"Peter."

He buried his face in a cushion. He was suddenly small, pale and unreachable, a pebble on the beach. How could she not have known? All these months, she had been merrily dispatching him there, sending him out to sea. All those months, he hadn't said. *She* hadn't asked. All those months, she thought he was "getting on rather well" and had been wondering, "Is his uncle ready to take him on full-time?"

"Peter, talk to me."

He wouldn't. He ignored her.

"Peter, Peter." As if saying a name could fix a problem. "I know what's been happening to you."

She could feel a change in the air. Electricity. The lump on the sofa that was Peter did not move, but that in itself seemed to speak volumes. Silence. She could hear the children out in the garden. Saturday morning outside. She would be called up to wicket soon. Or to play jacks.

"I read your...comic."

"I won't talk about it!" he snarled.

"I don't want you to talk about it," Clara lied. She did, of course, she did. She wanted to know everything. She wanted to know what she was dealing with here. How bad was it? She dared not touch him now. He had become vividly illuminated to her in his agony. She had not seen the true Peter before, he had been "one of the children." Now he was before her as someone who had been explicitly wronged.

On her watch.

"Just nod yes or no. That's all you have to do."

Deep breath.

"Is it your uncle? Does he hurt you?"

Nothing. And then after maybe twenty seconds or so, that tousled head under the cushion moved up and down. It was ever so slightly, but it was enough. Clara wanted to howl. *Her boy. Her boy had been hurt.*

"Don't tell anyone," he hissed. "Ever. Promise."

The ripple that went through her was like nothing she'd experienced before. Other things she had dealt with were in the daylight, but this, this was in the darkness.

Keep cool, keep cool.

Fortunately, it was Miss Cooper who answered the phone at the council and not Miss Bridges, who might have dug further. Perhaps Miss Cooper wasn't as worldly as she thought she was.

"Peter has left his schoolbag at his uncle's. I'll just pop round there and get it." Clara paused. She surprised herself at how easily she lied. "They get in trouble at school if they don't have all their stuff."

The little extra detail always did it.

Clara could hear Miss Cooper opening drawers, then leafing through papers. Clara's heart was racing. The damn paperwork. "Ah, here it is, yes—Woodfield Road, twenty-four. Got that? Okay, Miss Newton. Hope Peter doesn't get in trouble."

Hard to say what Clara was thinking when she went there. She wasn't thinking anything clearly. She was remembering how she had wound up here in Lavenham: a small advertisement in the *Evening Standard*. An offer of accommodation. A sweet nut of a salary. A job to get her away from her father. A test run of an interview.

This is why the changes, Ivor.

These are children here, children's lives.

Peter's uncle wasn't home. Afterward, Clara was relieved he hadn't been there—what on earth would she have said or done if he was?—but at the same time she was furious.

The aching protectiveness and sense of failure she felt toward Peter overwhelmed her. She could think of nothing else. Peter was not a baby, but a nearly independent young man. She loved them all dearly. But Peter. Oh, Peter. She didn't know what it was—that he reminded her of herself at that age, the hesitancy, the quiet unshowy kindness, or perhaps because he looked a little like Michael as a teen might have done, too tall for his own good, that bright carrot-top head. She wanted to sling a protective cape around his narrow shoulders. There was something about his features, his narrow frame, that made him different from the rest of the world—and she had let him down.

She could not be more appalled with herself. Waving Peter off like that week after week. Occasional flirtatious chats with the uncle as he tanned his elbow out of the driver's-seat window. Oh! Clara turned crimson at a memory: once he had asked how she managed looking after eight children and she had giggled, "You need a firm hand, that's all." Sometimes, when Peter got back, she had dreaded the morose tone of his boots in the kitchen and she had told him, "Put a smile on your face," or worse, "Cheer up, it hasn't happened yet."

She should die from shame. What had she been thinking? Call herself a housemother! She was complicit—if not by design, certainly by stupidity.

She had to talk to someone at the council. Another telephone call. Miss Cooper was now out with prospective adopters. Miss Bridges was at cemeteries. Some people were camping next to the graves and she'd gone to move them on.

Clara was passed around, until she found herself speaking to Mr. Sommersby, the actual head of children's services. She gulped.

"Shilling Grange, is it? Hello, Miss Newton. How's Mr. White? Did he tell you we were in the Home Guard together?"

"He did." She paused. "Thank you, he's well."

"What can I do you for?" he continued jovially.

"I...I have a child who doesn't want to see his living relative anymore. However, since he's nearly fifteen, I think we should respect his decision."

Mr. Sommersby sighed. "We're the adults, Miss Newton, we make the decisions."

"It's complicated but I feel the decision is the right one."

I'm not going to cry, I'm not. Please don't be kind.

Fortunately, Mr. Sommersby was not kind.

"Bring him in next week, fill in some paperwork. Sign a consent form."

"I have to bring him in?" Clara doubted Peter would agree.

"Yes, he has to be here."

"Right."

"It's just protocol. It can be done in minutes."

"Really?" This was a relief. And completely unexpected. "It's not...an unusual...request?"

"It's unusual but it's not unheard of."

"Great." She remembered taking Billy and Barry to the council offices after they had run away. That had been fine but this felt different.

"Looking forward to December, are we?"

"December?"

"Your wedding?"

Clara made the right noises before she hung up. There was something to be said for being on the side of the powerful ones. It was certainly better than the alternative.

CHAPTER THIRTY-SEVEN

On the wedding preparations rolled, like a Sherman tank mowing down everything in its path. It wasn't until December, for goodness' sake, but there was so much to organize. Julian took such an interest in all the details. Clara should have known, after all the fuss with the engagement party, but it was still surprising. He certainly wasn't one of those "leave it to the bride" types. (Michael had been! Michael was "whatever you want, sweetheart, is fine by me.")

Julian did make some funny decisions though.

"Mrs. Garrard will do the flowers. I know you don't like her, but she is awfully good."

"It's not that I *dislike* her, it's just she doesn't like me."

Julian chortled, "Well, she likes *me*."

"What's that mean?"

"Goodness, Clara. You *are* on edge today."

She *was* on edge. Ever since the Peter revelations—it was like a gray cloud obliterating everything.

And it wasn't just Peter she was worried about. Every single child was a concern for her now. What else had she missed? Some of the worries were old and worn, almost comfortable ones: Peg not speaking before or since the "cows" incident, Terry and her love of short trousers, Rita and her lament for her mama. These had become classic anxieties that Clara carried around with her permanently. Then there were the newer worries: the twins' lack of progress, how to afford Alex's new school uniform. As one worry subsided, others came into view. The inside of her head felt like a cuckoo clock sometimes.

Julian tried to interest her in some wedding menus—*Mrs. Wesley thinks duck, but it can be fatty*—but gave up before they got to dessert.

"I'll be fine soon," Clara reassured him, "I just want to get the council meeting with Peter out of the way and then I'm all yours."

"I wonder if Shilling Grange will *ever* be out of the way."

Clara was beginning to feel the same. Two failures now (because she hadn't forgotten Maureen, of course she hadn't). Probably more that were brewing. She had known she wasn't up to it ten months ago. And then, foolishly, she had thought she could make a difference. Well, it turned out she had made a difference, but not necessarily for the better.

Oh, Peter.

Clara began to regret agreeing to December. It wasn't as far away as she'd imagined, 21 December, the shortest day—or as Julian liked to say, with one eyebrow peaked, "the longest night." She should have stuck to summer or autumn 1950—but when she said maybe she'd rather be a June bride, Julian said relax, he'd take care of everything and Clara was a woman who looked divine in all seasons.

The issue was Clara didn't know what she was going to do after the wedding. The council would expect her to resign. Married women rarely stayed on in employment. Although he denied it, Julian probably expected it of her too. Ideally, she would continue as she was now for some months or perhaps share the job with another housemother, although she had no idea if this was a possibility or not. All suggestions seemed to involve walking away from the children but Clara was convinced there must be a way around that and she would find it.

Julian was already asking if she'd applied to get the week after the wedding off for their honeymoon in Bath. (Julian was sure she would love the Regency architecture—he was so thoughtful.)

She had not.

"For someone who likes getting everything down on paper, you're being remarkably lackadaisical about this, Clara!"

"All in good time," she said, but the thought of writing a request for time off right now was enough to make her head spin. What would Peter think, she asked herself. She couldn't abandon him now.

The wedding would be in All Saints Church. Julian promised her that the vicar there was charming and not at all pompous. Clara felt skeptical about this because Julian's version of not pompous was not the same as anyone else's, but in fact, the vicar *was* lovely and welcoming, and most importantly, he didn't scold Clara about the children's poor, that is, virtually non-existent, church attendance.

And yes, the church was beautiful and no, it didn't make her feel like an outsider.

The service would be followed by a reception back in Lavenham at the Cloth Hall, Julian's favorite place. Clara was not to worry about the rationing ("we have ways"); Mrs. Wesley was working on the cake—three tiers, icing, the lot. Clara was only to worry about making sure she was there. Looking—

"Marvelous, yes, Julian. I've got the message."

"Write it down then." He winked.

Clara had had some input into the music: a five-piece swing band from Norfolk. And *some* input into the photographer—

"Who do you want?"

"As long as it's not the man from the *Suffolk Times*—Maurice Selby, was it?—I don't mind."

"Ah."

"Julian?!"

"He's a friend of mine."

"You didn't say!"

"What *could* I say...? You were in such a fury, you wouldn't have listened to a word I said."

And the more Clara tried not to think about the wedding she had once planned with Michael, the more it intruded on her thoughts. This was a very different wedding indeed—well, naturally; not only was Julian a different man, but she was a different woman to the one she was back then.

"Can I see the guest list this time?"

"I have the list in here." Julian tapped his head, infuriatingly.

"I just want it written down."

"What difference does it make?"

Did it matter that she hadn't even heard of half the people coming?

Sir Munnings was coming though. "*I wouldn't miss the nuptials of my favorite person*," he wrote in his RSVP—at least she thought he did, his writing was worse than Alex's. (Julian was convinced the "my favorite person" meant him.)

"I have it on best authority that Sir Munnings' gift is going to be a painting," Julian told her.

"Not of a horse?"

"What else?"

Clara was going to say something about looking a gift horse in the mouth, but Julian had moved on to the wedding cars.

Judy was coming too. "I wouldn't miss it for the world," she said, but Clara didn't trust her because of the engagement party. "Will Alex be there?" Judy asked.

All the children were coming. Clara wasn't going to make the same mistake twice. And she wanted to give them roles too, although she hadn't worked out what yet. Everything was up in the air. You couldn't plan—Clara didn't feel like she could trust herself to decide anything.

Although perhaps the girls could be flower girls? Terry would hate that—perhaps she could be a pageboy? *What does a pageboy even do?* Maureen would have been a gorgeous chief bridesmaid. Perhaps this could tempt her back—only there was no way of telling her; she had not been heard of or seen since she vanished. Some of the children would love to perform—Rita especially, and the twins—but there were others who hated an audience. And then what would she do with the silent Peg?

She would like to ask Peter to give her away. Yes, she would do that. Give the boy something to focus on.

Julian's best man was going to be the creepy Mr. Browne. Clara said she was dreading his speech.

"How do you think I feel?" Julian countered.

Clara didn't know. There was a lot she didn't know about Julian, but she rather liked that. What was the point of knowing everything about someone upfront? It would be like reading the end of a book first. Where's the mystery? Where's the exploration in all that?

Anyway, she knew enough: he loved her.

And it worked both ways. He didn't know that she and Michael had been engaged or that she had been planning to go to America. He didn't know that her parents had abandoned her. He didn't know because he hadn't asked. She'd tell him all about it one day. It's good to be able to surprise each other.

She had already been to a dressmakers in Dedham. Glorious to think about a dress without the worry of coupons. While she admired the women who had made do and mended their wedding dresses during the war years—for Judy's wedding, Judy, her mother and her mother's friends had saved their coupons and the gown had been absolutely gorgeous; she remembered Arthur had cried—it was fortunate not to have to do the same.

Everything was going to be wonderful.

"It's more than I deserve."

That made Julian laugh. "No one gets what they deserve in this life."

"Don't they?"

They had been due to go out for a lunchtime ale, but Julian

said something important had come up. For a moment, Clara was suspicious. Julian had never given her cause to doubt him before, in that way, but now she sensed something shady about him. She made a face.

"Just work, darling, honestly."

"If you're sure."

There *was* something, but she supposed it was another thing to do with the wedding. He liked surprising her, that was all.

"I have a problem," Clara told Ivor when she nervously dropped in at his workshop on the way home. (She was never sure how receptive he would be nowadays.) "Peter needs to go to the council with me, to sign a few forms, but he is saying he won't."

Ivor looked up, confused.

"It's no big deal." Clara coughed, self-consciously. "It's just he doesn't want to see his uncle anymore and he needs to make that clear."

"If it's no big deal, why won't he do it?"

Clara couldn't say. She tried to make that clear with her expression.

Ivor chewed his lip. He didn't understand, but that was the thing about Ivor, he'd still try his best.

"So...Okay...Do you want me to talk to him?"

That was pretty receptive. "Please."

Later, Clara stood by the kitchen window watching Terry making daisy chains in the garden. Peg was playing jacks under the kitchen table, Rita was studying her face in the mirror, Alex was poring over the human skeleton in his book and the twins were wrestling.

Peter was in the parlor with Ivor.

Clara expected Ivor would be back within moments—Peter was hardly communicative at the best of times—but he didn't return for an hour or so. Clara had all the questions but decided not to ask them. There was only one that was important.

"Will he come?"

Ivor shrugged. "He's thinking about it."

"Oh, that's better than nothing, I suppose."

"I talked to him about how I got this." Blushing, Ivor patted the nub of his arm.

"Ah." Clara reddened. She always did when it was mentioned. It was the elephant in her mind. The twenty men he saved at Dunkirk. The medals. She realized he had never told her anything about it, not once.

"I've said I'll come along too, for moral support, if that's all right?"

Clara was going to say, "There's no need, it's just paperwork," but she liked the suggestion: it would be better if Ivor were there.

"Thank you."

"Peter *will* get over this." Ivor's cheeks were coloring again. "Whatever it is. He will recover and move on. He has a great sense of self. In the long run, it will help."

Clara felt a lump in her throat. *Oh, Ivor. He understands.*

"And in the short run?"

"In the short run, it is going to hurt. But he'll get through. He has a lot of people around him who love him: the other children, you, me. All of us on his side."

Us. Such a tiny word for something so powerful.

Clara was almost overcome by the sensation of wanting to kiss him. She immediately told herself not to be so daft. She was just getting confused by all the upset. Ivor wasn't her man. She had a winter wedding to Mr. White, solicitor, to plan. Nineteen fifty was going to be her best year yet. It was the year she would put the war, the grief and all the turmoil of the last few years behind her. She was going to be Mrs. White and this was a position of absolute privilege—think of the way Mr. Sommersby had been with her on the telephone! The idea that she would jeopardize it just for a thank-you kiss, well, *that* was ridiculous. Imagine what Anita Cardew would say. It was easy to mix up gratitude with attraction. They might look similar, they might act interchangeably, but they were very different beasts.

Later that evening, Peter sloped into the kitchen and pinched a cracker from a plate. He wouldn't meet Clara's eyes. When she asked him how he was, he addressed the floor.

"I asked you not to tell anyone."

Clara wanted to set him straight—she had not told Ivor the specifics, she had not betrayed him… Never. But it must have cost a lot for Peter to say even that.

"I didn't tell him much and I won't. But you will go to the council and sign the paperwork, Peter, promise? It's really no—"

"Big deal," he echoed. "So they say. All right, I will."

CHAPTER THIRTY-EIGHT

Peter, Ivor and Clara would leave at half past ten. Miss Bridges had offered to take them in her car. Clara had never before been driven by Miss Bridges—or any woman, come to that—and part of her was actually looking forward to it.

It was just before ten when she heard a clattering, then footsteps in the garden and a knock at the back door. She swung it open, expecting Miss Bridges even though it was early and even though Miss Bridges usually came to the front. It wasn't Miss Bridges, but a crouching young man in a cap pulled low over dark features. Clara *kind of* recognized his face but she wasn't sure where she knew it from.

"Can I help you?"

"Miss." His voice was surprising gravelly, like he had stones in his throat. "It's Maureen."

"Maureen?" Now she knew who he was. She had last seen him sauntering down the stairs, blowing kisses, when she had thrown him out of the girls' room. "Where is she?"

He pointed out to where the trees were at their densest. "There. Can I bring her in?"

"Oh my. *Maureen?*"

What a state the poor girl was in. She was writhing, bent double, clutching her stomach. Her hair was wild. Her eyes were fearful. She stumbled across the garden, then grabbed onto Clara.

"Oh, Miss Newton!" she said through tears.

She was bleeding too. Clara saw red blotches on her skirt.

"Oh, darling, you need the hospital."

"I want to come home," Maureen wept.

Clara led Maureen up to her own room and her own bed. She ran around frantically looking for a blanket, sanitary towels, a jug of water and an aspirin.

Moments later, Clara heard a knock and the front door opening. Voices. Peter must have let Miss Bridges in.

"Don't tell anyone I'm here," Maureen hissed. "Please, Miss Newton. No one must know. Please. We will get in so much trouble."

"It's only the woman from—"

"NO."

"She'll want to help you, Maureen. We all do."

"I will run away again if you tell anyone. No one must know."

Clara wiped her sweaty face. "But I'm going to have to call Dr. Cardew."

"No," insisted Maureen, then, still writhing in pain, "No one must know, or we go."

The boy stood behind, no sign of cockiness now. He took off his cap and wrung it silently between his fingers.

Miss Bridges was chatting with Peter in the kitchen and they both looked up expectantly when Clara came in. And then Ivor was there too, looking like a different Ivor, a dapper and professional version, in his suit. Clara knew he hated dressing smartly and her heart melted that he had gone to this effort. He was smiling encouragement at them all.

"Everyone ready?"

"I'm afraid there's been a..." murmured Clara. *What had there been?* "A setback."

"What? What's wrong?"

"It's fine. I've just got something important to do here."

Ivor was briefly lost for words. She watched him swallow, think, then say damningly, "More paperwork, Clara?"

"Not paperwork, just … I have to stay behind."

"Is this a joke?"

"No, you go ahead with Miss Bridges and I'll catch you all up in a taxi soon as I can."

Poor Peter had turned an agonized crimson beneath his freckles. Ivor was doing some side-to-side thing with his jaw.

"It's thirty minutes away. We need to get going now." He stood at the door ushering them. "Come on, everyone. Clara!"

"I can't."

"Of course you can."

He was trying not to show how furious he was, but it was quite clear.

"I will be there as soon as I can. You've got to trust me, Ivor. It's just signing the consent forms, that's all. A mutual agreement."

"This is the second time you've let them down. I knew it. I knew you'd never understand what it's like."

Peter put his hands over his ears. Miss Bridges was delving into her handbag, pretending not to listen.

Two times? He was still counting the Alex thing? Or did he mean Maureen? And was two times supposed to be a large number? What did he know about being relied on every single day, every single moment of a life? All he had to worry about was inanimate objects—his curtains and cushions—she was the one who was exhausted with carrying all the children. And she had to get back upstairs.

"You're not being fair."

"*I'm* not being fair?"

He stormed out of the back door, slamming it so hard the hanging cups trembled. Miss Bridges and Peter gave Clara limp smiles, then followed him out.

Once Clara heard the car had gone, she didn't go upstairs, but dashed down the street to the doctor's surgery. With each thud of her feet pounding on the pavement, she was thinking, *I can't cope with this, I can't.*

Clara was relieved when Dr. Cardew answered the door. She didn't want to have to go through Anita. Not today.

"It's Maureen. She's...she's in a terrible state. A miscarriage, I think."

"She's alone?"

"There's some boy with her, in my room. Can you come?"

"You go. I'll bring the car."

They arrived back at the Grange around the same time. Dr. Cardew raced in with his bag of tricks. He knew where to go, he'd been on enough call-outs before.

Maureen was thrashing around on Clara's bed, crying. The boy was uselessly petting her hair. "Everything goes wrong for me. I'm no good," she cried out.

Dr. Cardew took one look at her then said to Clara, "She needs the hospital."

To Maureen, he said, "Come on, Maureen, I'm taking you in."

But Maureen would not go. She would stay here. She would rather die than move, she said. Dr. Cardew took control, thank goodness. He crouched on the floor beside her, stethoscope dangling to his knees, and told her if she didn't go soon, she might well die and that would be on his conscience and Miss Newton's conscience forever and they might even go to prison for not helping her.

Clara wasn't convinced of this, nor was Maureen. *Thank goodness for the boy.*

"You'll be all right now, Mo," he said. "Listen to them. Hospital is the best place for you."

"You've got to come with me," Maureen cried.

"No," said Dr. Cardew, as though it were all decided. "He'll come tomorrow, right, son?"

The boy agreed. He kissed Maureen on the forehead and backed out of the room. Clara thought he might have been glad to get away. Maureen sobbed.

Clara could have hugged Dr. Cardew but after they loaded poor

Maureen into the back of his car, he surveyed her glacially. "You should have called earlier."

"I called as soon as I could."

She thought, *I can go to the council offices now and later I will meet them at the hospital.*

"I have to go to an important meeting," she explained. She didn't want him to think badly of her. "You'll look after her, won't you?"

Dr. Cardew stared at her in amazement. "You have to come." If she had admired his certainty before, now she didn't like it.

"I...will this take long?"

He didn't answer, just got in the driver's seat.

Clara clambered in the back, where Maureen grabbed her hand and wouldn't let her go. Clara gave her a handkerchief and this set her off again.

"I didn't do it on purpose," she moaned and in the rearview mirror Dr. Cardew raised his eyebrows. At first, Clara didn't know what Maureen meant, but then she whimpered, "Your photographs, they tipped off the desk and one smashed on the floor."

"And the files?"

"The files?" Maureen wasn't sorry about this. In a much stronger voice, she said, "You should have shown me them, Miss Newton, you should have. It's my history, not yours. It is my right."

Maureen's grip was so tight now, it felt to Clara as though her bones were being crushed. It was what she deserved.

"I know," she whispered. "I'm sorry, Maureen."

At the hospital, they put Maureen on a trolley and disappeared her down echoing corridors. "I'll be back as soon as I can," Clara called after her. For a moment it was all quiet and sanity, then Clara ran outside.

It's really no big deal, she reminded herself.

By the time she had found an idling taxi and the poor fella had got to Bury St. Edmunds, waited at all those damn red traffic lights and got stuck behind a rag and bone cart, it was too late; of course it was. Clara hadn't noticed it was such a windy day, but now the wind picked up bits of rubbish and threw them along the pavements. There was no sign of Miss Bridges, but Peter and Ivor were emerging from the great stately doors of the council head-quarters. She could see immediately from their tight expressions that it wasn't good.

Peter was paler than a ghost. Even his freckles had gone into hiding. He squatted down by the curbside. He looked like he was going to faint. A man in a bowler hat walked by and stared at him with such disdain, it was heartbreaking. Clara wanted to storm over and put him right.

Neither of them would look at her.

"Get your filing done?" Ivor snapped.

She ignored him.

"What happened in there? Ivor? Peter?"

Ivor's lips were set in a thin line. "They want to force Peter to keep visiting."

"No!"

"His uncle even brought in a solicitor to argue for him."

Peter let out a moaning sound. He had turned himself into a tiny ball on the pavement.

"And who do you think the solicitor was?" Ivor continued.

Clara felt like she was falling. No, she felt like she was being pushed. She knew who it was before he said it.

"It's Mr. White, Clara. Julian is representing Peter's uncle. And there's more. They want to apply for full-time adoption."

Peter threw up into the drains.

CHAPTER THIRTY-NINE

My dear Clara,

Thank you for your honesty with me, I completely understand how difficult it must be.

You are a beautiful young woman with so much potential to give the world. Of course you've moved on. Of course. This is natural. I don't want you stuck in the past like so many of us are. But I would love to stay in touch—if that's not an imposition on you. When I see an envelope with your writing on it, my heart sings, truly!

This Julian White—what a curious name!—is truly one lucky man. Tell him that from me! I hope he treats you how you deserve to be treated.

I feel proud that for a short time, I was able to call you "daughter." I know you will never forget "our Michael." He lives on in us.

Marilyn Adams

CHAPTER FORTY

Maureen was in hospital for three days and she refused to let Clara in for any of them, not one visit. Clara couldn't understand it. *She came to me first, so why won't she see me now?* She tried on the fourth day, Friday, but Maureen had already checked herself out. Dr. Cardew was the only one who knew about Maureen's reappearance but when she pleaded with him to tell her where she had gone, he said, "I can't tell you anything, Clara. Patient confidentiality, you know that."

Dr. Cardew didn't say it outright, but he seemed to think that Maureen had brought it on herself. Girls got judged harshly in this world, Clara realized, especially orphan girls.

"She'll come round eventually," Dr. Cardew said. "In the meantime, she doesn't want you to know where she is. And she has a right to privacy."

"I only want to know she is safe."

Dr. Cardew shrugged.

"And the boy? She let him in, did she?"

Dr. Cardew surprised her. "Joe Parker seems a nice young man. She could do worse."

Ivor was still furious. Clara thought he was avoiding her, which was good—*let him cool down*—but they ran into each other in the street one morning and he wouldn't stop talking.

"I don't understand why you couldn't be there for Peter." It was as though he had rehearsed his side of the conversation many times in his head before. "What were you thinking, Clara?"

Clara grew angry with Ivor too. She was surrounded by know-it-alls. Everyone thought they knew better than her.

"You've got to trust I did what I thought best at the time. Can you do that, Ivor?"

He shook his head.

And Peter, poor Peter, he just carried on, going to school, coming home from school, scrubbing the oven, laying the table quietly and taking baths for so long that the water must have been stone cold. There was something stripped-back about him now, raw and vulnerable. Clara desperately racked her brains to think of some way she could, if not *reward* him, then at least show that she sympathized with him, that she admired him, that she loved him.

In the end, she swapped the coupons she was saving for a pair of sandals for pencils and sketchbooks instead, then divided the pages into squares for comics—for he seemed to struggle with outlines—and left them neatly stacked by his bed.

As for Julian, Clara was burning with rage at him too, but at the same time she was horribly nervous about seeing him again. Would he try to talk his way out of it? His patter could be so charming, his smile so convincing. She *did* feel an irresistible pull toward him: not just him but their wedding plans, his lifestyle, his dog. Their dreams of the future. Everything about him appealed because it was so solid and undramatic. So permanent.

This was dramatic though, but she knew he'd pretend it wasn't.

And even when she knew he wasn't being nice, she still liked being with him. Being with him was comfortable in an uncomfortable world, she was a happy paper doll when she was in nice restaurants and tea rooms—and she hated herself for it.

Maybe he would say he was drunk when he agreed to take the

case. Maybe he'd come up with some other paltry excuse. Maybe she should have bribed him not to, with cushions and tea towels, maybe that's the way things were done here.

Julian was also capable of displaying staggering kindness: the first-edition Jane Taylor volume, the impromptu visit to the cemetery, the frequent cut flowers; so many small things. Wasn't it more likely that he was just a normal man born of human frailty?

But then why this—why would he do this to Peter, to them?

They were supposed to be seeing each other on the Sunday afternoon, but Clara was determined to get it over with before then; so, as any military planner would, she used the element of surprise.

Early on Saturday morning, she stealthily slipped over the road to his place. It was still misty, the grass and the hedges covered in dew. It was Terry's favorite type of morning and, while most of the children were fast asleep, she was already up and working in the garden. She waved at Clara, who waved self-consciously back.

Julian opened the door wearing a short and swirly-patterned housecoat that she'd never seen before—maybe he saved it for when she was not there. It struck her as the housecoat of someone who'd do dastardly things and for a moment, Clara couldn't believe he had ever impressed her. But then Bandit came bounding toward her, brigadier mustache at the welcome, and so warm and lovely. He never failed to melt Clara's heart. And Julian was so good with his dog, patting him and letting him lick his fingers. A man who loves a dog is irresistible.

Almost.

"You look ridiculous." He was all knees and thin white shins. "What *are* you wearing?"

"I'll get you one if you like. We could match. Well, this is a surprise, sweetheart. To what do I owe the pleasure?"

He smelled of last night's whisky and week-old cigars. Men's clubs and gambling halls in London. Or places with dancing women. Perhaps he *was* the sort after all, he was just better at covering it up than most.

He certainly didn't notice how angry she was with him. Pulling her into the hallway, he murmured, "Come to bed, Miss Newton, you know—"

"Get off me."

Peter's weary face, the tears pooling in his sad eyes, the trembling fingers. He had turned from a boy on the cusp of adulthood to a small and frightened creature. *Dear God.* He had put his faith in her and she had betrayed him. But Julian was worse.

She wondered if she was experiencing the same sense of fury that, only a few years ago, had propelled the Curtis Act founders to take action on the well-being of children; a feeling of righteous anger absorbed her, compelled and propelled her.

"How can you do this to the boy?"

"What?"

Playing the innocent party like she'd guessed he might. "Get involved. With the Peter thing. With his uncle."

"But you didn't go to the police, Clara?"

Clara stopped short.

"It wasn't a police matter, that's why."

"You should have. For all I know"—Julian was grinning as though this was one of their tit-for-tat tickle games—"you committed unilaterally to withdraw his only family from him. For no stated reason. It wasn't your best move. Legally."

"He's a bully and a..." Clara looked behind her into the street. There was no one there, but she still whispered it, a word she had never said aloud before. Peter would have to forgive her this. "Molester."

At that, Julian let out a yelp of laughter. "Oh, Clara, you can tell *you* never went to public school."

"What?" Bile rising. "What the hell does that mean?"

Julian must have caught the warning in her voice for he proceeded not on those lines but instead said, "You must see how it looks, Clara? You said that Peter could never see him again—you had no right to say that to a living relative!"

This was his *oh-so-reasonable* tone. She knew it well.

Bandit started barking. He couldn't stand a row any more than Clara could. Julian grabbed him by the collar and pulled him into the kitchen out of the way. When he came back, he was grinning. There was nothing he loved more than winning an argument; he'd told her this many times, but when she was on the same side as him it hadn't really mattered.

"Well, he can't see him again."

"He can."

"I just don't get why you are involving yourself in this? It's my work, it's my children and…why are you so against us?"

"I'm not against anyone!" Julian raised his hands in shock. "Definitely not you. Look, here's the thing. Peter's uncle—Mr. Courtney—and I go way back. We belong to the same club."

"What?"

"I don't *like* the man particularly, but the rule of law must prevail. We can't just have…what do they call you again, 'housemothers,' randomly decide who children can and can't see. It would set a dangerous precedent."

"For goodness' sake, Julian!"

At last, Julian seemed surprised at her vehemence. And why wouldn't he? She'd always been quiet as a church mouse with him. He began backtracking.

"That's not the *whole* reason I'm involved. That boy won't stand up in the witness box. You told me yourself he was 'trouble.' Your words, Clara. He stole from me. You said it—he sometimes skips school, he is unreliable. He has *bad blood*."

"I never said bad blood. I've never once used that ugly phrase in my life."

"But the rest of it."

"He abuses him, Julian. How could you ignore that?"

Julian laughed. He was in such an upbeat mood. "How do you *know* that though, Clara? You don't, do you?"

"Oh, we're going to fight this. Mark my words, he will never go to his uncle's again!"

"Look, you're going to be at the Grange, what? Six more months, a year at most. Give it up. I can give you a nice life, I promise. You won't have to mix with these low-lives any more."

It took just a little wiggle to loosen the engagement ring. The ease with which she could remove it said everything.

Julian looked as if he was in shock. He truly was a man used to getting his own way.

"Put it back on."

"No!"

"I'm not going to let some petty criminal come between us."

"*You're* the petty criminal, Julian. I wish I'd never set eyes on you."

"You can't mean this."

"I do."

"Let's get you out of that place. You'll see sense once you're out."

"No, I'm not leaving them. I won't. That's not going to happen."

Julian went quiet, then patted his forehead with his housecoat sleeve and said coldly, "Your father wrote to me, you know. After I wrote to him. He said I could do better than marry a girl like you. Me! He had never even met me before and that's what he said, '*You could do better.*' *Your* father, Clara, his words."

Clara could not let this slide. "You know *nothing* about my father, so don't..."

"He thinks you're a whiny little girl who likes playing the martyr and who has no idea about life in the real world. He said you would let me down—that you let everyone down in the end. I should have listened to him, shouldn't I?"

"My father abandoned me, he dragged my mother to Africa when she didn't want to go and he did not get her the medical attention she required. So, you want to tell me I let *him* down? I don't care."

With that, Clara left Julian and his skinny pale legs in his minuscule dressing gown at the door. This went way beyond normal human frailty. This chapter of her life was over and she was glad. How had she ever let it get so far?

CHAPTER FORTY-ONE

"Pamela Lewis is a gardener, which is why I thought of Terry straight away," said Miss Cooper. "The husband is a bookkeeper. The quiet type. They're an older couple. Early forties. Been through the wars, you know."

Despite Miss Cooper's excitement, Clara felt cynical. It wasn't like Terry's grandmother or Billy and Barry's excursion into "permanent family homes" had met with any success. As for Peter—his disaster was probably a direct consequence of the guidelines that come what may, children do better with their own families.

Sometimes, she wondered at the confidence that people like Miss Cooper or even Dame Myra had in their own decision-making. Was the Children's Act a move in the right direction or was it, as Ivor had always maintained, meddling, tweaking, money-wasting?

Clara still believed in her work, in their work, but she could see the downsides now. And the downsides were that there weren't the resources, nor the people or money to make as much difference as they wanted. And if there weren't enough resources, people or money, then all their ambitious plans were in vain.

"What do you think?"

"Do you want to arrange for them to come over?" Clara asked flatly. Miss Cooper clapped her hands. Clara wondered how she still retained so much enthusiasm for her job.

"I already did. Three o'clock on Friday. Can you see to it that Terry—"

"Looks clean and humble." Clara sighed. "Yes, we know the drill."

Pamela and Harry Lewis had a pot of tea in the garden and a slice of Miss Bridges' fruit cake. Although she hadn't expected to, Clara warmed to them immediately. Pamela was a bony woman who'd clearly made a great effort with her outfit, but was uncomfortable in it. She fiddled with the sleeves of her blouse and pulled at the pearls at her neck. She was like a child dressed up. Clara imagined she'd be far more relaxed in breeches and gardening boots. Harry was a foreign-looking man, with silver threads in his mustache. He was older than early forties. Reading through their notes, Clara saw that they had lost a son in the war and her heart went out to them. Still, she would not be bamboozled by emotions ever again.

"It will be quite something to go back to little children," Clara said.

"I know," Pamela replied shortly. She didn't add anything. She didn't need to. Clara thought, *she does know. I don't need to hammer this home.*

When the children came back from school, Clara intercepted Terry and told her that the someones they had talked about the other day had come to meet her.

"Ones who might want to take me?" The hopeful glow in Terry's eyes was painful to see.

"That's right."

By the time Terry had got cleaned up, Pamela was knee-deep in a flower bed, while Harry was ensconced in a newspaper and smoking a pipe. When they saw Clara and Terry come out, they both jumped to attention.

Pamela wiped her hands on her prim skirt. "I'm so sorry, I can't resist getting mucky. I saw some weeds over there and I just had to get stuck in."

Terry looked her up and down. "I'll get my tools if you like."

She scampered off to the shed and came back with her wheelbarrow and gardening set.

"What beautiful things," Pamela said. She wasn't just trying, she seemed genuinely impressed. "Will you show me around the garden?" she continued, to Terry's obvious delight.

It was lovely, and perhaps all the more lovely since they hadn't expected it. Terry was telling Pamela about her spectacles.

"I have some just like those for reading," Pamela was saying. "I'll show them to you sometime... if you like, that is."

"If we wear them at the same time, we'll look like twins," said Terry.

Harry was smiling indulgently at both of them. He looked over to Clara, who stood holding the tea tray, not sure what to do. She wasn't part of the beautiful group emerging in front of her. It was like watching a butterfly form, it was a transformation. Harry took the tray from her and placed it on the table.

"Thank you."

"Don't thank me," said Clara. "I didn't..."

"You're part of it," he said. "Please take your share of our gratitude. I grew up in a workhouse. Went in with my mother and never saw her again. We can never thank you enough for keeping these children safe."

As his warm hands squeezed hers, tears came to her eyes. It felt as though that was exactly what she hadn't done.

CHAPTER FORTY-TWO

If you had told her one year ago how children's laughter would affect her, Clara would never have believed it. But nowadays, when the children laughed, it warmed her through. This time it was Alex, chortling merrily to himself in the hall. She poked her head round the door to see him cross-legged on the floor, utterly captivated by a pop-up book of dinosaurs.

"Where *did* you get that from?" It wasn't one of the ones from the library. Alex had been through all the children's section and was now on the adults.

"Mrs. Martin sent it," he said. "Oh gosh, this is funny!"

Judy did?

"I didn't know. When did it come?"

"This morning. Here..." He pointed to one of the pictures. "It's a pterodactylus."

"How...kind."

How puzzling! Maybe Judy thought it was Alex's birthday or something. Or maybe Judy would explain on the telephone soon.

On Thursday afternoon, Peter's uncle's car rolled up outside the Grange. If Clara felt frightened, goodness only knew how Peter must have felt, looking out from his room. Clara stormed out into the street. She had to look strong even if she didn't feel it. For once, Peter's uncle had gotten out of his car and was marching toward the house as though all was well in the world.

"Stay away," Clara called, cursing her voice for its giveaway shaking.

"I have a solicitor's order. Peter comes with me."

Peter was now trembling next to her. Clara wished she'd warned him to stay inside. No point him being a witness to this. And he was a shrunken boy now, not strapping anymore but bent in on himself like a wizened old man. How could she have thought this was *just Peter. Just teenage stuff.* She hated herself. If Peter's uncle was a monster, what did that make her for not seeing it?

"If he doesn't come, I will bring this place to its knees." Peter's uncle was brimming over with self-confidence. He pointed to her. "And I will destroy *you.* No question about it."

Clara had no breath inside her. His finger remained fixed on her, as intimidating as he was.

"I'll go with him," whispered Peter. His hair fell over his eyes, but couldn't hide how petrified he was underneath.

"No."

"I . . . I have to."

Peter's uncle was enjoying himself. "I'll make sure you're finished here. All of you."

"You're not going," Clara told Peter firmly. "I won't let you."

But Peter was already making his way toward his uncle. It was as though he were being hypnotized, or tugged along by invisible strings.

"Hurry up," called the uncle, now certain of his triumph. He laughed at Clara. "There's nothing you can do about it."

"Oy!"

Ivor's voice. Ivor. Ivor had come out of his workshop, holding a chair leg, holding it like a weapon. His face was one big angry sneer. She had never seen the soldier Ivor before, or thought much about the hero label he didn't like to wear. Now, he moved like a hunter. He was so still, so stealthy, the air seemed to slow around him.

Clara couldn't take her eyes off him: the lines of his shirt, the braces, the cut of his gray trousers. He was mesmerizing. Him being there made her feel a hundred times safer. All was not lost yet. Forget Julian, Peter's uncle could not possibly win as long as Ivor was on their side. Ivor had saved twenty men. Now he would save one more.

Peter looked between them all. His hands were clenched down by his sides.

Ivor moved toward Peter's uncle. He didn't have the lopsided gait he often had.

But Peter's uncle just laughed. "Look who's here?! Oh, I'm not scared, he's perfectly 'armless." He searched around as though looking for an audience for his barbs. "Suffolk's answer to Douglas Bader."

"It's time you left."

"Where's wifey gone? Yankee Doodle Dandy land, is it? Couldn't keep her satisfied? That's what they say, isn't it?"

"Just go now." Clara was horrified. *Poor Ivor.* "Please."

"He's *my* nephew. He's coming with me."

"Over my dead body." Ivor was now inches away from Peter's uncle's face, the chair leg at shoulder level, ready to strike.

It felt like ages, but was probably only seconds, before Peter's uncle backed clumsily into his car. A slam of the door, then a roar, and the car careened off down Lavenham High Road, its exhaust spitting black fumes. He was shameless. Clara pitied anyone on the road that afternoon.

Clara tried to put her arm round Peter but he wouldn't let her. He pushed her away. He hated to be touched.

"What are we going to do?" His teeth were rattling audibly.

"We're going to get on with our day," she told him. "Go inside now."

A few seconds later, she heard the bath taps running.

Ivor had already turned toward his workshop. Clara called over to him, desperately, "Thank you so much, Ivor. I owe you."

"Put it in your next report."

He didn't even look at her, not once.

Okay, so he was still angry with her.

CHAPTER FORTY-THREE

Judy said they should go out for a pub lunch, then she'd come back to the Grange to see the children. Clara was both surprised and gratified—this was perhaps a sign that Arthur was being less controlling. She could ask Judy about Alex's book too. "I hope you don't mind, but I chose this place because it's famous," Judy explained at the frosted glass door of the Swan Hotel. "It's where the American forces who were based at RAF Lavenham signed their name on the walls before a mission."

Judy had read about it in the newspaper. "It's in the airmen's bar," she said. "And they did a drinking game called a boot challenge too, three and a half pints of ale in as quick a time as possible."

This was a shock to Clara—she hadn't been expecting any of this, and once again, as she had been at the American cemetery, she felt as though she were on the back foot.

Watching her carefully, Judy said, "We don't have to go in, but I thought it might be helpful for your...grief."

Clara hesitated before saying brightly, "Boot challenge, eh? That sounds like Michael!"

It was early in the day and the bar had only just opened, although already a few old men were standing at the counter. Clara joined the wait. Judy went over to the walls, traced them with her fingers as Clara readied herself to order their drinks. Judy looked well, Clara thought approvingly. Maybe Arthur had stuck to his word after all—though she doubted it.

Suddenly Judy called out, "Captain Michael Adams?"

"Yes?"

"It's here, Clara, his name is here."

For a moment, Clara couldn't breathe. The barman put the drinks in front of her with a paper menu. His face was sympathetic. She took the glasses over to Judy, trying to keep herself steady. She pictured herself dropping them to the floor and everyone making a fuss.

"Here. See…"

CAPTAIN MICHAEL ADAMS

In capital letters, bold and unfussy—just like him. He had been here. There was nothing there about her, of course, silly to hope there might have been. This was *his* big moment. He would have been off to work and he probably went completely into himself in the way she'd heard women who are about to give birth do.

"Oh, darling," said Judy gently as a sob escaped Clara. "Is it too much? I hope it's not too much, I just wanted to help."

Poor Michael, so full of life; sometimes it was impossible to imagine he was not alive. His notes were in her files in her room. Funny little doodles of planes and parachutes. Proper love letters. Although it was too painful to read them, she would never let them go.

How had he sat here—where she was right now—knowing he faced possible death?

Judy had everything prepared. She got out some fine paper and a pencil and helped Clara do a rubbing of his name. Tears dropped down her nose.

"I'll send one to Marilyn," Clara said, though the thought of that lonely lady across the ocean, examining that thin paper with the last writing from her only son, made her weep.

She was still crying as she sat with Judy on the red velvet bench. And as she cried, she remembered how Judy had always been there, she'd always been that shoulder for Clara to cry on, and that made her cry even more. Judy was such a good person.

"Michael would want you to move on," said Judy now, her hand on Clara's shoulder. And although the *what Michael would have wanted* line usually rubbed Clara up the wrong way, it didn't when it came from Judy. Judy knew Michael; and besides, it was true. He had once told her so himself. They were walking home having their usual argument about whether it was "cinema" or "movies." And he said, "If anything happened to me…" and she had hated the conversation so much, she had just said, "Nothing will."

Move on.

"Although not necessarily with Julian."

They burst out laughing and the barman looked over in surprise. Clara didn't tell Judy that it was Ivor Delaney who was increasingly on her mind, not Julian. Nor mention how quickly Julian had slipped out of view. Judy probably had guessed it though: it wasn't that Julian was a bad egg—well, he was, it was more that he wasn't the man for her.

"Don't cry, Clara. You picked yourself up before, you'll pick yourself up again."

"I'm crying because I'm going to miss Bandit."

More laughter. Clara remembered the time she and Judy had picked themselves up after a terrible night in the shelter. Walking across London, in streets that had been freshly bombed. They had found a leg sticking up from the rubble. Judy used to carry a whistle and she had whistled with all her might. It was awful. The ambulance workers had come and dug up the leg and it was a doll, nothing more than a child's doll. They hadn't stopped talking about it for weeks.

Scotch egg, ham, egg and chips, or pork chops.

Fingers crossed, thought Clara, it would be done well. She had been spoiled by all those nice restaurants recently. Julian would have chosen chops.

"I have something to tell you," Judy said suddenly. "I…Oh, Clara, I've been really down."

It all came tumbling out. Judy and Arthur had been trying for a baby and it hadn't happened. They hadn't even had a near-miss, not even a far-miss—just nothing. Ever since they had been married. Over three years now.

The dread Judy felt every month was just unbearable. It was like the dread of the air raid sirens, she said, but so devastatingly lonely too.

And she had just got her monthlies again, only yesterday. She had never hated her body in her entire life as much as she did now. It was destroying her.

"Why didn't you tell me?" Clara's first reaction was shame. She knew it shouldn't be—she should be more Judy-focused—but it was. She had leaned on Judy for all these years. It hurt that she had not provided a warm enough shoulder for her friend to cry on. The confidences, the comfort had all gone one way—and this said to Clara that they were not friends, not in the way she had thought they were.

"We *are* equal," Judy insisted. "You know I just don't like leaning on anyone."

"Not even me?" Clara felt choked.

"Not *anyone*. Not you, not Mum or Dad, not Arthur." More tears. "And it's a weakness of mine. I envy you, because you manage to ask for help."

Clara snorted. "I have to ask for help because I'm consistently in hot water."

"No, you do it because you are strong. You've always been able to do that and I've admired you for it—if you aren't good at something, you'll just move on or get someone else to do it. But me? I try to be good at everything and it cripples me, Clara, it does. I try to be perfect at everything—I try to appear perfect and I can't…I'm useless."

Judy thinks she is useless!

"You're not useless, Judy, don't say that."

"I can't even make a baby with my own husband. After all these years of trying."

"Oh, Judy, I had no idea."

"After everything he went through, I can't give him that. That one thing that could help heal us."

Oh, Judy.

"Conceiving is such a strange word, isn't it? A con, that's how it feels. I thought it would be easy and it isn't. And I'm a hateful person because I'm so jealous, I'm so angry with those people, those parents for whom it comes so easy and then it's easy to walk away. Like...like some of the parents of the children at the Grange."

"You are the loveliest person I know, don't hate yourself over a few bad thoughts. We all have them."

I should know.

"It's awful. Every single month, I hope and I pray and then nothing. How could my body fail me like this?"

"So, what do the doctors say?"

"'Keep trying.' It's been nearly four years, Clara. How long can I keep trying for?"

She threw her arms round Clara, her body trembling with emotion. Clara smelled the shampoo in her hair. Her best friend was going through agony and she hadn't known. This was a journey they hadn't been on together. No wonder their friendship had struggled.

"It's like we went through the war, all those years, and now I'm having my own private war. And I don't know which is worse. I look back on those days like they were the good old days and that makes me feel terrible because of all the dead."

"Judy, you can't help how you feel."

"It's wrong though. It's not a war, it's my stupid, stupid womb."

"I'm so sorry. If there's anything I can do to help, ever, let me know."

Clara would remember that moment forever, for the sun shafting through the window, catching Judy's golden hair like in an old Dutch painting. Then the barman came over and said, "Who's the Scotch egg?" and Clara put up her hand like she was in a classroom.

After they had admired how wonderful the food looked, Judy unraveled the cutlery from its scarlet napkin, then said in a serious voice: "Actually, Clara, there is one thing you can do."

"Anything, Judy, you know that."

"It's Alex. I think he's wonderful."

Clara cut through the orange bread crumbs surrounding the egg, smiled. It was a beautiful dish—a work of art. This was a great place—no wonder Michael used to come here.

"He is, rather. They all are, but he is special."

"Would you consider us for adopting him? Would you recommend us?"

Clara's heart plummeted. *Arthur. Arthur and Alex?*

"I've been thinking about it for some time," Judy went on. "Well, ever since I met him. No, since before that probably! Since I first heard you talk about him. It was like love *before* first sight, I just knew he was for me."

Judy set her knife and fork down again. Clara felt bewildered. She gulped. The yolk on her plate peered back at her.

"He's going to the grammar school in Ipswich, Judy. He's just got in and he's so excited, you know this."

Clara was floundering. She knew Judy was fond of Alex, but this? She hadn't expected this in a million years.

Judy's eyes were shining with possibility and she seemed animated and alive, more alive than Clara had seen her for a long time. She was like pre-married Judy. She was hopeful and she was excited.

"That's the thing. There is a grammar school near us, you know. The King John School is terrific, very high-performing. With his results, Alex could transfer across easily. I've already spoken to them. And we could help him—his science, his interest in the world, you know how curious he is. It would be a fresh start, for him and for us."

"Oh, Judy!"

Judy had spoken to a school?

Clara tried to order her thoughts. She remembered another night, when she and Judy had run to a shelter to be told to move on, there was no room. Bombs falling. The same confusion. Judy had known a place though, Judy always knew somewhere they could run and hide.

And Judy was going on. "I know this sounds crazy, but I feel like it's destiny, *he's* our destiny. You know my brother's middle name was Howard and so is Alex's? I know you're not superstitious, but it means something, see. It's another sign. And you know how I feel about dinosaurs—I always spend half a term on them, do you remember the papier mâché I did? I love that stuff. Think what I could do for him."

"I know," Clara said quietly.

More people were coming into the pub now. Not tourists like them, but locals who knew the barman's name: Matthew. Sweet name, suited him. She kept her fingers in the crevices in the table where once Michael might have sat. She held on to it like she used to grip his hand.

"So, what do you say?"

"I don't know."

"Well, that's okay. Just think about it for a few days then let me know."

Clara looked at her friend's excited face. She remembered her eye—both eyes. The sunset color of the bruises. Her ankle. *Silly sausage, it's nothing.* The migraines she wouldn't see a doctor about. The lies she had to tell her husband just to see her oldest friend.

Gently, Clara tried, "I don't think I can."

"What?"

"Put you forward for adoption. I don't think that's something I could do."

Immediately, Judy's face snapped shut like blackout curtains. A tremor went through Clara.

"Why not?"

"You know why, Judy," Clara whispered. "You *know*."

"Arthur would never hurt a *child*." Judy was hissing now.

"Judy…"

"He wouldn't. I know him. I trust him."

"But he might," Clara said lamely. Ridiculous trying to eat through this conversation; she pushed her plate away from her. "He wouldn't, you don't meet the criteria."

"I wish I hadn't told you. I wish I hadn't told you anything."

Clara wished she hadn't too. Six months ago, she was blissfully oblivious. But he had even managed to hurt Judy when Clara was there, sleeping nearby. That was bold, wasn't it? That was wrong. And yet part of Clara wasn't sure. Maybe that was normal behavior after the war. Maybe she was being foolishly idealistic again. The person she'd usually ask about things like this was Judy…

"So other people can have a baby without meeting 'requirements' but Arthur and I can't. Is that it?"

Clara bit her lip. "I can't bend the rules for you."

"I know how the system works. It *doesn't* work. No one cares about individual children. It's dog eat dog out there, you know it, I know it."

"It's not up to me though," Clara said. "I couldn't send him to you even if I wanted to."

As the words tumbled out, she prayed, *please don't pick up on that, please don't.*

Of course, Judy, wily as a fox, as an *injured* fox, would. "But you *don't* want to, am I right? After all these years—you *don't* want to. They sell babies in the newspapers, you know that? They send them all over the place to anyone. It's a booming business. And you're acting all high and mighty with me!"

They were closer than sisters. Judy's parents had been like a mother and father to her. Tea after work on Fridays, a quick clothes wash here, a snack there. They *saved* her. Not her life, but her mind. A warm family home after her own parents had left her.

And now she couldn't save Judy. Or wouldn't.

But she couldn't send a child from the home to him. She couldn't. She wouldn't. She might be wrong on this—but even if she was, she couldn't do it. The barman, Matthew, approached, confounded by the plates still stacked with food. "Is there anything wrong?"

"Not with the food," snapped Judy.

"It's lovely." Clara met his eye, attempted a soothing smile. "We're just not hungry anymore."

"I'll leave them with you for a bit, shall I?"

Won't he let us alone? Clara straightened her hand so it was palm down on the table. It was as if Michael was pulsing through it. Breathing through her. Michael. *What would he have said?*

"Thank you." She forced a smile and he walked away.

"What's with them?" someone asked him. *Does everything have to be commented on?*

"They wouldn't ask, Clara. And there is nothing to tell anymore anyway. All that is over now."

"I'd *have* to tell them."

"No, you wouldn't. Why would you want to be so cruel? After everything I've done for you. Is it money you want? Is that it?"

The whole conversation was out of the blue, but this was even more left-field.

"Never!"

"Oh, I *bet* it is. You're always wanting things for the home, I bet that's what it is."

"It isn't, Judy, why are you saying this? You know it's not about money."

"I could get a child, any child, from anywhere, but we want Alex and I could give him a good home, the best kind of home. And you know it too."

Clara couldn't reply.

"We could pay you."

"No."

"We'll go somewhere else then. He's special and I know it would work but he's not the only boy in the world. And you're not my only friend."

Judy stood up. In one swift movement, she grabbed her bag and her coat and headed toward the exit. Clara could see silhouettes outside the frosted glass. She got up and followed her friend. She had wanted to say goodbye to Michael's writing properly, but this was important.

"Please, Judy, be reasonable."

Judy was still shaking—in fury or disbelief, it wasn't clear.

"I can't believe you'd put your job over me."

"It's not a job, Judy, it's much more than that."

"Don't forget who helped get you your job. Me. I did. You've got such a short memory."

"No, Judy. *You* have." Even as she said it, Clara knew she would regret it, for as long as she lived. "Don't walk into any doors on the way out."

CHAPTER FORTY-FOUR

The children were disappointed not to see Judy.

"I thought—" began Billy but Clara made a gesture of zipping her lips and he piped down.

As Clara walked through the country lanes with some of the children later that afternoon, she went over and over the conversation. Each time, she was sure she had made the right decision. She remembered the Curtis Report, their goals and the childcare revolution. Protecting children came first, above all else. You couldn't send your jam jar to any old larder.

Alex babbled about the school trips offered at his new school, "all the museums, Miss Newton!" a subject that made Clara wince— even more so today. Peg ran ahead, dancing. Rita picked buttercups and made everyone check if they liked butter. Terry thumped iron railings with a stick. As he walked past them, from behind his hand, Mr. Garrard muttered, "Hello, Miss Newton, hello, children." This was progress, Clara supposed. A few yards behind him, holding Bertie the dog close as though they might be wanting to attack him, Mrs. Garrard averted her eyes.

When they passed Ivor's workshop, the children shrieked greetings and Ivor called back, but he didn't include Clara's name like he usually did. A quiet evening with leftovers pie. Vegetables ready for tomorrow's lunch. A quick cleanup with Terry. Times-tables practice for Rita, who did them aloud, and Peg, who wrote them down. Peter had another bath. Billy and Barry practiced making farting noises with their elbows. Rita asked to try on Clara's makeup and Clara was too tired to resist. Then Billy and Barry went to their room and thumped a ball against the wall. For the millionth time, she told them not to. Freshly bathed Peter was in the parlor, cartooning or dreaming of a better world.

Alex was poring over his new dinosaur book. Every so often, he'd rush over to Clara to show her something urgent: "This is amazing—look at the size of the diplodocus, yet its brain is pea-sized," and every time he did it, Clara felt worse. Poor diplodocus.

Clara looked through her files but found she couldn't concentrate. She could only think of Judy, the girl who had saved her. Clara had not exactly been an orphan, but she had felt like an orphan. She had been abandoned—she could see that now, through the lens of time—but back then, she had just been bewildered. Two ways of seeing the world, she remembered. Everything is a matter of perception.

It wasn't that the other girls at Harris & Sons were unkind, it was just they were busy, exhausted, wrapped up in their own worlds, to notice the secretary. Judy was different: she remembered Clara's name—"Is it Newt or Newton?"—thanked her when she made tea, eventually invited her out. Mr. Harris Sr. used to say, "factory floor and office workers don't mix," but the war had upended everything—now the men had gone and the women *did* mix.

Their friendship solidified when she met Michael. There was dancing and double dates for Judy that came to nothing but were fun nevertheless. Then Clara lost Michael. There was one day when she truly thought about throwing herself in front of a tram. Everyone knew someone who'd done it, a broken father, or a guilt-torn mother. Everyone knew someone who couldn't survive anymore. But Judy had been there, a hand, a shoulder, a friend: "You'll get through this, Clara. I promise you."

And what had Clara done in return?

Clara decided to telephone her. She was uncertain what to say even as she held the receiver, which was still sticky from someone else's breath, but she knew she needed to make amends. But the telephone rang and rang until after a while, it was just one long terminal drone.

Judy. Please.

She remembered Judy helping prepare her for her job interview: "And if they ask you, what do children need most?"

"I will say 'happy homes where they will feel safe and accepted.'"

They hadn't asked her that.

In the middle of the night, Clara woke with one of those ideas that if you don't snatch it up, act upon it right away, it will disappear into the ether. So, sitting at her desk in candlelight, she gathered her best writing paper and her favorite pens: she would not let this idea slip away. It was not the stuff of telephone calls and Clara felt glad she hadn't reached Judy earlier after all. Clara wrote with as much diplomacy as she could. It had to be legible, it had to be clean, but mostly, it had to be the exact right words. Then she blew on the ink, as much for luck as to dry it, folded it, then inserted it in an envelope to catch tomorrow's post. She knew the address by heart.

My dearest darling Judy,

I know it took a lot of courage for you to tell me what has been going on. I know you are a private person, I respect that.

I know how fond you are of Alex. And you would never cause him harm. But I can't send him to you two. I can't. Alex comes from a background of violence. I will not see him go back into one.

I can't change my mind. I know you are angry with me. More than angry.

You think the world of Arthur, but no one should ever do what he does to you. Never. I remember your face when you opened the door to me, so ashamed, so depleted. And your ankle, your migraines?

I'm sorry I said what I did. I was shocked and angry and not thinking straight. But I am thinking straight now: what if you were to split from him, Judy? People get divorced all the time now and you surely have good enough grounds and then we could work something out. Please consider this option. Perhaps this could be the incentive you need to leave him?

I love you and will do everything I possibly can to make this work.

Clara xx

In front of the postbox the next morning, Clara had hesitated, just for a moment, before letting the envelope go. Was she doing the right thing? In the middle of the night, she had been so sure she was, yet now that same certainty made her feel uncertain; certainty wasn't Clara's natural state. But sometimes you just had to swallow doubts down, like bad medicine; or perhaps you had to be like Churchill—you had to get out a smelly old cigar and just power on through. So, she dropped her idea, her dove of peace, through the mouth of the pillar box: it might not work, but at least she would have tried.

It was up to Judy to decide what to do now.

Clara also sent the rubbing to Mrs. Marilyn Adams, Michael's mother. She hoped that it would bring her some comfort.

CHAPTER FORTY-FIVE

Suffolk County Council
August 9, 1949

Dear Miss Newton,

We regret to inform you that we have reasonable concerns over your capacity to stay on as housemother at Shilling Grange Children's Home, Lavenham.

Please attend a tribunal at 10:30 a.m. on August 28 at Bury Town Hall, where we will discuss the matter further. Please bring any evidence you feel to demonstrate that you are competent and able to continue as an employee.

The council will provide evidence supporting their concerns.

Yours faithfully,
P. P. Sommersby

"Reasonable concerns." Clara read the words repeatedly and each time they felt like a stab to the heart. "Capacity to stay on." This was a *proper* rejection, a full-blown blitzkrieg on the things she held dear. She had given Shilling Grange Children's Home her all—and now it transpired her all wasn't good enough.

Miss Bridges had brought meringues to sweeten the blow.

"They want to get rid of me?"

"I don't think they *want* to." Miss Bridges opened the window and fanned herself. Whether it was through heat or embarrassment, Clara didn't care. Let Miss Bridges suffer a little too.

"I've lost my job?"

"Unlikely." Yet Miss Bridges' voice and her expression suggested otherwise.

"But it could happen?"

"Well, yes," Miss Bridges admitted. "But I've only seen it happen once…" She paused. "Or twice. And they were bad," she added. "If they were particularly violent toward the kids or withholding food, for example. That sort of thing."

"I don't see what I've done wrong."

Actually, she did. She just wanted Miss Bridges to spell it out.

"It's the Peter thing. They don't like how you dealt with it. Withholding a child from his living relatives—whatever the reason—is not on. You know how keen they are for adoption within the family. That's the main thing."

"On top of the Maureen thing and the Billy and Barry thing and the Terry thing?"

"Well, quite."

Miss Bridges peered at the letter again. "The date works for you?"

What would she say if Clara said no?

"I suppose."

It couldn't be *that* urgent if they were giving her nearly three weeks' grace.

"The children will be away for their two weeks' holiday. Lucky timing."

There was nothing lucky about it.

"So, you can stay for these last weeks, then?"

"And if they don't want me anymore?"

Miss Bridges, who had been such a kind mentor, sometimes ran out of patience.

"Well, if it doesn't work out, you've got places you can go, haven't you? What about that lovely friend you're always talking about, Judy? You could stay there, couldn't you? Chin up, Miss Newton."

The children were going to Lyme Regis for their holidays. They would stay in a mansion full of orphans from across the country. They didn't have their own suitcases and Clara had failed to put in a request to the council for them in time. Ivor would probably have helped, but they were still not talking. However, she happened upon Sir Munnings in the high road and he said he would lend her some, said it was the least he could do.

"Hear you've been having issues, old bean."

Who told him? Julian maybe?

"Stand firm. Those children charge past my house every day with their big beaming faces, squawking like seagulls. Warms my heart. They used to walk like a funeral procession in those dirty black capes, all doom and gloom. You've changed it."

"I hope the council see it like that."

"Funny places, councils." Sir Munnings screwed up his nose. "Like horses. Got to show them who's the boss."

The evening before the children left, Clara cooked a ham hock stew, Peg's favorite, and it went down well. Anita Cardew had dropped over some cinnamon-spiced apple crumble and there were mints from her relatives in America. It might be their last supper all together, but Clara didn't want the children to know that. She lit candles though and the children sensed it was an occasion; for once, Peter didn't slope off as soon as possible and Billy and Barry stopped arm-wrestling when she asked them to.

The suitcases were packed. After much deliberation, Molly Mouse was staying at the Grange where she would be safe; so was

Peg's beloved shell and Terry's plant Jockey, who was looking distinctly peaky. They made Clara swear over the Bible (as they'd seen in a film at Kids' Club) to look after them all. The twins had gone to say goodbye to the fish and Dr. Cardew had reassured them about how well they were getting on. Billy 2 in particular, he said, loved listening to classical music.

"What do you do there then, in Lyme Regis?" Clara asked.

"Dig," Terry said. Clara pictured the tunnels, the moats and the toddler traps that Terry would delight in creating in the sand. This would be Terry's last holiday with the children if the adoption with the Lewises went ahead. For a moment, Clara wished she could go away with them, but that had never been an option. It embarrassed her that she had nowhere to go—and no one to go with either.

"There is usually a contest for dancing," Rita said. "Peg likes that, don't you?" Peg nodded eagerly. "She might win the under-eights this year."

At this, Peg galloped around the room holding up the hem of her skirt. "Don't you go hiding," Clara warned her. One of her fears was that Peg would get lost. "Promise me."

Peg giggled.

"I like fossil hunting," said Alex. "You know, Dorset is one of the premier places in the country for archeology? I'd like to bring back a spectacular find."

"I don't think you're allowed to remove fossils, are you?"

Alex looked concerned. "I'll investigate further."

"Lots of games. Cricket. And rounders. And British Bulldog." Billy thumped his chest, ape-like. "Which *I* always win."

The next morning, Peter lay in his bed like a fossil waiting to be excavated.

"You have to go, Peter. You can't stay here."

Blank face and silence. Clara packed his pencils and papers in the bottom of his case.

"I want a comic please, Peter, a beautiful one."

He finally got up, moving in slow motion, stuffing his clothes carelessly on top of his art materials.

"It'll be fine."

It felt like she was preparing him for his execution. She accompanied them all to the train station. Mrs. Garrard was outside her shop, Bertie under her arm, disapproval dripping from her.

"Will you be here when we get back?" Billy asked abruptly in front of the ticket office. Clara was amazed. She didn't think she'd given anything about the tribunal away.

"Why do you ask?"

"I don't know if I told you before," Billy whispered. His knuckles were white on his case handle. "But they were really cruel. The nuns, I mean. They used to whip us and refuse us food. Sister Eunice was especially mean to Barry. And to Peg. I don't know why she picked on Peg. Peg tried so hard. I never could work it out. You never knew who would be next, but most often it was them. Once, she beat Barry so hard. She wouldn't stop even when he threw up, and held his head, she wouldn't stop. I thought he was going to die, but she wouldn't take him to the doctor. I prayed all night long."

Clara didn't know what to say. She had always suspected life at the Grange was worse than she knew, but to hear it laid out so starkly, from happy-go-lucky Billy of all people, was something else.

"It's better with you," he finished. "It really is."

Clara tried to hug him, because she would sob if she tried to speak, but he pulled away.

"Just thought you should know." He ran down the platform and leapt on Barry's back. They both collapsed on the floor.

Clara clutched the other children to her, except for Peter, who stood apart like he wasn't with them. She swished their hair and wiped their noses and gave away her handkerchiefs. She'd never have dreamed she would come to love them all so much.

Where the children had been, shame crept in. A hollowness replaced their noise. Clara had anticipated that the house would be quieter, naturally, but she hadn't expected that it would smell so different without the children in it too.

It was just horrible that she didn't know if she was staying or not. It was like that time when the country had gone to war, but actual war had not yet broken out so you weren't sure what was happening. Or like the word her parents used to terrify her with— Purgatory, that terrible state of in-between-ness.

How she used to hate her missionary parents for their self-righteousness, their commitment to improving the "lives of the savages." It was interference more like, they were nosy, busybody, patronizing do-gooders who didn't do good for anybody but themselves. The irony, she realized now, was that she had become just like her parents; only she was probably worse than they were, because where they had succeeded, she had failed. She had let the children down.

And she had lost her friendship with Judy too. And for what? Maybe she was wrong. Maybe Arthur *had* turned himself around.

Hadn't she started this journey virtually indifferent to children—and hadn't she fallen in love with every single one of them? Maybe she—who was capable of change—had not realized that others might be equally capable?

Arthur might have gone on his own journey. Judy promised he had. He might have come back from his war flaming with griev-ance, but he might have put the violence aside and learned to be sanguine; maybe he had learned some self-control or some respect.

But Clara supposed the point was that she didn't know. She couldn't be sure so she had erred on the side of caution. And that was the right thing to do; but this had cost her her most precious friendship, her most important relationship in the world.

She heard nothing from Judy. She continued to hear nothing every morning. Judy must have received Clara's letter by now and must have elected not to reply.

CHAPTER FORTY-SIX

Clara was so wrapped up in her woes, she forgot she had agreed to go to the Jane Taylor meeting at the library until Anita turned up at the door. Anita insisted she would wait while Clara reluctantly got changed. Much as she enjoyed the meetings, she wasn't feeling in the mood and if it weren't for Anita, dressed up to the nines, thrumming her nails on the kitchen table, Clara would have stayed at home.

At the library, Clara looked around surreptitiously. *Phew. At least Ivor isn't here.*

"He told me he was busy," said Anita, who was an annoyingly skillful mind-reader. *Or avoiding me?*

"Why don't you go and see him, Clara?"

"He knows where I am."

Initially Anita had struggled to accept that Clara's engagement to Julian was off, but now that she had done so, she made a little spitting noise every time his name was mentioned. It was quite satisfying. Julian had gone from eligible solicitor to devil's spawn in one small step. But now, ridiculously, Clara suspected Anita was trying to match-make her with Ivor. Not because she thought they would be good together, Clara realized, but because Anita didn't want Clara to leave Lavenham. She wanted her to have a further reason to stay.

"He could do with some encouragement," Anita said, making innocent eyes at her.

"Sssh." Clara pretended she was trying to concentrate.

*

Today, Mr. Dowsett the librarian was talking about how it was the setting to music that had made "Twinkle Twinkle Little Star" really take off. It became popular in musical boxes throughout the nineteenth century. "The birth of a lullaby," he said. "Some people suggested Mozart wrote the tune."

Clara thought of the pretty musical box she had given Rita for Christmas. She put up her hand.

"And would Jane Taylor have known how popular it was?"

"Unlikely. It wasn't popular in her lifetime."

Someone else asked, "Did Jane Taylor have children?"

"We think she wanted a family, very much, but there was maybe a betrayal, or a love affair gone wrong. She was, by all accounts, an involved aunt to her many nephews and nieces."

Clara thought again of Judy. She must call her, find out if she'd received the letter. They did go astray sometimes—especially the important ones. Judy must have had time to think by now.

The speaker continued on how, in Jane Taylor's lifetime, her work was not recognized—nor had it been since, really. Few people still knew, he said, that she was the author of this poem, and sadly, she died from breast cancer aged only forty, lamenting the stories she didn't get the chance to write.

"It's such a tragedy," said Clara after the talk.

"No," said Anita, "look what she gave us and at least we still talk about her"—she counted in her head, quicker than Clara ever could—"a hundred and thirty-three years later."

"But no one knows she wrote it—well, except for everyone here," Clara said.

"But still, what a gift to have left."

"Is it worth doing something if nobody knows it's you?" Clara mused as they left. She was thinking aloud and not expecting an answer, but Anita was smiling at her.

"Of course it is. The sun rises every morning—and it's beautiful whether you see it or not, isn't it? You don't do things for the recognition, you do it because it's right."

Anita Cardew looped her arm through Clara's and together they went back to the Grange for tea.

CHAPTER FORTY-SEVEN

The children had been in Lyme Regis for one week and there had been no postcards or letters. While away, children were encouraged to make a clean break. Contact might make them homesick, apparently. Clara understood the rationale, but she was still feeling glum about it when Ivor rang the bell.

He looked great. He was wearing his hat, his shirt properly done up, no needles between his lips. He handed her a bottle of her favorite gin.

Clara felt herself go weak at the knees and she hated it. She should have stuck with Julian, she thought, she could have made him reform. Julian didn't ever make her feel this wobbly.

"Did Anita tell you to come?"

He grinned. "Anita is a persuasive woman."

Clara was determined not to smile back. "I thought you weren't speaking to me."

"I wasn't." Eyes lowered. "Then I told myself you must have had a good reason not to be there for Peter that day."

"I did," she said indignantly. She wasn't going to forgive Ivor this easily. "A very good reason."

"Then I'm sorry. I should have trusted you." He was that rare man who didn't mind saying sorry and he didn't say it like he was swallowing Epsom salts either. He hovered in the doorway. She was still determined not to ask him in.

"I wanted to tell you, I read the Curtis Report."

"You did?"

Clara had forgotten he had it.

"The child? What happened to Dennis O'Neill—is it true?"

The young boy had been fostered, then abused, and eventually was starved to death—and no one had done anything to save him.

"It is all true, Ivor."

"It's terrible."

She had to invite him in after that.

They sat at the kitchen table drinking tea.

"Don't worry, Miss Bridges made them," Clara said as she offered the biscuits and was grateful when Ivor laughed.

"I would have taken one anyway and suffered later." Turning serious again, he said, "I can't believe how rotten it was for so many children."

"Horrendous for some. For many. And what we want is for that never to happen again."

"We?" Narrowing his eyes, he looked intently at her.

"Yes, *we*. You know, we talk about what the Nazis did, and what the Japanese did, and it's an affront to humanity—repulsive and evil, but at the same time, quietly, under cover, some terrible things have been done here, to children in our own backyard."

Ivor nodded.

"We are making pacts and deals and international laws to make things better between us all—and that's as it should be and my word, long overdue—but what about the suffering children? We had to do something. And what we have created now, it's imperfect, of course it's imperfect. And we will sometimes get it wrong and some children will still get hurt, but we still have to try."

Taking a biscuit, Ivor broke it in two. Crumbs rained onto the plate.

"It is better, Clara. I see that now. Just because the system is overloaded, just because there are mistakes, doesn't mean it's wrong to try."

"Thank you. It's not great. But despite all the muck-ups, the bureaucracy and how slow-moving it is, I do see it as progress."

"It's an improvement."

"That's right. And some of the childcare officers are not good and some of the housemothers"—*like me*, she thought—"aren't as good as they should be, or as good as the children deserve. But we will get there."

Ivor held out his tea and for a moment she didn't know why. His face was tilted toward hers, sunlight pouring through the window. At that moment, she trusted that face more than any other face in the world.

"To all the children."

"And to Dennis."

He clinked his cup against hers.

Ivor didn't ask how Clara was coping with the children being away. It was probably obvious. She had washed everything, made their beds, *lay* on their beds, swept and swept again. Shilling Grange had never looked so spotless. She had never been so industrious. It looked like a hotel—*eat your heart out, Lavender Arms*—immaculate for whoever was going to be there in September. Clara felt instinctively that it wouldn't be her but she didn't want her replacement to be able to say what a slattern she was, as well as everything else. She didn't want them to say she didn't care for those kids.

Ivor was about to leave when she asked, "Are you doing anything later?"

That awkward swing-back of the other arm. She could have predicted it.

"No...do you need something?"

"I just wondered...shall we open the gin over a game of Monopoly?"

Monopoly had been Judy's gift to her. Clara remembered playing it at Judy's family's house. Her father, her mother, her brothers, the one with the middle name Howard. The cheerful family arguments. She'd never known arguments could be so friendly. They didn't have to end in silence and slammed doors. *Will Judy ever speak to me again?*

Judy must know Clara was in the right; they would work it out. That's what friends did.

"Before I accept, I ought to warn you about something," Ivor said.

"Yes?"

"I'm a demon at board games."

"That's fighting talk, that is."

It's not a date, Clara reminded herself, or a "rendezvous," as Julian would have had it; but usually Ivor popped over on an errand or with something for the children. Or she nipped to his with a bag of socks or trousers. There was something about this that felt different.

Clara tried not to let herself dwell on the evening of the telescope because it was so intimate, so…private. That feeling of him close by in the darkness. She hadn't felt able to move. The smell of him. Sometimes, she thought about him that day at the market too; she had sensed him watching her sometimes, she wasn't imagining it; but that image was shattered by the memory of the old man talking about Ruby—*"She was a one."*

Was Ruby still on his mind?

Since those two occasions, they had rarely been alone. There was always an interruption: a child with a tummy ache or a lost marble or a tummy ache *and* a lost marble.

Clara found herself "getting ready." As she changed into a smart blouse and a fitted skirt with slip from her Harris & Sons days she felt like she was losing her looks. Usually it didn't matter. Today, suddenly, it did.

Don't forget, he's married, she told herself. Nevertheless, a spritz of Rita and Terry's homemade perfume wouldn't go amiss. Rita had forgotten to take this experimental bottle away with her. (Hopefully, it wouldn't bring Clara out in a rash.)

Ivor arrived promptly and it didn't feel like it was tempting fate to note that he too had made an effort. Freshly shaved and gorgeous, Ivor wasn't losing his looks; he looked like a man who had just found them.

She was the old boot. He was the racing car. From the moment the Monopoly dice was first rolled, they didn't stop laughing and chatting. Ivor liked facilities; he bought electricity and water. As she passed on the cheaper streets and instead pursued only the expensive areas—Mayfair, Park Lane—he said, "Clara, I had no idea you were so ruthless!"

Clara *may have been* getting a little tipsy, but he didn't seem to mind. He did seem to like her. She knew that. The question was: how much and what did it mean? At about nine o'clock, Ivor said he had to go back to his workshop. Clara's heart fell: *over so soon?* But it was just to fetch some more of the cider he had made last spring.

While he was out, Clara raced to the mirror. She hardly recognized her flushed face and excited eyes. Where had all this come from? She told herself that she wasn't falling for him but she was, of course, she knew that really. She had been falling for him for months now and she was gaining acceleration as she fell. She applied lipstick and powder, and combed her hair. If only she'd dyed it blonde... If only she looked a bit more desirable.

He had such brown eyes. Her favorite color for eyes.

She wanted him to say something like: *I'm glad you're not marrying Julian*, or *I can't stop thinking about you*, but there were no declarations. She wondered if he were waiting for a sign from her. But she couldn't think of a way forward that wasn't *too* forward. She still wanted a way back, if necessary.

What would Anita Cardew do? she thought before giggling to herself and deciding *whatever* Anita would do, she should do the exact opposite.

It grew later and darker. Ivor looked around for a clock, then gasped, "What? Is that really the time?" It was just before midnight. "I thought I'd have thrashed you by now." He grinned at her. "I'd better head off. I've got some early appointments."

It pained her, but although one part of her wanted him to throw caution to the wind—"to hell with them"—she liked that he didn't let people down. That was Ivor all over.

As he collected his hat, she had this ridiculous urge to put it on her own head and call out *ta-da* or to do something with jazz hands. Or to hide it in the closet and insist he look for it, or jump out at him—"Boo!"

Goodness, she *was* tipsy.

Too hot for his jacket, he laid it over his arm. "I've had a great evening, Clara."

Even the way he said her name was dreamy. She could listen to that sound forever: *Clara, Clara.* He said it how it was meant to be said. She had never thought about her own name before, but now, from his mouth, it was the most musical, most exotic word she'd ever encountered.

"Me too."

"Shall we do this again tomorrow?" Somehow, he managed to ask without looking directly at her.

"Tomorrow I hope to spend less time in jail."

Although Clara went to bed full of lightness and fluttering, replaying the sweet moments and shy looks, she had a terrible night's sleep. Maybe it was Ivor's homemade cider, or too much gin. Whatever it was, she had the most terrible dreams she had had in a long time:

She witnessed a child falling down a well, another getting into a fatal knife fight, children slipping into fast-flowing rivers or tumbling down stairs. She heard voices wailing for their mamas, others screaming for ambulances. Barry and Peg beaten to bloody pulps. And then there was Peter's uncle, smug, elbow spilling out of his car, "You need a firm hand," and then Ivor leaning in, only in the dream, his arm purple and misshapen, his mouth full of spikes, and Judy was there too, crying: *Trust me, why didn't you trust me?*

In the morning, Clara had just put on the kettle and was gazing out into the street, and at the faithful lights of Ivor's workshop, when the telegram boy appeared. He parked his bike against the garden wall, firmly straightened his cap, his jacket and his expression, then walked toward the door of the Grange.

Clara,

This is instead of telephoning because I can't find your number. Maybe it's better that I don't hear your voice. Deeply regret our beloved Judy was taken from us last Monday. Arthur has been arrested. Funeral arrangements to follow. Broken-hearted beyond measure.

Kitty Kislingbury

CHAPTER FORTY-EIGHT

Clara didn't know how long she had stayed at the kitchen table, the telegram beached in front of her. At about three o'clock, Ivor came over to resume the battle of the old boot versus the racing car. She didn't recall him placing down the tin he was carrying and cradling her in his arms. She did remember hugging him: the smell of his neck, his shoulders, and the bristle of his chin, and the softness yet strength that came with him and that it didn't matter one bit about his arm, not one bit. It was not monstrous, there were no needles in his lips, those were bad dreams; and yet, real life produced its own monster variants and needles of its own. She couldn't recall much else. The part when he disentangled himself from her to make her sweet tea, even that had felt like too long. He had tears in his eyes. He watched her drink as though she was a newborn and he was concerned she couldn't do it right.

He held her close again, he stroked her back, her shoulders, the bit between her shoulder blades, the tops of her arms, and she pressed herself toward him. She yearned to be closer to him, inhaling his smell, his shape, it was overwhelming—she had wanted this for a long time and it was good and she could feel there was maybe a kiss coming, finally they might actually kiss, she only had to raise her head and then they would kiss. It was like waiting for a train to come through a tunnel, it was like waiting for a tram to reach her stop. She closed her eyes and waited, enjoying the anticipation, enjoying the moment of melting, not an inch between them, not a centimeter, pressed against him, she was deliriously warm, deliciously, it was the only place she wanted to be in the world: she raised her face, just slightly, parted her lips and called him Michael by mistake.

He disappeared and she was alone in the kitchen again and it felt even worse than before.

Judy. Poor Judy.

Drinking tea and weeping, blowing her nose on her own sleeve.

"He'll be headteacher in eight terms." You utter bully, Arthur. You contemptible bastard.

Anita and Dr. Cardew appeared through the back door, the one they'd never usually presume to use. They came out of the blue as though they'd been pulled out of a hat and Clara did remember laughing—so inappropriate—at her surprise. How did they get there? How did they know? And how funny to see them together. United, she murmured. They buzzed around her distantly, talk of smelling salts, the possibility of Valium. She heard Anita, her all-too-loud voice, *she doesn't have any family*, and that seemed to echo so loudly that she thought she might never hear anything else again. She used to have family. Judy had family, Judy was the one who was loved by everyone who knew her—and Judy was gone. Clara should have been the one to go, no one would even have noticed.

Then she was tucked up in bed, a teacup on the table beside her, a kiss from Anita on her forehead, a promise to be back the next day.

At St. Mary's Church, Battersea, where Judy and Arthur had gotten married only four years earlier, Judy's sweet mother clung to Clara and Judy's bewildered father shook her hand and said, "Thank you for coming," three times, he was in such a daze.

Did they know she and Judy had the most God-awful row, or not? A row so terrible, the word "row" didn't seem to cover it. It was more like a cataclysmic split.

Clara tried to work it out; when would they last have seen Judy? But it was unclear, and it didn't matter, cataclysmic split or not. If they did know about it, they didn't care. Their daughter was dead.

Judy's grandmother came in unsteadily, leaning on a stick, with a group of young men fussing around her. She must have been ninety-five at least. Judy and Clara used to laugh about Judy's good genes. The shock was now etched into her grandmother's features, like someone had drawn lines all over her face.

"This will break her," someone in the row in front of Clara said as they watched her shuffle down the aisle. She had lived through the 1860s, they went on, she'd lived through the Spanish flu, her brother had died during the Great War at El Alamein. Clara wanted to correct them—it wasn't El Alamein, it was the Dardanelles, get it right—but why was it so important to get it right? The sentiment was the thing.

How could anyone come to terms with this?

Arthur did it. Arthur the bastard.

Clara didn't know how he'd killed her; her imagination ran riot. She was torn between wanting the details—it couldn't be as bad as she pictured, could it?—and wanting never to learn the truth about Judy's agonized last hours. Had he ever stopped the violence toward her, or had it been going on and on all this time? And what difference did that make anyway?

Clara had known. She had known what he was like and had done nothing. She looked around the church. Was she the only one who knew? The only one who failed Judy? Or was she sitting among more of them, a whole load of traitors?

Anita had offered to accompany Clara to the funeral, but from the moment she read the telegram, Clara had known that she would go on her own.

Anita had been a dear friend. Whenever Clara thanked her, frequently, Anita shushed her: "You'd do the same for me." Clara hoped that was true, but she felt so lost; she thought now that she was such a bad friend, she didn't know anymore what she would do. Her trust had all but gone—her trust in herself. Did Judy tell Arthur what Clara had said about her not having Alex? Was that what had infuriated him—was that the final straw?

If Clara had said yes about Alex, would Judy still be here today?

Such a slender coffin; could Judy fit in there? It looked feather-light, insubstantial, as they carried it down the aisle. A photo at the altar, of Judy looking very much not like Judy. Puffy-haired and serious of face. How much trouble had it been to find a recent photo of her without him in it? They would have had to discount all the wedding pictures. And they would have had to discount any with black eyes or cuts—not that Judy would ever have allowed herself to be photographed like that.

A small choir of children were singing, "He's Got the Whole World in His Hands," and then at the last verse, enthusiastically, they changed it to *her*: "She's got the whole world in her hands."

Clara wondered if the vicar would mind—she knew what vicars were like, the ones her father was friends with, anyway—but if he did, he didn't show it. His expression was serene. The people in the pews were laughing at the unexpectedness and crying at the same time, and something about that was so beautiful, it felt like it created its own Judy rainbow across the room.

A lot of the people there must have been teachers, Judy's—and Arthur's—co-workers. Some of them were dabbing their eyes too. Clara knew some of them by name but not face, but she did a good job of guessing who was who: that must be Mrs. Lewis, who once ran out of class because the children were so disrespectful, and that must be Miss Ballard, who wanted to be a singer, who might have been in love with him, Mr. Young, the teacher who was good at finger-painting, who Judy suspected was homosexual.

Afterward, there were cars—not to Judy and Arthur's house,

not the crime scene, no, no, but back to her loving parents' home. There, everyone agreed it was a beautiful service, or it was fitting or just right. It was what Judy would have wanted.

When Judy's mother asked Clara to come upstairs with her, Clara bridled. *Here it comes*, she thought. *She knows that I let down her daughter, she's going to scream, rail at me, tell me I was no friend.* But upstairs, Judy's mother was focused on some of Judy's things. She was bagging them up, frantically. There were piles of old clothes on the bed, piles on the floor.

"I took them from the house." Judy's mother rummaged through until she held up the thing she'd been looking for.

"The mink stole? You borrowed it for that interview?"

"I didn't wear it in the end." Once again, Clara hated herself for her sometimes ridiculous devotion to accuracy. But she couldn't not tell the truth to Judy's mother. If the other woman asked if she knew about Arthur and his violence, she would have to tell the truth about that too. *Was she going to ask?*

"Would you like it? I'd love you to have it."

"Thank you."

"And the shoes."

"I did wear those," Clara was happy to report. "And the gloves."

"She told me. Proud of you, she was. I know that's what she would have wanted."

Clara's lips trembled.

"How is it at the Grange?"

"I…" But now Clara found she couldn't tell her the truth—that it was nearly over and they had reasonable concerns about her capacity to stay on. "It's an experience."

Judy's mother had the same smile as Judy. "When I heard you had got the job, I knew you would be perfect. You, more than any-one, would understand how it is to be left. I knew you could do it. Judy said you were made for it."

I let Judy down, thought Clara. *At the last minute, in her hour of need, I let her down.*

She wanted to confess everything, but she could not. It would not be fair to put this on Judy's mother. And then Judy's mother lunged at her, nearly knocking her over.

"How could Arthur have done such a thing? Clara, how could he?"

In each of the downstairs rooms, sympathy cards stood on every surface. The sideboard, the windowsill, the fireplace. A teacher, with as much love in her heart as Judy had had, must have set the children to it. The cards fluttered: Clara thought it was as though they were working up to something as she paced around the room, picking them up, putting them down one by one.

My favorite teacher. You were the best. I love you, Mrs. Martin.

Those darling pictures. Sunshines. Stars. Trees. Sandcastles. Happy faces. Children eating ice cream. And perfect houses with green grass and blue sky and smiling stick families in front of them. All Judy ever wanted.

CHAPTER FORTY-NINE

Clara didn't see Ivor the next day, or the one after. Anita left her a heavily spiced goulash, which saw her through the next couple of days. Inevitably, she was reminded of the weeks after Michael died, which was its own kind of agony because most of what she could remember from that time was centered around Judy and her never-ending well of kindness.

When Ivor did come round, he was unusually formal with her, staying at the door as though he were stuck to the frame. Clara remembered how people became nervous when you were bereaved: like you had stepped into a different time zone from them, every-thing was at cross-purposes. Or like they expected you never to laugh again. She hadn't thought Ivor would behave like that. Not after they had held each other for so long. Although the thought of holding him or kissing him now seemed absurd and that was strange too.

He was just checking up, he said apologetically, said he was busy, then said he'd be away the next night, but not to worry. *Why would she worry?* He was on the way to Sir Munnings'. Something about a car and a driver. She wanted to say how sorry she was for calling him Michael, but that felt inappropriate, ill-timed, so she pretended to herself that he had forgotten or that he hadn't even heard, even though she knew he had.

The pink roses Miss Bridges sent brightened up the kitchen, but no one came round to see them and, as they still didn't have a telephone, there was no way for anyone to call. Clara found herself floating around at a loss; the Grange seemed to have doubled in size without the children and now she felt like she had shrunk. In the garden it was worse; she felt like a blimp. The children had kept her grounded—now, she was the *Hindenburg*, floating away before being seized by flames.

It was the day of the tribunal and Clara had a bad feeling from the moment she woke up. Eating leftover goulash for breakfast hadn't been her best decision ever: her mouth felt dry and her stomach bubbled. The last thing she wanted was a grumbling belly at the council, for goodness' sake.

She would be gone from Shilling Grange before the children got back and regretted not saying her farewells before they left. When Sister Eunice had gone, just like that, she had thought it brutal. Her departure would be even worse.

And she had no idea where she would go. She would be home-less again, only this time there was no family home, and there was no Judy's home. There was nowhere.

She was back to "do not pass go."

That wasn't her chief preoccupation though: this time the children were. *Well, there were always letters*, Clara told herself, and she began thinking what she would write. She suspected Peg and Rita would be the ones who at first might miss her most—but then they might also get over her quicker. *The younger they are, the quicker they forget*. It was another of Miss Bridges' sayings: "Children are resilient."

Hopefully, Terry was going to her permanent home soon. That was surely a good thing, not just for Shilling Grange and Suffolk Council's statistics; Terry would have the loving family that the dar-ling girl deserved. Clara would fade into just a fuzzy memory for her. And Peter was nearly of age to leave, in the next year or so. Billy and Barry had each other. They hardly needed anyone else, she told her-self, although deep down she knew it probably wasn't true. And Alex would cope. He didn't have much choice but to cope. And he had the tools: the intelligence, the ambition, the manners to cope better than most. But, oh Alex, he didn't know it, but he was at the heart of this maelstrom. He must never know it. How on earth could she explain *anything* in a letter, never mind everything?

Clara dressed in the same clothes as she had worn to her job interview almost one year previously, not just because they were lucky clothes, but because she didn't have anything else suitable. This time, she paired the outfit with Judy's mink as well as Judy's slip-on shoes. It was nice to smell of Judy. She looked fancy, which might go against her, but then she had a feeling that just about everything was going against her. She was on a downward trajectory.

Miss Bridges came to the house to drive her there. It was good of her, she didn't have to. She too was dressed more smartly than usual, in a tweed jacket and pearls, although she denied it when Clara mentioned it. She said, "Any questions, ask me. Some of these panels can get pretty technical." And she flapped her hands. She was hot, these days, always hot. It was her age.

"Remember, whatever happens, Clara, we just want the best for the children."

It seemed to Clara that Miss Bridges was suggesting this was not going to be a good outcome for her and to prepare to accept it. This feeling multiplied when in the car Miss Bridges asked her if she was thinking of taking a break somewhere. It would be a shame to waste the heat.

I'm not going to see the children again, Clara thought, and the prospect made her want to climb out of the car and run back to the house.

It wasn't the panel who had originally interviewed her. There was no kind-eyed stiff-haired lady. Clara recognized only one of them: Mr. Sommersby, Head of Children's Services, and she missed who

Mrs. McCarthy and Mr. Goodge were. Maybe she should have been relieved there were only three, but they were each intimidating in their own ways. They'd obviously pulled out the big guns for her.

A glass of water was set in front of her. She wondered idly why Ivor had needed a car. She was glad of Judy's mink stole. Miss Bridges might be boiling but the room was cool.

Mr. Sommersby was in the middle: "I am the chair," he said and Clara thought how the children would giggle at that. *He is a chair?*

"We have gone through the documentation you submitted. Thank you. Very thorough."

Thorough. That's what they'd put on her bloody grave.

"So, we are looking at your capacity to continue at Shilling Grange. And this has come to a head, if you like..."

Clara did not like.

"...because of the case between Master James Peter Downey and his uncle, Mr. James Courtney, and your decision to withhold the child from his only—"

"Living relative, yes."

"Who is now hoping to file for adoption."

"I...yes."

"Unfortunately, there are other issues too." Mrs. McCarthy shuffled her papers. She was about sixty, fiercely intelligent-looking, in a dog-tooth check skirt and pink blouse with a ruffle. "A veritable Pandora's box has been opened. If it were just...you're here for a series of repeated breaches of regulations."

Clara felt faint. She wished she'd agreed the window should be opened when they'd offered. Miss Bridges was examining the parquet floor as though her life depended on it. In the corner of the room was a little pile of dust that someone must have swept and forgotten to pick up. It was strangely compelling.

I belong there, Clara thought. *With all the useless things. That's my place.*

"Submission from Mr. White. According to him you left the

children alone on numerous occasions. You called the children 'feral.' You left the children in the care of a woman with dubious history."

This wasn't fair. "Mrs. Cardew doesn't—she isn't! She's a wonderful woman. There is absolutely nothing dubious about her."

"She was in Bergen-Belsen. She lost her parents and a sister there."

Clara took a sharp intake of breath. She had not known that. She forged on for her friend.

"Mrs. Cardew is perfectly capable with the children, beyond capable. I resent what you are insinuating here. What exactly *are* you insinuating here?" she added, growing stronger. They could insult her, but not her friend. And not for that.

"When you have the local solicitor sending testimony against you, you have to sit up and take notice, I'm afraid," said Mrs. McCarthy, and Clara was uncertain whether the *I'm afraid* meant she was sympathetic or not. "As for calling the children feral? Which children sometimes aren't?" she asked, smiling.

Clara nodded cautiously.

"I don't think Solicitor White's statement carries any particular weight. It rather looks like someone has a grudge."

That was clearer. Clara looked at Mrs. McCarthy gratefully, but she was too busy going through her papers to notice.

Mr. Sommersby continued. "Next, we have a submission from Mrs. Garrard. I quote: 'Miss Newton never struck me as a good influence from the moment she shouted, "paper, paper" at my husband and I in the street.' "

"She cannot be serious."

" 'On another occasion she smirked at Bertie when he was in my handbag.' "

Mr. Sommersby looked up. "Presumably Bertie is a dog, not the husband?"

Mrs. McCarthy looked over her half-moon glasses. "That does sound rather cruel."

"He didn't like being carried in it, and it looked funny." Clara added unconvincingly, "Anyone would have laughed."

"Anyway, this to me looks like another grudge," Mrs. McCarthy said and Clara agreed readily. "Which raises the question—how, in just ten months here, have you acquired so many people who have taken against you?"

Clara was unable to answer this. She felt like she was losing a game; time was running out and she was torn between wanting more time to win—to turn it around—and just wanting it all over now. To be misrepresented in this way was painful. She couldn't feel any fight in her.

Mr. Sommersby continued, "As I understand it, you didn't want the position at Shilling Grange; in fact, I'd go so far as to say you plotted to get away."

Clara could feel Miss Bridges shifting uncomfortably in her seat next to her.

"In several reported conversations you said, 'I don't think I can do it, I don't belong here.'"

"I had some doubts about my suitability at first," admitted Clara. "It's true. But these were minor. At the normal end of the scale, I'd say."

"You resigned," Mrs. McCarthy pointed out.

"Ah."

Miss Bridges' cheeks were flaming.

If this were Jane Taylor's time, Clara thought absurdly, *she might have fainted to the floor.* They might have gathered around her with lacy fans and smelling salts. As it was, she just had to sit tight and endure it.

Clara was trying to see everything through neutral eyes, but she could see that it looked bad. Everything looked bad.

"I'm so sorry," mouthed Miss Bridges. Tears came to her sad eyes. She took off her smart jacket and it was like she was trying to remove everything she had done.

"I don't know if that's the normal end of the scale, frankly—"

Clara interrupted Mrs. McCarthy. "But now I do want to be at Shilling Grange and I believe I am the best person for the children."

Mrs. McCarthy wrote something down, then smiled at her. "Why is that?"

"Why do I want to stay? Oh…" Clara suddenly felt tearful too. Her voice was trembling. She couldn't express the affection and the determination she felt for each one of her charges. Something inside her slumped. She dragged on. "I have worked on their reports and…everything."

Mr. Sommersby marked his file. Mrs. McCarthy frowned.

"And then we have the newspaper incident. We do try to keep our children out of the papers, Miss Newton. We don't plaster their photographs all over the front pages with details—erroneous, of course—of our accounting. This is a terrible breach of anonymity. What if one of the parents had seen it? We were lucky it didn't escalate."

Clara knew saying it wasn't her fault wouldn't cut it, so she just shook her head. The lines of the hangmen were well and truly drawn, it was clear; there were only a couple of letters to go.

"And the child who ran away? A Miss Maureen Amy Keaton?"

"I would do anything to have Maureen back with us. I…miss her."

Mrs. McCarthy handed over a pale blue handkerchief—Terry had taken all of Clara's on holiday—and Clara loudly blew her nose.

"Let's have a short break," Mrs. McCarthy suggested. "Back in thirty."

Miss Bridges offered to walk with her, but Clara told her she needed some time alone. She didn't need time alone so much as she had to accept that it was over and Miss Bridges, with the best intentions, would only talk over her or confuse her. Clara knew she would have to find something else to do. Somewhere with no children, no socks on pipes, no May Queens, no handkerchiefs, no school reports and no nits. Somewhere with no memories.

For a long time, she had avoided voluntarily going into a church, any church, even the one where she was supposed to marry Julian. But she had always loved beautiful old buildings and this church, not five hundred yards from the council offices, looked particularly old and beautiful. Thanks to Anita's goulash, she wasn't hungry so she walked in.

Immediately, she could feel herself clench up. All the anger she felt toward her father seemed to live on in these places. Even if it was a church he had never—to her knowledge—been to before. Even if she'd never been to it before. They all smelled of him, evoked him, called him. As Clara sat on a wooden pew not far from the entrance, she was flooded not only with anger but with sadness and regret. She was transported right back in time.

Clara remembered the weekly letters she had received from her mother. Without fail, the post prefect would call out, "Newton, Africa calling!" How the first letters were so long, full of questions and full of Mother. And then, as her disease progressed, they grew shorter, weaker and more distressed. As if she were actually trapped inside the writing paper.

Clara had begged her mother to come home, but her mother wrote that she couldn't: "Father wants to stay. Pray for me."

Clara wrote "Come back," every day, but her wishes were ignored.

Letters came further apart but at least they still came, with their postmarks, their exotic stamps and their faded writing: "God will provide." Clara kept each of them in a secret place and studiously replied to each one. They bound her and her mother together— until one day, maybe six, seven months in, Clara gave up. She stopped writing altogether—she was furious that her mother still hadn't come home. What good did all the letter-writing, all the pleading, all the rationalizing, all the sympathy do?

Nothing. Her mother was staying put.

Still, letters made their way to her: "Newton, Africa calling."

Please write, darling. You must understand how painful this is for me too.

Increasingly, there were no more stories, no more escapades, no more mention of her father even. These were notes from a sick person. Her mother was confined to some village hut, to four empty walls, and had nothing to say only, "It won't be long now," and "I hurt all over," and "I know you are angry, but I love you. We both do."

Then that final telegram from her father, explaining that it was over and that her mother was with God now; yet in the same paragraph he, *her father,* was furious at *her.* Raging at her for not writing to her mother, for not making her last few weeks "more palatable."

How dare you punish your mother in that cruel way?

In that one furious moment, Clara had destroyed all the letters her mother had ever sent. She could not read one without feeling remorse. She could not even look at them without the fear that someone would find out that—when her mother had most needed her—she had abandoned her.

What she hadn't realized at the time was that not only was she destroying the evidence of her stupidity, she was destroying the only things she had left of her mother.

Mama, Clara thought to herself in the church, *My mama.*

And for the first time, she allowed herself to feel the intensity of that great loss.

It was nearly time to get back. Clara was about to make for the door but changed her mind. Instead, she sank to her knees and prayed to be allowed to stay on at Shilling Grange. Whether she was praying to God, to Jesus, her mother, the universe, she didn't know. She just remembered that at that last awful meeting, Judy had said Clara *wasn't* afraid to ask for help—and that this was a good thing.

Well, she was asking for help now.

She had never wanted something so much in her life.

As Clara rose to her feet, she had a strange and overwhelming certainty that she was not alone. What exactly that sensation was, she didn't know—she wasn't a religious person—but she felt like she was immersed in a wave of acceptance. As if, while she might feel powerless, actually she was part of something much bigger than herself and all was not lost.

Clara was the first back in the room. Hopefully, Anita's goulash would see her through the next bit. How much longer could they be planning on spending on her? Couldn't they just give her her marching orders and let it be over with?

The panel trooped back in and took their seats. Mr. Sommersby had crumbs in his beard and the air smelled of corned beef.

"Right, I'm afraid, Miss Newton, that—"

There was a clattering at the back of the room. The door opened and there was Ivor. *Ivor?* He stood half in the room, half out, feeling his collar awkwardly.

"We're not too late, are we? We've come to talk to the panel about Miss Newton."

Who's we? panicked Clara. *Not the children. The children are on holiday.*

But then the door opened wider and the children pushed into the room. A quick head count: eight of them—eight? Even Peter was there, even...*Maureen?* Dear, dear Maureen, where had he found her? And Anita too, at the back, shepherding them forward, smiling that nervy smile she had.

At first, the children clustered together in the center of the room, but then Rita broke out, bowled over to Clara and gripped her round the waist. This set off the others, who all shuffled over, closer to her.

"Maureen, I missed you," Clara whispered to the girl, who smiled shyly. She was wearing a tea dress much too loose for her; she looked old and weary. Heartbreaking to think of her scared face that time, crumpled over in the garden and in the car.

To Ivor, Clara said: "They're supposed to be on holiday."

"They wanted to come back." Ivor was wearing his suit—his boots were polished and made a clacking sound on the floor as he shuffled toward her. "One day early. To support *you*, Clara."

Mr. Sommersby wasn't happy. "You took these children out of their once-a-year annual holiday—at great cost—to spend all day on a train and then in an office?"

"Yes, that's how important it is," Ivor said brightly. "Although we came in a car, not a train. And we're here to submit *our* evidence."

Clara remembered his fear of public speaking. That he had once told her, "It's worse than being chased by cows." Well, he seemed to have found his feet today.

"That's ridiculous. We can't have evidence from children! Facts are facts and we've already heard character references from Mr. White and Mrs. Garrard," said Mr. Sommersby.

Lunch hadn't helped his irritability.

"Yes, well, the children are the ones who know Clara—Miss Newton—best."

"Can you start by explaining who *you* are?" Mr. Goodge looked up from his papers with the air of a weary husband.

"He's our favorite neighbor," said Alex.

"He's an upholsterer," Billy shouted.

"Our favorite upholsterer," said Rita.

"It means he stuffs cushions," explained Barry. (He'd never gotten that before.)

"Although upholsterer means much more than that," Alex insisted. "It's a complex thing. What? I'm just saying. Definitions are important. Words"—the little professor looked around—"have meanings. You can't just change them to suit you, willy-nilly."

"Oy," warned Barry. "I hate being called nilly."

Anita stepped forward. She looked like a shop mannequin in a closely fitted navy dress with pleats and a beaded necklace, her hair styled into a pretty chignon. She looked like she belonged in Paris, not a tired town hall in Suffolk.

"I'm Mrs. Cardew." Her voice sounded foreign in this English chamber. "Dr. Cardew's wife."

Mr. Sommersby didn't say anything, but his expression squarely said, *what now?*

"Nobody informed my husband or me that we could make a submission to the panel," she said firmly. "He knows the children like his own hand. I have gotten to know them well too. Dr. Cardew will write a recommendation for Clara. And so will our other friends. Sir Munnings the horse painter, the lady from the post office and Mr. Dowsett, who is the librarian. None of us were asked but Clara has many supporters in Lavenham."

Clara's cheeks burned with embarrassed pride.

"This is unorthodox."

"It is unorthodox," Mrs. McCarthy agreed. "But I don't believe it's a breach of any kind. What else do you have for us, um, Mr...."

"Delaney. Well, we're not doing paper reports or er...written evidence. That's more Miss Newton's thing." Here, Ivor wore almost the same expression as he had when she had landed on Fenchurch Street after he had just acquired all four stations in Monopoly.

"But you have information pertaining to Clara's suitability as a housemother?"

"We have a verbal submission from a Mr. Garrard!"

Mr. Garrard walked into the room looking distinctly shady, as though he'd rather be anywhere but here.

"A few weeks ago, I was walking Bertie." He looked around the room. "My dog, a miniature schnauzer, lovely little thing. He was off the lead and I was calling him. He was among the cows. The cows came at us. I was frozen and Miss Newton helped me. She saved my life and quite possibly, Bertie's too."

Everyone stared at Clara. She shrugged, modestly. *Imagine if I hadn't*, she thought. "Anyone would have done the same," she said aloud.

Ivor stepped forward. "Now, the children would like to show you some of the things Clara has taught them."

Clara didn't know what this meant and the panel didn't seem to either.

"Ready?" Ivor said. "Terry, you go first."

Terry stepped forward. Now Clara noticed she was wearing a dress for the occasion. But what a dress. It looked like an outfit for a Victorian scullery maid. She also had a great whacking bit of plaster taped round the bridge of her spectacles. Clara inwardly groaned.

"I wanted to show you my gardening. Clara was the one who gave me my own patch, see? But we couldn't uproot the vegetables."

"Quite right," Mrs. McCarthy said. "Gardeners take a long-term view. It is their skill."

"So instead, you may have heard of Jane Taylor?"

"I haven't," Mrs. McCarthy said, looking around at the others' faces. Mr. Sommersby shrugged. Mr. Goodge shook his head.

"That's because you're silly," shouted Rita.

Goodness, that girl has a loose tongue.

"Rita!"

But Mrs. McCarthy took it in her stride. "That's what my grandson says too."

"Well, she lived in this town," Terry went on, glaring at Rita. "And I'm going to recite you a piece of her poetry."

Now Clara understood.

Terry began: "In the dark blue sky you keep, / And often through my curtains peep, / For you never shut your eye, / Till the sun is in the sky."

At the end everyone clapped, even Mr. Goodge clapped. Mrs. McCarthy dabbed her eyes. "That was lovely," she started, then gasped as Ivor, who had slipped out during the recital, pushed a piano on wheels into the room.

"And now, goodness, is someone going to play the piano for us?"

"Wait, wait. We have refreshments."

It was Maureen who had spoken. Pink-eyed and sulky as ever, she was holding a plate covered with a lace doily, which she whipped off dramatically.

"Plain scones and fruit scones," she announced.

She walked over to the panel, clearly enjoying their eyes on her.

"Now, let me tell you what I know about Clara—sorry, Miss Newton. She's a useless cook. So, if I wanted to have something nice for dinner, I quickly realized she wasn't the one to ask. She once made chicken soup so bad, we didn't recognize it as chicken. Another time, I didn't know if it was a nightmare or not."

"Thanks, Maureen," Clara said.

"Well, it's true. I thought all housemothers would cook well, so that did surprise me." Maureen shook her head dramatically.

Sarah Bernhardt, eat your heart out, thought Clara.

"But her *not*-cooking well, it gave me space to learn. And I did. I can't say I'm much good either, but I do like doing meself a cake. And these," Ivor handed her another plate, "are coconut ice. I often used to make them."

"Don't mind if I do!" For the first time, Mr. Goodge was quite animated.

Once they too were distributed, Maureen tiptoed over and put her arm round Clara and Clara knew right away she was going to ask for something, "Miss Newton, do you think I can come home? I'm still under fifteen."

It was music to Clara's ears but she had to be honest.

"I can't decide that, I don't have the authority. But whether you're there or not, and whether I'm there or not," whispered

Clara, suddenly getting choked up, "I will always do my best for you, Maureen."

Maureen kissed her on the cheek.

It was Rita who was going to play. She looked around the room and when satisfied she had everyone's attention, announced, "I think I want a kitten most. Or a puppy."

"Rita, concentrate." Ivor steered her firmly to the piano stool. "Show the panel what you wanted to show them."

"I didn't."

Ivor cleared his throat. "What you *said* you would show them... Remember?"

"This is supposed to be a disciplinary procedure—" reminded Mr. Sommersby.

"It *is* a disciplinary procedure," Mrs. McCarthy interrupted. "We put the children's welfare at the heart of everything, remember?"

Alex was standing next to Clara.

"Are you going to play too, Alex?" she asked.

"Still can't play a note," he whispered back.

"Neither can I!" admitted Clara.

"Mrs. Cardew says she's never met anyone so thoroughly tone-deaf," Alex said proudly.

"I don't think she should say that..."

"It's true though. Don't care. I can't be good at everything."

Clara laughed and put her arm round the little professor. Incredibly, she was almost enjoying her own tribunal.

Rita played Beethoven's *Für Elise* and she played it beautifully. Clara was astonished at how she had progressed. Away from the piano she could be a drip; here, now, she was a tornado. She bowed five, six, too many times, then shouted, "Now it's Peg's turn!" just as Ivor was about to speak.

Clara wondered for a moment if Peg would speak again;

perhaps she had been saving her words for today? The memory of that "COWS!" was a joyful one.

But Peg wasn't saying anything, she was skipping. She and Rita jumped in time with the rope, whipping on the floor.

"Teddy bear, teddy bear, turn around, teddy bear, teddy bear, touch the ground…"

Only Rita was reciting the words, but Peg's face was wreathed in smiles. Clara almost felt tearful. Darling Peg, she would get there in her own time.

"Ooh, I'm like the narrator too," said Rita. Clara had a feeling that this tribunal was turning into The Rita Show, but no one seemed to mind and Rita *was* quite the performer.

"So now, I present… Billy and Barry doing magic!"

Billy and Barry were both rosebud pink. They were wearing the rarely-seen tidy versions of their school uniforms, all tucked in, polished and smart. They had even Brylcreemed their hair. Billy showed everyone a top hat, Barry showed everyone a wand. Even Mr. Goodge was made to inspect it. Mr. Sommersby looked annoyed at first but then, unexpectedly, he laughed and said his father used to do tricks at the Railway Arms.

After much ado, a rabbit was produced from the hat. A *real* live rabbit. Everyone clapped, Mrs. McCarthy gasped out loud. Rita grabbed it, squeezing it to her cheek.

"I recognize that rabbit," Clara whispered to Anita.

"Got to earn his keep," Anita mouthed back.

Clara *was* enjoying this. Even if she was going down, at least she was going down with her head held high.

It was Peter's turn. He stood with his head bowed. He too was all dressed up, noted Clara. She didn't know where he'd gotten the clothes from. Wait, yes, she did—that was Ivor's tie. The rest of it was probably Ivor's too. How would she ever be able to thank him? For everything.

Peter fanned out some comics. "I made these myself," he said, blushing furiously. "For Miss Newton."

Peter? Peter had done this for her? If anyone knew what an effort it was for him to stand up there, she did. She covered her eyes. She *was* going to cry.

Mrs. McCarthy looked perplexed. She asked questions. Mr. Goodge looked annoyed. Mr. Sommersby idly flipped through the comics' pages. For a moment that was the only sound in the room. *Please don't dismiss him*, Clara thought, *not Peter, not now. He deserves so much better from all of us.*

"What does this prove?" he asked.

"Miss Newton encourages me," Peter said. He spoke quietly but with an assurance Clara hadn't witnessed before. "She found out I like drawing and she helped me. I like cartoons now. She is going to help me do work experience, I'm fourteen next year."

"That's not a way to make a living—"

"Actually, it could be," Clara interrupted.

"My nephew is an artist," Mrs. McCarthy said. "I wouldn't say he was rich but..."

"You could say Miss Newton is the one who let you down, though, isn't she? Vis-à-vis your uncle?" Mr. Sommersby continued. "She doesn't want you visiting him. And she is blocking your chance of adoption by a living human relative."

Peter's face was aflame. He wouldn't look up.

"She was entrusted to take care of you and yet—"

"Nothing is her fault."

"Well, why won't she let you see him?"

Peter stared at the floor. Clara knew how much he hated talking about it and her heart wept for him.

"If you refuse to speak..."

"Unless you say something," said Mrs. McCarthy in a kindlier tone than Mr. Sommersby, "then we have to assume it's just...it's just nonsense."

"It's *not* nonsense," Peter snapped. "My uncle hurts me, he does."

Ivor leapt over. "I don't know why you are doing this to him again. You know this."

"It's his word against..." Mr. Sommersby looked into his papers. "Mr. Courtney's."

"Children's welfare at the heart of everything," said Ivor. "I've studied the Children's Act—they would never, ever have wanted a child to go through this."

He looked at Clara and she looked back at him. *Thank you.*

As Peter walked away from the panel, he slipped Clara a paper folded into four.

A cartoon drawing, one scene, *pow, zap, ooff.* The hero was wearing a mask and a cape, but from the hair and the dress, Clara could tell it was her. A man was flat on the floor. In the top left square it said, "Meanwhile in a house in Lavenham, forces of good were gathering."

In the bottom left rectangle, in tiny letters, letters embarrassed, it said, "thank you for everything."

Mrs. McCarthy had stood up and was telling everyone to give them a few minutes, when Ivor, hand in his jacket pocket, called out, "Oh, I have one more character reference here. It's a written one."

He waited for quiet, then started to read.

Whatever you think about Miss Newton...

Clara watched, puzzled. Ivor seemed to have a lump in his throat. He couldn't read on. Very gently, Miss Bridges took the note from him and continued.

...and her idealism or her naivety, she always, always puts the children first.

"And that's from a Mrs. Judy Martin, teacher at Honeywell Primary School in London."

Clara couldn't afford to sob now, but her shoulders went up and down as she tried to keep hold of herself. Ivor's eyes were full of tears, yet he was gazing at her so sympathetically... She wanted to embrace him, like they had that time in the kitchen, only she wouldn't get his name wrong now, she wouldn't get his name wrong ever again. She wanted to lose herself in his broad chest and shoulders. Instead, she tried to pour all her thanks into a smile. He gazed straight back at her, his dark eyes locked onto hers.

Rita had leapt to the front of the panel again, dragging Peg by the hand.

"We got something else to say," she said, her nose up in the air.

"Go ahead, Rita, is it?" said Mrs. McCarthy warmly. "What is it you want to tell us?"

"Miss Newton takes care of all of us, like Mama." Then she put her thumb in her mouth, punctuating the sweetest of sentences with a full stop.

CHAPTER FIFTY

Peter's uncle's adoption application would be thrown out and he was forbidden to contact Peter again.

Miss Newton would be allowed back at Shilling Grange. Her contract would be renewed *indefinitely*.

Alex misheard, thought they said renewed *infinitely*. He was staggered!

Miss Newton was to report any instances of misbehavior—a fine euphemism if ever there was one—to the council straight away. No ifs, no buts, no cover-ups.

None of the other evidence would stand. In fact, they were appalling smears and would be discounted.

Mrs. McCarthy was holding Maureen's coconut ice. "Mm, this is my favorite. Maureen, you must give me the recipe."

Flustered, Maureen agreed.

"And won't someone get poor Miss Newton a telephone? It is nearly 1950 after all! We can't have her dragging up and down the road in dressing gown and slippers each time she needs to communicate with the outside world."

Mrs. McCarthy turned to Clara and smiled. "Why don't you go and tell your lovely man the good news?"

"He's not *my* lovely man." Clara was blushing but she knew who Mrs. McCarthy meant, of course she did.

Mrs. McCarthy laughed and picked at her coconut ice. "If I may be so bold—your neighbor, Mr. Delaney, is in love with you."

Although she tried to keep a straight face, Clara knew she was failing massively.

"Do you think so?" she squealed.

"I *know* so."

"I don't know where he is—"

"He's outside," interrupted Maureen helpfully. "Go on, Miss Newton. Ivor is mad about you."

"Toodle-pip. I'm going to get to know these children." Mrs. McCarthy finished her coconut ice, then clapped her hands with the easy authority of a head teacher. "Children, it's time to have some fun. Anyone know 'The Lambeth Walk'?"

Peg was the first one up.

Clara raced along the corridor. As the lift doors opened, she saw with horror that Julian was standing there. His expression didn't change as she got in.

"Floor?"

"Ground, please."

Clara couldn't think of another word to say to him. She wondered if he'd heard the news that she was staying. No, he couldn't have—yet Julian did have a knack of knowing things before other people did. She stared at her Judy shoes while he stared at his shiny brogues. It was interminable. It was the slowest, most excruciating two minutes of her life. Having worn out the sight of her toes, she turned her attention to her fingernails, praying the lift would not break down or, if it had to break down, that it killed them both instantaneously. Better to be crushed, quickly and brutally, than have to stand around for hours listening to him.

They arrived on the ground floor and he tugged apart the iron gates. Once they were open, he blocked her way.

"I need to tell you something about your father, Clara. He didn't write those things about you."

"I know."

"I should apologize. I was angry and—I wanted to hurt you."

He held out his hand.

"Friends?"

Clara did not think so, this man who had lied and conspired for her to lose her job, and who had deliberately collaborated with an abuser, but now was not the time. She shook his hand limply—the way she knew he did not approve of. Right now, she had bigger fish to fry. *Much* bigger.

The first time she had met Ivor he was singing about fish to Peg. She remembered leaning against him to watch the stars and how that felt. She remembered the kiss under the mistletoe.

He might think she was the hokey-cokey, but that's what it was all about.

You wouldn't go to all this bother unless you loved someone, would you? You just wouldn't. Mrs. McCarthy knew what she was talking about. She couldn't have gotten this wrong.

She had to apologize to him about the Michael thing, explain it was force of habit, nothing else, and then she had to tell him how she felt. How she had been feeling for a long time, a silly amount of time.

There he was, *her* lovely man. *Ivor.* She saw a flash of that oh-so-dark hair; he was looking at her, over the head of someone else. He was hugging someone in the middle of the street. He stepped away from the embrace. Then the someone else pulled away too, sensing they were being watched. It was a woman, a young woman, oh so pretty and so polished. *Much more polished than anyone around here. Much more polished even than London people.* Clara, who didn't often notice clothes, couldn't help noticing this woman's. She was wearing a green woolen coat, with a gold brooch in a butterfly shape, and a flared spotty skirt. Super-high heels, white with black stockings. She was more than wearing, she was modeling. It looked daring. She looked wonderful. So modern. Bleached Hollywood hair.

Clara was caught by the look of utter confusion on Ivor's face. *Is that dismay?* Or fear, that's what it might have been. Maybe it wasn't. Maybe she just hoped it was.

The woman saw Clara's approach, saw Clara's shock and looked quizzically at her and Ivor as if trying to decipher a code. Finally, she puffed out her shiny lips as though she was going to whistle.

"Ivor." She pronounced his name differently, the emphasis more on the *vor*. "Aren't you going to introduce us, *Ivor*?"

That deep breath Ivor took to compose himself. The giveaway protective swing-back of his arm, the thing he did when he felt shy. Clara had felt like she knew everything about him, and yet just at that moment, she realized she knew absolutely nothing.

"Ruby, this is Clara— Miss Newton. Clara, this is Ruby..." he hesitated, swallowed, then finished, "my wife."

CHAPTER FIFTY-ONE

Clara had wondered if Ivor would come over to the Grange that evening, but he didn't. She supposed they had a lot to catch up on: Ivor and Ruby. Ruby and Ivor *Delaney*. *Childhood sweethearts.*

She told herself Ruby was just here as friends or to pick up some things she left behind, but she was kidding herself: it was obvious Ruby was back for good. And the fact that Ivor didn't come over reinforced that.

Other people came to celebrate. Dr. Cardew and Anita, and Anita brought her violin. Some teachers and the high school headmaster came, Mrs. Deacon the postmistress and Mr. Dowsett the librarian. Miss Bridges was there, of course, equipped with plates of cakes, and Miss Cooper turned up too, with Socialist leaflets that Miss Bridges said weren't allowed, but she'd let her off just this once.

The cheek of Mrs. Garrard! She and her husband hovered at the front door, like uncertain bees.

"Can we come in, Miss Newton? Seeing as you're here to stay." She was as cool and unabashed as ever. "They say, if you can't beat 'em, join 'em."

In the parlor, Mrs. Garrard and Maureen bonded over their deep knowledge of the silver screen.

"She knows all the idols," Mrs. Garrard said to Clara with a new respect in her tone. "I might have just found myself a new cinema companion. Larry is terrible, he yabbers all the way through a film. *And* he likes to leave as soon as it ends."

Clara, who could never see the point of hanging around at the end of a film, sympathized.

"You have made it better here. Even I can see the children are happier. I know I complain, but it's only fair to applaud you for what you've achieved so far."

Clara, the guests and the children chatted and laughed all evening. Rita played the piano while Peg danced with the ladies in the garden. The boys disappeared, then reappeared sporadically, Maureen kept making drinks, which Peter shyly served up, and Alex told everyone about Samuel Pepys, a writer who had buried his Parmesan when the Great Fire of London broke out because he loved it so.

"The things we do for love," sighed Miss Bridges, her eyes on Clara. Between bites of coconut ice, Mrs. McCarthy had asked Clara if there was any reason she couldn't be more involved in policy-making and guidelines going forward. Particularly regarding child protection and everything she'd learned in that area.

No reason at all. Clara felt excited. Children *and* paperwork? These were a few of her favorite things. Her private life might be falling apart, but everything else was coming together. Perhaps it had to be that way.

The next morning, Clara hung out sheets in the garden. Peg had wet herself in the night. It was all the excitement, Clara presumed, and late-night tea-drinking and whatnot. But these incidents were definitely occurring further apart. Billy was green around the gills. He must have eaten something that didn't agree with him. Clara made him stick his fingers down his throat before he and Barry went tearing off into the countryside. Alex was researching cheeses. Rita was concerned that she'd forgotten how to yawn, Terry had mislaid her glasses, naturally, and Peter was sleeping in. He'd been washing up way past midnight. Maureen hadn't stayed and had refused to say where she was going, but promised she would be back for dinner on Sunday. She would help to cook it too.

"And is it all right if I bring Joe?"

Clara supposed it was. It hadn't been the best morning and yet, and yet... it was perfect. Clara still had her job. She had more than a job, she had a family. And it had been a wonderful celebration.

She knew Ivor would eventually come over—he had to. And he did; he knocked on the back door shortly after ten. How awkward he looked, how sheepish. He could have done with his hat, his hair was more disheveled than ever. He also hadn't shaved.

Rita got to him first and insisted on climbing up him. "Roly-poly," she cried with arms outstretched. When Rita had sufficiently roly-polied, he said, "Now, now, May Queen, let me have a quiet word with Miss Newton here."

Rita tucked her dress into her knickers, did one cartwheel, then skipped away.

"So..."

"So..."

"She came back then?"

"I don't know what to say."

"You don't need to say anything, Ivor. I'm happy for you," Clara lied and he made another expression that she hadn't seen before, which was all the more heartbreaking. They had so much more to find out about each other, but that wasn't going to happen. She looked up into his dark eyes, her favorites, and realized that he knew she loved him, she didn't need to tell him.

"I feel—" he began.

"Shh," she whispered. "Don't say."

There are two ways of seeing the world. In one, everything is fuzzy and blurry and Ivor and Clara are in love. In the other, the one in sharp focus, Ivor Delaney is married to Ruby and not her.

Clara put her hand out and touched the bit where his arm no longer was.

Ivor smiled at her, then leaned in. Clara held her breath. Very quickly, he kissed her cheek and she knew exactly what it was: he was kissing her goodbye.

A few days later, Pamela and Harry Lewis came with Miss Bridges for Terry. When Clara suggested sitting out in the garden first, Pamela jumped up. She was much more comfortable outside. It was a hot day for September. The lawn looked terrible from the ball games and the dancing, but if you ignored that, the garden was lovely; the trees were thick with leaves, the wildflowers were like an earthy rainbow and Terry's vegetable patch was thriving.

The couple would suit Terry, Clara was certain of it. Nothing to do with statistics. Clara had thought that after the events of the last few weeks, she might be scared to ever use her judgment again, but actually she wasn't. Case by case was the thing. Step by step. They had both been interviewed by a panel and had filled in paperwork. And Terry liked them too. Sometimes, when Terry was chatting to them, she looked up at Clara and her expression said, "Is it okay to like this?" and Clara nodded back, hoping her expression said, "It's fine."

Terry's bag was packed and by the door, so once everything was signed, there was little to do—except say goodbye.

"I'm not going to cry, I'm not," Clara murmured in Terry's ear and Terry patted her back, "It's all right, Miss Newton. It's for the best."

And then she was gone.

Miss Bridges made tea, murmuring, "there, there" as though her mind was on other things. Clara found herself speechless. Her lovely Terry had left. The jam jar had gone to a new larder. That sweet outdoorsy girl was gone. A few minutes later, Miss Bridges could contain herself no more.

"Three new children will be coming to you!"

"Three!" Clara exclaimed. "When?"

"Next month. It would have been sooner but everything was up in air with the... tribunal, you know."

"And you've got their paperwork?"

Miss Bridges winced. "Not yet. I think there are two ten-year-old girls."

"Sisters?" Clara hoped so. Siblings tended to hold each other up even when the world pulled them down.

"Don't think so. And a boy of eight." As that was sinking in, Miss Bridges made a gleeful face. "And at long last, we're getting you... ta-da! A telephone."

"When is the engineer coming then?"

"Ah, that. I've put in a report."

They smiled at each other. *I'll believe it when I hear it*, Clara thought. Miss Bridges leaned forward and patted her hand.

"Oh, and Clara, there is something else you may find interesting..."

A few days later, Clara walked down Lavenham High Road with a large cardboard box in her arms. Julian and Bandit were on the other side of the street but thankfully, Julian didn't notice her—or least he pretended not to—Bandit gave a friendly woof. Dr. Cardew and Anita waved as they left the surgery, deep in conversation, as did Mr. Dowsett the librarian and Mrs. Garrard. *Her friends in Lavenham.*

The box was only awkward to begin with, now it felt as though it were growing heavier by the second. She didn't regret it though, quite the opposite, she had thought she might burst if she had to keep the secret for much longer.

Outside Ivor's workshop, she rested her aching arms for a moment.

The doors, usually wide open to all, were now locked and the blackout curtains kept in all the light. Maybe someday in the future things might be different? Clara hoped so but she wasn't going to rely on Ivor or anyone else. She could stand on her own two feet. She *was* the world now, for the children at Shilling Grange at least. There were new adventures to be had. New children to prepare for. Old children to cherish. And Mrs. McCarthy had decided to make an exception in the guidelines for Miss Newton's children who had been through such a lot. As Clara waited in the kitchen, for the first time in a long while, she felt that she was in exactly the right place at exactly the right time.

Alex was the first through the door, Peg was the first to notice the box rocking on the table, but it was Peter, with those long legs, who got to it first. He picked up the little kitten and solemnly handed her to Rita, whose mouth was opening and shutting in disbelief. Bags and coats were dropped on the spot. The kitten yawned and batted air.

"Is it for us?" shouted Billy.

"Can we keep it?" yelped Barry.

"Yes, and YES!" Clara got out her handkerchief for the tears were now rolling fast down Rita's cheeks.

"Miss Newton," she murmured, pressing the cat to her, "I love her."

The story of Shilling Grange Children's Home and its occupants will be continued in Lizzie Page's next book.

AFTERWORD

A LETTER FROM TERRY

Dear all,

I have been with Pauline and Harry for two months and I am having the time of my life. (I told them I'm not comfortable with calling them Mum and Dad, and they were very nice about it.)

I go to a Catholic school, which is fun except we have to pray a lot. I have started praying to my plants. Pauline says it can't hurt.

I love the garden and I am growing lots in my own patch. I have a room all to myself too. The bed is very soft. Dreams can come true. Please tell the others, if there is a chance to be adopted by good people, take it. We have visited Kew and are planning a trip to Ambleside, which is the Lake District.

Give my love to everyone, especially Peg. I miss her very much and hope she will come and visit.

Lots of love,
Terry

PS. Miss Newton, please give Ivor a big kiss from me.
PPS. I have now broken three pairs of spectacles. Harry calls me a liability.

AN INSIDE LOOK AT THE MAKING OF *THE ORPHANAGE*

I have written several books about the experiences of women in the first and second world wars, and I have enjoyed writing about women who triumph against the odds or battle against hardships.

When I finished my last book, *The Wartime Nanny*, the Covid-19 epidemic was underway and I felt I needed to move away from writing about wars or hardship and instead, I wanted to write about a more positive atmosphere. I was looking for something more uplifting to get me through lockdown!

I was convinced that the late 1940s would be a good era to set a more upbeat kind of story. I decided to explore post-war Britain, a time when people were coming to terms with what they'd lost while also looking toward a brighter future. It seemed there were lots of parallels with my present-day life.

At first, I didn't know what the story should be about though. I had vague ideas for characters but nothing substantial and I had some ideas for plot but nothing that tied them together. And then, while researching the period, I came across the issue of children without parents. During and after the war, people had become increasingly concerned by the terrible conditions some children, especially orphans, were living in. The mass movement of children in the wartime evacuation had made people more aware of the deprivations suffered by children in other parts of the country. Then there were the children orphaned by war. Then there was also a tragic case in which a young boy, Dennis O'Neill, died at the hands of his foster parents.

Civil Servant and Academic Dame Myra Curtis was appointed to run a Government Committee investigation into the lives of children without parents. Her report, the Curtis Report, noted the fragmented care system and how children fell through the cracks, and it recommended big changes including smaller, more family-like children's homes and more careful adoption and fostering were the future.

The Curtis Report wanted all those involved in childcare to "view children as individual human beings with both shared and individualized needs, rather than an indistinct mass." The report's recommendations became the basis for the 1948 Children's Act and were part of a raft of social reform measures enacted by the Labour Government.

While I was reading, enthralled, about all this, in my head, I was also gradually building the foundations for this story: A nation in post-war recovery...a massive policy change, orphaned children, an inexperienced housemother, and maybe a love interest or two...

So this series, like my other books, is still very much focused on ordinary women doing extraordinary things but this time in peace rather than war. For the setting, I wanted a country setting not too far from London. A family visit to beautiful Lavenham with its long rich history and its important wartime connection to America convinced me that it was the ideal place. When I found out that there is an actual place there called Shilling Grange with its own long rich history, I felt like I struck gold.

I enjoy writing about children (fortunately!). I have done so in the past—with lovely Pearl in *When I Was Yours* or sweet Hugo in *The Wartime Nanny*. There is something about the bluntness or straightforwardness of children that never fails to make me smile, and I am constantly inspired by my children and their friends. Some of the children in *The Orphanage* are amalgamates of children I know and love—Some are entirely imagined yet with issues I have some experience of. I hope I've been able to shine a spotlight on some of those struggles and that I've done justice about how it may affect them *and* their caregivers.

Readers who've read my other books will know I can't resist putting real-life remarkable people in my stories. Not only does Dame Myra Curtis—the remarkable woman whose report was the basis of the Children's Act—get a mention but there is also a recurring storyline about the poet Jane Taylor—the author of *Twinkle, Twinkle, Little Star* and much more. She was a former resident of Shilling Grange and proves an inspiration to Clara.

I get truly moved when I find out about incredible yet almost forgotten women in history and I love to pass on and celebrate their stories.

I hope you have enjoyed *The Orphanage* and—although it did go a bit darker than I originally planned!—I hope it provided some positivity and brightness for you too.

If you love reading stories set in post-war Britain, I recommend:

Small Pleasures by Clare Chambers
The Librarian by Salley Vickers
Miss Graham's Cold War Cookbook by Celia Rees
Transcription by Kate Atkinson
The Diaries of Nellie Last and, especially, *Nella Last in the 1950s*
    (this is a memoir)

For information about the Children's Act and childcare in the 1940s and 1950s, I read:

Mother to Hundreds by Lucy Faithfull
Champions for Children by Bob Holman

And for anyone interested in the history of orphans a trip to the Foundling Museum, 40 Brunswick Square, London WC1N 1AZ is a must!

DISCUSSION QUESTIONS

1. In the book, the job advertisement for a housemother mentions "Do What Women Do Best—Caring." This ad is based on something I saw during my research. I hope we've moved on from the idea that women are naturally good at being caring or that it's what we do best. Have you seen or experienced adverts or statements like this? What are your thoughts?

2. Clara is a reluctant housemother at first. She says, "I'm an empty shell of a woman. I don't know how to look after people, emotionally." I think this changes throughout the book but which of Clara's qualities make her a good housemother? Which of her qualities make her less good at the role?

3. The Orphanage is set in 1948, when Britain was still very much struggling with the aftermath of the war. Have you read any books set in this time period? What are common threads found in books set in this postwar time period?

4. I know we're not meant to have favorites—but which of the children in *The Orphanage* is your favorite and why? (You can't say Bandit. 😊)

5. What impression did you have of the relationships Clara has—first with fiancé Michael and then with neighbor Ivor?

6. I wanted to convey that although the changes brought about by the Children's Act were good—this was still (and still is today) a very imperfect system. Do you have experience with the care system and if you were in charge what would you do to improve things?

7. Clara believes "the effects of musical education can be transformative." Do you agree? Why or why not?

8. Clara also bends the rules to get the children a pet. What do you think children—and especially orphaned children—need most?

9. "Judy would rescue her. Like she did in the Blitz." Judy always helps Clara but when Judy asks Clara to help them adopt, Clara can't do it. Do you think Clara did the right thing? Could she have handled it better? What were your thoughts on what happened to Judy?

10. Did you expect Ruby to return? What do you predict will happen next?

ACKNOWLEDGMENTS

Thank you to the people who created this great shift in the care of vulnerable children—and to those today who work tirelessly to protect children's rights: foster carers, social workers, teachers, charity workers, the police and more. These tasks are not glamorous and the work is so often only noticed when something has gone wrong. The care and protection of vulnerable children needs to be talked about, thought about and acknowledged a lot more.

Thank you to all the gorgeous children who've inspired me. Other people's kids are fascinating and I've loved meeting and watching my children's friends and my friends' children grow up—keep on keeping on, you lovelies—you give me faith in the future.

Guess I'd better mention my own kids too. Thank you, Reuben, Ernest and Miranda for being you. I thank my lucky stars that you are in my life. Continue to enjoy yourselves (work hard too). Thank you also for your writing and marketing ideas. They're not all totally bonkers.

Thank you to my darling husband, Steve—we made it through lockdown together. It must be love.

Thank you to Lenny the Dog for getting me out of the house when I don't really fancy it.

Thank you to my sister and gorgeous nieces who bring me such joy.

Thank you to my fabulous supportive friends—I've loved our lockdown walks and/or Zoom chats.

Thank you to all the coffee shops in Leigh-on-Sea and Westcliff. My rotation of coffee from Saltwater, Millys, Temple Cafe, Birdwood, Anke's keeps me happy and sane. Love you all and your cappuccinos with chocolate sprinkles.

I love being part of the writing community. I've made such lovely friends through writing, it is absolutely awesome. It's been fantastic meeting people I can relate to, people I get, people who make me feel happy and have good plot ideas too.

Bookouture is such a lovely publishing company to be part of and I am massively grateful to them for everything. I'm scared I'm going to forget someone and annoy people, but here goes:

Huge thank-yous as ever to the brilliant Kathryn Taussig, who planted the idea of *The Orphanage*. I think she said something like "You write children well," which was super nice.

She's a wonderful, imaginative editor—and an expert reassurer too.

These are big shoes to step into and Rhianna Louise has— Thank you so much for helping birth this book, Rhianna.

Thank you to all the copy editors, proofreaders, designers and those working behind the scenes on *The Orphanage*.

And of course, a massive thank-you to the dynamic marketing department, cheerleaders and counselors—Kim, Noelle and Sarah. So nice to know you and to work with you.

Thank you to my brilliant agent, Thérèse Coen—without her, I wouldn't be writing this. I really struck lucky with Thérèse and I couldn't be happier than to be part of Susanna Lea Associates.

Thank you to bloggers and reviewers who post the most gorgeous photos on Instagram (I have tried to take similar lovely photos and failed—it's much harder than it looks), reviewed on Amazon, Goodreads, or retweeted about books on Twitter. It's all so helpful and so encouraging. You make such a difference.

No thanks to social media for distracting me. My attention span is now shorter than it's ever been. Weep.

Thank you to everyone who sells or loans my books.

Finally, thank you readers, everywhere. After years of wanting to write stories, the thought that there are people out there reading my books is enough to bring a tear to my eye. Thank you, readers, thank you. Where would we be without you?

ABOUT THE AUTHOR

USA Today bestselling author Lizzie Page lives in a seaside town in Essex, England, where she grew up. After studying politics at university, she worked as an English teacher, first in Paris and then in Tokyo, for five years. Back in England, she tried and failed at various jobs before enjoying studying for a master's in creative writing at Goldsmiths College. Lizzie loves reading historical and modern fiction, watching films, and traveling. Her husband, Steve, three lovely children, and Lenny the cockapoo all conspire to stop her writing!

You can learn more at:
X @LizziePageWrite
Instagram @LizziePageWriter

YOUR
BOOK
CLUB
RESOURCE

VISIT
GCPClubCar.com

to sign up for the **GCP Club Car** newsletter, featuring exclusive promotions, info on other **Club Car** titles, and more.

 @grandcentralpub

 @grandcentralpub

 @grandcentralpub